Ah, and she felt good there, her breasts soft against his chest, her lips parting under the relentless pressure of his. No gentle kiss this, but an act of need, of possession. Boldly he thrust his tongue into her mouth, and felt her hands clutch at his neck, felt her arch up against him. She was his! He felt it in his heart, his soul. His, and no other's. His kiss gentled, became almost playful, nibbling at her lips, her cheeks, her nose. "You're mine," he said, his mouth tracing a path down her neck, suckling softly on her white skin. "Mine."

"Yes," she gasped, arching her head back to give him better access.

"Say it." He stared into her eyes. "Say it."

"I'm—yours."

"Aye, *leannan*." His mouth swooped down upon her again. "That you are."

In A
Pirate's Arms
~

Mary Kingsley

A TOPAZ BOOK

TOPAZ
Published by the Penguin Group
Penguin Books USA Inc., 375 Hudson Street,
New York, New York 10014, U.S.A.
Penguin Books Ltd, 27 Wrights Lane,
London W8 5TZ, England
Penguin Books Australia Ltd, Ringwood,
Victoria, Australia
Penguin Books Canada Ltd, 10 Alcorn Avenue,
Toronto, Ontario, Canada M4V 3B2
Penguin Books (N.Z.) Ltd, 182-190 Wairau Road,
Auckland 10, New Zealand

Penguin Books Ltd, Registered Offices:
Harmondsworth, Middlesex, England

First published by Topaz, an imprint of Dutton Signet,
a division of Penguin Books USA Inc.

First Printing, March, 1996
10 9 8 7 6 5 4 3 2

Printed in Canada

Part I

Chapter 1

~

Out in the harbor the ship stood rigged and ready, awaiting only the morrow to sail. Rebecca Talbot took one last look at it, the ship that symbolized the end of her life as she knew it, and then turned away, hunching her shoulders. It was nearly teatime. Father would wonder why she wasn't at the Donner town house, where she was staying with him and Amelia, her sister. Never would he understand that she had fled to escape discussion of the voyage she dreaded so; never would she understand why he so wanted to be rid of her, no matter her past sins. She knew only that if she didn't return soon, there'd be the devil to pay.

And so she turned her back on the turquoise harbor and its surrounding rings of green, green hills and islands, and began walking, away from the quay, past the warehouses with their narrow alleys, past the quaint pink fortress. In spite of herself, Rebecca's spirits lifted at the chaos and babble of the market. She adored Charlotte Amalie's main street, the Dronningens Gade, a curious mixture of Caribbean color and the old world stateliness of the Danish who had colonized the island. The people fascinated her: the tall, burly, blond-bearded Danes; short, swarthy sailors from all countries; even the occasional British soldier sweltering in his red wool uniform, for the British patrolled the waters of the Caribbean against the French. From shops on the ground floor of pastel-colored houses with second-floor balconies of lacy wrought iron, dark-skinned natives selling fruit and vegetables called to her with a musical lilt as she walked by. Rebecca had to force herself not to answer in kind, not even to smile. Among all the color and noise, the bright cottons, the red-roofed buildings, she stood out, a proper, quiet woman in a walking gown of good gray twill and sturdy boots, with a bonnet of dull gray silk shading her face. Her walk, however, belied the image; her strides were much too long and free. Nor would a proper lady be without gloves. At the moment, Rebecca didn't much care what was expected of her. Tomorrow her life would change, and she would never be free again.

The street narrowed as she left the marketplace behind, and the slope sharpened. The Donner town house was built high on Government Hill, which meant she had a long, arduous climb before her. She'd arrive perspiring and out of breath, earning a scold from Father, and that thought was enough to make her quicken her steps on the steep, cobbled street. Besides, she didn't like the looks of her surroundings. On either side pressed shabby buildings, likely containing taverns rather than more reputable shops. The colorful population of the marketplace had been replaced by disreputable-looking sailors. Even so, Rebecca wasn't frightened; merely wary. Long ago she had learned to draw a cloak of respectability around herself, so that she was rarely accosted, even when alone. But then, few men would accost a woman such as she, too tall, too old, and, quite simply, far too plain.

Only a few paces ahead, the door to a tavern opened outward with a resounding bang, and two men flew out into the street. Rebecca stepped back just in time as the first of the men pounded past her, pressing herself against the wall of the tavern to avoid being trampled. She had a quick image of brawny shoulders in a snowy linen shirt, dark hair that curled past his collar, and, surprisingly, a smile flashed at her as the man ran by. Behind him his pursuer, yelling obscenities at the top of his lungs, held a wickedly long knife high in his hand. His shirt was of coarse, dingy homespun, and his teeth, what there were of them, were bared in a grimace rather than a smile. Altogether a most fearsome sight, and the first man was unarmed. Before she could stop herself, Rebecca thrust out her foot as the man thundered past her. Howling with surprise and rage, he sprawled to the ground, his knife flying from his hand.

Mercy! Rebecca stared blankly at the man lying supine at her feet. He had fallen so hard against her that she had nearly lost her own balance, and had saved herself only by clutching at the walls of the tavern. Why in the world had she done such a thing? She raised dazed eyes to see the first man facing them, his pursuer's knife in his hand. In his other hand was another, equally lethal-looking knife, its mother-of-pearl handle and silver hilt accenting, rather than softening its danger. He stood easily, feet planted apart, and he looked quite as dangerous a rogue as she had ever seen. The image she had of him, of lean, masculine strength matched with curly hair many a girl would envy, was confirmed. The only thing she hadn't noticed during his headlong flight, and which she now viewed with astonishment, was his eyepatch.

"Well, boyo," he said, his voice soft and with a lilt far different from the Indies, "and do ye plan on gettin' up? No, don't be thinkin' of going after the lady." This as the second man stirred, casting Rebecca such a murderous glance that she pressed harder against the wall. "Next time watch where you're going, boyo. Not polite to knock down ladies." He inclined his head toward Rebecca, and in that moment she knew why she had done what she did. It was because of his smile. "Now, Simms. Will ye be gettin' up, or do I have to make ye?"

Simms looked up again, and his eyes widened with fear at the sight of the knives the other man held so casually. "Cap'n, I didn't mean," he began, scrambling to his feet.

"Oh, didn't ye, boyo?" the man called the captain said and threw Simms's knife.

It flew toward Simms, now the hunted, who pressed back against the tavern a few scant feet from Rebecca, hands splayed against the wall. It started its downward flight, just grazing Simms on the stomach, to land in the dirt between his feet, the point embedded deep, the hilt quivering. "Christ, Cap'n!"

"The next one goes higher, boyo," the captain said, his voice still soft, still deadly. "Unless you take back what you said."

"You ain't no liar, Cap'n," Simms babbled. Perspiration beaded on his forehead, and his eyes remained fixed on the captain's remaining knife. "No, you ain't no liar."

The captain stalked closer. "And ye'll never try to cheat me at cards again, will you, boyo?"

"No, Cap'n. I swear." Simms's face paled even more as, with swift grace, the captain bent and scooped the knife up from the ground. Slowly he brought it up, the blade making a soft, snicking sound as it brushed against the buttons of Simms's waistcoat, the tip moving higher, caressing his chest, his chin, his nose. There it paused. Simms arched his head back, away from the deadly threat, his eyes crossed in a desperate attempt to see the knife. "Cap'n, I swear!"

"Do ye, boyo? Good." The captain flicked his wrist, and the knife flew up into the air. It twirled several times before it started down again, landing hilt-down in his hand. With a click, the blade recessed into the handle. "A fine blade. Mind ye use it for other purposes. Here." The captain tossed the knife up again, and this time it landed in the dust of the street. "You'll need it aboard ship."

"Aye, Cap'n!" Simms scrabbled in the dirt, shoving the knife into his breeches pocket. "Thankee, Cap'n, and I'm sorry. I'll jist go now."

"Do that," the captain said affably, and stood there, legs braced, arms akimbo, and a broad smile on his face. For a man who just a moment ago had been in danger of being killed, he looked remarkably composed. And he had let his assailant go!

"I shall never understand men," Rebecca said, her voice clear in the hush of the street.

The captain started, and turned to her. Still he smiled, but something in the nature of his smile changed. "Ah, *leannan*, I forgot about ye. Forgive me. You're not hurt?"

"No, no thanks to you." Rebecca stepped away from the wall, straightening her bonnet. "You did nearly knock me down."

"Ah, well, when you deal with ruffians like that—"

"Deal with! You were running for your life."

"Not at all. I was looking for a good place to fight. The lane's too narrow." His smile softened. "Still, *leannan*, I do thank ye. 'Twas a brave thing you did."

"Brave, or foolish." She brushed at her skirt in a vain attempt to remove the dust. "I don't know why I did it."

"Don't you?" He tilted his head to the side, his smile displaying even white teeth in a sun-darkened face. He was, she realized again, very handsome, the eyepatch only adding to his rakish appeal. He was also quite aware of it.

"I suppose I don't like seeing someone helpless being chased."

He clamped his hand to his heart. "Now you wound me, *leannan,* you really do. Do I look helpless?"

Anything but. Not with those shoulders, or his arms, which even through his shirt stood out lean and corded with muscle. "He had a knife."

"Aye. And I've a better one. Never mind, *leannan.* 'Twas brave, ye were. We'll leave it at that."

"What does that mean?"

"What?"

"What you called me. *Leannan.*"

" 'Tis the Gaelic." He smiled down at her. "Ye've a look of the old sod to ye, yourself. Red hair and green eyes."

"Brown and hazel," she said, repressively. "And I freckle." Now why had she said that?

"Aye, like an Irish lass. Yet you're American, *leannan?*"

"Yes, from Georgetown, near to Washington City." And that was entirely enough information to give him. She must remember who she was, where she was. "I must go, sir. If you will let me pass?"

He stepped back, crooking his arm. "Allow me to see you home, *leannan.*"

"Mercy, no!" She eyed him with undisguised alarm. If Father saw her with this man, any man, there'd be the devil to pay. "Thank you, but no."

"As you wish." He frowned a bit, perhaps at the vehemence of her protest. "But I'll suggest, *leannan,* that if ye choose to walk out tomorrow ye pick a safer place."

"I won't be here tomorrow," she blurted out. "I sail for England in the morning."

"England." He was very still, his face expressionless. "Ah. And you came here to take ship, because your country forbids trade with England. But why is a good American lass like yourself going there?"

"Family business. I really must go now. Good day, sir."

He eyed her for a moment and then stepped back. "Good day, *leannan.*" Before she could react, he caught her hand in his and lifted it to his lips. His hand was large, square, calloused, dwarfing hers in a grip too strong to break. "You don't wear gloves."

"No, I detest them—no, don't!" she protested, but too late. His head was bent, his lips just brushing the back of her hand, scalding hot. "Oh, please."

"Ah, *leannan*. Such pretty hands." With surprising gentleness he turned her hand over and dropped another kiss in the palm, a longer, firmer kiss. His breath tickled at her wrist, and gooseflesh broke out at the back of her neck, making her shiver.

"Please," she said again, faintly this time, and he lifted his head. His one good eye met hers, and for a moment their gazes held, with no barriers between them. In that moment she felt she *knew* him, as she had never known anyone before. It was so frightening a thought that she took an involuntary step back.

Instantly he released her. She stepped back again, cradling the hand he had kissed in the crook of her arm, as if it were injured. It wasn't pain she felt, however. "So be it, *leannan*. Have a safe journey. And"—his eye twinkled suddenly—"watch out for pirates."

"What!" she exclaimed, but he was gone, striding away with a loose-limbed, lean-hipped grace that was both arrogant and supremely male. He reminded her of a tiger on the prowl. Quite likely he was just as dangerous, too, she reminded herself tartly. Certainly he wasn't for someone like her, who preferred the safety and familiarity of her home. Though sometimes, just sometimes, she wished—well, never mind that. Wishing had caused her trouble more than once. High time she went on her way. She had her own life, and today's incident had no part in it.

Still cradling her hand in her arm, she turned and trudged away. It had been an astonishing incident, but it was over. It was quite foolish for her to dwell on it, or to remember the startling moment when she had gone against all her upbringing to help a handsome stranger. Even more dangerous to think of the astonishing feeling of his lips on her hand. Such was not for her. Rebecca was resigned to the truth. She would never see him again.

Brendan Fitzpatrick strode along the Dronningens Gade toward the quay, looking neither to right nor left, the black cloak he affected even under the warm Caribbean sun swaying from side to side. There was nothing overtly threatening about him; no weapons were in evidence and his face wore a pleasant, if watchful, expression. Yet even the stoutest men fell back at his approach, while respectful greetings followed in his wake. The women weren't quite so intimidated; they smiled and called out greetings, for Brendan was, in spite of his eyepatch, a fine-looking man. He was also said to be uncommonly generous to any woman he took to his bed, and not just with money. Brendan returned the greetings with a smile, the more ribald comments with sallies that set them all to laughing. Not once did he stop, however. He had a purpose this fine May morning, and he would not be dissuaded from it.

The harbor was filled with crafts of all description, from the very smallest dory to the largest, lumbering ship of the line. In these days of constant war St. Thomas was unique, a port that had managed to stay neutral and thus welcomed ships of every flag. Briefly his eyes touched on a ship anchored further out, a sleek, black-painted brigantine, and his face softened. Aye, but he wasn't there to admire his own vessel. There were more vital matters on his mind. Much of what he planned depended on what he would observe today.

Closer in was another ship, a trader, square-rigged and broad-beamed. The *Curlew*. She rode low in the water, as if heavy laden, the Union Jack floating from her stern. Even from here Brendan could see the activity on her deck as the crew made ready to hoist anchor. Aye, she'd be sailing soon. He stood very still, studying the ship as another man might study a woman he desired, noting details of rigging and hull and armament. Six guns, maybe, and she wouldn't be fast, not with those bluff bows and heavy bulwarks. Easy pickings. Still, Captain Smithers, her master, was a good seaman. Brendan would do well not to underestimate him.

A small group of people stood on the quay, three men and two women, awaiting the captain's gig to bring them to the *Curlew*. Aye, there was Smithers, grizzled and portly. His passengers must be important, to merit his personal escort. The man standing with him was tall and cadaverous, dressed in rusty black. Brendan had never seen him before, yet he recognized him from the description he had been given. So his information had been good. Neville would indeed be aboard the *Curlew*. The hunt was on. Brendan smiled grimly. He was rather looking forward to action.

As for the other passengers. Brendan's gaze flicked over them assessingly. A middle-aged man, a young woman, whose blond curls peeked out from under her high-crowned, stylish bonnet, and—*the devil take it!* Brendan drew back a pace. *She* was there, the woman from yesterday who had been quite convinced she'd rescued him, the woman with eyes so deep and so clear they'd haunted his sleep, yet which nevertheless held secrets. Devil take it, she was going to be aboard the *Curlew*. It was almost enough to make him give up his mission.

He had seen all he had come to see, all he needed. He turned, the cloak swirling about him, and at that moment the woman looked up, her gaze locking with his, making him stop dead in his tracks. No, he hadn't imagined those eyes, eyes that seemed to see straight into him. Without conscious volition he stepped onto the quay. *You're pressing your luck, boyo,* he told himself, but still he walked, drawn by a force he didn't understand. For the life of him, he couldn't stop.

Rebecca went very still, watching as the man with the eyepatch walked toward her, his gait rolling and easy. Something sparked to life within her, a curious flicker of excitement deep in the pit of her stomach, and her breathing became shallow. He was all she was aware of, all she could see, and the joy of seeing him again, when she had never thought she would, sparkled through her.

Beside her, Mr. Neville, who had been talking, broke off in midsentence, though she didn't notice. Following her gaze, he, too, watched the man approach, his eyebrows raised. "Who is that fellow?" he said, and both Captain Smithers and Ezra Talbot, Rebecca's father, turned.

Smithers turned pale under his tan. "Good God," he muttered, and stepped away from the passengers, intercepting Brendan before he could come closer. "Captain Fitzpatrick," he called in his booming quarterdeck voice. "To what do I owe this pleasure?"

"Mornin', Smithers." Brendan exchanged bows with Smithers, a lazy smile on his face. "Fine day to weigh anchor, it is."

"So it is, so it is. Let us pray the weather is with us across the Atlantic."

"You're for England, then?"

"Aye." To Rebecca, Smithers seemed to hesitate. "And you?"

"Where the wind takes me." Brendan's smile didn't quite reach his eye. "What is your cargo?"

Smithers turned even paler. "Nothing unusual. Tobacco, sugar, some cotton. Mixed goods."

"Sounds an excellent prize." Brendan's teeth flashed in a smile. "Oh, don't worry, boyo." He clapped the other man on the back. "It's bigger fish I'm after."

Amelia had sidled over to Rebecca and was clutching her arm. "Who is he?" she whispered.

"I've no idea." Rebecca was surprised at how calm she sounded. It was him. His image had haunted her dreams last night. Yet memory, clear though she'd thought it, paled next to the reality of the man. His long black cloak accentuated the breadth of his shoulders and rode over his bent elbows, framing him in darkness and throwing his shape into stark relief. He wore a loose shirt of white linen, open at the throat, disclosing a strong, corded neck and a chest liberally sprinkled with dark hair. Close-fitting black breeches were tucked into well-worn boots, while his hair, tousled from the wind, glinted blue-black in the sun. His strong, even teeth gleamed as he talked with Captain Smithers, and the lean planes of his face were shadowed with beard. His eye, however, was bright and alert, turquoise that rivaled the sea behind her. He was all lean, dangerous male, vital and virile and alive, and she knew somehow that he was as aware of her as she was of him.

"He's rather frightening, isn't he? That dreadful eyepatch. But dashing, too. I wonder who he is. Oh!" Amelia's face lit up. "I wonder if he's a pirate."

"Don't be silly," Rebecca snapped. "He's an ordinary sailor, like Captain Smithers." Ordinary. Hah. There was nothing the least ordinary about him.

Amelia pulled away. "I want to meet him."

"Melia," Rebecca protested, and her father, who stood nearby, turned, in time to see Amelia reach the two men. "Oh, mercy."

"What is she doing?" Ezra demanded.

"I tried to stop her, Father, but—"

"I've no patience with your excuses! You're supposed to look after your sister. Good gad, girl, must you always be as flighty as your mother was?"

Rebecca hunched into her pelisse. "I'm sorry, Father."

"Well, go and get her! Good God, I am having serious doubts about your accompanying her to England."

Then let me come home, Father! she thought, though she

knew better than to say so aloud. She had tried, oh, she had tried, reasoning first, and then begging, but nothing worked. Father was determined that Amelia would not travel to England alone, even if he didn't always consider her a suitable companion, with her soiled past. Of course, she knew that Amelia needed a companion; of course she thought it should be herself, since she stood almost as a mother to Amelia. What hurt was that she herself was expected to stay there, in exile.

Amelia was chattering animatedly as Rebecca drew level with her. Captain Smithers looked harassed, but Captain Fitzpatrick was smiling down at Amelia. As well he might, Rebecca thought. There was no one lovelier than her sister in Georgetown, with her cornflower blue eyes and her cornsilk curls. That she was sweet and genuinely friendly only added to her appeal. But did he have to look at her in quite such a way? she thought, and was immediately appalled. Never before had it bothered her when a man admired Amelia. It must be because this man was hardly presentable.

"Amelia." She touched her sister on the sleeve. "Father would like you to go to him, please."

"Oh, Becky!" Amelia turned to her, her curls dancing. "Captain Fitzpatrick tells me I will like England ever so much."

"Does he? How nice." She kept her eyes down, afraid to meet his again, afraid of the power of his gaze. "Come, Amelia. Father wants you."

"And who is this charming young lady, sir?" she heard Captain Fitzpatrick say as she turned, and she stiffened. Charming! She knew she was no beauty, certainly when compared to Amelia, but he needn't mock her. "Please introduce us."

"Miss Talbot?" Captain Smithers looked at her, and she gave in.

"By all means," she said.

"Miss Talbot?" Brendan was studying her, his head tilted to the side. That devastating smile was on his face, a dimple creasing his cheek. She hadn't noticed that before. It made him look younger, almost boyish, and yet it enhanced his masculinity, rather than detracting from it. In spite of herself, she felt the beginnings of an answering smile on her lips. "Ah. You are sisters, then."

"Miss Talbot, Captain Fitzpatrick," Captain Smithers mumbled.

"And a pleasure it is to meet you," Brendan said, bowing.

Well. At least the man had manners. "You, too, sir," she said, and saw the glint in his eyes brighten.

"Ye travel to England, too, Miss Talbot?"

"Harumph. She does," Captain Smithers interrupted. "Ladies, we should be getting to sea."

"Yes," Rebecca said, as if Smithers hadn't spoken. "I believe my sister told you she is betrothed?"

"Aye." He didn't smile, precisely, but his dimple was quite pronounced. "To a viscount, no less."

"Yes." Wretched man, making her want to laugh at a time like this. "I will be staying with her."

"In England? Ah, but ye'll not like it there, *leannan*."

"What does that mean?" Amelia put in.

" 'Tis my country ye should visit. A poor land, true, but of great beauty, and poetry. Do ye like poetry, Miss Talbot?"

"Aye—yes." Mercy, what was the matter with her?

"Sure, and I thought ye might. Ye've the soul for it."

"Captain Fitzpatrick—"

"Oh, what a lovely thing to say!" Amelia exclaimed. "Oh, I do wish we could stay here longer, now that we've met you. Will you be coming to England, sir?"

His face went very still. "I am sorry, lass, but no true Irishman goes willingly to England."

"Never?"

"Never." His smile included them all impartially, and Rebecca felt abandoned. "I must be off. 'Tis time and beyond ye were gone."

"Aye." Captain Smithers smiled for the first time. "Good day, Fitzpatrick."

"Good voyage, Captain. Oh, and Miss Talbot."

Rebecca looked up, and was again caught by his blue, blue gaze. "Yes?"

"Watch out for pirates," he said, winked, and strode away, the folds of his cloak billowing about him.

Rebecca stared after him, mesmerized by his easy grace. "Whatever did he mean by that?" Amelia asked.

"Come, Miss Talbot, Miss Amelia." Captain Smithers mopped at his brow with a capacious handkerchief. "Best I return you to your father, now, or there'll be the devil to pay."

"But who is he, sir?" Amelia said, dancing alongside him on the quay. "And what did he mean about pirates? Sir!" She stopped, hand to her heart. "Are we likely to meet pirates?"

"No!" Smithers spoke just a little too loudly. "There's the gig. We can go out to the ship."

"Rebecca." Ezra's face was contorted with rage. "What did you mean, allowing Amelia to speak with that man?"

"I'm sorry, Father," she said hastily. "He was polite enough."

"Polite! Hah! His kind don't know how to be polite. If this is the care you take of your sister, I fear for her safety, I truly do."

"That's not fair!" Rebecca protested, stung. "I watch after Amelia. You know I do."

"Do not speak to me in such a way, girl."

Rebecca's eyes lowered. "I'm sorry, Father."

"But, Daddy"—Amelia took her father's arm and smiled up at him—"he was very charming. Who is he?"

"Ahem." Mr. Neville stepped forward, pulling at a cravat that was already loose and wrinkled and dingy at the edges. "A most dangerous man. Do you not know?"

"No. Who is he, sir?"

"He is believed to be the Raven."

"The Raven!" Amelia exclaimed.

"The Raven," Rebecca said, more weakly.

"Aye," Captain Smithers said, his voice heavy. "The Raven. And I pray I never encounter him on the open seas. Come. Let me help you into the gig, Miss Talbot."

Rebecca gave her hand to him almost automatically, stepping from the stone quay into the dancing, rocking boat. The Raven! Good heavens. Even in quiet Georgetown his name, and his exploits, were known. What she hadn't heard was how handsome he was, how charming and compelling. The stories instead concentrated on his daring, infamous raids at sea. For Captain Fitzpatrick, the Raven, was the most notorious pirate ever to prowl the Atlantic.

Chapter 2

~

"Oh, Becky!" Amelia whirled into the tiny stateroom aboard the *Curlew*. "Is this not exciting? We are finally on our way. I did think this day would never come," she went on, sinking down onto the bunk. "But, only think! One month more and I'll be with my dear Stephen." She frowned, thoughtfully. "I wonder if he is as handsome as his miniature makes out?"

Rebecca glanced up from unpacking, and felt a small spurt of sympathy for her sister. Imagine traveling across the great wide ocean, to marry a man one knew only through letters. She couldn't do it, especially knowing that Stephen, the Viscount Blaine, so badly needed money that he would deign to marry the daughter of an American tradesman. In the miniature his eyes appeared watery and his chin, weak. Not at all like the merry blue eye and determined features of Captain Fitzpatrick. No, she wouldn't think about him. "Do please move, Amelia, so that I may open the drawers," she said, her voice sharper than usual, and busied herself with stowing away her belongings in the drawers built into the base of the bunk. "You do not even know the man."

"But I do!" Amelia protested. "He writes such wonderful letters. I know you don't wish to go, Becky, but I think it's horrid of you to try to spoil things for me."

Rebecca's face softened. "Dear Melia, I am sorry." She rose and sat on the bunk, putting her arm about Amelia and drawing her head down onto her shoulder, as if she were a little girl. "You're right, I don't wish to go, but that's no reason for me to be cross with you. It isn't your fault." She paused. "I only wish you knew the man better."

"Papa knows him. He wouldn't have agreed to the betrothal if he thought it was wrong for me."

"I know," Rebecca said, though privately she wondered at her father's motives. True it was that he always had been an ardent lover of all things British; true also that, over the course of several journeys to England he had made friends there, including the viscount. Why he was so determined for Amelia to marry into the aristocracy, however, was something Rebecca couldn't fathom. "It will all work out, I imagine."

"Of course it will. You'll see." Amelia straightened, her face brightening. "You won't have to play maiden aunt, Becky. We'll find someone for you to marry."

"I hope not," Rebecca exclaimed. "Then I'll have to stay there forever."

Amelia drew back. "But, Becky. Aren't you staying? You are, aren't you? Don't tell me you'll leave me there."

"Hush, Melia. Of course I'll stay for awhile. I would never leave you while you needed me. But, Melia." She turned to face the younger girl. "Soon you'll have a husband and a family of your own. You won't need me."

"But, Papa said—"

"Yes, I know Father intends for me to stay with you." Her eyes darkened. "That way, I'll be off his hands."

"Oh, no, Becky! I'm sure Papa will miss you terribly."

Would he? Rebecca wasn't so certain, and it hurt. Oh, how it hurt. "Perhaps. I doubt, Amelia, that I'll belong there. It's not home."

"You'd really rather stay in Georgetown? Even though everyone knows about—"

"Yes, I really would."

" 'Twill be all right." Amelia slipped her arm about Rebecca's waist. "You'll be happy, you'll see. And if you are not—well, you'll just have to return to Georgetown. Yes." She nodded. "I shall speak to Stephen about it."

"Thank you, Amelia," Rebecca said, amused and touched by her sister's sudden show of maturity, and rose. "We'll be sailing soon. We must go say good-bye to Father."

"Oh, yes!" Amelia jumped up from the bunk. "Do let me straighten my bonnet, first. Pity there are no eligible males sailing with us," she chattered, as they left the stateroom and climbed the narrow stairway that led to the deck. "Mr. Neville and Captain Smithers are much too old for you."

"As I am on the shelf, Amelia, that hardly matters."

"Don't be silly! But I do wish there were someone for you." Her eyes took on the soft, faraway look Rebecca had long ago learned to distrust. "Now, if we were sailing with Captain Fitzpatrick—"

"He's a pirate," Rebecca snapped.

"Yes, and how romantic that is," Amelia snapped back. "You're blushing, Becky. Were you thinking the same thing?"

"There you are, Amelia," Ezra said, smiling at Amelia as they came out on deck, saving Rebecca from answering that question. "Is all to your liking? Will you be comfortable?"

"Oh, Papa!" Amelia hugged him around the neck. " 'Tis ever so exciting! But I do wish you were coming with us."

"So do I, daughter, but you know I cannot leave my business." His face darkened. "I would take you on my own ship, if our government wasn't so idiotic as to forbid trade with England," he rumbled. It was much to Ezra's annoyance that the United States had placed restrictions on trade with England, because of that country's policy of boarding American ships. For that reason, they had come to St. Thomas, traditionally a free port, for the girls to take ship for England. "I dislike sending you alone."

"I'll watch out for her, Father," Rebecca murmured.

"See that you do, girl," Ezra said, and turned away, nodding to Captain Smithers. "Watch over my daughter, now."

"Aye, Mr. Talbot. I'll look after both your girls."

"Captain," Amelia broke in, her eyes sparkling, "do you think we'll have any trouble from the Raven?"

"I hope not, miss." Smithers' voice was heavy. "I've heard tales of those who've tangled with him—but you needn't worry. We're not carrying anything he'd value."

Into Rebecca's mind flashed the image of a sun-washed street and the sharp flash of a steel blade. She had seen herself how the Raven dealt with his opponents. "Captain, if the man is a known pirate, why is he still abroad? With the British patrolling these waters, I'd think he'd have been arrested by now."

Smithers gave her a look from under his brow. "It's been tried, young woman, many a time. Fast he is, in that ship of his. No one can catch him. Even ashore the fellow has the devil's own luck." He looked from one to the other. "Last time it was tried, a young lieutenant, name of Dee, I think it was, took several soldiers and went to a tavern where they'd heard the Raven was, waited outside for him. Plan was, when he came out, they'd grab him. Aye, and it might have worked."

"What happened?" Amelia asked, her voice breathless.

"The Raven did come out, but it's as if he knew. He had his knife ready. Powerful skilled with a knife, he is. Before the soldiers could close in he'd disarmed one and kicked the other in—well, the man was disabled. Then he let out a whoop—he's an Irish savage, and the yells they make make your blood run cold—and all the riffraff poured out of the tavern. Many a man ended in gaol that day. But not the Raven. Last anyone saw of him he was laying about with the best of them, and laughing. All Lieutenant Dee got for his pains was a slash on his cheek. Bears the scar today, so I hear."

"Was he hurt?" Rebecca said, so urgently that the others looked at her in surprise.

"Dee? Oh, the Raven. Nay, not he. Some say they saw a blackbird flying away, but 'twas a drunken fancy, most like. No one knows where he went. Wasn't seen in St. Thomas for a long while after that." Smithers frowned. "Come to think of it, he disappears for months at a time, no one knows where. Only time you see him is when he's after prey. 'Tis why his face is not so well known ashore. But seamen know him, aye, and take care to stay on his good side." He stared back at the shore, and then shook himself. "But this is no talk for ladies such as yourself. Be assured you're safe from him. You'll get to England in one piece, aye, or my name's not Bob Smithers."

England. It sounded like a death knell. So absorbed had Rebecca been in Captain Smithers' story that she had forgotten, for just a moment, what lay ahead. "Father," she said, turning.

"I'll be going," Ezra said and caught Amelia up in a hug. "You be good, daughter." His voice was gruff. "Make a good marriage."

"Oh, Papa!" Amelia wailed, clinging to his neck. "I don't want to go. Let me stay with you. Please?"

"Now, Amelia." Ezra stepped away, his own eyes suspiciously moist. "No crying. You're a big girl, now."

Mr. Parker, the first mate, approached. "The boat is ready for you, sir, and the ladder's been lowered."

"Thank you." Ezra reached out to touch Amelia's cheek, and then abruptly turned away toward the railing, where the rope ladder hung.

It was too much for Rebecca. "Daddy," she called, her voice breaking, and took a step toward him.

Ezra turned from the railing. Something flashed in his eyes, regret, perhaps, but then was gone, leaving his face stony. "Take care of your sister, girl," he said, and climbed out onto the ladder.

"Papa!" Amelia cried, starting forward. Rebecca's arm shot out and caught her about the shoulder.

"Hush, Melia," she murmured.

"But, Becky, he's leaving—"

"Shh." Rebecca hugged her, staring ahead, her eyes dry. She never cried. Long ago she had learned tears did no good.

"I don't want to go to England," Amelia sobbed. "I don't, I don't!"

"Stop it." Rebecca spoke sharply. "You are making a spectacle of yourself. Besides"—her voice softened—"I'm with you. I'll take care of you."

Amelia sniffed, looking up at her. "I'm sorry, Becky. You're not mad at me?"

How, Rebecca wondered, could Amelia manage to look so pretty in the midst of a storm of tears? Her cornflower blue eyes seemed larger than ever, and her lips trembled appealingly. Not for her the red nose and blotchy cheeks that Rebecca suffered when she cried. Life, she reflected without anger, was sometimes prodigious unfair. "No, of course I'm not mad."

"You're so brave, Becky." Amelia sniffled, digging into her reticule for a handkerchief. "I could never be as brave as you."

Brave? Hardly, but for Amelia's sake she would pretend to be. *Daddy!* The silent cry came from her heart. Holding on to her sister, as much for her own solace as for Amelia's, she watched as the small boat headed toward shore. Her father was leaving her. Never in her life had she felt so alone.

With a fair wind and a following sea, the *Curlew* sped toward England. Rebecca marked each day in her journal, uncomfortably aware that with each mile she came closer to her dreaded destination. With each mile, she was farther and farther from home. She missed her father and her familiar surroundings with an ache that never left, missed the house she had grown up in, the people she knew, the peaceful cemetery on the heights above Georgetown, where she had often spent sunny Sunday afternoons. All behind her now, and what lay ahead did not bear thinking of.

Not that she had much time for thinking. Once their ship left the harbor and encountered the northeast trade winds, Amelia took to her bunk, her face sickly green and her spirits low. Even Rebecca's stomach rebelled as the ship bucked the waves caused by the head winds, but she fought against it. Caring for her sister was something she had always done. She would continue to do so now.

They were a week out of St. Thomas when Amelia came out on deck, pale and shaky but otherwise, to Rebecca's relief, fine. Even after a week of illness, Amelia looked charming, in a high-waisted day dress of white dimity that draped demurely over her slender figure. Over that she wore a spencer in a shade of blue that rivaled the sky, and her high-crowned chip straw bonnet was trimmed with flowers to match. Next to her, still in her good gray twill gown, cut full to conceal, rather than reveal, Rebecca felt dowdy and just a little resentful. There had been a time when she had dressed stylishly, too. "How good it is to breathe fresh air," Amelia said, sinking onto a bench. Rebecca joined her. With the stern cabin housing behind them, they were sheltered from the wind. "Goodness, look at that man, Becky!" Amelia pointed to the top of a mast. "What is he doing up there?"

Rebecca shaded her eyes against the brightness as she looked up, and involuntarily shuddered at the height. "He is the lookout. You wouldn't know, since you were ill, but we have sighted several ships. All quite friendly, by the by."

"Of course. We are on a British ship. 'Tis why Papa put us aboard, instead of one of his own."

"One of the reasons. Or have you forgotten that we are not supposed to trade with Britain?"

"Oh, pooh, that is boring talk! I will not let you go on about it on such a fine day." Amelia stretched out her legs and regarded her feet, daintily shod in the latest style, soft black slippers with crisscross ties. "I do miss Papa."

"So do I," Rebecca said after a moment.

"But, oh, we shall be so happy together in England. I promise you so."

Rebecca's smile was forced. Of course she would never have allowed Amelia to travel alone, but must she really be banished so far away? Surely her crime hadn't been that terrible. Surely she had paid enough, over the last seven years.

"Ladies." Mr. Neville ambled over to them. "A pleasure to see you up and about, Miss Amelia."

Amelia dimpled up at him. "Thank you, sir. It is good to feel better, at last. There were times I thought I would die."

"Seasickness can be distressing," he agreed, quite as if he hadn't spent the first days of the voyage in his stateroom. "It is a shame you had to miss so much."

"Why?" Amelia's eyes sparkled. "Have we met with pirates, sir?"

"Amelia," Rebecca reproved.

"Well, I would still like to know what Captain Fitzpatrick meant, telling you to watch out for pirates."

Uncharacteristically, Rebecca flushed. She had her own ideas as to what that meant, and they had more to do with a flashing smile and a lilting brogue than being captured at sea. Dangerous, either way. "He was funning us, Amelia."

"I hope so." Neville frowned, looking rather like a black-visaged bird in his dark, rusty clothes. A crow rather than a raven, Rebecca thought suddenly, and just as quickly tamped the thought down. Much too fanciful. If she'd once had the soul for poetry, it was long gone. "May I join you ladies?"

"Oh, please do!" Amelia shifted on the bench to make room for him. He sat, his thigh pressing much too close to Rebecca's. She edged away.

"I doubt not that he was bluffing," Neville went on. "We are not the type of prize to attract such as he. After all, we carry no coin or bullion, just simple merchandise. May I say you're looking especially lovely this morning, Miss Amelia. And you, too, Miss Talbot," he added, as if in afterthought. Rebecca noticed, however, that his gaze had strayed to her bosom, and she edged away again. She didn't like Mr. Neville. He hadn't actually made any advances toward her, but the way he looked at her and his tone of voice were advance enough. Mercy, why he'd chosen her as an object of flirtation and not Amelia, she couldn't imagine.

Amelia dimpled. "Thank you, sir. Though I am persuaded I must look ghastly after having the mal de mêr."

"Not at all. You could never be less than beautiful."

High time the topic was turned, Rebecca thought. "Do you know of the Raven?" she asked briskly, and then bit her tongue. Now why had she said that?

"But, dear lady, who does not know of him? He is a legend. Infamous, of course, but there it is. Why, in these civilized days, who would expect pirates to roam the seas?"

Amelia leaned forward again. "What has he done, sir? Please, tell us."

Neville's lips pursed. "I'm not sure 'tis a story fit for ladies' ears, but—oh, very well. No one knows where he came from, you know. There's a tale that he is from an aristocratic family in England, but I don't credit that. He suddenly appeared one day in his black ship and attacked a helpless British trader. Took her and all her cargo as a prize. None knows where he went after that." His gaze was distant. "He disappears for long periods of time, reappears only when he needs more money. Some say he has his own island in the Indies, where he hides when he is not marauding."

"Then why was he on St. Thomas, sir?" Rebecca said tartly.

"The man likes to court danger, I believe. He once took on a British warship."

"No!"

"Yes, and took off men for his own crew. Some say they saw him at the top of the mast"—his gaze went up to the topmast, high above—"and he was laughing. Laughing at the mightiest navy on earth!"

Rebecca felt the oddest urge to cheer. "A most dangerous man," she said, primly adjusting the folds of her skirt. "I am glad we shan't be encountering him again."

"Yes." He leaned forward, his face scant inches from Rebecca's. "He is utterly ruthless, and he will not let anything stand in his way. Or anyone."

Rebecca pulled back. "Has he killed, then?" she said, surprised at how detached she sounded.

"I fear so, dear lady. But that isn't the worst. He has been known to employ torture on his captives."

"Torture! But why?"

Neville's eyes gleamed. "To get them to give up their valuables, of course. But I also fear that he enjoys it."

"Mercy," Rebecca said faintly. It couldn't be true. It didn't sound like the man she had met so briefly. Dangerous he might be, but cruel? She couldn't credit it.

"He shows none. And he is no gentleman. I hear that on the last ship he took, there were ladies aboard."

Amelia leaned forward. "What happened to them, sir?"

"No one knows." Silence lay heavy between them. "He took them aboard his devil-curst ship, and they've not been heard of since."

Somewhere a bell sounded, and Rebecca counted the strokes with relief. Eight. That meant it was noon, and time for luncheon. Odd, the way hours were kept on ship. "Well." She rose, shaking out her skirts. "I believe that's enough pirate stories for one day. There's the bell for luncheon. Shall we go below?" she said, and at that moment a cry floated down from the top of the mainmast.

"Sail ho!"

"Where away?" Captain Smithers' voice boomed out from the quarterdeck.

"Three points off starboard quarter, Cap'n, and comin' fast."

Smithers raised his spyglass and put it to his eye. "A dispatch boat, most like," he muttered, but he was frowning when he lowered the glass.

"Oh, Becky, another ship!" Amelia exclaimed, catching Rebecca's arm and drawing her over to the rail. "How exciting! Do you suppose we'll have company?"

"Some naval officers for you to flirt with, Melia?" Rebecca said, but she smiled. Amelia was still very young. Let her have her pleasures while she could.

"Oh, look!" Amelia pointed as they crested a wave. Momentarily, far behind them, they saw the flash of a white sail. Then it was lost, as they went into a trough. "Oh, bother, it's too far away. He'll never catch up."

"Gaining on us, Cap'n!" the lookout called.

Rebecca turned to look at the quarterdeck. Smithers hadn't answered, but still stood, glass to eye, watching the other sail. His face was grim. In spite of the day's warmth, Rebecca felt a sudden chill. "Amelia, luncheon is waiting—"

"Ladies," Neville said behind them. "Can you see the other ship?"

"Oh, Mr. Neville, 'tis ever so exciting!" Amelia turned shining eyes on him. "Almost like being in a race."

Rebecca shifted away from the hand Mr. Neville placed on her shoulder. "I wonder who it is."

"No one you need to fear, ma'am." Mr. Neville smiled, showing yellowed teeth with spaces between. Irrelevantly Rebecca remembered another man, and a laugh that displayed strong, even teeth, on a sunny St. Thomas street. As before, she banished the image. "We are on a British ship. No one would dare to attack us," he went on. "Had we been foolish enough to travel on an American ship, we might be exposed to the unpleasantness of being boarded."

Rebecca looked up at him. "Do you not feel it is wrong, that England feels free to stop American ships and board them?"

"Of course not. England's navy is only after those sailors that have deserted."

"But many of the men they impress are American, sir."

"So they say."

"And you are American, as well. I wonder that you feel this way."

"I have no quarrel with England. No right-thinking person should." He smiled at her again. "But, there, I don't expect you to understand. You should leave these matters to men. We are more suited to understand them."

"Mr. Neville, if you think—"

"Can you make him out?" Smithers' voice boomed out as he called to the lookout, cutting off the rest of Rebecca's reply.

"Aye, Cap'n," the lookout called back. "Looks to be a brigantine, flying the Union Jack."

"There, ladies, see?" Mr. Neville nodded. "We are quite safe."

"I never doubted we were, sir," Rebecca said tartly, her gaze straying back to the captain. If their pursuer were indeed a friend, why did he still look so grim? Again that chill of unease swept down her spine. "Amelia, I believe we should go down to luncheon—"

"Good Christ!" Smithers exclaimed at the same time. "Mr. Parker!"

Mr. Parker, the first mate, who was supervising the crew, sprang forward. "Aye, Cap'n?"

"Call all hands, and be quick!"

"Aye, Cap'n! All hands on deck! All hands on deck!"

"What is it?" Amelia asked, looking up at Mr. Neville as if he could provide an answer.

"What is it, Cap'n?" Mr. Parker called.

"Trouble," Smithers said. "Get the guns out, and be quick. And get those landlubbers below! We've no time to spare for them."

"I'll take care of this." Mr. Neville took the two girls' arms, steering them toward the companionway that led below. "Is someone chasing us, Captain?"

"Aye." Smithers lowered his spyglass and folded it with a short, sharp motion. "You might as well know the worst. I believe it to be the *Raven*."

Chapter 3

The *Raven* dipped into a trough, and for a moment all Brendan could see was the deep, green sea and the sky above. But then the ship crested the swell, and his quarry was again in sight. Standing far above the deck on the foretopsail yardarm, one arm wrapped around the mast for support, Brendan grinned fiercely. Through his spyglass he could see the white flutter of sails that he knew to be the *Curlew*. He'd been tracking her for days, careful always to stay out of sight. Now, a week out of St. Thomas and with no other ships near, it was time to strike. Within a matter of hours, the *Curlew* and all she held would be his.

His smile dimmed for just a moment. No, he would not think of eyes as green and deep as a sunlit sea, or a smile that had so unexpectedly charmed him. That Rebecca Talbot was a passenger on the *Curlew* was an accident of fate. He had a mission to perform. Best he concentrate on that.

"Five degrees starb'd," he called down to the man at the helm, and felt his ship respond to the turn of the wheel, rolling to port as her course was changed. She was a fine ship, a sweet ship, his *Raven,* and if anyone had told him when he was a boy he'd someday be skippering her, he'd have thought they were insane. Not when he'd seemed destined to live his life on a small, rocky tenant farm, struggling to eke out a meager existence. Not when he'd envied his distant cousins their wealth and ease, not when he'd gone to market in Bristol and seen the ships on the Avon, their utilitarian beauty making his heart ache. Aye, he'd never even let himself dream of something like the *Raven,* not until his life had changed so drastically and completely.

The grin faded again, and his lips tightened in the grim line that was familiar to many an English captain. Leaning perilously far out, he caught hold of a line and rode it, sliding down to the deck. He met the ship's movements easily, legs spread, arms akimbo, and gazed up at the sails, gauging his ship's speed. Aye, they'd got the wind now. Soon enough, they'd catch the *Curlew.*

A giant of a man came into his vision, arms crossed at his chest, and at his inquiring look Brendan nodded. "Ahead and to port. Three, four hours at the most, Sam. Crew all ready?"

Sam nodded. Brendan stood at ease, comfortable with the silence. Most had thought him daft when he'd signed Sam up as first mate, a mute, and black at that. After all, one of the mate's jobs was to repeat the captain's orders to the crew. Sam had his own way of communicating, however, with clicks and whistles and gestures, and the crew not only caught on to his meaning, they also quickly learned to obey. Besides being a decent navigator and a superb seaman, he was more than capable of running the *Raven* if for some reason Brendan couldn't. He'd trust Sam with his life, aye, that he would. But not with the truth. That he told to no man.

"Call all hands," he said tersely, and Sam let out a sharp whistle, making a chopping motion with his hands at another man. The command was hollered and repeated, and the sounds of feet pounding on decks and companionways echoed throughout the ship. Men came from the rigging, from the deck, from crew's quarters, alert and ready for action. They crowded the deck, fully one hundred of them, enough to man this ship and yet another, enough to fight. They were trained, seasoned, and they knew what was expected of them. As Brendan talked he saw heads nodding, eyes gleaming in anticipation, and knew that he would win the upcoming battle. He had a sweet ship, a fine crew, and his own skills. He needed nothing more.

Within moments the *Raven* was stripped and readied for action: all hatch covers battened down; the eight nine-pound carronades run out, along with the six long guns, and put in place with the men to arm them; the foc's'le cleared for use as a surgery. Pistols were primed, knives placed to hand in belts, and, here and there, the occasional saber clanked. The *Raven* was going to battle, and she intended to win.

It was chaos. Utter chaos, and Rebecca had never seen the like in her life. Within a moment of Captain Smithers' announcement a ripple of panic had spread through the *Curlew* and grown. It showed in the crew's faces, in their voices, in their words. The *Raven*! It was a name from nightmares. Remembering Mr. Neville's stories, which a moment ago had seemed like fairy tales, Rebecca felt the same panic welling within her. Dear heavens. If the Raven captured this ship, what would become of her sister and her?

She had barely a moment to contemplate that before a sailor grabbed her arm and hauled her and Amelia toward the stern cabin. "Wait," Rebecca protested, twisting her head around, seeking Captain Smithers and some measure of reassurance. "I want to—"

"Get below," the sailor snapped, shoving her toward the door. "You, too." That, to Mr. Neville, who was staring in the direction where the *Raven* had been sighted, a look of horrified fascination on his face. "You're in the way."

"Oh, Becky!" Amelia wailed. "We shall all be killed!"

"Nonsense," Rebecca replied, the need to protect Amelia asserting itself over her fear. "Captain Smithers won't let him get us." Would he? Her last glimpse of the deck as she stumbled down the companionway to the passengers' quarters, hampered by her long skirts, showed the men scurrying to and fro, climbing into the rigging, bringing out the big cannons in preparation for a fight. In that brief glimpse she saw fear and grim determination on the faces of the crew. Heart sinking, she remembered again the times she had met Brendan Fitzpatrick. She remembered again seeing him in action on a narrow dusty street near a tavern, and she could at last believe all that had been said of him.

The door to the stern cabin banged shut, a terribly final sound. Amelia wailed again, and in the gloom Mr. Neville struck a lucifer match, though light filtered down from the skylight above. They were in the saloon, which served as dining room and parlor for the captain and his passengers, and now seemed like a trap. "I say. They could at least let me join the fight," he said without conviction.

Rebecca pulled off her bonnet. "Amelia, do stop screeching. We've no time for it."

"But, Becky, we're going to die or worse—"

"Stop it!" she snapped, and Amelia stared at her in surprise. If she allowed Amelia to fall into a panic, then she would, and nothing would be gained by that. "We'll be safe."

"Fear not, ladies." Mr. Neville came out of his stateroom, thrusting an oilskin-wrapped packet inside his coat. Rebecca felt unreasonably disappointed. She had hoped he'd gone for a weapon. "I shall protect you."

"Oh, Mr. Neville, you are so brave," Amelia said, her eyes huge. "Do you think we'll fight them off?"

"I would think so, dear lady." He patted her hand. "Now let us go into our staterooms and do our best to protect ourselves."

Rebecca stared at him. To protect himself, he meant. She had little confidence in Mr. Neville. His first concern was for himself. That meant that she and Amelia were alone.

What little courage she had left drained away, leaving her shaking. *Oh, Father!* she thought, almost in prayer. When he had sent them on their long voyage, he surely hadn't envisioned them like this, in danger with no one to protect them. If he had, however, he would expect her to do what she always had. He would expect her to take care of her sister.

The thought steadied her. She couldn't go to pieces with Amelia relying on her. No matter what happened, she had to make certain her sister was safe. Papa would expect it of her.

The *Curlew* was in sight. Even the men on the deck of the *Raven* could see her without the aid of a spyglass. Three miles ahead, two miles, now one. She was bending on sail, Brendan noted from his perch at the foretopsail yardarm, but she didn't seem to be making much headway. That was as he'd planned it. He'd waited for just the right conditions of winds and waves, for calm seas and a wind to the quarter, or side, of the ship. For the *Raven* it was the most favorable wind direction, but the *Curlew* was full-rigged and did best with winds coming from dead aft. To make headway, she had to tack constantly, swinging back and forth in a zigzag line. It not only lost her precious time; it meant too many of the crew had to be involved in sailing the ship. Brendan smiled grimly. Good. His victory would be that much easier.

From the *Curlew* there was a flash, a puff of smoke, and then an echoing boom. The cannonball flew through the air, splashing as it fell into the sea, far short of its mark. So. Battle was joined. "Hold your fire," he called down to the deck. The carronades were accurate at close quarters, but not at this distance. No use wasting precious shot. His men were well-trained, gunners in the Royal Navy before deserting, and he intended to take full advantage of their skill.

Closer now, and closer, and he could see the *Curlew*'s crew scurrying about on her deck. Even from this distance they had the look of frightened men, and that was good. Frightened men made mistakes and defeated themselves. He wanted to get out of this encounter with as little bloodshed as possible.

The *Curlew*'s cannon boomed again, and again the ball fell short. But now it was time. The other ship was in range of their long guns. "Mr. Wright," he bawled down, and a grizzled man wearing a red-and-white striped shirt and dirty white trousers looked up. "Prepare port guns to fire."

"Aye, Cap'n! Ready guns."

"Mr. Goldrick." This to another grizzled veteran, in the bow of the ship, standing near the long gun set on a pivot. "Fire when ready."

"Aye, Cap'n!" The gunner set flame to the cannon's fuse. It fired with a roar that shook the ship and made Brendan grin fiercely as he slid down the line to the deck. A cheer went up from his crew, ragged but heartfelt, and he whipped around to see what had caused it. Their shot had taken down *Curlew*'s mainmast, effectively crippling her.

It was the first victory in an afternoon of victory. Commanding from the stern of the *Raven*, Brendan experienced it all with crystal clarity: heard the crashing of gunfire and the screams of men dying in agony; smelled the acrid odor of gunpowder, hanging like a pall over both ships; saw his own crew scurry into the rigging to take positions on the yardarms and rake their opponent with small-arms fire. Swiftly the *Raven* edged up to her quarry, her guns firing and her crew yelling in the fierce exultation of battle. The *Curlew* fought back, her crew raking the *Raven* with shot of their own as the two ships came abreast of each other. Some found their mark; near one of the *Raven*'s guns, a man fell, screaming, and one cannon ball flew clear through the mainsail, leaving a ragged hole. But they weren't defeated. "Port tack," Brendan yelled to his crew, and the *Raven* shifted, sheering away from the other ship, fast in spite of the ruined mainsail. The first action of the battle was theirs.

Again they came around, and again, and the *Curlew* fought desperately on, until, at last, Brendan saw what had been inevitable from the beginning. The *Curlew* struck her colors, taking down the Union Jack from her stern. Another cheer went up from the *Raven,* followed by a louder one when the white flag of surrender fluttered from the *Curlew.* Brendan grinned. They had won the day.

"The shooting has stopped," Rebecca said, raising her head. She was crouched on the floor of her stateroom, Amelia, hands shielding her ears, held close to her. The roaring of the cannon had stopped, and the subsequent shaking of the ship, and yet Rebecca still shuddered as if the battle continued. "I think it's over."

Amelia raised her head. "Did we win?"

"I don't know," she said just as someone pounded on the door. She stiffened, clutching Amelia closer. If someone tried to break in, there was no way she could stop them.

"Miss Talbot?" a voice said from outside.

Rebecca relaxed and rose, though Amelia clung to her, and opened the door to see Neville, his cravat askew and his hair standing on end. "Is it over?"

"It appears to be." He patted his shoulder, as if to reassure himself that his packet was safe. "I don't know if we won, but, fear not, dear lady. I'll protect you and your sister."

"Thank you," Rebecca said with absolutely no trace of irony as she stepped out into the saloon. If they had lost, who else could she depend on?

"Becky," Amelia whimpered.

"Hush." Rebecca briefly laid her cheek on Amelia's hair, feeling far more like her mother than her sister. " 'Tis all right. It seems to be over."

"Did we win?"

"I don't know. Mr. Neville? Should we go on deck to find out what is going on?"

"We'll know soon enough," he said, making no move, and at that moment the door to the deck banged open. The noise made Rebecca cringe almost as much as Amelia did.

"You, down there." It was the first mate, strained and dirty-looking. "Are you safe?"

"Yes," Rebecca called and was ashamed of the way her voice wobbled. "Did we win?"

"Stay there," he commanded and moved off.

"Mercy." That didn't sound hopeful. "I wonder if we should go see what's happening."

"We're safer here," Neville said. The light revealed him crouching against the wall, his eyes glittering.

Rebecca glanced about the saloon. An eerie quiet pervaded everything, and broken glass from the skylight crunched underfoot. Here was a measure of safety, and yet the suspense of not knowing their future was unbearable. "I have to know," she said and stepped onto the first stair of companionway.

"Becky!" Amelia threw herself at her. "Don't leave me!"

"I'm not, Melia." She pulled Amelia's hands from about her waist. "I just want to see what's happening."

"B-but—"

"Stop whining! I'll be but a moment," she said and began to climb, exasperated both with Amelia and herself. Her sister couldn't help what she was; she'd been sheltered from life and had never had to face any of its harsh realities. Rebecca, however, hadn't the luxury of giving in to her fears.

She had reached the top of the companionway, and for the first time wondered at the wisdom of what she was doing. It was eerily quiet above her, the mingled odors of blood and gunpowder making her gorge rise in her throat. Dread curled in her stomach, and yet something stronger urged her on. Taking a deep breath, she eased her head out the door.

The harsh sunlight and the pall of smoke made her eyes water, so that it was a few moments before she could take everything in. The mainmast lay on deck, a tangle of rope and canvas and splintered wood. Sickeningly, a man's leg protruded from under the wreckage. More men lay on pallets, some moaning, some too quiet. And the deck ran red. Rebecca swallowed, hard, and looked away, over the ship's rail. There, just a few yards away, was the *Raven*.

Oh, she was a fearsome sight, black as the devil's soul, sharp and sleek as glass. Men were in her prow, in her rigging, knives at the ready in their teeth, a sight made even more frightening by the absolute silence. Even the normal sounds of a ship at sea, the creak of rigging, the splash of waves, were muted. The *Raven* seemed almost a ghost ship as she drifted closer, except for her savage-looking crew.

And him. Standing in the bow, one foot braced on the rail and looking not one bit ruffled, was Brendan Fitzpatrick.

Her breath caught in her throat. Fear, of course, for he looked devilish, and as black at heart as the bird of prey for which he was named. The light of battle glowed in his one good eye, and tension was lined in every part of his body. He looked ready to spring from one ship to the other at a moment's notice, and as if he would soar while doing so. It could mean only one thing. The *Curlew* had lost the fight.

Abruptly she pulled back, scurrying down the companionway. "Into the stateroom, Amelia, and hurry!" she gasped, flying across the saloon to her sister. "We must find some way to protect ourselves. I think—oh!" Her voice broke off as a great, grating sound echoed through the ship, and a jolt made the floor tilt crazily. Rebecca flung her arm out to maintain her balance. "What in the world—we must have collided."

"The *Raven*?" Neville said, crouching near the wall.

"Yes. I think—"

"Are we sinking?" Amelia asked.

"No. But we'll be safer in the stateroom, if it comes to a fight."

Amelia's eyes widened. "B-but I thought it was over."

"It is. In with you, Melia." She hustled her sister into the stateroom and slammed the door behind them, looking around for something to bar the door. It was futile. All the furniture was bolted down. "It's over, and we're safe. See? We aren't hurt at all."

"B-but the pirates—"

"Won't hurt us." She spoke with far more assurance than she felt. "The Raven knows who we are. He won't dare harm us." Amelia shivered, and so she rushed on. "At the worst, he'll want to ransom us."

"Do you mean he'll take us prisoner?"

"No, of course not," she said soothingly, though that was exactly what she thought. "I imagine he wants the cargo."

Hope crept into Amelia's face. "Do you think so?"

"I most certainly do." Rebecca hugged her, mentally praying for forgiveness for her lie. No matter what happened, no matter what it took, she would protect her sister, she thought, and repressed a shudder. Now was not the time to break down. Now, with her father's admonitions ringing in her ears, with Amelia depending on her, was the time for her

to be brave. Tightening her arm about Amelia, she raised her
head and prepared to face the fury of the Raven.

The ships' hulls groaned and complained as they grated
together. Before they were completely still Brendan leaped
across to the *Curlew*'s quarterdeck, making nothing of the
green water below. From the *Raven* his men were throwing
grappling hooks, securing the ships together. All was calm,
orderly, and very tense. While Smithers' face wore the
white, sagging look of defeat, his crew still stood ready and
armed. It would take little for them to erupt, Brendan
thought. An accidental jostle, a word spoken in haste, and
he'd have another battle on his hands. Fortunately his men
were well trained; they swarmed over the side, calmly and
quietly taking up their stations. One man went to the helm;
others took up posts at the guns, silent now, while still others
collected weapons. And still the tense, tight silence pre-
vailed.

"Captain." He spoke briskly as he approached Smithers.
"My compliments on a fine fight."

"It was one I could have done without," Smithers rumbled. So there was a spark of fight left in the man yet.

"I'll have your papers, and your bill of lading. And don't
be thinkin' to foist a false one on me," he said at the look
that appeared in Smithers' eyes. "I've seen that trick before,
boyo."

"I am a man of honor, sir. I would not think of such a
thing."

"Good lad." Not that it would matter if he had. The *Curlew* was Brendan's now, aye, and all she held. "And your
passengers?" he asked.

"For the love of God, man! They're helpless women,"
Smithers erupted.

"Ye've my word, they'll not be harmed."

"The word of a scoundrel."

"Careful, boyo." In a lightning quick move, the blade of
his knife snicked out, posed at Smithers' throat. " 'Twould
be wise not to insult me."

Smithers swallowed, but his gaze remained steady. "What
do you plan to do with them?"

"Return them for ransom, of course. Sam." He snapped
his fingers, and Sam glided quietly to his side. "Find Mr.

Neville and gather his belongings. I'll see to the ladies myself."

"I'll come with you," Smithers said stiffly.

"As you wish." Brendan turned away. Below him, on the main deck, some order was being returned to the chaos. Those of the *Curlew*'s crew who were still able to stand had been gathered together in a small, ragged group, while his own men cleared away the debris from the fallen mainmast and helped those injured who lay beneath. "Who among you is American?" he called, and silence fell over the ship. "Speak up, now. I know some of you are."

"Why do you want to know?" a voice came from below.

Brendan braced his hands on the quarterdeck railing. "You, boyo. Come here. From New England, are ye?"

The sailor who had spoken pushed his way forward, taking his time. He was tall and lanky, and his red hair spilled over his soot-smudged face in an untidy hank. "Ayuh. From down east. Maine."

"What is a good New Englander like yourself doing on the enemy's ship?"

"I was impressed." The sailor stood at ease, hands tucked into trouser pockets, shoulders slouched back. A likely lad, showing courage at a time like this, Brendan thought, though he kept his face impassive. "Shipped out of Boothbay for Cathay, and we were stopped by a ship of the line." He spat, and Brendan's impression of him went up a notch. "Limeys pretended not to believe me when I said who I was."

"So what are you doin' here, boyo, when it's home you could be? Or on one of your own country's ships?"

"And be impressed again? And this time be flogged for deserting? Thought this would be safer." The contemptuous way his eyes flicked toward Brendan showed what he thought of that course now. "Besides, no work at home. Jefferson's dambargo closed all the ports."

"Aye." President Jefferson's embargo, along with the various obstructions to trade since, was much hated in the seacoast states. "What is your name?"

"Tom Corby."

"Well, Tom Corby, you're free now. Stay if you wish, or join with me."

"You?"

"Aye." Brendan almost smiled at the scorn in the man's voice. "At least I'm not British, boyo."

"Ayuh. I'll think on it."

"Do that. Any other Americans here?" He surveyed the crew, but no others came forward. "Well, then. Any deserters from His Majesty's Navy?"

"Not on my ship!" Smithers exclaimed as several sailors stepped forward.

Brendan ignored him. "You're free to go or stay, too, lads. The rest of ye'll be brought back to the Indies. Mind yourselves and ye'll not be hurt. Now." He turned back to Smithers. "About your passengers."

Smithers' face had gone from the pallor of defeat to the purplish red of outrage. "You are no gentleman, sirrah."

"Aye." Brendan's teeth gleamed in a lazy smile. "But then, I never claimed to be. Your passengers, sir?"

Smithers glared at him a moment longer, and then his shoulders slumped. "They're below. But let me come with you," he added as Brendan turned away. "They're gentlewomen, easily frightened. If I'm with you they'll feel safer."

Brendan inclined his head and followed Smithers across the main deck to the hatch that led below. The younger Miss Talbot might scare easily, but the older didn't strike him so. Still, Smithers had a point. With him there taking them would likely be easier. God spare him from hysterical females.

The saloon was dark. From one stateroom came Neville's rusty voice, raised in protest. Brendan held back a smile. Sam would be implacable, gathering up all of Neville's belongings, and that was what mattered. This other business, with the Talbot sisters, was trifling, a minor inconvenience.

"Miss Talbot." Smithers was pounding on a door. "I must request that you and your sister come out."

There was silence for a moment. "No." It was Rebecca, sounding clear and unafraid. Brendan held back another smile.

"Miss Talbot, please." Smithers cast a look back at Brendan and wiped his forehead with his hand. "Captain Fitzpatrick has given his word you'll not be harmed."

"His word!"

"Aye, *leannan*." Brendan stepped forward. "It may not be much, but 'tis all I have."

"Ha!"

"Miss Talbot, please," Smithers said again. "I'm afraid there's no choice."

"There's always a choice, Captain. One can fight on, or one can give in."

"Or one can retreat to fight another day," Brendan said.

There was a pause. "That sounds like a challenge, sir."

"No, lass. Just pointin' out the folly of resisting."

Another pause. "Are you alone?"

He glanced at Smithers. "Aye."

"Very well." There was a click as a key turned in the lock. "You may come in."

"Thank you." He set his hand on the door handle, distrustful of this sudden acquiescence. Miss Talbot had shown herself to be capable of surprises before. 'Twould be wise for him to be prepared now.

He opened the door and stepped into the stateroom. The portholes were covered, and it took a moment for his eyes to adjust to the gloom. The younger girl crouched in a corner, her eyes wide with fear and what he suspected might also be excitement. A lovely lass, he thought detachedly, but it was not on her that his gaze stayed. For, there before him, hunched over as if prepared to fight, was Rebecca, and in her hand was a knife.

Chapter 4

~

Brendan's first reaction was to laugh. Reprehensible, since she was obviously frightened, but there it was. She looked like nothing so much as an angry kitten, puffed up and spitting at an opponent too large for her. Aye, an angry, tawny kitten, with hair like fur that would be soft to the touch. . . .

But that was not what he was here for. "Is it that you don't trust me, *leannan*?" he said, stepping forward.

"Keep away." The knife slashed through the air, bringing him to an abrupt stop. He doubted she knew how to use a knife, and that made her dangerous.

He took a cautious step. "You'll not be needing that, *leannan*."

"Keep away, I said!" The knife slashed through the air again. "And don't call me that ridiculous name."

"Ridiculous, is it?" Arms crossed, he leaned against the wall, giving the impression of relaxed amusement. In reality his muscles were coiled and his eyes were alert, searching for any faltering in her movements. If he acted hastily or wrongly, she could be hurt. For himself he had no fear. "Ah, lass, d'ye think you're a match for me with that?"

"No." A lock of her hair had fallen over her shoulder, and she brushed it back impatiently. "But I will use it, I assure you."

"Maybe if I talk with her," Smithers said, and Brendan motioned him to silence with a sharp wave of his hand.

"I've no doubt ye do, but there's no need."

"No need? When you've come to take us captive and do

God knows what with us? No, thank you. I will, as you warned me, watch out for pirates."

"Ah, so ye remember that, do ye?" Never taking his eyes from the knife, from her, he slipped quietly to the side.

"Much to my sorrow."

"Then ye'll remember how I disarmed a man who was more of a threat than ye'll ever be, *leannan*."

"I told you not to call me that."

"No? Suits ye, it does." He took another sideways step, and another, until he faced her directly. "D'ye know of my land, Rebecca? D'ye know of the green, green hills, and the soft mist that always falls? D'ye know the poetry, and the sorrow? Ye'd like it there, lass. 'Twould suit your soul."

"Leave my soul out of this," she said, so tartly that he chuckled.

"And the temper, aye, ye've that, too. A poor land, my country." He slid forward, so silently and slowly it was almost imperceptible. "Rocky and barren in too many places, but rich in so many ways." Another careful, cautious step forward, his gaze never leaving hers. Keep talking, keep her listening, distracted, and in a moment he could reach out and grab the knife from her. "Ye need a temper to survive, but ye need the poetry, too. Have ye heard it, *leannan*? *'Rom-lín múich i n-ignais Éirenn.' "*

She looked interested in spite of herself. "I—what does that mean?"

"It is 'Colum Cille's Lament.' 'I ever long for the land of Ireland.' " And while he spoke he took advantage of her distraction, closed the gap between them, and clamped his fingers on her wrist.

Instantly she went wild, bucking and fighting against him. "No! Let me go!"

"Drop the knife, Rebecca." It was softly spoken, but a command, nevertheless.

"Never. I'll—ah!" She gasped as he abruptly tightened his grip. Her fingers relaxed, as if suddenly nerveless, and the knife clattered to the floor. With one smooth movement he bent to retrieve it, and then caught her against him. Her eyes were huge and luminous with pain and frustration and defeat. She held herself rigid, and yet he was aware of her, of the surprising softness of a figure he'd thought was angular, of a scent in her hair he couldn't define. Danger. "A lesson for ye, lass," he said. "When I give an order, 'tis wise to obey."

Rebecca gaped at him. He had disarmed her so easily, and not just with the knife. With his teasing smile, his lilting voice, he'd gotten past all her defenses, making her forget for a moment that he was the enemy. Defeat rose bitter in her mouth, and she twisted away. She would not show weakness before this man. "It is easy to overcome someone weaker than you."

"Smaller, perhaps," he said. She looked back in surprise. Surely that wasn't admiration she'd heard in his voice? Before she could ponder that, however, he was speaking again. "Ye'll be transferred to the *Raven,* ye and your sister, and ye'll be ransomed." His glance flicked over to Amelia. "Come out, lass. There's no danger to ye."

Rebecca studied his face. He seemed sincere, but how could she know? Amelia, though, would be safer with her.

"Melia," she said, holding out her arm.

Amelia didn't move. "I—I'm scared."

Rebecca turned toward her sister, but stayed in place; no telling what the unpredictable man behind her might do should she move too fast, and she didn't want Amelia scared even more. "I'll be with you, Melia. Papa trusted me to take care of you, didn't he?"

Amelia stirred. "Y-yes," she said, and at last rose to her knees from her huddled position. Keeping as far from Brendan as possible, she scuttled across the stateroom to Rebecca's sheltering arm.

Brendan made an ironic bow. "After you, ladies." He gestured toward the door and followed behind the two girls as they stepped out into the saloon. Amelia clung to her sister; Rebecca held her head high. He felt reluctant admiration for her. He doubted he would have been so brave in such circumstances.

As he stepped into the saloon, his gaze met Sam's. Sam shook his head, his grip on Neville's arm tight. So. Sam's search hadn't been successful. Brendan nodded in return, and he saw Sam's gaze shift to Rebecca. Sam's eyes grew reproachful, a look which Brendan ignored. In spite of his muteness Sam communicated his feelings remarkably well, but Brendan was not about to apologize for what he had done. Some things were necessary.

"Miss Talbot." He made his voice abrupt. "Sam will see you safely to the *Raven*."

Rebecca glanced back at him, and her hold tightened on her sister. In no other way, however, did she show any fear, and his respect for her grew. "Very well," she said, her voice as brisk as his.

"B-but, Becky," Amelia protested.

"Hush. 'Twill be all right, Melia," Rebecca said, and, head high, climbed the companionway to the deck.

Neville made as if to follow. "No, Neville, not you," Brendan's voice cracked out, and the other man glanced quickly around, his features sharpened by fear and cunning. "We've things to discuss, boyo."

For the second time in—could it possibly be just a few minutes? Rebecca looked out at the deck, this time stepping out. So much had happened, so much had changed, that it felt as if many lifetimes had passed. All about her, in the very air, lay the carnage and detritus of battle: the ruined mast; the coppery smell of blood; the groans and cries of the injured men. Yet at some point a strange calm had descended upon her, adding brilliant unreality to all she saw. This couldn't be real. She couldn't really be standing on the deck of a ship taken captive by a pirate, wasn't really being guarded by a mute, frightening giant of a man, didn't really have to cross that narrow plank from one ship to the other. For the first time, fear for herself assailed her, fear of heights, fear of what lay below. The board that stretched from the *Curlew*'s bulwark to the *Raven*'s railing dipped and swayed with the movement of the sea, not at all a secure foothold, so much like the gangplank from which she'd fallen as a child. She hunched her shoulders. Surely it would slip if she stepped on it, surely it would sag and fall, and—

A hand touched her arm, and she looked up to see Sam regarding her. He had nice eyes, she thought irrelevantly, strange in a pirate. Liquid brown eyes that regarded her with what surely couldn't be concern. "The—the plank," she said, swallowing hard. "Must we cross on that?"

Sam inclined his head gravely. "Is it—are you sure 'tis safe?"

"Oh, Becky!" Amelia wailed, burrowing closer. "I don't want to go on it, I'll fall, I know I will."

"Hush, Amelia!" Her own fear made her voice harsh. To

her surprise, Amelia quieted, making her feel momentary regret for her harshness. Of course Amelia was frightened. Her own paltry fear of heights was nothing next to Amelia's terror. "I'll cross first."

"Oh, no, don't leave me—"

"Stop being a ninny!" she said, impatient again. "One of us must go, and would you rather go on the *Raven* first?"

From under the safety of Rebecca's arm, Amelia peered toward the other ship and saw what Rebecca herself was all too aware of: a crowd of dirty, leering men, making a mockery of all Brendan Fitzpatrick's assurances of safety. "N-no. But I don't want you to leave me, Becky."

"You'll be right behind me, and then we'll be together. I promise. Don't cling." She freed herself from Amelia's clutching fingers. "I trust our belongings will be brought over?" she said, looking up at Sam, and again he inclined his head. "Thank you. Very well. I am ready."

There was a sudden sharp, piercing whistle, making her jump. Looking up, she saw Sam holding two fingers to his lower lip. It must have been some sort of command; instantly men on both ships leaped to the plank, holding it steady on either side. Small comfort; they were dirty and disreputable and would probably try to look up her skirts. But at least it was an attempt to make the crossing easier. Squaring her shoulders, she let Sam hoist her onto the plank.

Her stomach lurched. *Don't be silly,* she scolded herself. She wasn't really that high up. *Take a step. Don't look down. But if I fall—no, don't think of it.* The plank rose with the motion of the ships, so that she was going uphill one moment, down the next. She concentrated on keeping her footing. If she looked down, she'd be lost. If she allowed herself to remember how narrow the plank was, how slight the margin between her and disaster—*No! Stop thinking that way, or you will fall. And then who will take care of Amelia?*

The thought strengthened her, gave her something to cling to. She adored her sister, always had, from the moment of her birth. When Amelia's mother, Rebecca's stepmother, had died when Amelia was just a small girl, Rebecca had taken over her care, though she was still a child herself. Amelia depended on her. More importantly, her father depended on her. She could not let him down. She could not—

Strong hands grasped her elbows and swung her into the air. She gave a small cry, but then there was a solid surface beneath her feet again. It moved with the sea, true, but at least it was broad and substantial. There was also a hand on her posterior. Without thinking, she glared at the sailor who stood behind her, and, grinning, he moved away. It was unsettling. Men didn't pay her that kind of attention. It made her fear for her safety, and her sister's.

Looking up, she saw Amelia, face deadly pale, on the plank, and her heart flew into her throat. If she fell—but Amelia made the crossing safely, to be swung down to the deck by the same two men who had caught Rebecca. She moved swiftly to Amelia, glaring again at the sailor who had accosted her. They were together again. They were also, dear God protect them, aboard an infamous pirate ship.

She hadn't heard Sam cross the plank, but suddenly he was there beside her, taking her and Amelia by the arms and leading them across the deck. The crew parted for them and yet pressed close, making Rebecca uncomfortably aware of how alone she and Amelia were, and how far from help. She caught glimpses of soot-darkened faces and gap-toothed grins, and earrings worn barbarically in one ear, or, in one astonishing case, in the nose, of men of all shapes and sizes and colors. Their odors pressed upon her as, head down, teeth clamped together, she passed through the gauntlet, hearing whistles and catcalls and muttered comments about her attributes that made her face turn a fiery red. Worse was the feeling of being stared at, an almost tactile sensation that made her skin crawl. Much as she wanted to see how her sister was faring, on Sam's other side, she didn't dare look up. To do so was to face madness.

Before her yawned an open hatch. Before she could quite comprehend what was happening, Sam pushed her into it, down a ladder steeper even than the companionway aboard the *Curlew*. Amelia stumbled down behind her, and in the dim light they looked around, finding themselves in a dark, narrow passageway. Amelia clung to her, but was mercifully silent. Sam came last, and lighting a lantern that hung suspended to the ceiling, led them down the passageway, stopping at a door. Inside, Rebecca could see a tiny room, with two pallets on the floor and little else. The porthole was heavily glazed and barred and let in little light, and another lantern swung from the ceiling above. If the room had been cleaned recently, it certainly didn't look it; it smelled of sweat and human despair.

From somewhere, Rebecca found courage. "Surely this can't be right," she said, facing Sam. In return he grunted, and indicated the room. "But—oh, very well. I suppose if we don't go in ourselves you'll push us in."

"B-Becky." Amelia's teeth chattered. "I don't like this."

"I'll see what I can do about it later, Amelia," she said soothingly. "At least if the door's locked we'll be safe. You will lock the door?"

Sam inclined his head, and for some reason Rebecca felt oddly reassured. Grasping Amelia's hand, she stepped into the room, the darkness overwhelming her. The last thing she saw before the door closed behind him was Sam's eyes. Odd. She could have sworn they held regret.

The key turned in the lock, and Sam's footsteps echoed as he trod away. Rebecca and Amelia looked at each other and then fell into each other's embrace, shaking. They were alone and, for the moment, safe. But for how long? For they were, against Rebecca's worst fears, captives on a pirate ship.

A scraping noise jolted Rebecca from sleep. Sitting bolt upright, she rubbed at her eyes, dizzy and disoriented as the pallet beneath her rocked back and forth. Where was she—oh. On the *Raven*. Dread settled deep in the pit of her stomach. Mercy, how could she ever have fallen asleep?

Beside her, Amelia stirred sleepily. "Becky?" she murmured.

"Shh." Rebecca laid a hand on her shoulder, sensing danger. It must be evening. The light had faded since they had been thrust into this room. Against the darkness a small, square space showed high in the wall opposite. It took her a moment to realize she was staring at the door, which evidently had a window set in it. The scraping noises she had heard had probably been the cover being pulled back.

"They in there?" a gruff masculine voice said from the other side of the door, and she jumped.

"Can't see them." A man's face peered in, making both Rebecca and Amelia shrink back. It was an evil-looking face, bristling with beard, with a walleye and a grin that displayed rotted stumps of teeth. "Sam brought 'em here, though. Saw that myself."

"Cap'n don't usually take prisoners," the other voice said. "Least, not women. Wonder what he's got in mind?"

His companion laughed, as evil a sound as his face. "What do you think? 'Bout time we had a bit of sport on this ship."

Amelia whimpered, and Rebecca squeezed her shoulder. Somehow it was imperative that the men not know she could hear them.

"He won't share." That was the first speaker. "Cap'n keeps to himself. Stands to reason he'll keep these two to himself, too."

"Yeah, but if he doesn't." He leaned into the room. "Can't see 'em now, but did you get a look at 'em when they came aboard? That tall one, she's a little too long in the tooth for me, but the other one." He muttered something too low for Rebecca to catch, but the other man's coarse laughter told her it hadn't been pleasant.

"Yeah," he agreed. "Fact, if we could get the door open right now—"

There was no sound, but all of a sudden the little window in the door was filled by a dark, menacing shape. Amelia let out a little cry, and Rebecca hugged her harder, biting her lips to stifle her own exclamation of fear. Dimly from outside she heard the two men talking, almost babbling, and she opened her eyes again. "Becky?" Amelia whispered.

"Shh." Rebecca cocked her head toward the door, listening intently.

"We weren't doin' nothin'," one of the men said in something close to a whine.

"We was just looking," the other man chimed in. "Nothing wrong with that, is there, Sam?"

For a moment there was an ominous silence. Then the first man spoke, nervously respectful. "Didn't mean no harm, Sam."

"Yeah," the other man echoed. "We'll get back on deck, Sam. Leave 'em to the cap'n."

"C'mon," the first man muttered, and the sound of hasty footsteps told of their departure. Rebecca let out her breath. The menace was gone. She held her head high as Sam looked in. He was their enemy, but for now he was also their protector. From somewhere she found the courage to meet his eyes, until he looked away.

"Sam," she called on impulse, and he turned. "My sister and I are hungry. May we have something to eat? And please tell the captain I'd like to see him."

Sam studied them for a moment, and then nodded. Rebecca sagged in relief as he closed the window on the door. They weren't safe, not by a long measure, but for now no one would accost them. Sam would see to that.

"Becky," Amelia said, her voice very small. "Did you hear what they were saying?"

"Don't worry about it, Melia." Rebecca settled back on the pallet. "I think Sam will keep them away from us."

"I'm not a child!" Amelia flared. "I know what pirates do to women."

Rebecca stared at her in surprise. "Amelia—"

"Maybe those two won't do anything, but what about him? Sam? What about," her voice cracked, "the Raven?"

Rebecca closed her eyes. "I don't know, Melia," she said, though she very much feared she did know. They were both in for a difficult time. Unless—

She straightened, stunned by the idea that had just come to her, and at that moment Amelia spoke. "The viscount will never want me after this."

"Oh, Melia, of course he will," she said without any conviction. The viscount would want a spotless bride, not someone who had been corrupted by a pirate. And Father—Rebecca's breath caught painfully in her chest. Father would never forgive her if she allowed any harm to come to Amelia. It would be another sin to add to her long list of transgressions, and no amount of penance would ever expiate her guilt in his eyes. She had to protect her sister, and she thought she had a way. "I'll take care of it, Melia," she said softly. "I promise."

Brendan leaped nimbly from the *Curlew* onto the deck of the *Raven,* glad to be back, glad this business was over. In his cabin had already been deposited the gold bullion Smithers had carried; in his pocket crackled papers, documents for the *Curlew;* documents, as well, that served a vastly different purpose, and were worth more than the bullion. His mission had been a success.

The lines that held the two ships together had already been loosed. Aboard the *Curlew* his own men had taken command, and were jury-rigging a new mast. Once the repairs were done the *Curlew* would return to the West Indies. There in that chain of tiny scattered islands, they would put in at a harbor known to only a few, and the ship's cargo would be broken up and sold. Smithers and Neville, now locked in their cabins, would be set free beforehand. Brendan trusted that Neville would speedily return to Washington City with the messages Brendan had given him. Soon Mr. Talbot would know his daughters had been taken hostage, and would make arrangements to pay the ransom.

Brendan frowned, so fiercely that a seaman nearby, sprinkling heated vinegar on the deck to wash away the smell of blood, glanced at him nervously. The plight of the Talbot sisters left a sour taste in his mouth. He rarely took hostages, having found they caused too many complications, but his instructions had been clear. This mission was too important to jeopardize; the hostages were to be used to cover its real purpose. That they were women was incidental, and, he admitted to himself as he went down to his cabin, a problem. He would have to maintain strict discipline so that they would not be bothered by his men.

"Was it a success, Cap'n?" Tyner, his steward, asked when Brendan walked into his cabin.

"Aye." Brendan crossed the room and unlocked a cabinet, carefully stowing the papers inside. "Neville didn't part with them easily, though."

"What'd he think, ye asking for his papers?"

Brendan sat down at the table. "Thought it was an odd thing for a pirate to want, until I assured him I planned to sell them to the highest bidders." He grinned wolfishly. "English or American."

Tyner grinned back. Success for the Raven meant success for the entire ship, and in more than just profit. "A good day's work, then."

"Aye." Brendan's face sobered. "Except there were six men lost on the *Curlew,* and we've four injured."

Tyner shrugged. "The perils of war, Cap'n. Now. Be ye hungry? Cook's made a fine fish stew."

"Aye. I've a hunger to sink a ship." He smiled at the unintentional irony. "Tyner," he said, and the steward stopped in the doorway. "How are our passengers?"

Tyner's smile faded as he turned, hands on hips. "Proper scared, and what else did ye expect? What d'ye think you're doin' with them, Cap'n?"

"Orders, Tyner."

"Aye, well, I don't like it. Sam caught two of the crew lookin' in at them before."

Brendan sat upright. "Who?"

"Marley and Stevens. Sam took care of 'em, but it won't be the end of it, Cap'n. Not with two ladies aboard."

"Devil take it." Brendan got up and paced over to the wide stern window. The trouble was happening already. "Make it known that anyone who so much as looks at those girls the wrong way won't get his share of the profits."

"That'll cause a mutiny, Cap'n!"

"Oh?" Brendan turned, and he was no longer the affable captain, but the Raven, muscles bunched for action and a deadly gleam in his eye. "And who's going to challenge me, boyo?"

"Someone ye don't expect," Tyner said, not at all impressed. "Miss Talbot wants to speak to ye."

Surprise flitted across Brendan's face, and then he smiled. "Now why didn't I expect that? Very well, Tyner. Bring her here. And just her, Tyner. Not the other."

"Aye, Cap'n." Tyner turned to leave. "Maybe ye'll start showin' some sense," he muttered, closing the door behind him.

Brendan let out a sharp, short laugh. No respect for the Raven here, not from Tyner, and not from Sam. But then, they'd known him long before anyone had ever heard of the Raven, even he himself. Together they'd faced many an adventure, and they'd face this one, too. Women aboard his ship. And how, Brendan wondered, sitting down again, would he manage that?

The door to the cell, for that was how Rebecca had come to think of the little room, clanged open with such abruptness that both she and Amelia started. "Cap'n'll see ye now," a small, bandy-legged man announced. "Come on with ye."

Rebecca rose on unsteady legs. "Very well," she said, managing by sheer will to sound calm. "Come, Amelia."

"Cap'n said just you, miss."

Rebecca stared at him, her arm going around Amelia's shoulders. "I can't leave my sister."

"She'll be watched."

"No." She felt like sitting down and crying, and that would never do. "We'll both go to the captain."

" 'Fraid not," the man said, closing the door.

Rebecca's bravado crumpled. "Wait! Don't go."

The door opened again, and he stuck his head in. "Ye willin' to come alone?"

"Yes."

"Becky!" Amelia wailed. "You can't leave me."

"I have to, Amelia." She took her sister's chin in her hand. "We can't stay like this. Perhaps I can talk the captain into giving us some protection."

Amelia's eyes, luminous with tears, gazed up at her. "Do you really think so?"

"Yes," she said, though she had her doubts. She had little to bargain with. Little, that is, that the Raven would want. "You must be brave, Melia."

"I will be." Amelia straightened, squaring her shoulders. "Papa would be proud of you."

Rebecca hugged her briefly. "Thank you," she said, touched by the words, dismayed by the thought of her father's reaction should he learn what she planned to do. "I won't be long, I promise. Look after her," she added to the man, sailing past him into the passageway.

"Sam'll do that. I'm to take ye to the cap'n. Up here, miss, and then down that hatch." He led her onto the deck, and only the knowledge that the crew was staring kept her from stopping to enjoy the air, so fresh after being held below. "I'm Tyner, miss," he added, leading her down another companionway, this one not as steep as the first.

Rebecca nodded. "Tyner." She stepped off the last stair. "And do you enjoy being a pirate?"

"Now, miss." He stopped as he reached a white-paneled door opposite the companionway, his eyes filled with what she could have sworn was reproach. "I only do as I'm told." He opened the door. "Miss Talbot, Cap'n."

"Aye, and so it is." Brendan's voice came out to her, making her stop dead. What in the world was she doing? He'd never listen to her. "Well? Come in, Miss Talbot. Or will ye be tellin' me you're scared?"

"I'm not scared," she retorted, stepping over the threshold into the Raven's cabin. He sat at his ease in a wooden armchair behind a table, shirt opened at his throat to expose tanned skin stretched over taut muscles. Rebecca swallowed, her mouth suddenly dry. She would die before she let him see how frightened she was.

"No? Then ye are either very brave, or very foolish, *leannan*."

"Don't call me that."

"As ye wish. Now. What is it ye want?"

Rebecca clasped her hands primly before her. "It's more a matter of what you want, Captain."

"Oh?" He tilted his head. "And what is that, Miss Talbot?"

Rebecca glanced over her shoulder, to where Tyner was watching. "I'd prefer to speak with you alone."

Brendan waved his hands. "I've no secrets from Tyner."

"Perhaps I do," she snapped.

"A feisty one, isn't she, Tyner?" he said, looking past her. "Not scared of the Raven. Imagine that."

"Pray don't mock me, Captain."

"I wouldn't dream of it, *leannan*. Excuse me. Miss Talbot." His eyes gleamed at her. "Very well. Tyner, see to my supper. And don't be too quick."

"But, Cap'n," Tyner protested.

"Now, Tyner," he said, and after a moment Tyner went out. "Well, Miss Talbot? What is so important?"

"I demand to know what your plans are concerning my sister and me."

"Demand, do ye? Not many people demand things of the Raven."

"Oh, don't they? Well, I will. I'm not afraid of you."

He rose. "Aren't you, *leannan*?" he said, stepping closer to her.

Rebecca swallowed again and held her ground. "No."

"Ye should be, ye know." His knuckles grazed her cheek, and she flinched. But not from fear. "Have ye not heard of me?"

"Yes. You are a dastardly pirate, sir."

"Dastardly, is it?" His eye twinkled, and he reached up to twine a lock of her hair, come loose from its tight bun, around his finger. "Ye've beautiful hair."

"Dastardly," she repeated, her voice wobbling. "You prey on any ship, Lord knows how many. They say you've killed a score of men yourself."

He tugged on the curl and then released it. "Do they, now."

"Do you deny it?"

"Oh, likely enough, 'tis true," he said, stepping away. Rebecca took a deep, shaky breath. The immediate danger had passed, but it was there, and it wasn't just in him. It was in herself. She didn't like the way she'd trembled when he touched her cheek, the way her mouth had gone dry when he played with her hair. Oh, she was wicked, wicked, and here she'd tried so hard to destroy that part of herself. The part that enjoyed a man's touch.

She was so caught up in self-recriminations that she didn't realize he'd gone on speaking, until he called her name. "Miss Talbot?"

She blinked, coming back to herself and the position she was in. *Here* was the danger, evoking those old feelings within her. She should run, she should flee while she could, but she knew she wouldn't. "W-what?" she said, her voice unintentionally husky.

"You wanted to speak with me. Very well. I'm listening."

Vaguely her mind registered that in that moment his brogue had lessened, but she had other things to worry about. "I came here to make a bargain with you, Captain."

"Oh?" With almost feline grace he sank into the chair, his hands behind his head. "And what have ye to bargain with?" he said, his gaze roaming almost insultingly over her body.

She flushed. Oh, mercy, this was even more difficult than she had expected. "I would like my sister to be moved to a better cabin, and I would like her to be well guarded. In return ..."

"Yes," he prompted when she didn't go on. "In return?"

"Will you promise she will not be bothered?"

"Mayhaps. In return, Miss Talbot?"

She raised her chin. Difficult or not, she had to go through with this. She had to protect her sister. "In return, for the duration of the voyage, I will be your mistress."

Chapter 5

For a moment Brendan sat very still, startled into silence. "A remarkable offer, lass," he said finally, throwing an arm negligently over the back of his chair. "Are ye sure ye mean it?"

Rebecca thrust out her chin, valiant and stubborn. "Yes."

"I see." Idly, he rubbed his chin, stalling for time. "Almost, you tempt me."

"Then you agree?" she said coolly, surprising him yet again. He had expected at the least annoyance at the insult.

"I did not say that." Leaning back, he studied her. What the devil had prompted her to make such an incredible offer? And what the devil was he going to do about it? She wasn't his usual type, far too sharp and bright, not at all the cuddlesome armful he usually chose. Taking her to bed would be penance for both of them: she likely suffering in silence; he, taking no pleasure from her martyrdom. But then he remembered how she had felt against him when he had taken the knife from her, unexpectedly soft and warm and womanly, and his body reacted with a surge of heat that unnerved and intrigued him.

You're playing with fire, boyo, he told himself, but still he studied her at his leisure, seeking out the treasures that lay hidden beneath the shapeless gray gown. To her credit, she stood still under the scrutiny, though her face was flushed. Hard to tell, but there might be the curve of a breast, there, and the fullness of a hip, there. Tall, too; he wouldn't have to bend to kiss her, and her long legs would wrap around him when—

"Have you seen enough?" she said tartly as he fought against another stronger surge of heat within him. Fire, indeed, and likely he'd be burned. But it was a challenge she offered him, and he did not back down from a challenge.

"Nay, lass." He leaned back. "Take down your hair."

She stared at him. "What?"

"Ye heard me. Take down your hair."

"Why?"

"I've a desire to see it." More than a desire. A pulsing, pounding mindless hunger to see that glorious flame-colored hair loosened from its tight knot, spreading in waves across her shoulders, across the white linen sheets of his bed. Hair that held fire in it, he thought, and that was enough to bring him up short. When he began weaving poetry, 'twas a bad sign. "Come, lass," he said impatiently. "Ye offer to lie with me, but ye will not even unbind your hair?"

She remained standing still, staring at him, and her eyes were as deep and unfathomable as the sea. For some reason, that nettled him. "You mean to begin now?"

"Begin?" He leaned back, swinging his leg up onto the table and reaching for his knife. "Nay, lass. 'Tis simply a wish of mine, to see your hair."

" 'Tis a wish of mine to see the back of you," she blurted out, her eyes on the knife, held casually and competently in his hand.

"Careful, *leannan.*" His voice was deadly soft. " 'Tis not wise to insult me when I have ye in my power."

Her gaze flicked to the knife again. "Are you threatening me with that?"

"This?" He followed her gaze and saw with some surprise that he'd flicked the blade of the knife open. A habit of his when danger was imminent; dangerous, in this instance. "Mayhap," he said carelessly and began to clean his fingernails with the tip of the blade. "If ye don't desire me, lass, why are ye here? It is"—he looked up—"a surprising thing ye suggest."

"I've told you." Rebecca shifted her feet, her attitude very much that of a teacher struggling to get a lesson across to a recalcitrant pupil. For the first time the humor in the situation struck him. "For my sister's sake."

"Generous of ye, lass." He sat up, flicking the knife closed and securing it at his belt. "Are ye certain she'll thank ye for it?"

Two spots of color appeared high in her cheeks. "She knows I'll protect her."

"Protect her? But what if I agree to your bargain and then decide to take ye both?"

"You wouldn't," Rebecca gasped.

"Wouldn't I? But ye forget, I'm a pirate, lass." His smile was ironic as he leisurely swung his legs down and rose, stretching. It had been a prodigious long day, and yet he wasn't tired. Far from it. All his senses were alert, awake to the danger that this woman posed to him, and to what he needed to accomplish. The mission was the important thing. He had no desire to see innocents hurt in the fulfillment of that mission. He was, after all, a man of honor. Aye, but he was also a man, he reminded himself as he slipped from behind the table to stand before her. He had to end this farce now, or the devil knew what the consequences would be. "And are ye certain it's not for yourself you're here?"

Her head jerked up. "I've never heard anything so insulting in my life—"

"Haven't ye, lass? Turning missish on me, then, are ye?"

"I'll have you know, sir, I have never been the least bit missish in my life!"

She sounded so indignant over this insult, far more than over his suggestion that she desired him, that he couldn't help himself. He grinned, the humor and absurdity of the situation striking him at its fullest. She was a prim spinster; he, the Raven, as notorious with women as at sea, resisting what was freely offered. Except that this would have a price. Everything did. "Nay, lass, I didn't really think it of you."

"You're laughing at me," she said, and for the first time sounded uncertain.

"No, Rebecca," he said, reaching out to grasp her chin. "Believe me, I take this very seriously."

"Then why do you hesitate?" she demanded. "Don't pirates plunder and pillage and"—she swallowed—"rape?"

"Ah, lass, but it would not be rape between us." As he had before, he let his fingers stray, feeling her skin satin soft to the touch, hearing her breath catch. "Would it?"

She stared straight ahead, only the rise and fall of her bosom betraying any agitation. He watched it with quickened interest. "I would be willing."

Brendan laughed, genuinely amused. "Spoken like a true martyr."

"Don't mock me!" she exclaimed, flaring up at last, and

again he felt that surge of heat go through him. Mocking her was the furthest thing from his mind.

"Nay, lass, I don't." He stared into her eyes, deep into the green depths. "Take down your hair, Rebecca."

She swallowed, licked her lips, took a deep breath. So did he. He doubted that she was aware of her unconscious sensuality and its effect on him, prim spinster that she was. God help him, he wanted her, he admitted at last, his pulse speeding up as her fingers hesitantly rose to untie the strings of her cap. She fumbled with the knots, and then the cap came free. He swallowed, too, as she raised her arms again, raising her breasts at the same time; watched intently as her fingers felt at the thick knot at her neck for the pins concealed there; felt the blood thrumming in his veins—

And there was a loud, peremptory knock on the door.

"The devil take it!" Brendan exclaimed as Rebecca startled away from him. "Who is it?"

"Me, Cap'n." Tyner walked into the cabin without so much as a by-your-leave.

Brendan stepped back, hands riding his hips. "This had better be important, Tyner," he snapped, watching Rebecca as she stooped to retrieve her cap. Another movement, and that glorious hair would be covered again.

"Aye, Cap'n. Ship bearin' down hard from so-souwest, Cap'n, carrying the Union Jack. Thought ye should know."

"Aye. Tell Sam to call all hands," he said lazily, aware that Rebecca's face had jerked up, her eyes huge. "And Tyner."

Tyner, just opening the door, stopped. "Aye, Cap'n?"

"Next time do not enter without my permission."

"Aye, Cap'n." His glaze flicked back and forth between them. "Anything else, Cap'n?"

"Yes," Brendan said, wondering just how much Tyner had seen. "Have Miss Talbot's belongings moved in here."

"To yer cabin, Cap'n?"

"Yes, to my cabin. Go now," he commanded, and Tyner went out, closing the door very quietly behind him, making clear to Brendan just what he thought of this situation.

Brendan's lips thinned. Devil take it, this was a bad enough fix, without Tyner standing in judgment on him. "Tyner will see that you're comfortable," he said abruptly.

"You won't escape." Rebecca's cap was back in place, along with her composure. "They'll catch you and you'll be hanged."

"Bloodthirsty wench, aren't ye?" Pulling out his keys, he unlocked the cabinet where he stored his pistols.

"No. I merely wish to see justice served."

"It will be." Locking the cabinet, he strode across the room to her and caught her chin in his hand, placing a swift, hard kiss on her lips. She started in surprise, and it was only by a great effort of will that he pulled himself away. That, and the pounding of feet overhead as his crew ran to their stations, preparing for action. This was not the time. "This isn't finished, *leannan,*" he said, and left the cabin. And Rebecca, her knees suddenly too weak to support her, collapsed in a puddle of gray twill on the cabin floor.

A long time later, the door to the cabin again opened. Rebecca, her mind and face blank, looked up to see Tyner, staring back at her. "Be ye hurt, miss?" he asked.

"No. No." Belatedly brought to her senses, Rebecca scrambled to her feet, stumbling in her haste. All this, over one kiss. Shameful. "No, I'm all right."

"Easy there, miss." Tyner reached out a hand to steady her, and she shied away. "Cap'n's orders are for you to stay put," he went on, turning and dragging a trunk into the cabin. Her trunk, she saw with surprise. "Likely we'll outrun the limeys, but he don't want to take no chances with ye."

"No chance I'll escape, you mean," she said tartly.

"Now, miss." Tyner looked up from placing the trunk by the bed. "No one'll hurt ye."

"You think not? You don't know your captain very well."

He grunted. "Know him about as well as anyone does. When ye've unpacked, miss, I'll come back for the trunk."

"Wait!" she said as he turned to leave. "My sister, I must go to her—"

"Cap'n wants ye to stay here, miss."

"But she's never been without me before—"

"Cap'n's orders, miss," he repeated.

"But she'll be so frightened. Please, just let me reassure her—"

"She'll be moved into the cabin next to this one, miss." That stopped her. "She will?"

"Aye, miss. Cap'n's orders."

"And the captain's word is law."

"Yes, miss. Sooner ye learn that, the better for ye."

"Oh, yes," she murmured.

If Tyner heard the irony in her tone, he gave no sign. "I'll be needed topside. Be ye needing anything else, miss?"

Rebecca glanced quickly around the cabin, taking nothing of it in. Above her were the shouts and pounding feet of men preparing for battle, their second of the day, and she doubted they'd lose. Soon she would have to go through with her promise. "No," she said with a short, bitter laugh. "I cannot think of a thing I need at this moment."

Tyner nodded, taking her at her word. "I'll be back later, miss," he said, and went out, closing the door firmly behind him. A moment more, and there was the click of a key in the lock, stopping Rebecca in midstride. If she had thought to leave the cabin, she was mistaken. The Raven apparently took no chances with his captives.

Captive. The word struck a chill deep into her heart. For that was what she was, now, she and Amelia, captives for him to do with as he would. She had only made matters worse by offering herself to him. But, oh mercy, what else could she have done? From long experience she knew well that men would always choose Amelia over her. Usually she didn't mind. Usually they were safe enough suitors. To think of her dainty little sister in the hands of a pirate, however, was terrifying. Amelia would not survive such an ordeal. Rebecca, however, would.

At that moment, she surprised herself by yawning. She was tired, she noted with a strange detachment. Hardly surprising, considering the day she had had. Maybe she would just lie down—but one glance at the bed, and she looked hastily away. This time she took in more of the cabin, though the light was fading. She stared blankly at a cabinet, at the table with rails about its edges, at the unlighted lamp swinging overhead with the motion of the ship, but always her attention returned to the bed. She was tired, so tired, and yet if she lay down she would awaken only heavens knew what kind of ideas in the Raven's mind once he returned; though she had offered to share his bed, it wasn't something she looked forward to. Longingly she looked at the bed, the mattress high and soft, imagining how it would feel under her, and then turned away. It would be better if she sat at the table instead.

Fate decided for her. Though Rebecca had long ago gained her sea legs aboard the *Curlew,* the sudden movement of the ship as she heeled, turning hard, caught her unaware. The angle of the floor abruptly sloped upward, and, off guard, Rebecca lost her balance, tumbling backward, throwing out her arms to save herself. For the first time that day she gave in to her panic, letting out a shrill little shriek that ended when she fell, most emphatically and yet softly, onto the bed. Lying on her back, she blinked with surprise at the ceiling as the ship continued to heel, the angle increasing and making it impossible for her even to sit. Oh, mercy, the bed was as deep and as comfortable as she'd imagined. The Raven apparently did not stint on his own comforts.

Even thinking of him, however, was not quite enough to rouse her. While men shouted overhead, while a distant cannon boomed and sail flapped in the wind, Rebecca's eyes drifted closed. Worn out, beyond caring anymore, she slept.

Full dark, and the pale slice of moon shone down on the great trackless sea. Above, the night sky pressed down like a spangled velvet blanket, and in the wake of the ship's passing, the water glowed with phosphorescence. From his post in the foretopmast, Brendan scanned the sea once more and grinned. Long ago they had left the British frigate behind; though she had carried a full press of sail, she was no match for the nimble *Raven* or her crew. More importantly, the frigate had been diverted from the *Curlew,* for Brendan had deliberately used himself as bait to draw the other ship into pursuit. Now they were safe. The long day was done.

Reaching over, he caught a line and rode it down to the deck. A good day for the most part. That men had died today because of him was something he would live with forever, and yet his mission had been necessary. Now he had only to wait until his demands for ransom were answered, and he would be done. For now.

A few words to Starkey, his second mate, in command of the watch, and Brendan headed aft, letting out a prodigious yawn as he climbed nimbly down the companionway to his quarters. Devil take it, but he was tired. He'd be glad to seek his bed, and—

The devil take it! At the base of the companionway, he stopped. In the excitement of the chase he'd forgotten the events preceding it. What the devil was he going to do with Rebecca? In the ordinary way of things, it wouldn't be a problem. This situation was far from ordinary, however. The Talbot sisters were hostages, and special ones, at that. No harm was meant to come to them, not from his crew, and not from him. That was one reason he had agreed to have Rebecca move into his cabin, and her sister into the one which usually belonged to the first mate, just down the passageway. Women on his ship were a rarity, a temptation to men who would not see land again for many weeks. With them under his eye, he could better protect them. If he was honest with himself, however, he would admit that that wasn't the only reason Rebecca was now in his cabin. Not at all.

Eyeing the door, he pulled out his keys and started toward it, bracing himself for what would happen next. He had just placed the key in the lock when Tyner appeared from the shadows to his left, where the pantry and storerooms were located. "Left the limeys standin', aye, Cap'n?" he said.

"Aye." Brendan glanced at the door again and let out another yawn. "A good chase, and no one hurt. And the prize is safe."

"Good, good." Tyner's gaze followed his. "They've been quiet."

"Good. No trouble?"

"No. The younger one screeched a bit when we moved her—"

"Aye, I heard that," he said wryly. Miss Amelia Talbot had a carrying voice.

"—and her sister demanded to get out, at first, but since then, they've been quiet. But we'll be havin' trouble with them, I'm thinkin'."

"Mayhaps not." Another yawn. "I'm for bed. Good night, Tyner—"

"Cap'n." Tyner stepped closer, hands on his hips and chin thrust forward. "What be ye thinkin' ye're doin' with her? Movin' her into yer cabin and all?"

Brendan smiled a little. "Believe it or not, Tyner, it wasn't my idea."

"Nay, I don't believe it. Not knowing ye as I do. And I'll tell ye, Cap'n. This one's not like your usual lasses. This one could be trouble for ye."

"She won't be," Brendan said, suddenly annoyed. "I know what I'm doing, Tyner."

"Not this time, I don't think ye do, Cap'n. This one's a lady. Ladies expect things of their men."

Brendan let out a bark of laughter. "Are ye thinking she's looking at me as a husband, Tyner?"

"No, Cap'n, but—"

"Enough of this," he said abruptly. "Good night, Tyner."

Tyner stepped back, apparently knowing defeat when he saw it, and his voice when he spoke was flat. "Good night, Cap'n."

"Oh, and, Tyner." Brendan paused as he turned the key.

"Aye, Cap'n?"

"Bring me a hammock."

"A hammock—aye, Cap'n!" Tyner exclaimed and scuttled off up the companionway.

Brendan watched him go with mingled amusement and annoyance, and then opened the door. Caution, inbred and long-fostered, made him pause just inside the room, caution and the memory of Rebecca wielding a knife against him. He waited, letting his senses become attuned to the darkness and the silence, stretching his mind in search of menace, and finding none. The room was dimly lit from the waning moon streaming in through the wide stern window; the only sounds were those to which he was so accustomed he barely noticed them anymore, the creak of rigging and sail, the rush of waves at the bow, the tread and voices of men on watch. And soft, even breathing. He relaxed. Unless she was a very good actress, Miss Rebecca Talbot was sound asleep.

Striking tinder, he lit the oil lamp that hung on gimbals over the table. Its mellow light banished the darkness and scattered shadows across the room as it swayed with the motion of the ship. It shone softly on the woman curled up on her side in his bed, asleep, one hand pillowing her cheek. Without quite knowing why he did so, Brendan moved to the side of the bed, gazing down at her. She looked different in sleep, not so fiercely protective, and much, much younger. Her garments still disguised her shape, and her hair, he noted with amusement, was still tightly bound, but without the lines of worry and fear her face was soft, smooth, guileless. Her features were regular, her lips full, and the spiky dark lashes that lay against her cheeks were sinfully long. She was pretty, he realized with surprise. Until this moment he had not known an attractive woman lurked behind the facade she presented to the world. It made her doubly dangerous.

Abruptly he turned away, his jaw grinding. Devil take it, he was a man of honor, though that was difficult to remember at this moment, with the blood thrumming in his veins. Who would ever have thought that prim, starchy Miss Talbot would cause such a reaction within him? It had to be, he decided, turning away to stow his pistol in the cabinet, because he was so tired, and yet still so restless from the day's action, because certainly she wouldn't tempt him normally. At least—but he remembered a sun-washed lane in St. Thomas, the brief, fleeting thought that this time he really had had it, and then the astonishing intervention by the girl asleep in his bed. And the way her eyes had gazed up at him afterward, puzzled and yet intrigued, with something in their depths that drew him.

The door opened and Tyner came in, a canvas hammock slung carelessly over one shoulder. "Where ye be wantin' this, Cap'n?" he said cheerfully, and Brendan spun around, a finger to his lips. Tyner glanced from him to Rebecca, and a grin lit his face, crinkling his eyes. "Sorry," he said, his voice lower, and began stringing the hammock up. "Ye surprise me, Cap'n. Aye, that ye do."

"Quiet," Brendan whispered irritably, hanging up the other end of the hammock. It now stretched the width of the cabin, parallel to the bed. Not as comfortable, but he'd slept in worse quarters, and at least here he'd be removed from temptation. Devil take it, he'd never forced a woman in his life. He'd never had to. Taking her tonight would be force, no matter how willing she appeared. And that, more than anything else, more than his orders or thoughts of his mission, was what had made him decide not to take her up on her offer.

"Aye, Cap'n." Tyner stepped away from the swaying hammock, his eyes still crinkled. "Good night, Cap'n."

"Good night." The door closed behind Tyner. Letting out another yawn, Brendan pulled his shirt over his head, scratched his chest, and turned back to his hammock—to see Rebecca, lying absolutely still, watching him.

In the beginning the sounds were part of Rebecca's dreams, the door opening, the voices, loud at first, and then whispered. They whirled together with all the other images of this day: of a battle, in which she somehow took part; of a narrow plank beneath her, miles above a fathomless sea; of nightmarish, leering faces. Yet somehow she felt too heavy, too relaxed to move, until the sound of the door closing again penetrated at last into her mind. Not a dream, none of it. It had all happened, and she was in a pirate's stateroom in his bed—

She opened her eyes. Oh, mercy. *He* was there, locking the door and then turning away, yawning, and—*oh, mercy!* Pulling off his shirt. Quickly she shut her eyes, but as if they had a will of their own, her lids opened again. Dear heavens, she hadn't realized he was quite so large, or that his arms, brown from the sun, were quite so heavily muscled. He was brown everywhere, his chest liberally sprinkled with black hair that curled and whorled down to the waist of his breeches, and his shoulders were so broad. They would loom over her, and—

And he turned and saw her watching him.

Instantly a tide of color rose in her face. "Well, lass, and do ye like what ye see?" he said, hanging the shirt on a wooden peg set in the wall.

"I might have known you'd not be a gentleman about this."

He let out a laugh, sounding genuinely amused. "Ah, but what did you expect, lass? 'Tis sure that I'm a pirate, after all." He came to stand by the bed, hands on hips, grinning down at her. She wanted to close her eyes, but decided not to give him the satisfaction. Instead, she fixed her gaze beyond him, valiantly ignoring the blatantly masculine chest and the charm of his smile. She had made the offer, yes, but she would not—would not!—give into him.

"What is that?" she said, spotting the hammock.

Brendan scratched his chest again, and in spite of herself Rebecca's eyes followed the motion. "A hammock."

"Why?"

"To sleep in." His eyes twinkled. "Will ye share it with me, lass?"

"What?"

"Never mind." He moved away, yawning. " 'Tis too tired I am, to be playing games."

Rebecca leaned up on her elbow, frowning. This was no game to her. "You're sleeping in that?"

"Aye." He paused in the act of turning down the lamp's flame. "Now is it that you're wanting me in bed with ye?"

"I—I thought—we made a bargain, and you accepted."

Brendan doused the lamp, and abruptly the room was plunged into darkness. "Ye overrate yourself, lass," he said, almost gently, and the ropes creaked as he climbed into the hammock. "Good night."

Chapter 6

~

Rebecca stared into the darkness toward the hammock. Of all the possible things she had imagined happening this night, she had not expected this. Not from a pirate, not when he had seemed so willing, so seductive, so—desirable.

No. With a little sniff, Rebecca flounced onto her side, facing away from Brendan. He was an unprincipled rogue and so was not at all desirable. Certainly no woman of virtue would think so. Ah, but that was precisely what she no longer was. If she'd ever needed proof of it she had it now, in her own reactions and responses. For when the Raven had snuffed the light and jumped into his hammock, she had felt, for just a moment, strong, irrational disappointment.

And he, the wretch, was sleeping! She could hear his even, regular breathing, deepening into soft snores, quite as if nothing had happened. Overrated herself, had she? Perhaps she had, but it was galling of him to say so. Well, he'd see. When he finally got around to their bargain, they'd just see what would happen. She would not cooperate with him. He was a vain man, was the Raven, and *he* had vastly overrated his charms. Perhaps other women had been fooled by him, but she wasn't. She would not let him best her.

Taking a deep breath, Rebecca composed herself for sleep. She had lived through difficult situations before; doubtless she would again. But what, she wondered, would happen when the Raven came to claim her?

"Good morrow, miss," a cheery voice called, and Rebecca shot up in the bed, startled from sleep. For a moment she

stared, dazed, at Tyner, standing with a pewter dish in one
hand and a tankard in the other, and then it all came rushing
back to her. She and Amelia were captives on a pirate ship.
"I fell asleep," she said.

"Aye, miss, that ye did," Tyner said, smiling genially and
placing the dish on the table. "Breakfast here for ye. Be ye
hungry?"

"No—yes," she said as her stomach suddenly growled.
Had she no sense of shame? A proper lady would be pining
away at the horrors that had befallen her. Discreetly she
swung her legs over the side of the bed. "Is my sister well?"

"Aye, miss. Be ye wantin' water for washing?"

"Yes, thank you." She nodded, the unreality of the situation compounded by his cheerfulness and her politeness.
"When may I see her?"

Tyner's face sobered. "Sorry, miss, Cap'n said you're to
stay in the cabin."

"But my sister needs me—"

"She's well taken care of, miss. Don't ye fret, no harm'll
come to her."

Rebecca bit her lip. Amelia was safe because of the bargain she had made. The bargain the Raven seemed disinclined to keep. "Where is the captain? I would like to ask
him for myself."

"On deck, miss. Now. There's porridge, and bacon, and
coffee—hope ye like it? No milk for it, I'm afeared, but 'tis
good and strong. And an orange. Not many of those left."

In spite of herself, Rebecca drifted over to the table, lured
by the smells. The hammock Brendan had strung up last
night was gone. Would he be sleeping in it again tonight?

Her stomach lurched at the thought, making her grab the
back of a chair for support. "There, miss, don't doubt you're
weak with hunger," Tyner said, reaching for her arm, and
she flinched away. "Just ye sit down and eat, and I'll get water for ye. It'll have to be seawater, I'm afeared. Fresh water's in scarce supply at sea."

Rebecca raised dazed eyes to stare at him, near the door.
"What kind of a pirate ship is this?"

Tyner looked up from sorting through his keys. "Miss?"

"This." She gestured toward the food. "Breakfast, and
now you're bringing me water."

"Is that all right, miss? There'll be soap, too."

Rebecca let out a short, sharp laugh. "Why, of course

there will be. I have gone mad," she said, and sank her head into her hands. "Do you treat all your captives so well?"

"Nay, miss. But ye're special, ye and yer sister. Now, eat your breakfast, miss, and I'll be back with your water." Before Rebecca could protest, he was gone, his key clicking in the lock.

Rebecca gazed at the door, and then, suddenly tired, sat down. For Amelia's sake, she had to keep up her strength. She picked up the spoon and forced down some porridge. Why, it was good, she thought with surprise, flavored with brown sugar and a spice she couldn't quite identify. Her stomach growled, and greedily she swallowed more, following the porridge with the bacon, smoky and sweet, and the dark, rich coffee. Finally sated, she sat back, letting out a sigh of pure contentment. She had, she realized with surprise, consumed everything set before her, even the orange, and this under the most trying circumstances. She most definitely was not a proper lady. But then, that had been established long ago.

The food she had eaten with such relish now lay heavy on her stomach as she rose, desperate to escape. But there was no way out, not from this room, not from herself. Eager for distraction from her thoughts, she gazed about the cabin. It wasn't so very different from what she'd grown accustomed to in the *Curlew,* or in her father's own ships. Perhaps it was more luxurious, as befitted the captain's status, but it was small and simply furnished. The table where she had eaten faced the door and was circled by four chairs, bolted to the deck. Above was the oil lamp she'd noted last night, and a skylight to let in light and air. Cabinets lined one wall, one with glazed doors, and the wall next to the bed held pegs, from which hung the Raven's clothes. Rebecca's gaze slid uneasily over these, and encountered the bed.

Her lips tightened. Nothing simple about this piece of furniture. Of carved mahogany, it was piled high with a feather mattress and downy, colorful quilts that had been carefully, lovingly stitched. By one of the many women in the Raven's life? Rebecca flushed and turned sharply away. Best not to think about that, about what had gone in that bed and would yet go on in it.

At the foot of the bed the stern of the ship curved in a graceful arc of tiny, paned windows. Beneath it was a bench, padded with a red tufted cushion. Rebecca knelt on it to look out, seeing not a sight of land, not a sign of another sail. Only the restless sea and the ship's white, foaming wake tracing their course. It was calm today, the swells slight, the ship rocking only slightly beneath her, and yet she judged that they were making good time. But to where? With the trackless sea between them and land, it would be a long time before she and Amelia were ransomed. If ever.

She was sitting, hugging herself against a chill of fear when the door opened and Tyner came back in. "Ye've a good appetite, miss," he said approvingly.

"Yes." The fear slowly drained away. Tyner, at least, had been kind. "Why are my sister and I special?" she asked.

Tyner was busy clearing the table. "Why, because of the ransom ye'll bring, o' course."

"Oh. Of course."

"Every man jack aboard'll share in it, ye see," he went on, seemingly unaware of the irony in her voice. "Times are hard for seamen, miss, and the money'll be welcome."

"Is that why you do this? For the money?"

Again his eyes flickered. "Of course, miss. What other reason is there?"

"But you're English, Tyner. Why not serve in their navy?"

"Bah." Tyner made a face. "Aye, I'm English, and what good did it ever do me? No, miss, the best thing that ever happened to me was meeting up with the captain. I'm my own man now, ye see?"

"Oh." She didn't understand. Who was the Raven, to inspire such loyalty? "Have you been with the Raven long?"

"We don't call him that here."

"Oh? By what name do you call him?"

"Cap'n Fitzpatrick, o'course. A good cap'n, he is, but hard on himself. Ye won't see him belowdecks when his ship needs him, not to eat or even to sleep," he said admiringly. "Someone has to look after him."

The thought of the Raven needing to be looked after was ludicrous. He could well take care of himself. "I'd think there'd be women to do that."

"Oh, no, miss. Not at sea," he said, sounding shocked, and glancing at the bed. "Never at sea."

"You relieve my mind enormously," she said dryly.

"Yes, miss." He beamed at her. "Be ye needing anything else?"

"Yes." Rebecca raised her chin, amazed at how self-assured she sounded when all her emotions were in turmoil. "Please ask the captain if I may see my sister."

Tyner's lips pursed. "He'll not allow that, miss."

"Please! She needs me, and I—"

"I'm that sorry, miss," Tyner said, his expression genuinely apologetic. "When the cap'n gives an order, that's it."

"Then, please, won't you ask if I could have paper and a quill?" She was pleading now, her feelings openly displayed, and she didn't care. Amelia needed her. That was all that mattered. "At least ask if he'll let me write a message."

Tyner's lips pursed. "I'll try, miss," he said and went out, locking the door behind him. Setting the dirty dishes down in the pantry just under the companionway, he scuttled up to the deck, squinting against the sun as he searched the sails. Aye, there was the cap'n, as usual high in his perch, the wind ruffling his raven black hair like feathers. "Cap'n!" he hollered, cupping his hands about his mouth. Brendan looked down. A moment later he slid down to the deck and walked over to Tyner, his stride rolling, meeting every dip and swell of the sea.

"Aye, Tyner? What is it?"

"A request from our guest, Cap'n."

"Our guest?" Brendan grinned. "Do ye disapprove of her then, Tyner?"

"Ye know how I feel, Cap'n. I think takin' them was a mistake—"

"It's done," Brendan said, his voice slashing across Tyner's. "Now. I've little time for this. What is it she wants?"

"To see her sister, and—"

"No."

"Aye, Cap'n. She would like a sheet of paper, to write her sister a note."

Brendan pondered that. "Aye, let her have all the paper she wants, and a quill, too, if it'll keep her quiet."

"Not that one," Tyner muttered. "She's trouble, Cap'n."

"Get her what she wants, Tyner," Brendan said sharply, and after a moment, Tyner nodded.

"Aye, Cap'n," he said and scuttled away.

Trouble. Aye, that she was, Brendan thought, though not in the way Tyner thought. The crew seemed not the slightest bit disgruntled that he had access to a woman while they did not, but instead seemed to approve, several going so far as

to give him winks and sly smiles. He grimaced. While trying
to protect his captives, inadvertently he had boosted his reputation as a marauder. All to the good, but what no one realized, what he hadn't expected, were the complications
caused by Rebecca's presence in his cabin. Even he wasn't
sure quite what they would be yet, but of one thing he was
certain. She was, in her own way, very much a threat to him.

On impulse he turned on his heel, striding along the deck
and clambering down the companionway to his cabin. Madness, what he was doing, seeking her out, but then he never
had been one to run from danger. And a danger she was, in
spite of her prim ways and her austere appearance. He'd
seen that last night, when she had lain defenseless in sleep,
and again this morning. The sight evoked an odd, nameless
feeling within him, but that had driven him almost to stroke
her hair, touch her cheek. Only his finely tuned sense of
danger had saved him, and yet now the memory brought
forth the same, undefined feeling.

Bah. Twisting the key in the lock, he banged the door
open with more force than he had intended. Sitting at the table, Rebecca looked up, startled, and the pen she held flew
from her fingers, spattering ink across the paper. "Oh,
bother! Now look what you've made me do," she exclaimed.
"This paper is quite ruined."

"There's more, *leannan*," he said, biting back a grin. No
fainting or hysterics from her. Instead she challenged him,
provoked him, as if he inspired no fear in her. And yet, he
knew that wasn't true; he could see the wariness in her eyes,
in her posture. She was a brave one, his Rebecca. *Bah.* Not
his Rebecca at all.

"I told you not to call me that." She sounded disgruntled
as she dabbed at the ink with a piece of blotting cloth. "I
don't suppose you'd allow me a penknife to sharpen the
quill?"

"Nay, lass, I'm not that daft." Crossing the cabin, he
opened a cabinet set high in the wall, its door set with heavy
glass, and took out a book at random. "Likely you'd try the
knife on me. Not that it would avail you anything." He
sprawled onto the window seat. "Are ye writing to your sister?"

"No." She gazed at him, her expression defiant. "I have
decided to keep a journal."

"A fine occupation for a lady."

"I intend to document every single thing you've done, Captain."

"I'd expect no less of ye, lass," he said, opening the book and pretending to ignore her.

"I—you'll allow me?"

"Aye. I see no reason why not."

"But it will be evidence against you."

"Ah, but they have to catch me first." He bent his head to the book, only then realizing he held it upside down. "I'll leave ye to your writing, lass."

"Oh." For a moment, there was silence. Brendan could feel her gaze on him, but he continued to concentrate on the book. Only when he sensed her turning away, returning to her letter, did he quickly turn the book the right way, to realize that he had opened to a poem by John Donne. An erotic one, written to his mistress. He didn't know whether to groan or to laugh. Under the circumstances, with a woman in his cabin and his own hunger growing in a way he couldn't explain, he could not have made a worse choice. He was caught now, though. Rather than risk catching Rebecca's attention, he stretched out his legs and grimly began to read.

Sheer torture, as Donne cajoled his mistress into taking off her clothes. What did Rebecca look like beneath that shapeless gray gown? Not as angular as he'd first thought, not from the way she had felt against him yesterday. Soft, white skin, a shape he could only guess at, and that hair, crackling fire as it spread over her shoulders, over his pillow. He shifted on the bench as a surge of heat went through him, making his breeches uncomfortably tight. And this because of a woman who may have offered herself, but whose stance and expression, whose very being warned him away.

"You read poetry?" Rebecca said, breaking into his thoughts, and gladly he looked up, away from the images the poetry evoked, into another temptation. His gaze locked with hers, now the murky green of a stormy sea, hinting at emotions he could only guess at. A storm, was it? Aye, but he welcomed storms, as he welcomed danger. More fool he.

"Aye, lass," he said and cleared his throat, annoyed beyond measure at the huskiness of his voice. "That I do."

Her brow wrinkled. "I didn't think—I mean, I didn't even think you could read."

"A high opinion ye have of me, lass," he said, closing the book. "Did ye take me for an illiterate fool?"

"No. Oh, no," she said earnestly, as if concerned for his feelings. "But with your being a pirate, I just assumed—"

"Ye know nothing about me, lass."

"No." Her eyes widened as he rose. "I don't even know why you took us captive."

"But ye do, lass. For the ransom."

"I don't think so." Her eyes remained on him, sharper now. "I think you've reasons of your own."

"Some dark, nefarious purpose, d'ye mean?"

"Yes. And how a pirate knows such words, I don't know."

"There ye go again, lass, assuming ye know me." He picked up the book, to put it back on the shelf, and then, seized by a mischievous impulse, stopped. "Do ye read poetry, lass?"

"Why, yes."

"And are ye familiar with John Donne?"

Her brow wrinkled. "A bit. 'Death be not proud, though some have called thee—' "

"Ah, his sacred period. Nay, lass, I was referring to his earlier poetry. Like this." He flipped the book open to the poem he had been reading. " 'License my roving hands, and let them go, before, behind, between, above, below—' "

"Mercy!" Rebecca clapped her hands over her ears, her face scarlet. "You're no gentleman, to say such things to me!"

He laughed, genuinely amused in spite of the tension stretching between them. Ah, 'twas a mistake to tease her so, when he was the one ended up burning. "But as we've established, lass, I'm no gentleman. And I very much doubt"—he tilted her chin up with his fingertips—"that ye are a lady."

"Of course I am!" she protested, but she didn't pull away. Nor did he. God help him, he couldn't, not with their gazes locked together as they were. He knew well the sexual attraction that could spring unbidden between a man and a woman, but this was beyond his experience. "I was raised properly, sir."

"Were you?" He was hardly aware of what she said, of what he answered. His senses were filled with her, with the softness of her skin beneath his fingers, of the fire of her hair, and, most of all, her lips, full, pink, eminently kissable.

God help him, he was playing with fire, but never had he wanted more to be burned. "Ah, *leannan,* the words of the poem—I'd like to do them with you," he said abruptly.

"You presume too much, sir!" Rebecca said, almost falling off the chair in her haste to get away from this mesmerizing, maddening man. Dear God in heaven, that poem he had read! She could still feel the warmth of it in her body, down deep in her stomach. Oh, she was wanton, and she must never forget it, must never forget as well that this man was a threat to her.

"Do I, lass?" He remained where he was, an odd smile on his face. "But then, 'tis your idea, or so I believed?"

"Yes, but—not like that." Pressed up against the wall, she licked lips gone suddenly dry, and saw his eyes flicker. "But if you're going to do it, then do it!"

Brendan laughed, the tension leaving his face, and leaned against the table, his arms crossed. " 'Tis a sadly practical streak ye have, *leannan.* Is there no romance in ye?"

Rebecca's lips thinned. "There is no room in my life for romance, sir."

"No?" He regarded her, his eye bright and curious. "Now why is that, I wonder? Is it that you're not interested? Nay, I doubt that." His smile was wicked, knowing. "Not the way ye react to my touch."

"I do not react to you, sir! Not in that way."

"Ah, then ye do know what I mean? There was romance there once, wasn't there?" he said, his gaze and voice both suddenly sharper. "Is it that some man hurt ye, Rebecca? Is that it?"

" 'Tis none of your concern," she snapped, feeling the color rise in her cheeks.

"Isn't it, now?" He straightened, still studying her. "Why aren't ye afraid of me, lass?"

Rebecca licked her lips again. "I am."

"Ye don't act it."

Oh, but she was afraid of him. Afraid of him, and of her response to him, and what that meant about her. "If I did, you'd call me missish."

He laughed again. "Care for my good opinion, do ye?"

"Certainly not! I never have understood the need for hysterics and the vapors."

"Have ye not? A rare woman ye are, then. Most women use tears to gain what they desire."

"Tears have never availed me anything."

"For example," he went on, as if she hadn't spoken, "if ye cried, I just might leave ye alone."

There was silence for a moment. "I'm not going to cry," Rebecca said softly but determinedly. She would not show any weakness before this man. "You'd like it if I did, wouldn't you? Would it make you feel like a man, then? That you made a woman cry in fear of you?"

"You should be afraid of me, by God!" he roared, whirling around and slamming his hand on the table. Rebecca flinched and blinked, and for a moment there was tense, tight silence between them. Their gazes held, and subtly, slowly, something shifted in the atmosphere around them. Something changed. He was not a man with power over her of life and death, but just, simply, a man. And a dangerously attractive one, with his shirt loose at the neck and the corded muscles in his neck standing out. He looked away first, and she was relieved.

"Ye should be afraid of me," he repeated, turning away. "I'm the Raven, by God."

"Yes, I know," she said, almost gently.

"Ye mock me?" he demanded, glaring at her.

"No. Oh, no." But neither did she quite fear him anymore. She had just snapped at him, defied him, goaded him, and he had not reacted as she'd expected. He had not struck her, but had instead held on to his temper with great restraint. "I'm sure your reputation is well earned. Remember," she hurried on as he opened his mouth to speak, "I've seen you in action, as it were."

He stared at her a moment longer, hands on his hips, and then, incredibly, he smiled, displaying the dimple she found so incongruous, and so entrancing. The smile turned into a grin, and then a chuckle. "Ah, *leannan,* you're a rare one. And don't say I'm not to call ye that," he said, flicking her cheek with a fingertip. "This is my ship, and I'll do as I wish."

"Of course," Rebecca murmured, looking down at her hands, linked tightly before her. She still felt his touch on her cheek, and a little sting that burned out of all proportion.

" 'Of course,' " he mocked. "Why do I doubt such meekness?"

"Well, I can hardly stop you, can I?"

"Ah, now that's my lass. A good, proper waspish tone."

"You make me sound quite a shrew."

"Nay, lass." His eye twinkled. " 'Tis remarkably forbearing ye are."

"Have I a choice?"

He cocked his head to the side. "Is it really so bad here?"

She stared at him in astonishment. "So bad? You hold me captive on a pirate ship—"

"Aye. Better than going to England, is it not?"

"Better than—!" She closed her mouth with a snap. "It most certainly is not! You had no right to interfere in my life that way. And you look not a bit ashamed," she went on. "You, a godless pirate."

"I think I like ye better when you don't preach, *leannan*."

"But I am right, and you know it. Let us go," she said, suddenly, not caring that she begged. "Put us aboard a ship to England, and we'll not say a word against you. I promise."

He stood, hands on hips, appearing to consider her request. " 'Tis what you want? To go to England?"

"Yes."

"Ye lie, lass," he said very softly.

"I beg your pardon!"

"Ye no more want to go to England than I do. Admit it, *leannan*." He leaned his hands on the table, bending close, too close, and for the life of her she could not look away. Had she really thought he was only truly dangerous in a temper? Oh, no, for how much more danger he posed now, close enough to touch, to smell the scent of the sea and the indefinable essence that was him, to touch the coarse linen of his shirt and his bronzed skin. . . . Rebecca jerked back, and his hand shot out to grab her chin, imprisoning it, his gaze holding hers. " 'Tis not the life ye want. Ye want to be wild and free—"

"No," she protested weakly.

"Aye, lass. Ye do, deep inside. Free, with no one to tell ye what to do, to live your life the way ye please. Aye, to run barefoot if ye wish, to let your hair down and laugh. And," he said, his mouth hovering near hers, "ye want me to kiss you."

Chapter 7

~

Rebecca stiffened. "You've no right to speak to me in such a way."

"Let us get one thing understood, lass." He leaned closer yet, his face almost touching hers. "This is my ship. If I want something done, it will be done. If I give an order it will be obeyed." He stared at her, and she could find no trace of softness, of kindness, in his eye. "D'ye understand?"

"Y-yes."

"Good. Just ye remember it." Brendan straightened and turned to the door. "I'll leave ye in peace."

"Wait," she called as he swung the door open. "May I visit my sister?"

"No," he said curtly, and slammed the door shut. And, inside the cabin, Rebecca collapsed against the back of the chair, shaking uncontrollably. She was trapped. There was no escape from this ship, or from him. God help her, which prospect frightened her more?

Brendan ran up the companionway with the ease of long practice. Aye, he'd had a narrow escape, he thought, bursting out onto the deck, startling the seaman who lounged nearby. "Why aren't ye at your post?" he snarled, and the seaman jumped up, his eyes flashing white.

"I'm not on watch, Cap'n, I swear! Ask the mate."

Brendan gave him one murderous glare and then spun on his heel, leaving the hapless seaman to quake in both relief and terror that his days were numbered. "I'll be aloft," he said to Starkey, the mate on watch, who nodded uninterestedly. Nettled as much by the lack of response as he would have been had there been one, he began climbing the fore-mast shrouds, the tangle of lines that made up the standing rigging, higher and higher, surrounded by an ocean of canvas, a sea of sail. When he was a child he'd climbed to the top of the tallest tree, pretending he was on a ship, pretending that the wind sang through the rigging, rather than whistling softly through leaves. He'd been very young, he thought, with only a trace of bitterness, reaching his destination at last, the topmost yardarm. There he swung his leg over a spar and leaned back against the stout mast, swaying easily with the roll of a ship and lazily holding on to a line. Aye, he'd been young, and naive. As naive as the girl in his cabin, for all her show of bravery.

His lips tightened. God help him, if she didn't know what had sparked between them just now, he did. He knew well the ways of man and woman, knew that in that moment he'd wanted her more than he'd ever wanted another woman— and she had felt the same. Innocent she might be, but the passion was there, banked deep, and if he awakened it he would be singed. Burned. For that reason alone he should avoid her for the rest of the voyage. But he wouldn't.

From his perch, life looked simple, uncomplicated. Below him was his ship, and all about him, the sea. This was the easiest, and dullest, part of the adventure. Or, rather, it should be. With the northeast trade winds blowing steadily, with no sails in sight and with no set destination, running the ship required little of him. His mates and crew were well-trained; they knew to keep them on this empty stretch of sea and to watch for other ships, changing tack as necessary to keep to the meandering course he had set. The only danger he could see at the moment was the chance of a storm, in the clouds massing on the horizon far astern. That, and the woman in his cabin. Even in sleep he was aware of her, of her breathing and the little sounds she made in her sleep, aware that she was close, his for the taking. And that was something that bothered him out of all proportion.

Brendan stayed on deck the remainder of that day, and the next, preferring the simplicity of life from the yardarm. Time passed, however, and with the sun well up in the sky, it was nearly time to be taking the noon sights, to fix their position. Swinging onto the shrouds, he scampered down, as nimble and silent as a cat, so quiet that two seamen below him weren't aware of his descent. Not on watch, they stood near the rail, one idly whittling, the other spitting into the sea. "What I say is," the man who was whittling said, shaving another piece of wood off an already unrecognizable sculpture, "is why he's got them both holed up below if he's not doin' anything with them?"

The other man spat again. "Aye, and why he took the old one in with him. Don't know what joy he gets from her," he said, and they both laughed coarse, harsh chuckles.

"I say, if he don't want 'em, he should share," the first man said, and Brendan, momentarily frozen, returned to life. If they were discussing the two women openly, then all the crew likely thought the same thing. It was a threat, not just to the Talbot sisters, but to his own power. To himself.

"I'll take the little one. You can have the old one," the second man was saying, when seemingly from nowhere Brendan landed on the deck between them. Both knife and wood flew from one man's fingers, and flecks of spittle spattered on the other's face. "Christ, Cap'n!" he exclaimed.

Brendan said not a word. He didn't have to. His gaze, his very presence, said it all, that and the memory of all the past misdeeds it was rumored he'd committed. "Ye were saying, lad?" he said, his voice dangerously soft.

"I—nothin', Cap'n," the man who had been whittling babbled, while the other one began to edge away. "We was just talkin'."

"See to it that's all it is, boyo." Brendan's gaze was unflinching, and though the other man didn't look away his head reared back, as if in escape. "Because I protect what is mine." His eye flicked down to the knife, still lying on the deck, and then back up. "By whatever means necessary."

"Aye, Cap'n," the man babbled, bending down and scooping up knife and wood fragment in one fumbling gesture. "Beggin' yer pardon, I'll jist go and have me dinner—"

"Do that, boyo." Hands on hips, Brendan watched as he scuttled away, throwing nervous glances over his shoulder. Good. He'd put the fear of God in him, and in everyone on the ship. He was the Raven, by God, and he did protect what was his. Be damned if he'd share.

Still smoldering, he strode across the deck and rattled down the companionway. Aye, the cabin was his, too, and yet he'd let a mere woman chase him from it. No more, he thought grimly, turning the key and pushing open the door. *His* ship, *his* cabin, and his woman, and . . .

Rebecca, sitting at the table, looked up, startled, and the wary look in her eyes deepened. His? He stopped in his tracks. Good God, no! His prize, yes, his responsibility, but not his in the possessive way he'd thought just a moment before. He must have been mad.

"Captain?" she said when he didn't move, and it released him from his paralysis. She had courage, he'd say that for her. His men had scuttled, and yet there she sat, placid as a ship becalmed. "Is something wrong? Is it"—her hand crept up to her throat—"my sister?"

"Your sister is fine," he said rudely, jerked back to reality. Not his, by God. His keys jangled as he unlocked the cabinet and took out his sextant. "Ye'll not question me."

"I wasn't—"

"And ye'll not argue with me, either." He rounded on her. "D'ye understand?"

"I wasn't—no, of course not." Her hands, which had fluttered nervously into the air, now settled onto the table, two small birds folding their wings.

"Huh," he snorted and went out, banging the door behind him.

Rebecca stared at the door in mystification. Mercy, what was that about? She hadn't done anything to provoke him that she knew of. She glanced down at her journal, and then back at the door, and went still. She hadn't heard him turn the key in the lock.

As quick as that, she was up and across the room, her fingers on the handle. Mercy, it turned, it was opening, and— Tyner stood in the passageway, a pewter plate in his hand and a quizzical look on his face. "Miss?"

Rebecca made a futile slashing gesture through the air and turned away, disappointment sharp within her. Escape was impossible, but if she could only get out, could only see Amelia and reassure her, ease her fears. . . . "What is it, Tyner?"

"Dinner, miss." The door was again closed; the keys were held firmly in his hand. Rebecca eyed them hungrily. "Cap'n's in a rare taking," Tyner went on, setting the dish onto the table. "Best you eat. No tellin' what he'll do in this kind of mood."

Rebecca shuddered, her appetite gone. "What has happened, Tyner?"

"Don't know, miss." He turned the key in the lock, opening the door, and Rebecca tensed. If she moved quickly, caught him off guard. . . . "Never seen him quite like this, not in all these years."

Impossible to overtake him, Rebecca thought, the mad impulse leaving as fast as it had come. Tyner was small and scrawny, but his shoulders were broad and his arms ropy with muscles. Better to bide her time and find another way to gain her objective, as she always had to do with Father. And the first thing to do, she thought, realizing suddenly what Tyner had just said, was to get information. "Have you been with Captain Fitzpatrick long, Tyner?" she asked.

"Aye, long enough. I'll leave ye to your meal—"

"No, please, wait."

He stopped by the door. "Cap'n'll want me topside."

"I know. But please, tell me. How does my sister fare?"

Tyner paused and then half turned to her. "She's not eating, miss."

"Oh, drat," she said softly. Refusing to eat was a ploy Amelia often used when things weren't to her liking. Effective against their father, and occasionally against Rebecca herself, but it wouldn't work here. "She has to eat."

"Aye. We'll see to it that she does."

Rebecca stared at him. "You will?"

"Aye. The cap'n'll want her healthy for the ransom."

"Oh, drat the ransom!" she cried, and with a sweep of her arm spun the pewter dish across the table, scattering its contents of fish and bread and potatoes. "Her life is at stake, and all you care about is the money? What manner of man is your captain?"

"A hard man. Best ye remember that." Tyner frowned at the mess on the table. "And he don't like tantrums."

"If you think this is a tantrum, just wait until I get started. I'll—"

"And what's all this?" a voice said in the doorway. Rebecca looked up to see Brendan, and felt her face fill with color. "The food's not to your liking, Miss Talbot?"

"The—the food is fine," Rebecca got out, inwardly cursing her clumsy tongue and her earlier fit of temper. Mercy, what had gotten into her? "I would like to see my sister."

"Sorry, lass." Brendan shrugged as he opened the cabinet, putting away the sextant. " 'Tis not possible."

"Ye've taken the sights already, Cap'n," Tyner said.

"Aye. Sam wrote down my readings. I expected to see you, Tyner."

"I was busy putting down mutiny, Cap'n."

"So I see." Brendan glanced over at the table again, and unforgivably his lips twitched. "You're forgiven, Tyner. This time. Now see to my dinner."

"Aye, Cap'n," Tyner said and scuttled out.

"It wasn't his fault," Rebecca said into the silence.

Brendan turned from the cabinet. "D'ye think I don't know that, lass?"

"I—I lost my temper."

"Aye, so? Best ye clean that mess up, or ye'll miss your dinner."

"I'm not particularly hungry," Rebecca said, but, cheeks aflame, she returned the larger morsels of food to the plate.

"It doesn't matter, lass. Tyner has his orders." All levity had left his face. "And if ye interfere with his duties again, I'll have to punish him."

Rebecca looked up, shocked. "But he wasn't to blame—"

"No matter. He knew I expected him on deck." He sat down at the swivel chair at the head of the table, watching her, face set and eye slightly narrowed. "Let that kind of thing go, and before ye know it ye've mutiny on your hands."

"What—what would you do?"

"Hm?" Brendan looked up from writing some numbers on a slate. "Use the lash, I suppose."

"What manner of man are you?" she burst out, appalled. "To do such a thing to an innocent man!"

"A pirate, lass," he said and, unbelievably, smiled. "And don't ye be forgettin' it. Eat your dinner, now."

Rebecca sat down and stared at the food without seeing it. She was in the power of a madman. No matter his charm, no matter his looks. If he could so calmly consider whipping a faithful servant, then he was a monster.

They sat at opposite ends of the table, Rebecca and the pirate, she picking at her food, he continuing to write, and yet very aware of her, so near; so silent, and yet so disapproving. Aye, and he supposed she had a point, he thought, forcing himself to concentrate on the numbers on the slate so that he could figure out the ship's position with some accuracy. He didn't need a shrew of a woman to distract him, or to make him feel unwelcome remorse for his behavior. Of course he wouldn't punish Tyner; he wouldn't have to. Tyner was shrewd enough not to make the same mistake twice. He'd not allow himself to be distracted by Rebecca again. Unfortunately, Brendan thought, he couldn't say the same. "Bah," he said and threw down the slate pencil.

Rebecca looked up, startled. "What is it?"

He eyed her for a moment, seeing her cheeks still flushed and her hair tousled, as if she'd just arisen from bed. A surge of heat went through him. *Devil take it!* "Eat your dinner," he ordered curtly, and returned his attention to the far less interesting, but far safer calculations.

Tyner came in with Brendan's meal, which he ate distractedly, still working. Rebecca finished her dinner at last and stacked both plates together for Tyner to remove. Brendan ignored her. Frowning, not knowing why she was so annoyed, she drifted over to the cabinet that held his books, bracing herself with one hand against the wall as the ship rolled. All those lovely books, and, behind the locked door, as unattainable here as at home. Father didn't approve of secular reading; his meager library contained various political treatises, several volumes of sermons, and, of course, the Bible. His daughters' reading was similarly constrained. Wistfully she took in the titles: *The New American Practical Navigator,* a complete book of Shakespeare's works, the poetry of John Donne, Knickerbocker's *History of New York.* Why would a pirate read such books? Even more surprising was what was next to the volumes. "A chess set," she said, surprised.

"D'ye play, lass?" Brendan said behind her.

Tears unexpectedly surged into her throat. "Yes, I—once I used to play with my father. But it's been years." Many years ago, when she had been more to him than just a chaperon for Amelia. When her father had loved her.

"Fancy a game, d'ye?"

She turned. He was leaning back in his chair, hands linked behind his head, grinning at her for all the world as if earlier he had not been in a temper. "Not particularly, no," she said reluctantly. She loved chess, but to play a game with him would be like playing with the devil himself.

"I didn't take ye for a coward, lass."

"I'm not a coward!"

"No?"

"No." She closed her mouth firmly. She would not allow him to goad her. She would not.

"Is it that you fear you'll lose, then?"

"I wouldn't lose."

He laughed, throwing back his head and displaying again his strong, even white teeth. "Such confidence, *leannan*."

"Pray don't call me that."

"What d'ye say we play a game? For stakes?"

"A wager?"

"Aye." There was a devilish twinkle in his eye. "Don't tell me it's never crossed your mind."

"Never."

"Liar," he said without heat. "I know ye, lass. Ye aren't as innocent as ye'd have me think."

Rebecca froze. What did he know? What could he know? "Wagering is wrong."

"Even if the wager is—" He leaned back, toying with the slate pencil. "Ah, let's say, a visit to your sister?"

"Oh, would you?" she burst out.

"Aye, but only if ye win, lass. While if I win—"

"What?" she said, distrusting the twinkle in his eye.

"Why, lass, ye'll have to give me a kiss."

Rebecca stared at him for a long moment. Then, unable to help herself any longer, she let out a laugh. "Now if that isn't just what I should have expected!"

"Aye, lass. After all, I am a pirate," he said, though his eye still held the surprised look that had flashed into it at her laugh.

"Oh, yes." She turned, her back to the bookcase. "Of course, a kiss is something you could have had this age."

"Nay, lass. Not the kind of kiss I'm thinkin' of." His voice was soft, liquid. "All warm and wet and willing—that kind of kiss, lass."

"No," she stated, appalled at the surge of heat his words evoked within her.

"Aye, and ye'd enjoy it as much as I."

"I never would!" She turned her back. "I will not play chess with you. Not for any reason."

"What is one kiss, *leannan*, when ye've offered me so much more?"

She kept her back to him, her shoulders rigid. "There was a reason for that."

"Aye, and there's a reason for this, too, if ye win." He paused. "Unless ye fear ye'd lose."

She looked at him over her shoulder. He was grinning at her, cocksure and confident, and that, more than anything else, decided her. "No. I would not lose."

His grin broadened, dazzling her. "Then get the chess set down, lass, and prove it."

Involuntarily her fingers went to pull on the cabinet door, and then stopped. "Isn't it locked?"

"No. Ye can read any book ye wish," he went on as she opened the cabinet, "including the Donne. If ye've a mind."

"No, thank you," she said frostily, bringing the chess set over to the table where he already sat. "And is this more pirate's plunder?"

"Aye, what else?" he said, carelessly returning the pieces to their proper positions from the problem he had set up. The set was small, the entire board no larger than the length of her forearm, and each square had an indentation for the base of the chess pieces. The pieces themselves were the traditional black and white: rare ebony, fine ivory. Plunder, indeed, she thought, and then quickly frowned at the thought of a pirate, not only playing chess, but setting up chess problems. "And where does a pirate learn to play chess?" she asked, sitting down across from him.

"From his captives, of course. Ye may have the white, lass." His teeth gleamed in a smile. "I prefer black."

"So I noticed," she said dryly and advanced a pawn two squares out onto the board. Battle was joined.

Brendan studied the board for a moment and then, grinning, countered by moving a pawn of his own. "There. Not a fancy beginning, but a beginning, all the same."

Rebecca quickly glanced up at him through her lashes. So. He thought she couldn't play? True it was that she hadn't played in many a year, but chess was a favorite game of hers, and her father a pitiless opponent. As long as Brendan was unaware of that, however, she held the advantage. She was not going to give him his kiss, no, not the way he'd said! Warm and willing and wet, as if she were some kind of wanton.

Biting her lips, frowning, she reached out to a pawn, retreated, reached out again, and settled, finally, on the bishop.

"Bishop to king's bishop four," she murmured, forgetting her opponent for the moment.

"Are ye sure ye want to do that, lass?" Brendan said, and she looked up, still biting her lips. He was smiling still, but in his eyes was a look she distrusted, the look of a hunter after prey.

"I—I think so," she said and sat back, as if uncertain, when in reality she had put out the bishop to protect her queen. And to draw him in.

He clicked his teeth, as if in concern. Out came a black pawn, and what his intentions were, she could not guess. She needed only to remember that chess was a game of tactics, and he was a master tactician, as shown by his many captures.

Again, seemingly hesitant, she reached out her hand, and this time it was the queen she brought out, though not very far. Brendan said nothing, only looked at it with narrowed eye. She tried to keep her own face guileless, wondering if he'd see what was so clear to her: that by moving his pawns he'd cleared a space in front of his king, and thus a direct path for her queen. Hardly daring to breathe, she watched as his hand came out, hovered over a pawn, and then settled firmly on the knight, moving it out into the center. "There, now, lass, more moves like that and I'll control the middle."

"I don't think so," Rebecca said, almost gently, and moved her queen across the board to the space diagonal to his king. "Checkmate."

"What?" He stared blankly at the board. There was no doubt about it. The black king was blocked from any movement by the white queen. Rebecca had won. "I will be damned. The Fool's Game," he said, and she could no longer contain herself. She let out a laugh, full and rich. "I will be damned," he said again, and this time she caught the change in his inflection, the lack of poetry in his voice as, using her queen, he knocked his king over in the traditional gesture of defeat. Was it just because he'd lost? "Ye play well, lass."

"For a woman?" she said and laughed again, relieved. If he was angry, he wasn't going to take it out on her. "Has no one beaten you lately, Captain?"

"No. Not at sea, or at chess, or"—his gaze fastened with disconcerting intentness on her lips—"at love."

She was suddenly serious, aware of the tension so strong between them again. "I believe I won the wager, sir."

"Indeed, you did. Unless you care to make it best two out of three?"

Rebecca hesitated. She had won. She would be allowed to visit her sister. Something in his eye tempted her, though. "Oh, why not," she said recklessly. "Let's set them up again. But, whatever happens, I may visit my sister."

"Then we play for a kiss only," he said, and it wasn't a question.

"Very well." Her head was high; her eyes sparkled in a way he'd never seen before, with life and laughter and fire. Aye, he'd be burned if he played at this game much longer. "I warn you, however. You shan't get it."

"That remains to be seen, lass," he said almost absently, studying the board and planning out his strategy. So she wished to join in battle with him? So be it.

The second game was a very different affair from the first. And an affair it was, Brendan realized very early on, though he suspected Rebecca didn't. The goal of chess might be to capture the king, but this was about wooing the queen. Wherever Rebecca moved, he moved, too; where she went he followed. When he took one of her pieces, he touched it caressingly; if her queen came out onto the board, he was certain to be there. For she was the queen, the most powerful piece on the board, and while he wouldn't consign himself to the fate of being king, who must be protected, he was at the least a match for her. And not just in chess. If there was fire here, if he was to burn, then so be it. Watching her intent face, her brow wrinkled, her eyes serious and her lower lip caught in her teeth, he would, he knew, welcome it.

Her queen, and not so incidentally her king as well, was soon surrounded by a fawning, admiring crowd of pawns and knights and bishops. Her frown briefly deepened, and then, with a little laugh, she knocked her king over. "You have me," she admitted.

"Have I, lass?"

At his words, she looked up, startled, and her breath drew in. "No, I—I mean you've won this game. You play very well, Captain." She busied herself with setting up the pieces.

"Aye. For a pirate." Seduction was over for the moment. There was the matter of a wager between them, to be settled by the next game.

"Why do you say that?" she asked, and he looked up to see her watching him, a puzzled frown crinkling her brow.

"Because it is what I am, lass. I believe I take white this time."

"Yes. Yes, you are, but—"

Danger. He looked up from adjusting the board. "But?"

"I don't know." Her hand waved in the air helplessly. "You're not what I'd ever thought a pirate would be."

Definitely danger. He didn't know what she was thinking, what she had seen to say such a thing. Whatever it was, he needed to disabuse her of the notion, and quickly. "I captured your ship." He moved out a pawn. "I believe that qualifies me as a pirate."

"Yes, but—"

"But?" he said again, alert, tense. He'd left her alone in this cabin. Devil take it, what had she seen?

"But you haven't taken advantage of me."

Relief made him almost light-headed, made him want to pick her up and twirl her around. Made him wish that he had, indeed, taken advantage of her offer. "Know this, Rebecca," he said, leaning over the table, his head close to hers. "When this game is over I will kiss you. And it will not be taking advantage."

"You need to win first."

"I will."

He'd answered with such certainty that he expected her to look frightened or, at the least, apprehensive. Instead, she merely looked thoughtful. "We shall see," she said and moved a pawn out as well. "Where did you learn to play chess?"

"At home," he said absently, totally concentrated on the game now, his mind working ahead, running over her possible moves and his strategy. "Long ago."

"And where is home?"

Danger, his instincts screamed again, and he looked up to face an entirely different kind of danger: her eyes, large and luminous and, unbelievably, interested. In him. Not in the Raven, the pirate, but in him alone. " 'Tis a long time ago, lass," he said, returning his attention to the board and startled to find he'd moved a rook out. Now why had he done that?

"Ireland, I suppose."

"Aye." Now what was she doing, moving her knight out like that? Frowning, he looked up and again encountered her eyes. Danger! "Where, ah, how did you learn?"

"Oh, my father taught me." She sat back and then, almost nonchalantly, made her move. For the life of him he couldn't figure out what her strategy was. One thing he had learned, though, and that was not to underestimate her.

"Ye are close to your father?"

"I was." Her voice lost all animation. "I mean yes, of course, I am."

"But he sent ye away." He concentrated on her, the game forgotten for the moment. "Why did he do that?"

"Oh, Amelia needed a companion, of course," she said breezily, but he wasn't fooled. For the first time her hand had faltered as she reached out to make a move.

"He sent you away," he repeated flatly.

"No." She sat back, studying the board. "There's nothing left for me in Georgetown." Her face was impassive, but he thought he saw pain in her eyes for just the briefest moment.

"No one, *leannan*? No admirers? No suitors?"

"For me? Heavens, no! Your move."

"Then the men must all be fools."

"I am old, plain, and on the shelf." She frowned. "Are you certain you want to do that?"

"Yes," he said, moving out his queen and annoyed at the question. This wasn't about chess, any more than the previous games had been. "Surely ye know you're beautiful, *leannan*?"

"Beautiful? Me?" Her eyes were astonished, and in spite of himself he was caught by their spell. Caught, and lost.

"Yes, lass," he heard himself say. "You."

"But—" As if seeking refuge she looked down at the board, and he knew in a flash of understanding what her strategy was. It had nothing to do with chess. It did have everything to do with distracting him. He wanted to laugh and yell at the same time. She might use her wiles on him, yet she didn't believe him. He found her beautiful. And when that had happened, he didn't know.

"I'm not, you know." Her voice was prosaic.

"We'll not argue this, lass." His anger was gone, replaced by amusement and desire. "There's a game to be played."

Rebecca didn't meet his gaze. "So there is."

The earlier camaraderie of the game was gone. There were no more questions probing his past, no more huge green eyes fluttering up at him—somewhere along the way she had learned to flirt, deny it though she might now—

nothing but utter concentration. There was only the game, and the realization of what winning, and losing, meant. She was good, he'd grant her that, he thought, moving up his knight to a diagonal to her king, a trap she hadn't seen. Very good, but no match for his determination. "Checkmate," he said quietly, and her hand, which had been raised to move a piece, suddenly dropped. "I believe you owe me a kiss."

She looked up, and he could read nothing in her eyes, not sorrow or fear or even anger. There was only resignation in her sigh, in the set of her shoulders. "I believe I do," she said, not moving.

He rose, stepped away from the table. "Come here, Rebecca," he ordered. She bit her lips, and then rose, walking to him, her head bent. "Look at me, lass." He put his fingers under her chin, forcing her head up. "Look at me." Still nothing in her eyes, except perhaps the slightest flicker of apprehension. "Ye've been kissed before, haven't ye?"

She licked her lips, and he wondered if she realized how incredibly enticing a gesture it was. "Yes."

"I thought as much." He ignored the way her gaze swept up to him as he slid his arm about her waist, drawing her to him. Under his hand her waist was trim, firm, and curved exactly as it should be; against his chest he could feel her breasts, fuller than he'd expected. The heat that he'd been holding at bay all afternoon surged within him. The devil take it, she was a beauty. Why did she hide behind shapeless dresses and severe hairstyling? "Put your arms around my neck, lass." He braced himself as she obeyed, her breasts moving against him, forcing himself not to clutch at her, to pull her closer. For he wanted what he had said to her earlier. He wanted her all warm and wet and willing. "Are ye frightened, lass?"

"Of a kiss? No."

"Mayhap ye should be." Gazing down at her face, he allowed his fingers to slip along her chin, tracing the outline of her lips slightly, lightly, with the tip of a finger. Her breath caught; her lips parted, and it was suddenly too much for him. "Ah, *leannan,* don't you know you were made for this?" he said, and his lips swooped down upon hers.

Chapter 8

~

There was no warning. One moment Brendan was looking down at her, and the next he had captured her lips like the marauding pirate he was. He gave no quarter, but demanded all of her, kissing her openmouthed, warm and wet, and, oh, yes, she was willing, though she didn't want to be. A part of her stood aside, watching as the hands she had so reluctantly put around his neck tightened, grasping at his shoulders as if for support. And somehow she was detached from the woman who pressed up against him, all of him, desperate and eager for an embrace too long missed, too long desired. It was her body that willed her to do those things, to open her mouth to his seeking tongue, to reply in kind, as aggressive in her own way as he was. And surely it was her body that made her head arch back when his lips, greedy and impatient, sought a course down her throat; surely it was her body that shifted when his hand slipped up between their bodies to cup her breast—

Mind and body abruptly merged. Warm, perhaps, but no longer willing, Rebecca went still. This was wrong. What she had offered to him had been out of expediency, but this need, this wantonness, was wrong. No matter that everything within her clamored for more. Her body was weak, and what she had allowed was wrong. Her only defense against him, against herself, was coldness.

Brendan looked up, his gaze unexpectedly keen. "Is it not to your liking, *leannan*?" he said softly, and it was too much. Wrenching herself from his arms, she whirled away from him, standing at the stern window and hugging herself to still the long, slow shudders within her. Oh, yes, it was very much to her liking. That was the problem. "Rebecca?"

"Go away," she said, her voice muffled.

"Ah, now, *leannan*, I can't do that. 'Tis my cabin, after all." He sounded apologetic, but she heard the underlying note of triumph. "Come, lass, never say you're scared."

"I—I'm not." Not of him, at least.

"Then what is it, lass?"

"I do not desire you." She had meant the words to sound cold. Instead, they came out shaky.

He chuckled. "Ah, lass, do ye not?" The hair at the back of her neck prickled. He was nearing her. She could sense it, and oh, how she hoped he would reach up and touch her, stroke her neck, place a hand on her shoulder and turn her, persuading her, taking the choice away from her. "Admit it, lass, that I was right."

She held tighter onto herself. If he touched her, she would shatter. If he didn't, she would die. "About what?"

"The kiss. Warm and wet and willing."

She jerked away, though there was no place to go. Oh, yes, he was right. It had been all those things, and more. It had been wanton. And that was something she couldn't face. "I will never be willing, Captain," she said, and this time her voice was steadier.

"You offered yourself, lass." The teasing, coaxing note was gone from his voice. "You could be mine at any time."

"Not all of me." Her strength was returning with the ebbing of desire. She had spent years resisting passion; what was a few more hours? "There are parts of me that you will never have, because I will never give them."

"Sail ho!" The cry was distant, and faint enough so that Brendan was certain Rebecca didn't hear it. But he did. He jerked his head upward, looked at the beamed ceiling as if he could see through it to the man at lookout, to see the sail with his own eyes. Friend or foe? Given who he was, the latter was more likely.

"Rebecca." He made his voice patient. He knew what he was dealing with here: a virgin who had just discovered passion in his arms. The wrong man's arms. In this, though, he was the right man. He would have to proceed carefully. While that was frustrating, it also added spice to a game that lately had lost some of its excitement. He wanted her more, now, than he could remember ever wanting a woman. Such passion, such fire, under her prim exterior. "I didn't mean to frighten ye, lass."

"You didn't." Her voice was almost completely calm now. "But if you are going to take me I wish you would do so and be done with it."

"Be done with it!" That was too much. He stomped away. "Be done with it? By God, lady, that kiss was more than just being done with it! What the devil do you think I'm made of? Do you think you can kiss me like that and not expect more? Be done with it." He snorted. "No, Rebecca, what's between us won't be settled that easily."

Rebecca had turned and was staring at him wide-eyed. "You can't want me," she stated.

"The hell I can't—the devil take it, what is it?" he roared as a knock came on the door.

"Beggin' yer pardon, Cap'n." It was Tyner. "A sail's been spotted. Sam thinks ye should see it."

"The devil take it." He pulled open the cabinet door so hard it rattled, taking out the spyglass. "All right, Tyner. I'll be right there. And you." He turned, looking grimly at her. "We're not done."

She raised her chin. "What do you expect there could ever be between us, Captain?"

What did he expect—! It was his turn to stare at her. Had she, or had she not, kissed him with equal fervor? Had she not moaned, oh, not very loudly, but hadn't she, when his fingers had touched the underside of her breast? Oh, there was something between them, much as she might wish to deny it. "You'll see," he said, darkly, and slammed out the door.

Aboard HMS Cardiff

From his station on the quarterdeck, Lieutenant Jeremiah Dee collapsed the spyglass he had trained to the southeast. "It's him," he announced.

Captain Lancaster, in command of the HMS *Cardiff*, a fourth-rater carrying fifty guns in service to His Majesty's Navy, frowned. "Are you sure? Even my lookout can't tell." Damned if he would chase all over the sea in pursuit of a sail that likely belonged to a trader minding his own business. Not that he didn't want to come up against the Raven, mind. There wasn't a captain in the navy who didn't want that. He was not, however, too confident in the abilities of the young man standing beside him.

He was a strange one, was Dee. Aboard the *Cardiff* with the duty of capturing the Raven, he kept to himself, and was disliked by all who met him. Well, that was all right, one didn't have to be liked to do one's job. But there was a look in Dee's eyes that Lancaster distrusted, an intent gleam that bordered on fanaticism whenever the Raven was mentioned. In the past few days, that had been a great deal. Two days ago they'd spotted a ship, almost hull down under the horizon; a short time later they'd come across the man floating in the water, clinging to a piece of wood. He was a crewman from the *Curlew,* out of St. Thomas, and he'd jumped overboard when the *Cardiff* had been sighted, in hopes of reaching her. Though nearly drowned, he had gasped out the tale of the awful recent events aboard that ship, and the passengers that had been taken captive. By then the *Curlew,* the ship they'd sighted, was well out of sight. Besides, the seaman had given them a valuable clue: the Raven's last heading. For the last two days, they had been cruising in pursuit.

"It's him," Dee repeated, that same satisfied note in his voice. "I can feel it."

Lancaster shifted uneasily from one foot to another. There were more important considerations than chasing pirates in his estimation, the French for one, and those upstart Americans for another. He had his orders, however, and this latest atrocity added urgency to the search. Bless his soul, two young women captives of that villain! They'd be lucky to escape with their lives, let alone their virtue. The Raven had to be found.

Beside him Dee had raised the spyglass again, searching for his elusive quarry without success. Still, he was smiling when he brought it down again, a strange smile, feral, wild. *I have you now,* he thought. *You're there, I can feel you, and soon I'll have you. And you'll pay.* Unconsciously his fingers went up to touch the scar on his cheek, a too-vivid reminder of his prior brush with the Raven. He'd pay for that, with his life, if possible. The Raven was within his grasp, and he would never give up. Never. "Oh, yes," Dee said softly, no longer aware of the captain or crew. His attention was only on his quarry as he braced his hands on the quarterdeck railing, gazing far off to see. "This time, Raven, you'll not escape me. And you'll pay."

* * *

"Ye're ready, miss?" Tyner said.

Rebecca smoothed down her skirts one more time. "Yes, Mr. Tyner. Quite ready."

"Just Tyner, miss," he reminded her again.

"Yes, Mr.—sorry. Tyner." Her smile was strained as she watched him unlock the door. At last, after three days, she was going to see her sister, and she didn't for the life of her know why she was so nervous.

It was the aftermath of that incident with the Raven, she decided, following Tyner into the passageway and waiting while he fumbled with his keys. For a time this afternoon she'd forgotten how truly formidable an opponent the Raven was, until he'd shown her. Trust a man, she thought bitterly, to use that weapon against a woman.

Tyner unlocked the door, and after tapping on it, swung it open. "Company, miss," he called into the room and then turned to Rebecca. "Go on in, miss. I have to lock ye in. Understand?"

"I wouldn't expect otherwise, Tyner."

Unexpectedly, he grinned at her. "Aye. Yer a game 'un, miss, and no mistake."

"Tyner!" she said, astonished.

"When you're done, just bang on the door," he said, not at all abashed by her shock. "I'll be in the pantry, there."

"Thank you, Tyner." At last she stepped over the high coaming into the room to see her sister. "Melia!" she exclaimed, and rushed across the room, her arms outstretched.

"What are you doing here?" Amelia said, and the flatness of her voice made Rebecca stop dead.

"I came to see if you're all right. This does look comfortable enough." Amelia was standing at the far end of a very tiny stateroom. Tiny, but Rebecca saw to her relief, clean and bright. A bunk set against the wall had drawers set into its base and a cheerful quilt atop, while tucked into the corner was a washstand. Much of Rebecca's worry fled. "Oh, Melia, I'm so glad to see you safe."

"Are you? Then why haven't you been to visit me before this?"

"I wasn't allowed. Oh, do let me hug you, Melia! I've missed you so."

"I didn't ask you to come here," Amelia snapped.

Rebecca blinked. "Melia. What is wrong?"

"I don't want you here." Amelia turned her back. "Go away."

"Melia," Rebecca said, stunned rather than hurt. Amelia had always depended on her, been close to her, and except for the past three days, Rebecca had always protected her—ah. Relief coursed through her. Of course. Amelia was upset at what must seem like abandonment. "Amelia, truly, I had no choice," she said. "I asked to see you every day, and I wasn't allowed."

"And now you are."

"Yes." There was an odd note in Amelia's voice. "Come, let's sit down and talk. You're being treated well?"

"For a captive? Yes." Amelia turned, and her eyes flickered scornfully over Rebecca. "You look the same. I wouldn't have thought it."

Rebecca frowned. "Why shouldn't I? Oh. You were afraid perhaps he'd beat me? No, nothing like that—"

"You went with him," Amelia spat out. "I didn't think he'd like old tall Megs dressed in gray."

That hurt. It shouldn't, but it did. "Amelia! I don't think I deserve that. Besides, he hasn't—"

"Oh, you deserve it for the way you've acted." The words tumbled out. "I've kept my virtue. But you—"

"What else was I to do?" Rebecca cried. "Look where we are, Amelia! I did the only thing I could think of to keep us safe. To keep you safe." She swallowed hard. "If it's any comfort, he hasn't so much as touched me."

"Liar." Amelia stood with her arms crossed, looking so like their father it was uncanny. "You're exactly what our father said you are. A whore."

Rebecca's head snapped back as if she'd been struck. "Oh, Amelia, that's so unfair—"

"I don't want you here." Amelia turned her back again. "I want you to leave."

"Melia—"

"Now."

Rebecca bit her lips at the contempt in Amelia's voice and turned, blindly, stumbling to the door and clutching at the panels for support, before raising her hand to knock.

Tyner opened the door a moment later. "Done so soon?" he said, looking at her in surprise. "Cap'n said you could have an hour."

"I—I am unwell, Tyner," Rebecca said, stumbling past him into the passageway. "I would like to rest."

Tyner shrugged. "All right. But I doubt the cap'n'll let ye see her again soon."

A little hysterical bubble of laughter rose in Rebecca's throat as he opened the door of the Raven's cabin for her. Sanctuary. And wasn't that a ridiculous thought? "It doesn't matter, Tyner," she said, and still dazed, collapsed onto the bench under the stern window.

A long time later, Rebecca stirred, sitting up and wiping at her face with her fingers. She had cried and she had raged, but neither had done her much good. Her much-beloved sister had rejected her in the cruelest way possible, and how was she to live with it? Especially when she knew she deserved it. For if she might not be guilty of her sister's accusations in fact, in spirit she was.

Squeezing her eyes closed, she put her head in her hands. It wasn't the first rejection she had ever suffered, nor was it the most painful. Her father's had been that, and for the same reason. Because she was wicked, wanton. She carried the curse of it like a badge, and she would never be free.

The light had faded. Tyner had brought her supper a while ago without saying anything, and then, just as tactfully, had collected her untouched plate. Now it was late, and she was exhausted. She had gone through too much this day, too many emotions, from fear to passion to absolute, wretched dejection. Rising, she fumbled her way across the cabin, falling onto the bed, not bothering to change into her nightgown or to braid her hair. Nothing mattered anymore. If the Raven came to her that night, if he touched her and made her body respond in ways she couldn't control, she no longer cared. Nothing mattered.

Brendan yawned hugely as he unlocked the door to his cabin. A nuisance, this, not being able to come and go as he pleased. If he'd had any hopes of being able to ignore Miss Rebecca Talbot, they'd been dashed that afternoon. Nor could he simply put her in a cabin with her sister until they were ransomed, not after what Tyner had told him. It looked as if he was stuck with Rebecca for the duration of the voyage.

Faint moonlight spilled into the cabin, fading now, but Brendan's night vision was very good. He could see, well enough, Rebecca sprawled on the bed, still dressed, her eyes puffy, and he was suddenly, irrationally furious at her sister. What Rebecca had done was out of love for Amelia. Her sister had taken that gift of love, and flung it in her face.

Not that he'd helped matters. God knew he'd made Rebecca pay for her act, he thought dispassionately as he strung up the hammock. He made no effort to be quiet, but she didn't awaken. What had happened this afternoon must, in its way, have been as shattering to her as her sister's rejection. He smiled humorlessly. Imagine finding yourself attracted to a pirate, when you were a most prim and proper young lady.

Groaning slightly, he threw himself onto the hammock. Aye, he was tired, and why not? It had been a trying day for him. Delightful at times, with the chess match that was about so much more than chess, but difficult, restraining himself from reaching out and taking her when he wanted her so much. Even now, when he was worn out, his loins ached with desire for her. 'Twas the closeness, he told himself. Aye, and wouldn't making love be a good distraction right now, too?

For there was the matter of the sail spotted that afternoon. At most other times Brendan wouldn't have been concerned, but three days had passed since he'd captured the *Curlew*. Anything could have happened in that time; the *Curlew* could have been recaptured by the British. Whatever had happened, he'd had an uneasy, crawling feeling between his shoulders when he'd looked through the glass and seen the sails for himself. Danger. Square sails, like on a trader, or a man-of-war. Likely the latter, his instincts told him, and he'd learned to ignore them at his peril.

All through the day the other ship had played cat and mouse with him, sometimes coming nearer, sometimes dropping below the horizon, but always there. He could feel it. If the *Curlew* had been retaken, then his last heading would be known. In the letter he'd sent with Neville he'd set the rendezvous with Ezra Talbot for four weeks hence, at a specific latitude and longtitude. It was the only way he could have arranged it.

Now there was a chance that all his planning had gone for naught. If that was the case, what was he going to do? Groaning again, he put his arm over his eyes. He couldn't bloody well show up at the rendezvous, unless he wanted to be captured. His best option would be to put the Talbot sisters onto another ship, and then disappear. If he did that, however, he risked mutiny. His crew was looking forward to sharing out the ransom.

Ah, well, whatever happened would happen, he thought, with Irish fatalism. Likely he'd awaken and find that the other ship had disappeared. The matter was out of his hands.

As quickly as that, he pushed his worries aside, falling into a deep, untroubled sleep. Sometime later something pierced his consciousness, a little mewling sound, as of someone in pain. Instincts honed by years of being on guard brought him to instant wakefulness. No need to ask what the sound was, or where it was coming from. In the bed next to him, Rebecca was crying.

"What is it, *leannan*?" he asked softly, so as not to frighten her. When there was no answer he swung out of the hammock, but all light had faded and he couldn't see her. Frowning, he found tinder and flint, and at last lit the swaying oil lamp suspended from the overhead. Only then did he turn back to the bed. "Rebecca," he said in that same soft voice and saw immediately why she hadn't answered him. She was fast asleep.

It wrenched at him, an almost physical pain, twisting deep inside. What hurt her so that she could cry so heartbrokenly, and yet not awaken? What pain was there inside her? Aside from whatever pain he'd caused her, he thought with a grimace, sitting carefully on the bed. Aye, 'twould be best to put her and her sister on another ship, best for her, best for him. No matter how hard it might be.

"Rebecca." He laid a hand on her shoulder. Her breath caught, and then ebbed out again on a sob, and still she didn't awaken. Now what did he do? Crying women were the devil's own nuisance, but this—this was doing something to him. He couldn't sit by and let her suffer through this alone.

"Easy, lass," he murmured, slipping an arm under her shoulder and lifting her against his chest. He should soothe her back into sleep, he knew, but he couldn't. He had to stop whatever was causing her such pain. "Easy, now, Rebecca, 'tis all right. Wake up, lass."

"Nooo," came from her in a long, low moan, and she moved her head against his shoulder. She was shaking it in denial. "No! Oh, Robbie." The last syllable rose and broke. "Robbie."

Brendan sat quite still. Robbie. Here he sat, holding her, and she cried for another man. A fine fool he was. "Wake up, lass," he said again, louder now, shaking her shoulder a bit harder. "Rebecca. Wake up."

"No," she said again and then went very still. He was quiet, too. She had acted like an outraged virgin this afternoon, when all the time there was another man.

Rebecca raised her head, her face bewildered. "I—what is it?" she asked, her voice rough.

"You were crying in your sleep."

"I was? Oh." She seemed to realize for the first time that he held her, and she jerked away. He should have let her go, but even now, knowing what he did, he couldn't. Warm and sleepy, she felt good next to him. Too good. "I—had a dream. Thank you for waking me."

"Aye." He inclined his head. "A bad dream, by the sound of it."

"Yes. Excuse me, I wish to get my handkerchief." Again she tried to pull away, and this time he let her go, watching as she fumbled in the pocket of her crumpled dress. He stayed beside her, somehow unable to move. "I'm sorry. I never cry."

He inclined his head. "Ye've been through enough these last days."

"No, it wasn't that—yes." She forced a smile. "Thank you for waking me."

He inclined his head again, watching her. "What was your dream?"

"Nothing. Thank you, Captain. I'm sorry I disturbed you."

"Aye," he said and rose at last, any closeness he'd felt toward her gone. "Just one thing, lass."

She looked up, mopping at her eyes. "Yes?"

"Who is Robbie?"

Rebecca went very still, and then finished drying her eyes. "How do you know about him?"

"You said his name." He stared down at her. "Like your heart was breaking."

She looked away, biting her lip. "It is."

He didn't want to ask the next question, but he had to. He had to know. "Someone you love?"

"Yes," she said, and sighed. "You might as well know. There's no reason for you not to." She looked up at him, her eyes clear and candid, and yet filled with pain beyond bearing. "Robbie was my son."

Chapter 9

~

"Your son!" Brendan jerked back. "But you're not—"

"Married. I know." A wry smile twisted her face. "It happens, Captain. I surely wouldn't be your first woman."

"Well, no, but—that's different."

"Of course." She looked down at her hands. "Different." Men were allowed such things. Women were condemned for them. "So now you know."

"I don't know anything." Brendan sounded bewildered as he rose and began to pace the cabin. "All I thought I knew—"

"Come, Captain, we're hardly that close."

"Brendan." He swung around. "My name is Brendan."

Her eyebrows rose. "The Raven has a name?"

"Stop it." He stood in front of her, glaring at her. "We're close to each other, lass, whether ye like it or not. Circumstances have forced it."

Rebecca closed her eyes. Oh, yes, circumstances, and if things were different, he would never have looked at her twice. She was not, she had learned in the most painful way, a woman who attracted men. But they were close. There was no denying it. In the past few days she'd come to know him in an oddly intimate way. Never mind that she actually knew little about him; never mind that he was a pirate. They were close. The fact that the closeness had been forced on her would make little difference to the gossips back home. "I'm your captive," she whispered.

He swore, making her eyes open wide. "You're more to me than that, and you know it."

"No, how can I?" Her temper flared. "You hold us and

plan to trade us for ransom. That you've treated us well"—
she slashed through the air with her hand—" 'tis because of
that ridiculous bargain we made."

"I've never touched you, lass."

"And you never will. I want no part of this." She clambered off the bed, impeded by her full skirts, all the old hurt,
all her self-loathing rising within her. "I'd rather go back to
my cell than stay with you now."

"The devil take it!" he erupted. "Have I treated you
badly? Hurt you?"

"No." Her voice was very quiet. "You only expected me
to be a whore."

"By God, Rebecca, that's the last thing I expected of you!
I thought—"

"You thought I was a virgin," she said when he didn't go
on. "And it bothers you. Mercy! It does, doesn't it?"

"The devil take it, yes, it does." He rounded on her.
"What kind of a game have you been playing with me?
Playing the innocent when all the time you—"

"I never said I wasn't experienced." She sat down, her
hands folded in her lap, her anger gone. It would solve nothing. What was he to her, anyway? What could he ever be to
her? "Do you know, when you're angry you lose your
brogue?"

"Then ye'll know when I'm in a temper, won't ye?" he replied instantly, his eye startled.

"Oh. Yes." She looked down at her hands. "Please let us
go." Her voice was low. "This does no one any good."

"I can't, lass." He sat in his swivel chair, watching her.
"You're too valuable."

"Me? If it were only me I doubt my father would pay the
ransom."

"What happened, Rebecca?" he asked quietly.

His face was serious, and for the first time, Rebecca felt
that she knew him, that she could trust him. Very odd thing
to feel about a pirate. "I—well, you might as well know. I
had a child when I was seventeen."

"And not married?"

"No." She bit her lips again. "My father sent me away, to
my mother's family in the country, so no one would know.
He didn't want me to keep the babe."

"The father—"

"He died," she said quickly. It was true, as far as it went.

"I'm sorry."

"Thank you." She took a deep breath. " 'Tis past. 'Tis only that I dream about it from time to time, when I'm upset."

"Aye. And your sister upset ye this afternoon. Oh, don't look so surprised, lass," he went on as she blinked at him. "I know everything that goes on on my ship."

"I don't doubt it." Rebecca concentrated on pleating her skirt into precise little folds. "I'm sorry I woke you."

"Ye were crying, lass." There was an odd note in his voice. "Your son? What happened to him?"

Rebecca took a deep breath against the sharp pain in her chest. After all this time it shouldn't hurt so much, but it did. "He was a beautiful baby," she said softly, remembering, savoring the memory of the moment when her son had first been placed in her arms. A moment that had more than made up for the difficult months before. "Healthy, fair like his father, and good-natured. Most of the time." Her smile was rueful, wistful. "I stayed in the country so I could keep him. I didn't care what my father said, Brendan." She looked up at him, gaze fierce. "There was nothing sinful about him, nothing shameful. He was three months old, smiling at everything, beginning to gurgle and to reach out and . . ."

"And?" he prompted when she didn't go on. "Ye had to leave him behind when ye left for England?"

"In a manner of speaking." Again she took a deep breath, steeling herself against what was to come. So long since she had talked about this. So long since she'd even allowed herself to remember. "He died."

"Jaysus—"

"There was no reason. No hint it would happen," she went on relentlessly, ignoring him, lost in the horror and the guilt. "One day he was healthy. The next morning I went to get him up from his cradle and he wasn't breathing."

"Jaysus, Rebecca." He held out his hand, stunned by her words, by the lost look in her eyes.

"I'm all right. 'Tis long ago, now. But sometimes I wonder what I did wrong." She sounded bewildered. "I've gone over it and over it and I don't know what I did wrong. I took care of him, fed him, made sure he was warm—"

"Rebecca—"

"No, don't touch me!" She jerked back. "He was—gone. And it's my fault."

"Why?"

"Because I didn't get up to check on him!"

"Did he cry?"

"No," she said reluctantly. "But I should have checked on him—"

"How could you have known?"

"I should have! I was his mother. I should have known."

"I'm sorry," he said awkwardly.

"I know." She nodded. "It's been hard. I went home after that. No one knew, though everyone suspected. My father felt I'd disgraced him."

"This is more than disgrace, Rebecca."

"Yes, I know." Her head was bent. "It almost ruined Father."

"The devil take your father," he said impatiently. "You didn't deserve to lose your child."

She looked at him blankly. "I believe we're speaking of two different things. But it doesn't matter," she rushed on. "It's in the past."

"If that's so, why did your father send you away?"

"Mercy, that had nothing to do with it!" she said with forced lightness.

"No?"

"No. And, to be honest, 'tis rather a relief to make a new start."

Brendan frowned. Her words were light, but under them he could hear a vast, deep pain. Aye, a new start, until he'd taken her captive. Whatever the scandal she'd faced in the past, this would be far worse. Not to mention the effect on him. He was beginning to suspect that taking Rebecca hostage was among the worst mistakes of his life. "It's late, lass," he said, remembering just in time to thicken his brogue. If she hadn't said anything, he wouldn't have realized that his accent slipped when he was emotional. But then, until she came aboard he rarely had become emotional. "Best we both get some sleep."

"I—yes." Her eyes were uncertain as she rose. "I—we did make a bargain."

He stopped in the act of dousing the lamp, as stunned as he had been by any of tonight's revelations. "I won't touch ye, lass. Not unless ye wish it."

"What? A gallant pirate?"

"Nay, lass," he said very gently, because he had learned tonight that self-mockery was how she dealt with her pain.

" 'Tis just what I said. 'Tis late, and we're both tired." And, truth be told, he wasn't certain that he did want to bed her. Not just now, at least. Appealing she might be, but tonight she had become more than an inconvenient hostage to him, more than an unexpectedly amusing pastime. She was a woman, with hurts and dreams, and he was, as he kept reminding himself, a man of honor. Though what honor dictated in this situation, he didn't know. "Go to bed, lass. I'll take a turn on deck for a time."

She stayed standing where she was. "I—would you rather I went in with my sister?"

"Nay, lass," he said, though that would make matters vastly easier. "Go to bed." And with that he went out, closing the door behind him.

Rebecca stared at the door, and then sank down on the edge of the bed. He hadn't locked the door, but that no longer mattered. Where was she to go, should she escape? Telling her story tonight had brought home to her just how difficult her life had been the last few years, and how empty the future seemed. Only during the few days aboard the *Raven* had she felt alive. Frightened, angry, even wanton, but alive in a way she hadn't been in far too long. And all because of a pirate.

"Oh, no, you don't," she said aloud, rising and pacing about the room. She would not allow herself to be attracted to a pirate. Not what she'd expected a pirate to be like, true. She frowned, rubbing a thumb across her lips. He hadn't taken advantage of her, though she'd given him every opportunity; he was literate, intelligent, quick-witted, and tonight, when she'd faced the vast emptiness left by Robbie's death, he'd been unexpectedly gentle. Shocked by her story, of course, but that wasn't surprising. No, not at all how one would expect a pirate to behave. Who was Brendan Fitzpatrick?

Thoughtful now, she returned to the bed, automatically taking down her hair and braiding it into a thick plait. Dangerous, the path her thoughts were taking. Yes, he'd been gentle with her, and yes, she was at peace with herself in a way she hadn't been in many a year. Dreams of Robbie usually left her feeling unsettled, miserable. Guilty. Not tonight, though. Tonight she was distracted by a pirate. It was not to be borne. With quick, decisive movements, she peeled off the wrinkled gray gown, making a face at it, and let her nightdress settle around her. Robbie was in the past. Whatever she had done wrong then she could not undo, no matter how frantically she might wish to. The Raven, however, was another story. She was not going to make the same mistake twice.

Lips firmed, she turned down the wick on the lamp and climbed back into bed, arms crossed on her chest. Tonight she might have seen a side of the Raven that few knew existed, but it didn't mean anything. It couldn't. She was his captive, nothing more. And if he thought she would be a passive, timid captive, she thought, turning over and punching the pillows, he would soon learn differently. Brendan Fitzpatrick at last had an opponent. The battle between them was joined.

At horizon's edge, the rim of the sun appeared, slowly, almost tentatively, before bursting up in a display of color and light that dazzled any watchers. Brendan didn't notice. Perched high on the foremast, he kept his spyglass trained aft. North, where he'd sighted that elusive sail just a few moments before, fluttering just above the horizon. It had disappeared again, but it was there. He could feel it, and he didn't like it. Not when they'd changed course in the night to escape this elusive pursuer.

The wind shifted, and he looked up at the royal, the highest sail, frowning. Still fair, but if it shifted the *Raven* could be in trouble. She was a fast ship, but with a following wind a large square-rigger could catch them up easily. If that happened, more than his freedom would be in jeopardy.

Raising the glass to his eye again, he scanned the horizon, and came to a decision. Whoever was behind them had to be shaken off. He grabbed a line and rode it down to the deck. "I'll take the helm," he said to the man at the wheel, taking the spokes confidently in his hands. "Prepare to come about!"

"Aye, Cap'n," Starkey, the mate on watch, answered, and yelled the order to the crew. They scrambled to their positions, uncoiling the lines that secured the mast yards and the big mainsail, standing ready to his command.

"Ready about."

"Ready about!" Starkey bawled to the crew.

Brendan's eyes were on the sails, gauging the wind, the current, his ship. "Any moment now. Any moment—now! Hard alee!" he said, and put the helm down, changing the ship's direction ninety degrees. The big main boom swung over, the yards creaked in protest as their angle was changed, and for a breathless moment all was still, except for the shaking of the sails. Then, with a cracking of canvas, the sails caught the wind, bellied with it, full and white against the brightening blue sky. They were away on a new tack, and a new course.

Brendan stepped away from the wheel. "Maintain course," he said to the helmsman, standing back and studying the sails, feet braced, hands on hips and eye narrowed. Aye, they'd caught the wind, and a fair one, at that. The *Raven* would show that ghost ship her heels.

Well satisfied with the morning's work, Brendan strode across the deck to the hatch that led below. Time to break his fast. Aye, and time to face Rebecca again. The thought made him frown as he scrambled down the companionway, blinking to adjust to the darkness below. Devil take it, this escapade was becoming a lot more complicated than he'd ever expected. Bad enough he'd had to take hostages, but it was too much to expect him to deal with a weeping female as well. God knew, he thought, pushing a hand through his hair as he stood outside his cabin, how she'd react to him this morning. God knew how he'd react to her, and that was the real problem.

The door to the pantry opened, and Tyner came into the passageway, a pewter dish in his hand. "Mornin', Cap'n. Be ye wantin' breakfast?"

"Aye." Brendan looked again at his door. "That for her?"

"For Miss Talbot? Nay. For the younger one." Tyner scowled. "Proper riled up, she is. Started banging on the door at six bells and demanding to be let free."

"Did she, now." Brendan looked consideringly at the door down the passageway, and then nodded. "Give me that, Tyner," he said, reaching for the plate. "I think it's time Miss Amelia and I had a talk."

Aboard HMS Cardiff

"Lost 'im, Cap'n!" the lookout bawled down from the crow's nest.

Captain Lancaster frowned. "Where away?"

"Last time, heading due south, Cap'n."

"Due south," Lancaster muttered to himself. "Could be a trader heading to the Brazils."

"No." Lieutenant Dee, standing next to him, shook his

head. "It's him. We can't let him go. Change course, Captain. Due south."

Lancaster gazed dubiously at the soldier with the young face and the old, zealot eyes. "I am still in command, Lieutenant," he said dryly, "and any course change is my decision."

"There's no decision." Dee's eyes burned with dark fire. "Catch him, and the world will call you hero. Let him go, and . . ."

Lancaster's face turned thoughtful as Dee's voice faded. Damme, the man had a point. In times of war action was frequent, and promotions, swift. Lancaster had come to command after the battle of Trafalgar, however, when the British Navy had proven to all its superiority. His war had been spent in the relatively tranquil Caribbean, with little action and thus little chance of promotion. Why, he still captained the same fourth-rater he'd begun with, when it should be clear to all that he could handle a first-rater superbly. It was due to his enemies at the Admiralty, he thought darkly. But if he captured a prize such as the *Raven*—"Lieutenant Burke!" he barked, and Burke, his second in command, standing on the main deck, jumped.

"Aye, sir?" he said, looking up at Lancaster on the quarterdeck.

"Change course to due south."

"Aye-aye, Captain."

"We'll get him, Lieutenant," he said to Dee, smiling grimly. "Don't you doubt that."

"I don't, Captain," Dee said, and he smiled, too, a smile that made his eyes burn even more fiercely. "We'll get him."

The pewter dish slid back and forth on the table in the captain's cabin, in rhythm with the sway of the ship, spilling some of its contents with each move. Only the railings around the edge of the table kept it from slipping off altogether. Rebecca, head resting on her hand, watched it without interest. In the morning light her resolution of the night before seemed futile. Nothing had changed. She was still a captive; she still was who she was. She could resist him all she wished, but one thing remained the same. She was attracted to a pirate, and if that didn't prove the basic wantonness of her nature, she didn't know what would.

The door opened, and she looked up with the same lack of

interest she'd shown her food. Tyner, of course, but behind him was—"Amelia!" she gasped, rising and forgetting everything, the food, last night, the past.

"Becky." Amelia stood just inside the door, biting her lips. "I'm sorry! Can you forgive me?"

"Oh, Melia." Rebecca flew across the room, catching her sister up in her arms and barely aware of Tyner going out again, locking the door behind him. "Of course I can. You were upset. I can understand—"

"No." Amelia pulled back, shaking her head. "I was wrong. He made me see that."

"He? Who?"

"The Raven. Oh, Becky, when he came into my stateroom this morning I nearly swooned, he looked so fierce! I didn't know what was going to happen to me."

"Did he hurt you?" Rebecca demanded, caught up in Amelia's dramatics in spite of herself. Of course Brendan wouldn't hurt Amelia.

"No." Amelia looked down at her feet. "But he did read me a terrible scold."

"A scold?" Rebecca frowned and took her arm. "Come, sit here by the window. Why did he scold you?"

"Well." Amelia settled onto the bench beneath the stern window. "About how I treated you. I daresay I deserved it."

Rebecca stared at her in astonishment. "About how—no." She looked away. "Everything you said to me was true."

"Oh, no." Amelia leaned forward, brow wrinkled, clasping Rebecca's hands. "He made me see how wrong I was."

"What did he say?" Rebecca asked, still unable to face Amelia. Why in the world had the Raven gone to her defense?

"He told me that you'd moved in with him to protect me."

"I told you that, Melia."

"Yes, I know." Amelia's eyes were averted. "He also said you'd resisted him at every opportunity. Oh, Becky!" Amelia's eyes came up, huge with tears. "How brave of you!"

Rebecca's mouth opened and then closed again. Mercy, why had he told Amelia that? She had certainly responded to his kiss. If she had resisted him, it was only because he hadn't tried very hard. Lowering thought, and not just because of what it said about her. Apparently even a pirate didn't find her attractive enough to bed. "I don't know about brave," she said slowly, knowing she couldn't tell her sister the truth. " 'Tis what I had to do. But, you!" She turned to face Amelia. "Are you well? Have you been treated all right?"

"Yes, and yes. But I've been so scared, Becky."

"Yes, I know." Rebecca gathered her close again. "So have I. But I don't think there's any reason to be. I think—"

The door opened, and Tyner came in. "Be ye wantin' more breakfast, miss?"

Rebecca glanced blankly from him to the table and realized that she hadn't touched her food. "No, thank you, Tyner. May my sister stay with me?"

"Aye, miss, for a time. Are ye sure ye don't want more breakfast?"

"No—yes!" Rebecca said, suddenly ravenous. "Oh, thank you, Tyner!"

"Me, miss?" He looked startled. "Nothing I had to do with it," he said and whisked out the door.

The day was almost pleasant, spent in catching up with her sister. Brendan didn't return to the cabin all day, for which Rebecca was grateful. That she became a little lonely in the evening, when Amelia was back to her stateroom, was something she refused to dwell upon. Being lonely for a pirate was absurd, she told herself as she readied for bed. She should be grateful he was leaving her in peace; she should be giving thanks that he had yet to take her up on her offer. What she should not be doing was fighting off sleep, waiting for him to return, but that she couldn't seem to help.

The lock clicked, and then the door opened very quietly. Five bells had struck not long ago; ten-thirty at night. Rebecca willed herself to stay still, feigning sleep, but then, as she heard tinder striking flint, rose up on her elbow. "Hello."

Brendan glanced over at her in surprise. His hair was disordered from the wind; his shirt, as usual, was open at the neck. A feeling almost of pain went through her. Pirate or not, he was the most appealing man she'd ever met. "I thought ye'd be asleep, lass," he said.

"I tried. I'm restless tonight."

" 'Tis late." He made his voice gruff as he turned away. Of all the sights he had expected to encounter upon coming into his cabin, this was not one: Rebecca, looking sleepy and tousled, her face relaxed and her prim ruffled nightgown buttoned high, while her hair—the devil take it! She hadn't bound up her hair. "Go to sleep."

"I will." She flopped down on the bed, and he couldn't help

himself. He looked back at her. Oh, God, her hair was all he'd thought it would be, spilling over the white linen like liquid fire. "You didn't braid your hair," he heard himself say.

"Didn't I? Oh." she sat up, her hands reaching to her hair to braid it. Her breasts swayed with the movement, and he hastily glanced away, swallowing hard. "Of all the silly things—I forgot, there was so much I was thinking of. I have to thank you, Captain."

"Don't."

She looked up, surprised. "Don't thank you?"

"Don't braid it."

Her hands stilled. "Is that an order?"

"Aye." His voice held a husky note of tenderness that appalled him. Devil take it, but he couldn't let her affect him like this. "And on a pirate ship, disobeying an order carries severe punishment."

Her smile stretched wide. "You talk a lot of nonsense, Captain," she said, but her fingers combed through the hair she had so recently plaited. His eyes followed every movement. God help him, but he couldn't help but watch that glorious hair, or the rise and fall of her breasts, unfettered beneath her nightgown. He wondered if she was aware of the effect she had on him, if her first lover had taught her—

Abruptly he turned away. Devil take it, but he didn't like to think of her with another man, even in the past. That it had happened, he could accept; after all, who was he to judge? But that someone else had touched her, run his hands through that hair, kissed her full, sweet mouth—no. That he could not accept. Devil take it, she was his, he thought, and swung back toward her. "You're playing with fire," he said bluntly.

She blinked. "I am? Why?"

"Sitting there in your night rail with your hair down, waiting for me. Is that how you always behave?"

She stared at him, eyes huge, clutching the quilt to her chest. "I—I'm sorry. I know I'm not very attractive, and I thought—"

"Not attractive!" It exploded out of him, and she flinched. "Ah, lass, don't." Swiftly he moved to sit on the edge of the bed, reaching out to touch her cheek. She edged back, but he continued with the caress, needing to do something to ease the pain in her eyes, in his heart. " 'Tis me. I'm that sorry. I should never have said such a thing."

"I—I didn't mean to be wanton," she whispered, looking

down at her hands, knuckles white where she grasped the quilt.

"You're not, *leannan*." He covered her hand with his, painfully aware of her soft breast beneath. " 'Tis me."

She hesitated. "Why?"

"Because I do not like to think of him," he said, and rose, restlessly pacing the cabin.

"Him?"

"Your lover."

"For heaven's sake, why should that bother you?"

"I don't know, but it does, lass." He turned to face her. "It does."

"How very strange," she murmured. " 'Twas long ago."

"I know."

"More than seven years." She opened her mouth, as if about to say something, and then appeared to think better of it. "I do have to thank you, Captain."

"For what? For insulting you?"

"Oh, don't be silly. For letting me see my sister."

"Aye, well, ye won the wager."

"And for telling her what you did."

"Only the truth, lass. That I haven't touched ye." He swung toward her. "But I didn't tell her how much I want to, no, that I didn't."

Her eyes grew round with surprise. "Oh."

"Devil take it, Rebecca, what have you done to me?" he accused, facing her with hands on hips. "Do you know what I thought about today, when I should have been concentrating on my ship? You, lass. Don't laugh," he growled as she bit her lips. "It's been bloody hell. Thinking of how you look now, yes, right now, thinking of how your lips tasted, how you felt in my arms, how you would feel in my bed. I'm telling you, don't you dare laugh."

"I—I'm not." She was staring at him now, her eyes huge. "But—I don't know what to say. We did make a bargain—"

"The devil take the bargain!" he roared, and stalking across the room, hauled her into his arms.

Chapter 10

~

Rebecca made a little noise, an *mpf!* of surprise, but after a moment's initial resistance she came willingly into his arms. Ah, and she felt good there, her breasts soft against his chest, her lips parting under the relentless pressure of his. No gentle kiss this, but an act of need, of possession, to drive all thoughts of the other man from her head, from his. Boldly he thrust his tongue into her mouth, and felt her hands clutch at his neck, felt her arch up against him. She was his! He felt it in his heart, his soul. His, and no other's. His kiss gentled, became almost playful, nibbling at her lips, her cheeks, her nose. "You're mine," he said, his mouth tracing a path down her neck, suckling softly on her white skin. "Mine."

"Yes," she gasped, arching her head back to give him better access.

"Say it." He reared above her, staring into her eyes. "Say it."

"I'm—yours."

"Aye, *leannan*." His mouth swooped down upon hers again. "That you are."

Her fingers clutched at his shoulders as his hand slid around from her back, gently cupping her breast. "I—oh!"

"You like that, *leannan*?" he said, his voice low, his thumb stroking over her nipple.

"I—yes—I didn't know."

That made him look at her. Her eyes were closed, and her face was washed with color. "What, lass?"

"Nothing."

"No?" He caught her nipple between thumb and forefinger, and her breath drew sharply in, making him feel absurdly pleased. Whoever he had been, the other man, he must have been remarkably clumsy, not to have taught her the joys of lovemaking. It meant that, in a very real way, he was the first. "Didn't know what, lass? That this could feel so good?"

"It—it shouldn't."

He leaned back to watch her, to see his hands, both busy pleasuring her now. The sight of her, dazed and flushed with passion, was enormously satisfying. "Aye, lass, it should."

"A good woman shouldn't feel such things."

"Rebecca." His hands stilled. She made a little noise, of protest, perhaps, and her eyes fluttered open as he reached up to frame her face with his hands. Aye, he'd been clumsy indeed, that other man, and a fool. "You are, in every way that counts, a good woman."

Her eyes were dazed, darkened by passion to the color of a stormy sea. "Word of a pirate?"

He couldn't help it. He laughed and caught her to him, rocking her back and forth. "Aye, word of a pirate. You are a delight, Rebecca."

"It has been my dream in life, to delight a pirate," she said, her voice muffled against his chest, and he laughed again.

"Aye. You do, Rebecca." He nudged her chin up with his hand. "I think—devil take it!" he yelled as a knock sounded on the door. "Who is it?"

"Tyner, Cap'n," Tyner said from the other side of the door, sounding not the least perturbed. "Lookout's spotted running lights due north."

"Damnation." He rose, raking a hand through his hair. "All right, Tyner. I'll be right there. God knows why this has to happen every time we—"

"Lights?" Rebecca interrupted, looking up at him, tumbled and tousled and utterly desirable. Devil take it, but it was probably just as well. "Another ship?"

"Aye. There's been one chasing us all day," he said absently, tucking his shirt into his breeches. Ah, now he remembered her hands frantically pulling at it, and the thought sent heat surging through him. "A damned good thing it's dark, after what you've done to me!"

"What I've done?" Her gaze followed his down his body,

to where his desire for her was obvious. "Oh!" she exclaimed, quickly looking away, color flooding her cheeks.

"Aye. What ye've done." He took her face in his hands, planting a swift kiss on her mouth, red and swollen and very sweet. "Ye might as well go to sleep. No tellin' how long this will take."

"But—"

"Go to sleep, lass," he said and closed the door behind him.

In the passageway Brendan took a deep breath. If the situation weren't so serious he'd turn around and join Rebecca in bed, making her hers in all ways, every way. Devil take it, but he was like a randy boy, ready to explode at the touch of his first woman. And that wasn't good.

His grin faded as he emerged onto the deck. "Due north?" Sam nodded and handed him the spyglass. There she was, dim lights in the distance. Damnation. Who was chasing him? He returned the glass to Sam, shrugging. "Nothing we can do but keep on," he said and turned away.

Hands tucked into pockets, he ambled aft toward the helm, casting a shrewd eye up at the sails. Drawing well, making maybe eight knots. Good speed, but not good enough, not with another ship on his tail. It worried him. An ordinary trader would have been about its business by now, but this one continued to follow, closer than before. At the same time, he was glad of it. Strange thought, but there it was. Had he not been interrupted he would be making love to Rebecca by now. Pleasurable though that would have been, it would also be a mistake. For seeing the other ship reminded him painfully of who he was, and who she was. He wanted her. Lord knew he did, with a hunger that demanded appeasing. But she was his hostage, to fate, to his enemies. He couldn't allow himself to get close to her. He couldn't hurt her in such a way.

Muttering an oath, he took the wheel, as always feeling better with his ship under his direct control. He could outrun the other ship, of that he had little doubt. It wasn't that which troubled him. How was he going to outrun Rebecca, and his yearning for her? For the life of him, he didn't know.

Rebecca turned over in the bed and snuggled her head against the pillow. Early morning light flooded the cabin, and silhouetted against it she could see Brendan, his back to her, just pulling up his breeches. Not quite awake, she closed her eyes, but as if of their own volition they opened again, to see that he was now fastening the buttons. "Enjoying the view, lass?"

"What?" She blinked up at him. "Oh! As if I would!"

"You did," he said, and though his back was to her she could tell he was grinning. She burrowed her head deeper into the pillow. If it were possible to die of embarrassment, then she would. "Turning missish on me?"

"Go away," she said.

"Soon enough, lass."

His back still to her, he picked up his eyepatch and tied it in place. Embarrassment forgotten, Rebecca watched. What did he look like without the patch? "The other ship?"

His lips thinned. "Distant, but there."

That roused her. She leaned up on her elbow, pushing her hair out of her face. Mercy, it would be a job to comb it this morning. "Who is it?"

"Can't tell."

He was worried. His voice sounded clipped, and he was frowning. "British Navy?"

"Maybe."

"Good."

That made him look at her. "Good?"

Rebecca pounded the pillows and sat up, pulling the covers modestly about her. "Yes, of course."

"Are ye hoping I'll be caught?"

She nodded, very seriously. "Caught, and hung."

"Bloodthirsty wench, aren't ye?"

"You deserve it, after what you did to me last night," she said severely.

"Rebecca." His eyes were wary, and she looked away, biting her lips against a smile. So she wasn't the only one feeling uncertain this morning. "What is it you think I did?"

If that was meant to disconcert her, it didn't. "You left me," she said, and waited for the reaction.

It was a moment in coming, so obviously had he expected something else. Then he grinned. "Ah, so ye think I should finish what I started?"

It was her turn to be wary. "I—don't know. Do you?"

"Aye, lass." His grin was wider, making her regret starting this. "But ye'll have to wait till this evening."

"Oh." She looked down at her hands, not knowing what to

answer, not knowing what she wanted. Propriety and her upbringing demanded she repudiate the feelings he'd awakened
in her; something else, deep within her, urged her to accept
those feelings, to rejoice in them. She felt so alive! Never
before had she felt this way, not with any other man, not
even when holding Robbie. Only in a pirate's arms. Her pirate's arms.

She raised troubled eyes to him. "It can't happen again."

He reached out to touch her cheek, and the heat of it
branded her. "What can't, lass? Our loving, or my leaving?"

"Both. Neither! Oh, I don't know." She buried her face in
her hands. Because she didn't know which she feared, or desired, more. "Oh, please do go away."

From above came a cry, faint, distant. "Sail ho!"

"Damnation," Brendan said, glaring at the ceiling. "I am
beginning to get very annoyed with this ship."

Rebecca hugged herself. Odd, but she suddenly remembered that moment on the deck of the *Curlew,* when the ship
that had been spotted was the *Raven;* odd, that same feeling
of foreboding shivered through her. "Can't you outrun him?"

Brendan, near the door, turned, startled. "Do ye not want
to escape, lass?"

"Of course I do!" she declared with more force than necessary. "And if you can outrun him, I won't."

"I will, Rebecca." He paused, hand on the door handle.
"But if I'm caught, I won't give up easily."

"I wouldn't expect you to." What would that mean for
her, and Amelia? What would it mean for him? "Mercy, not
another battle."

"Are ye concerned about what will happen to me, Rebecca?"

"What, a pirate? Of course not."

His eye gleamed. "So ye say."

"And so I mean! Do please go."

"Aye. But we shall see, Rebecca. Tonight," he said and
went out.

Rebecca flopped back onto the pillows, staring at the ceiling. Tonight. Oh, mercy! She wouldn't think about it.
Wouldn't remember the hard pressure of his mouth on hers,
or the warmth of his body, so close, or the feel of his hand
touching her breast—

Stop it, she told herself firmly, turning over and bunching
the pillow under her head. She should get up, she supposed.

Tyner would be bringing her breakfast at any time, and her upbringing had inured her to such hedonistic luxuries as sleeping in. There was, however, no place for her to go, nothing for her to do, and the bed felt good, soft and deep. Besides, she had a great deal of thinking to do. After last night, everything had changed.

Within only a few minutes, however, she threw back the covers and rose. No matter that she'd intended to think long and hard on her predicament; her unruly thoughts kept returning to what had passed between her and Brendan last night, and what might very well transpire tonight. She was uncomfortably warm, uncomfortably restless, and she certainly didn't want to contemplate doing such things with a pirate. Even if that pirate were Brendan.

In the act of splashing water on her face, she stopped. At some point she had stopped thinking of him as the Raven, and had started using his name instead. It wasn't a welcome change. To call him the Raven distanced him; using his name brought him closer. Made him into just a man, instead of a pirate. Dangerous, that. She must never forget how he had disrupted her life. And yet, she thought, toweling her face dry, one thing had changed. She was no longer afraid of him.

She was thoughtful as she dressed, aware of the difference in sound topside. In the past week she'd grown accustomed to the tramp of men's feet overhead, and the sounds of their voices, but this was different. It sounded as if Brendan had mustered the entire crew, who spoke with an urgency she hadn't heard before. The other ship! Her hands stilled on the buttons of her brown walking dress. The other ship must be near. But that was surely good. It would mean release from captivity, so long as she and Amelia weren't hurt. If only there were some way to advertise their presence ...

Brendan hadn't locked the door. The memory slipped clearly into her mind, of his walking out. She couldn't remember hearing the click of the lock. If she had a chance of escape, she had to take it.

Before she could stop herself she had crossed the room. The door handle turned easily under her fingers, and she stepped into the passageway, waiting, watching. Nothing. Not even Tyner. Her sister's stateroom was close, but she dared not stop. At any time she might be discovered, and there would go all chance of escape.

Biting her lips, she crept up the companionway, sticking her head cautiously through the hatch. After the enforced confinement of the past days the air was heavenly fresh, and the sun, even filtered through clouds, so bright that she blinked. She'd been right. There were a great many men on deck, some holding onto a line, for who knew what purpose, others up in the rigging. They blocked her view of anything beyond the ship's rails, and so she went up another step, still cautious. She could see over the railings now, and she looked, ahead, behind, side to side, to no avail. The other ship was nowhere near.

Relief flooded through her so strongly it staggered her. But no, she shouldn't feel relief, she was thinking when abruptly her arm was seized. "Devil take it, how did you get up here?" Brendan roared.

"You forgot to lock the door, Captain," she said sweetly, and a sailor nearby sniggered.

Brendan's face grew even darker, and he tugged on her arm, yanking her onto the deck. "Damnation. I haven't time for this. Tyner!" he yelled, dragging her across the deck with him. Now the rest of the crew was watching, all smiling, some even laughing.

"Really, Captain, you don't have to manhandle me so," Rebecca protested, smiling back at a sailor, who was surely little more than a boy. "I can hardly escape."

"I never know what you're going to do," he growled, thrusting her to the side and taking the wheel. "Stay there. I haven't time to deal with you. Sam! Where's Tyner?"

Sam came over, and though his face was solemn his eyes held the same amusement as the rest of the crew. "Hello, Sam," Rebecca said, smiling at him.

Sam inclined his head, the gleam in his eyes more pronounced, and then pointed downward. "He's below? Then get him." Brendan glanced at Rebecca. "And I'll read him the riot act about keeping an eye on you."

"I'll stay out of the way. You won't even know I'm here."

"Not likely. You're going back below."

"I thought the other ship might be nearby."

"Ah." He glanced at her again, and for the first time his face relaxed a bit. "Thinkin' of jumping ship?"

"Of course."

"I warn ye, Rebecca, I'll not let ye go that easily. And the other ship? Bah." He snapped his fingers. "Too far to see from here."

At that moment Sam, crossing to them with Tyner in tow, stopped dead, staring past Brendan's shoulder. Brendan turned to see what he was looking at, and swore. "What is it?" Rebecca asked.

"Damnation. Sam, take the wheel. We're at the crest of the wave," he muttered, raising his spyglass. "Maybe that's why—hell and damnation!"

Rebecca caught his arm as he abruptly lowered the spyglass. A moment ago she had caught the flutter of white on the horizon, recognizably a square-rigged ship. "What is it?"

"The wind's to his advantage," Brendan went on to himself, ignoring her. "Sam! Ready about!"

Sam nodded and spun, remarkably quickly for so large a man, and that chill of foreboding went through Rebecca again. "Brendan," she said urgently, "what is it? Tell me."

"Well." He turned to her, his eye a flat blue. "It seems ye may have your wish, madam."

"My wish?"

"Aye. To see me hung. That"—he jerked his head in the general direction of their pursuer—"is a British man-of-war."

Chapter 11

~

In the captain's cabin, Rebecca huddled on the bed with Amelia in her arms, while overhead the preparations for battle went on. It was eerily reminiscent of the capture of the *Curlew*—could that have been just five days ago?—and yet there were differences. Then she'd heard panic in the crew's voices; now she heard urgency, but no real fear. She also suspected that Brendan was a far better mariner than Captain Smithers, and that the *Raven* would be hard to catch. One thing remained the same, however: her fear of being caught.

From far off came a faint boom, and, closer, a splash, almost drowned out by the savage yells overhead. Amelia shuddered and huddled closer to Rebecca. "They're firing at us."

"Yes, but they missed," she said soothingly, brushing back Amelia's hair.

"Is it much bigger than us?"

"No," Rebecca lied. The wind was from the north, and that wasn't good, Tyner had told her as he'd escorted her back to the cabin. Ordinarily the *Raven* could outsail any ship afloat. A square-rigger with the wind dead aft, however, could easily outdistance a fore-and-aft rigged vessel like the *Raven*. But she shouldn't worry, Tyner had added with a grin. He'd seen the cap'n get out of tighter spots than this. "They're British, Melia."

"Then they'll rescue us." Another boom. Amelia shuddered again. "If we're not killed first."

"We won't be."

"I hope they catch us," Amelia said with sudden vehemence.

"Y-yes."

Amelia pulled back. "You don't sound very sure."

"Of course I'm sure. I hope they catch us, too." Overhead a gun roared, followed by the eerie whistling of the round shot. The ship veered crazily, and Rebecca threw out her arm, bracing herself against the wall. "Mercy! What is he doing?"

"Because if they catch us they'll catch him," Amelia chattered, and Rebecca had no doubt she meant Brendan. "And he'll hang."

"No!" The word slipped out involuntarily.

"He deserves it, after what he's done to us."

Rebecca's eyes squeezed shut against the image of Brendan's lifeless body swinging at the end of a rope. Dear God. She swallowed hard, tasting bile. Dear God, but he'd come to mean more to her than she'd realized. If he died, it felt almost as if she would, too.

Again the ship veered, and this time she and Amelia toppled to the floor, both of them crying out. Oddly enough it was Amelia who recovered first, rising to her knees and reaching out to help Rebecca. "I'm—are you hurt—Rebecca!"

"What?" Rebecca sat up, her glance following Amelia's to the stern window. There, so close it seemed they could touch it, loomed the other ship, the cannon in her bow flashing fire.

"Get down!" Rebecca gasped, grabbing Amelia and pushing her to the floor. But again there was a splash as the ball missed, and after a few moments she cautiously raised her head, staring at the other ship, Union Jack fluttering from its stern, in horrified fascination. A British ship, under other circumstances symbolizing order and authority and safety. For Rebecca all it meant was doom.

Amelia sat up beside her. "Do you think they'll fire again?" she said in a very small voice.

Rebecca's eyes were fixed on the ship and the stormclouds beyond. Or were they only clouds of smoke? "Yes." The British ship would fire, and with Brendan standing defenseless at the helm, that would be that.

This time she sensed the ship's veering before it actually happened, giving her a chance to grab Amelia and brace them both against the sudden slanting of the floor. The ship slewed around, and through the window she could no longer see the British ship; just the sky. Those *were* clouds, scudding across the sky. From the south! If a storm was coming, then the winds would shift—

Abruptly there was a volley of shots overhead, shaking the ship to its timbers, and savage cheers. Then the *Raven* was slewing around yet again, and picking up speed. Rebecca crouched on the floor, Amelia's head buried against her shoulder, and stared out the stern window. No sign of the warship, but distant cannon fire, followed by shuddering, told her the *Raven* had been hit somewhere. If Brendan were captured and hanged, how would she survive?

Another volley of shots, and another cheer, and again the *Raven* turned. Grabbing onto the table to keep from tumbling across the floor, Rebecca looked up slantwise through the stern window, able to see, again, the warship, now broadside to them. Forgetting Amelia, ignoring even her own safety, she clambered to her feet, hope clawing at her at what she thought she'd seen. Could it be—"Yes!" she exclaimed, running to the window and bracing one knee on the bench. The warship grew ever more distant, but even so Rebecca could see that on her decks was a tangle of masts and spars and canvas. The *Raven* had crippled her, and escaped.

"Oh, yes!" she exclaimed again, and jumped down from the bench, doing a little dance of joy. "He's safe, Melia! Safe!"

"Becky." Amelia sat up, staring at her. "What are you talking about? Who's safe?"

Rebecca froze. "Father," she said, the first person she thought of, knowing she could never tell Amelia who she had really meant. "He's safe, Melia!"

"Papa?" Amelia climbed to her feet. "Is he—oh." This as she caught sight of the warship, far distant now. "Oh, Becky! They didn't catch us."

Rebecca put a comforting arm around Amelia's shoulders. "I know, Melia."

"Then we're still captives—Becky, was Papa on that ship?"

"No, Melia."

"Then why—"

"I meant he's safe, thank God he's safe at home," she babbled, knowing she made little sense. "If he were here—two battles, Amelia, and we lost both—well, you know he has a tendency toward apoplexy!"

"But, Becky." Amelia leaned against her. "When he finds out where we are, what will he do?"

"He'll get very angry, I imagine," Rebecca said, calm now that Amelia seemed to have accepted her nonsensical explanation. "And then he'll come after us."

"But we're still captives."

"I know. But I'll keep you safe, Melia. I swear."

The door behind them opened, and Tyner looked in. "All right and tight, miss?"

Rebecca turned. "Yes, Tyner. We're away?"

"Aye, miss." Tyner's eyes lit up. "A splendid battle, miss, splendid! Never saw the cap'n in finer fettle, that I haven't."

"He's all right?" she said before she could stop herself.

"Him? O' course. Has the devil's own luck. Ball came this close to his head," Tyner held up thumb and forefinger a scant inch apart, "but it just flew by, and he laughed."

"Oh," Rebecca said faintly. "Was there any damage?"

"Some, but not much to signify. Don't ye worry 'bout it. The cap'n will get us away."

"But we didn't want to get away!" Amelia cried, her eyes filled with frustrated tears, and they both turned to her.

"Melia," Rebecca began.

"Well, miss, could be worse," Tyner interrupted. "A girl like you don't want to get mixed up with a bunch o' limeys."

Amelia stamped her foot. "But they would have *rescued* us."

"As for that, miss, ye're safe enough. Now if you'd—"

"Becky." Amelia turned to her. "Can't you make him understand? They have to go back and let us go."

"Aye, and if we do that, miss, we'll all be caught and hanged, and ye wouldn't want that, would ye? Now, seeing as how we missed dinner, I'll see if Cook has something for ye."

"Becky," Amelia protested again.

Rebecca laid a soothing hand on her arm. "There's no help for it, Melia. It looks like we won't be rescued yet. But I'm sure we'll be fine."

Amelia stared at her. "You trust—him?"

Somehow Rebecca knew she meant Brendan. "Yes, Melia," she said softly. "I do."

Her words drifted back to her later, after they had eaten dinner and Amelia, worn out from the morning's excitement, had fallen asleep on the bed. She did trust Brendan, not only with her life, but with her sister's. It said much about how she had changed since she'd been taken captive. For she'd learned a great deal about him in the past few days. She knew he was not the simple, evil pirate he appeared, but a complex man, intelligent, quick, charming when he wanted to be and dangerous when it was needed; capable of great anger, but also of laughter and poetry. And tenderness. The way he treated both her and Amelia was proof of that. Not a monster, but a man who tried to hide who he really was, for some unknown reason. A man who had quickly become important to her. Frightening thought, but as she looked at Amelia sleeping with one hand under her cheek she knew one thing. She would not rest until that man, her man, stood before her, safe and sound and unhurt.

Aboard HMS Cardiff

The grim task of cleaning up after fighting and losing, a major battle went on as the ship's surgeon tended to the wounded and the carpenter oversaw the rigging of a jury mast. Standing on the quarterdeck, Jeremiah Dee saw none of it. His thoughts were far away, ranging across the sea where the *Raven* had fled. Lost now, and all because of Captain Lancaster's incompetence. If that cannon shot had been just a few inches to the left, they'd no longer have Brendan Fitzpatrick to deal with, and he, Jeremiah, would at last be at peace.

The last time Jeremiah had encountered the Raven, he'd been left with a scar, a nagging sense of familiarity, and a deep, burning hatred. This time he was luckier. There'd only been a glancing blow to his head from a falling spar. It had made everything fuzzy for a time, but the surgeon had assured him he'd recover. His only other injury was a cut on his arm. Not his sword arm, for which God be thanked. He'd need that arm, to do God's own work.

Jeremiah's hands tightened on the quarterdeck railing. The world must be freed from the scourge of the Raven, and he, Jeremiah, was the man to do it. It was his divine mission.

He'd seen it just now, in those few disoriented moments after receiving the blow to his head, a vision of light and terror, an angel with a sword. His duty and his mission.

Dee looked up to heaven, briefly said a prayer of thanksgiving for having been vouchsafed such a vision, and added a solemn vow. He would not give up. Somehow, someday, he would find the *Raven* again, and his mission would be fulfilled.

Brendan had hardly stepped into his cabin when a warm, soft form threw itself against him. "What the—Rebecca?" he said, staggering back.

"Of course it is." She flung her arms around his neck, glad, so glad, for the sight of him, the feel of him. "You're not hurt."

"Nay, lass. But let me catch my breath. Ye've knocked it out of me."

"Oh." She turned away, eyes downcast as he closed the door behind him. Her silhouette was outlined against the soft lamplight; the curve of her breast, her hips, and the soft flow of her hair—dear Lord, her hair was down.

"Not that I didn't like the greeting, lass," he said, his voice husky.

Rebecca, eyes uncertain, looked at his open arms for only a moment before launching herself at him. This time his arms closed around her, and held. "I was so worried. Tyner told me you were unhurt, but still, I was so scared."

"Were ye, lass?" Brendan gazed at her, absurdly pleased. "I thought mayhap ye'd want to see the end of this pirate."

"No. Oh, no. At least"—she pulled back, her face stiffening into primness—"not that way."

He laughed, and her face relaxed again. "I'm glad of that. And ye, Rebecca? You're not harmed?"

"No, except for a few bruises." She grimaced. "Did you have to turn the ship so fast?"

" 'Twas the only way I could come about to escape in time. And I had to escape." His eyes were suddenly serious. "You know that."

"Yes, I know." She looked down. "And—I'm glad."

His eyebrows rose in surprise. "Are ye, lass?"

"Yes." She faced him defiantly.

"Well, imagine that," he mused. "Turning pirate on me?"

"Oh, don't jest about it! I was terrified you'd be caught and hanged."

"Lass." His voice was husky again as he caught her chin in his hand. "I didn't think ye cared."

"I don't," she tossed out, but her eyes said something different. "I don't want your death on my conscience."

"Nor would I," he said fervently, remembering the sound of the cannon shot whistling by his head. It had been close, indeed, closer than she knew. "Lass, if ye stay pressed up against me like this, I'll have to be kissing ye."

"Oh?" She looked up at him, eyebrows arched, and then, with deliberate provocation, leaned her breasts against his chest. "Then why don't you?"

He couldn't help it; he laughed. But the laughter quickly changed to something else as she surged up against him, catching his lips with hers for the very first time and finding him unprepared, but very ready. Their tongues met, his seeking, hers retreating, and then advancing again in a battle neither could lose. Dear God, he wanted her. It thrummed in his veins as his hand caught her hips, dragging her against him, her softness to his hardness. He was alive, alive, and he wanted her as he'd never wanted another woman. As he would never want another. The knowledge shot through him, cooled his ardor for a moment, awoke him to what was happening between them. It wasn't what he had planned, it was something he'd struggled against, but, God help him, it wasn't wrong. He couldn't bring himself to believe that.

"Rebecca," he gasped, wrenching his mouth away while he still could, his breathing ragged as, diverted, she began to press kisses on his neck. "Do you know what you're doing?"

That stopped her. She looked up at him, some sense creeping into the mindless, blind desire that had swamped her when he'd pulled her close. Seven years ago she hadn't known what she was doing, but now she did. She knew the possible consequences all too well, and she didn't care. What mattered more was that she wanted, no, needed this man, in a way she had never before needed anything, and she could not resist. It went deeper than mere desire, into her heart, her soul. Something had happened to her today, making her see things in their shining essence. He was no longer a pirate, or she a prim spinster, but a man and a woman. Oh, yes, she knew quite well what she was doing. "Might as well be hanged for a sheep as a lamb," she said, startling a laugh out of him.

"What is that supposed to mean, lass?" he asked, his eye twinkling.

"That everyone will believe I've lain with you anyway."

He laughed again, his head thrown back to reveal the throat she had so recently kissed, and wanted to again. " 'Tis a rare compliment ye pay me, *leannan.*"

"What does that mean?"

He shook his head, bending to kiss her. He meant it to be a brief kiss of affection, but the moment his lips touched hers the flames flared again, and somehow his hands were ranging over her body, stroking her breasts, her waist, her thighs; somehow her hands were at his shirt, pulling it free of his trousers. *"Leannan. Mo cridhe,"* he muttered, nudging her head with his chin and planting openmouthed kisses on her throat. Beloved. My heart. "I want you."

She made a noise that might have been agreement. Suddenly he needed to know that this was by her choice, and not just because they had once made a bargain. "Rebecca. Look at me."

She raised her head, her lips already puffy, her eyes glazed. "Y-yes?"

"I want you. Do you"—he moved his hips against hers, evoking again that little sound from her—"want me?"

She gazed back at him, her eyes no longer dazed, but alert, aware, giving him her answer before she spoke. "Oh, yes," she said, and, at her words, he scooped her up into his arms and carried her to the bed.

Chapter 12

~

Rebecca turned her head into Brendan's shoulder, feeling, not thinking. If she did she would remember the last time she had let her emotions run away with her, and the disasters that had followed. No matter that this was time out of time and a place that was not quite real. The consequences would be real enough.

Brendan bent to set her on her feet, slowly, slowly letting her body slide against his, making her exquisitely aware of his body's reactions. He wanted her, old, plain Rebecca Talbot, she with the soiled past and the tarnished reputation. But he had a bit of a reputation himself, her common sense asserted, and that made her look up at him, seeing him gazing intently at her. It was as if he were trying to see through her in some way, and it was unnerving. Unable to meet that bright, blue look, her eyes drifted away, encountering the stark fact of his eyepatch and what it meant. Without quite thinking about it, she did what she'd wanted to do for a long time: raised her hand and brushed her fingers across the patch, gently, caressingly.

Brendan flinched, his head rearing back, and his eye turned wary. "Havin' second thoughts, are ye, lass?" he asked softly.

"Yes." She looked down, but that was almost as bad; her gaze lit unerringly on the triangle of skin exposed by his shirt, warm and tanned, with just a hint of crisp hair showing. "But not"—she made herself look back up at him—"for quite the reasons you're thinking."

That intent look was back, this time holding puzzlement as well as ardor. "How do ye know what I'm thinkin', lass?"

Oh, she knew. She knew quite well what he now thought of her, that she was wanton, shameless. "I'm not like other women you've known," she said primly.

To her surprise, he chuckled and drew a finger down her cheek. The touch burned, making her jerk back. "Aye, lass, but I knew that already."

"Don't—please don't mock me."

"I wouldn't, Rebecca," he said and bent his head, taking command again. Oh, he kissed so well, his lips moving so persuasively over hers, making her melt. She could feel him against her through the skirts of her gown, hard and pulsing, and yet there was no force in the kiss. No demand. Not yet, and it was that, as much as anything, that made her finally capitulate. This was going to happen. She had agreed to it, and the moment was here.

"What I meant," she said, gasping, tearing her lips from his, her breath coming in uneven spurts as his mouth sought the side of her neck, "is that I'm not as experienced as I might have led you to believe."

"Don't fret about it, *leannan.*" His lips moved along the line of her jaw, making her swallow convulsively. "I'll take care of you."

That confused her, but then there was no time for thought, for his lips were on hers again, this time demanding; needy, and hot. *Be damned with the consequences,* she thought hazily, in a rising swell of passion, feeling his hands slip over her back to her hips, holding her intimately against him. She'd deal with them later.

He knew the exact moment, the exact heartbeat, when she became his. He felt it in her kiss, in the way her knees suddenly sagged, and he lowered her slowly to the bed until they were sitting together, their lips still clasped. Ah, but he couldn't have enough of her, the taste of her, the warmth of her against him, the silk of her hair, tangled in his fingers. A strand slipped free, and his touch followed, to her neck, her shoulder, and then to her breast, feeling the satin of her hair against the prosaic roughness of her cotton dress. He had touched her there before, aye, but never would he have enough, never would he have his fill of her in his hand, round and plump, the hardened tip protruding impudently through her layers of clothing. His gaze followed the path his hand had taken, and suddenly just touching her wasn't enough. He had to see her.

His fingers fumbled as they searched for the hooks which fastened her bodice in the front. Intent on his task, feeling her warm under his hands, he yet saw her eyes drift closed with a little flutter of nervousness. Ah, poor lass, this wasn't easy for her, even if she was made for it. For him. But he would show her, he thought as the outer half of her bodice fell open, if his fingers would stop shaking, if he could just untie the laces that fastened the underpart—there. The bodice fell back with a soft whisper of fabric, revealing the bandeau that supported her breasts, and a plain white linen chemise. Willing his hands to steadiness, he slid his thumbs under the edges of the bodice and peeled them back over her shoulders and down, until her arms were free and the upper half of her dress puddled about her waist. There was only her underwear to deal with, and that, without any frustrating hooks or laces, was easy in comparison. It joined her dress, and she sat revealed to him.

"Ah, Rebecca," he whispered. Once he'd thought her thin, angular, shapeless. Then, feeling her against him, he'd known that wasn't so. Even so, he wasn't prepared for the lush fullness of her breasts, firm and white and rosy-tipped. Unexpected in a woman who tried so hard to be prim. "Ah, lass, you're lovely," he murmured, his hands caressing her lightly, his thumbs stroking those velvet nubs. "Beautiful."

She arched her head back as his mouth sought her neck again. "Am—am I?"

That made him look at her. "Don't you know?"

"I—want to be. I want to please you."

"Oh, you do, *leannan*. You do," he said and dropped brief, fluttering kisses on each nipple. Her breath drew in surprise, and her fingers clutched at his hair. Aye, he'd been a fool, that other man, he thought, bending his head to his task again and lightly taking her nipple between his teeth. A fool not to awaken her passion and avail himself of it. Brendan was not going to make that mistake. She was his.

Urgency grasped him, and in its grip he forgot about patience, about slowness. Instead he bore her down onto the bed, his mouth suckling her, his hand pleasuring her other breast, while her hands tangled in his hair, clutched at his neck, his shoulders. A growl of impatience, and he sat up, tearing off his shirt and then returning to her, his mouth hard, demanding on hers, drawing on her tongue as it darted and retreated in his mouth. More quick impatience, and he was skimming her gown and petticoat over her hips, her thighs, until at last all he touched was her satin-soft skin. His, all his, and as quickly as that, the urgency was gone. Aye, his, and he would love her so thoroughly, so completely, that she'd never forget it.

Rebecca lay in a daze of feelings, hot, urgent, radiating from her breasts, throbbing from his attentions, into her belly, and from there into a part of her body that modesty rarely let her think about. Dear heavens, she was naked before him, and she shouldn't feel shame, she should want to cover herself—but she didn't. She exulted in the greedy way his eye feasted on her, adoring her, making her feel as she never before had: beautiful, and wanted. She rejoiced in the feeling of his hard, calloused hands sliding over her, grasping her hips, gliding over her thighs, parting them. Willingly she opened for him. No, no shame in this, only glory, and love. For that was what it was. Love.

It was an easy realization, natural and right, as if she'd known it for a long time, deep in her soul. She loved this man. He gave her no time to dwell on it, though, for his fingers were brushing against the soft curls at the juncture of her thighs, his voice whispering in broken words that she couldn't understand and yet which resonated inside her. Her hips arched upward without her conscious volition but very much with her will, and his fingers slid deeper, oh yes, there, working magic on her such as she had never imagined. She bit her lips against crying out at pleasure so great it was almost pain, and then bit them again when his touch was withdrawn. But it was a brief respite, time enough only for him to struggle out of his breeches. Rebecca hurriedly closed her eyes, not quite as brave as she'd thought, and so she was unprepared to feel him settle above her, his chest to her breasts, his legs between hers and his manhood pressing against her softness. Unprepared, but willing. She put her arms around his neck and waited.

"Look at me, Rebecca," he said, his voice harsh. "*Leannan,* look at me."

Rebecca opened her eyes to see him looking down at her with that same intent expression. And, at the same time as his gaze penetrated hers, he entered her, and this time she did cry out. It had been so long, and he was larger than she'd expected. It hurt, but it was an exquisite kind of pain, a stretching to accommodate him. Without quite realizing it she opened herself wider to him, her hands clutching at his shoulders, feeling the ache within her. A different ache, of need, not of pain. Her knees drew up around his hips and he

began to move in quick, shallow strokes, making her breath
come in pants. Oh, she couldn't take this, she couldn't, if he
kept on she would surely die—but he seemed to know that,
seemed to know when she had reached her limit. And then
he filled her fully, moving in her with sure, confident
thrusts, and she was moving with him, the ache growing, in-
tensifying, consuming her as he was consuming her. She was
his, and he was hers, and at the thought the ache tightened.
It held, and she poised, trembling, on the brink of some mar-
velous discovery, eager, desperate, and yet frightened.
"Brendan," she gasped, holding to him, her only security.

"Ah, Rebecca. *Mo cridhe, leannan,*" he answered, his
voice rough, and it was enough. The ache abruptly let go,
and it was wonderful and frightening all at once, sensations
rippling over her like waves. She bucked against him, a
harsh little cry issuing from her lips, and he abruptly grasped
her hips, holding her tight to him. His cry echoed her own,
hoarse and wordless and yet filled with meaning, and dimly
she was aware that he had reached his release, his warm
seed spilling inside her. He collapsed atop her, and her last
coherent thought as she spiraled back to reality, was that she
was right. She was his, and he was very much hers.

A long time later Brendan lay on his back, Rebecca nes-
tled close by his side while his fingers idly stroked her bare
arm. He couldn't remember when he'd last felt this good, he
thought, looking up at the overhead. If this was a mistake, it
didn't feel like it. It felt real and right. Under other circumstances he wouldn't have looked at Rebecca twice, and yet
now she lay beside him. He was glad of it. He felt at peace,
as he hadn't in too long a time.

Beside him Rebecca shifted, and then turned over, rising
up on her elbows. Her hair spilled in glorious disarray over
her shoulders, her lips were full and red, and her eyes—ah,
her eyes. A sparkling, emerald sea he could drown in. "Ah,
leannan, you're beautiful," he said, lightly running a finger
along her shoulder and smiling when she shivered.

"So are you," she answered, making him grin. Aye, that
was his Rebecca, he thought, forthright and brave. No halfway measures for her; she had given herself to him wholeheartedly. Who would have thought it, back on that dusty
street in St. Thomas? "Do you ever take it off?"

"What?"

"The eyepatch."

"Nay, lass." He kept his gaze steady. "What's underneath isn't pretty."

She reached out as if to touch it. He caught her hand in his, bringing it to his lips. "How did it happen?"

"The eye?" He was tasting the soft skin of her wrist and was distracted. "During a battle. Spar came down, hit me on the head."

"You're lucky to be alive!" she exclaimed, pulling her hand back and rising just enough for him to see her breasts. He grinned, enjoying the view. "Oh, why must you do it? Why are you a pirate?"

"Rebecca—"

"The way you sail, surely you could captain any ship you please."

"Like in the British Navy?" he asked, tilting his head.

"No. I thought you hated the English."

He sighed and tugged her down to him. "So I do, lass. So I do." He paused. "I'd be hung for desertion before being given a command."

"What!" That made her rise up again. "You did serve in the British Navy?"

"Aye, lass. I've the scars to prove it."

Her voice was a whisper. "Scars?"

"Aye. On my back," he said prosaically. "Ye didn't notice?"

"No," she said. "But how—"

"The lash, Rebecca. All too common on a warship."

"The lash—"

"Aye. Which I will not wield on any ship I command."

She shuddered and settled against him again, her arm across his chest, hugging him tightly, as if to keep him safe from harm. "What did you do?"

"Nothing so very much. Dared to question the lieutenant's ancestry." His eye twinkled. "He didn't much like it."

"He flogged you for that?"

"It seemed necessary at the time. Tyner saved my life."

"How?"

"Kept me from going after the lieutenant. For that, he got the lash, too. He was a mean bas—man, the lieutenant." He stared up at the overhead, remembering. "If I'd attacked him, likely he'd have flogged me to death. Aye, and enjoyed it, too."

She shuddered again. "Why in the world did you go into the navy in the first place?"

"Lass, do ye think it was my choice? I was impressed. Just like the lads on your country's ships are." His lips thinned. "Aye, taken by a press gang, and when I woke up there was the King's shilling in my pocket, as if I'd agreed. And me the only support of my mother."

"But that's terrible."

"Aye, lass, it is." His face hardened. "I never saw her again. Only her grave."

"Oh, no!" She stared at him, eyes huge. "No wonder you hate them so."

"Aye. Soon as we could desert we did, Tyner and I. Been together ever since."

"And became pirates," she said in a small voice.

"No, not right away. But 'tis the most profitable thing I've done."

"Profitable!" This time her shock was directed at him. "How horrid, when it means people's lives—"

"Lass." He laid his fingers on her lips, stilling her. "D'ye not realize why I do it?"

"No. And it doesn't matter. It's wrong."

"Mayhaps." Her face was set in stubborn lines. He sighed inwardly. If he could tell her the truth—but that would jeopardize too much. "Ye'll not reform me, lass. Giving me your body doesn't give ye that right."

"Oh, you're horrid!" she exclaimed, tossing onto her side away from him. "That's not why—"

"I know. Here, don't leave me." He caught her about the waist, pulling her back, though she stayed stiff and unyielding. "And I don't mean to belittle it." He paused. "It meant a great deal to me, Rebecca."

"It did?" Her voice sounded uncertain.

"Aye, lass. It did."

"But there's no future in it," she whispered.

He stared at the overhead again. No, no future, not between a pirate and a respectable lady. "I'd not have thought ye a coward."

"I'm not!" She turned to face him, her forehead creased. "What does that have to say to anything?"

"No future," he murmured, lifting her hand and measuring his own against it. A small hand, but square, capable. "We only have now, lass. Are ye brave enough for it?"

Her eyes met his, and in them he saw acceptance and a sad wisdom. "Yes," she said and lowered her mouth to his.

In later days, Rebecca would look back on the following three weeks as among the happiest of her life. Strange, considering that she was held captive on a pirate ship; but it didn't feel that way. For in loving Brendan, a part of her that she had never known existed had broken free, was soaring. It was this part of her that accepted that there could be no future for them, that this was an interlude out of time. Of course it would have been, anyway, even had Brendan been engaged in a respectable occupation. Aboard a ship, far from any sight of land, the concerns of ordinary life seemed distant and unimportant. Now was what mattered. Now was to be treasured.

Treasure it, she did. She wasn't certain, but she thought he might, as well. He spent a great deal of time with her, and not just at night. During the long, lazy days when the *Raven* sailed aimlessly about the southern Atlantic, there was little for Brendan actually to do. They read aloud to each other from Brendan's volumes of poetry and played endless games of chess; he taught her some rudimentary navigation and pointed out stars; and they talked. Oh, how they talked. Rebecca sometimes thought she liked that best of all. He told her of his childhood in Ireland, growing up on a poor, rocky farm and losing his father young, and of the joys that life had nonetheless held. She talked of home, of the mother she had lost so young and the stepmother she had adored, and once, only once, she talked about Robbie. If there were things in his past he never brought up she didn't point that out; if she hadn't told him anything about her child's father, he didn't ask. Both knew instinctively that their time together was too brief to be spoiled by any unpleasantness. There was just one thing that would have made everything perfect for Rebecca: to know that Brendan loved her. He had yet to say it.

Rebecca awoke from sleep one night to see him bending over her, his face creased with concern. "Rebecca, wake up—ah. Ye are."

She looked up at him, befuddled. Dawn was breaking, and the light in the cabin had a pinkish glow. "Yes? What is it?"

"Ye were having a bad dream, *leannan*," he said and touched his fingers to her cheeks. Abruptly she realized that her cheeks were wet, and as abruptly remembered her dream. "About your son?"

"Yes," she said and went into the shelter he provided with open arms, burrowing her head into his shoulder. Oh, yes, she had dreamed about Robbie, and it had hurt, but before that had come the part of the dream he didn't know about. Robbie's father coolly telling her he was betrothed to another, that she had been a diversion, nothing more. Only this time it had been Brendan saying the cruel words. He was her life, but for him she was likely no more than a passing fancy.

" 'Tis past, lass," he said, stroking her arm.

"You have dreams sometimes," she pointed out, though he had yet to share them with her. "Is it past for you?"

He was silent for a moment. "No."

"I dreamed I heard him crying. That's the worst dream."

"Why?"

"Because when he—when it happened, he didn't cry. Oh, maybe he did, but if so, I didn't hear him, and sometimes the thought of that—"

"Rebecca. Hush," he murmured, laying his fingers across his lips. She kissed them lightly, glad of his presence.

"A baby can be so demanding," she went on, driven to punish herself. "I was so tired. There were times when all I wanted was to sleep the night through. Do you know what I thought that morning?"

"No, *leannan*. What?"

"How good it had felt to sleep without interruptions."

"Normal, I'd think."

"Yes, but—what if he cried for me and I didn't hear? I think of that and sometimes I think I'll go mad."

"Rebecca." Again he touched his fingers to her lips. "There's naught ye can do about it."

"I know. Oh, I know. But I can't forget, either."

"No, I don't see how you could." He looked at her consideringly. "But mayhaps it's time to forgive yourself."

"Forgive?" she said, startled.

"Aye, lass. Forgive. Ye might think about it," he said and yawned, scrubbing his hand over his eyepatch.

Instantly Rebecca's attention was diverted. "Is it paining you?"

"No." He went very still, his good eye wary. "Itches sometimes. Another thing that can't be changed. But, lass"—his voice had taken on the husky note that was already so familiar, and so dear to her—"we have now."

"So we do," she said and went into his arms.

Brendan fell asleep after the loving, his body heavy atop hers, and it was only by pushing at him and twisting away that she at last lay in some comfort, her back to his front, like a spoon. By then she was wide awake, lying in his arms, watching the sky outside grow progressively lighter. The fire of their loving had burned away the night's regrets. He was right. There was only now.

Carefully she turned so that she could see him, studying and cataloging each feature against the day when they would be parted. Her gaze drifted over his thick, black hair; the stubble of his beard across his strong chin; the broad set of his shoulders, and the eyepatch. She frowned. It was the only part of him he hadn't revealed to her. She could understand that; she wanted to be beautiful for him, perfect for him, and she empathized with his need to hide his flaw. But, oh, he didn't need to hide it from her! She would not mock it, or shy away in disgust, or, worse, pity him for his loss. When she had given him her love, she had done so wholeheartedly. He had flaws, not the least of which was his occupation, and yet she loved him anyway. She would love him no matter what lay under the patch.

The cords of the patch tied at the back of his head. Her fingers were reaching for the knot before she stopped, appalled. Yes, she would love him in spite of everything, and yes, he should know that. This wasn't the way, though, this sneaking effort to remove his patch while he slept. What she should do was challenge him to show her. He couldn't seem to resist a challenge.

But he might resist this one, she thought, and again, her fingers crept toward the knot. This time she let them, working on the string with exquisite, patient slowness. It wouldn't do to have him awaken during this, and—there! The knot was undone. Now all that was left was to lift the patch away.

At the thought, she quailed. It wasn't right of her, and it wasn't fair. Something stronger than scruples drove her on, though. She reached to lift the string—and gasped as her wrist was caught in a hard, fierce grip.

Chapter 13

~

"What the devil do you think you're doing?" Brendan said, his voice deadly cold, deadly calm.

"I—I—please let me go." Rebecca pulled her hand back as he relaxed his grip ever so slightly, not looking at him. Mercy, what had she been doing? "I'm sorry."

"I should bloody well think so." Brendan twisted away from her, tying the patch in place with quick, practiced motions. "This is private, Rebecca. None of your concern."

"I know. I—" She took a deep breath, forcing herself to look at him as he paced away from her, his back muscles bunched and strained with tension, all lean, magnificent male. In spite of the situation she felt a thrill of admiration and pride that she belonged to such a man, if only for a little while. "I meant no harm, Brendan. 'Tis only that sometimes I feel you're hiding behind the patch."

He shot her a look as he pulled up his breeches and began buttoning them. "D'ye think I'd wear it if there were no need?"

"No. No, of course I don't think that. But you don't need to hide anything from me," she said, leaning forward in her need for him to understand. "I wouldn't spurn you because of it."

"I didn't think ye would, lass." He sounded more in control of himself as he pulled on his shirt. "But pity me? Aye, that I think ye might."

"I wouldn't mean to."

"Aye, lass, but ye would. And I'm not a man who takes kindly to pity."

"I'm sorry," she said again, looking away.

"Rebecca." He knelt on one knee on the bed, his fingers coming under her chin, forcing her to meet his gaze. "Ye'll have to trust me on this. 'Tis not something ye wish to see."

She searched his face. "I do trust you, Brendan. But do you trust me?"

He laughed, a short, bitter sound. "You forget something. We're enemies, you and I."

"Oh, how can you say that, after what we've shared!"

"I took you captive, Rebecca. Remember that."

She flinched. "I can hardly forget, can I?" she said, her voice low. "What we've been to each other these last weeks—it was all part of the bargain, wasn't it?"

"Devil take it, no, Rebecca!" He stared at her, frustrated, and then turned away. "I don't know what it is."

That hurt, and yet she should have expected it. When she was ransomed—and give him credit, he'd never claimed to need her for anything else—he'd go on his way and forget about her. While she—well, she would pay the price. The woman always did. "You're not the man you pretend to be."

He turned again. "Oh, yes, I am, Rebecca. I am exactly how I seem."

"No." She looked up at him, trying to see past his fierce facade to the man below. The man who made such sweet love to her. "You've kept us safe, Amelia and me, and given us every possible comfort. You promised me we wouldn't be harmed, and we haven't been. I think"—her voice softened—"you are a much better man than you'd have people believe."

He gave that bitter laugh again. "Aye. A common pirate, but a good man."

"You are!" Wrapping the quilt around herself, she climbed off the bed and went to him. "But you hide behind that eyepatch. Please." She touched his shoulder. "Take it off. You need have no secrets from me."

He stood still, and she could sense his indecision, in his frown, in the way he looked away. Then his face hardened. "You asked if I trust you. The plain truth, Rebecca, is that I do not."

"Oh, Brendan—"

"Because ye'll go back someday, lass."

"I wouldn't say anything!"

"No?" He cocked his head. "Maybe ye wouldn't mean to,

aye, I give ye that. But if they keep after ye, Rebecca . . ." He shook his head. "Better for ye that ye don't know everything. Better for me, too."

Rebecca frowned. If she did see beneath the patch, what could she tell about him, after all, except that he lacked one eye? "What would happen if I did say something?"

"It would mean my life, Rebecca."

Her breath caught from the horror of it. Brendan, swinging from the end of the rope. But why would her paltry knowledge of him cause such a thing? He was hiding something from her, and for the life of her she didn't know what. "I won't tell. Oh, Brendan!" She threw her arms around his neck, and the quilt fell to the floor in a jumble of color. "Don't you know I'd never do anything to harm you?"

"I believe you believe that," he muttered and brought his lips down on hers. It was a hard, demanding, desperate kiss. Something within Rebecca responded, making her rise to her toes and tangle her hands in his thick hair. His hands swept over her, touching her everywhere, molding her to him, and when he swept her up into his arms she made no protest. In the past weeks they had learned each other well. This time there was no need for slow, careful wooing or seduction. She was his for the taking, and she gloried in it.

She rained kisses on his throat and jaw as he carried her across the room and dropped her onto the bed, and then raised up on her elbows, watching as he rid himself of his breeches. No more shyness, now; she reached out, enfolding his hard length in her hand as he came down onto the bed with her. He groaned, capturing her mouth for another long, ravaging kiss, and when at last he released her she reared back, catching his head with her free hand and holding it so that she could press kisses to both his eyes. She loved him, oh, she loved him, whether he had perfect sight or not, and as if sensing it he groaned again, hauling her up against him. "Put your legs around me," he commanded, and a second later she felt him thrust within her. No slow, gentle loving, this, but a quick, fierce mating, her legs wrapped around his waist, her hips rising and falling with his rhythm. She was hopelessly lost, no longer knowing anymore where she left off and he began, for he possessed all of her. She cried out as the climax swept over her, and clung to him when he, too, reached his completion, knowing in that moment that she possessed him, too.

"God." Brendan raised himself on his elbows a few moments later, staring down at her. "Did I hurt you?"

She smiled, a secretive woman's smile, and traced the outline of his lips with a fingertip. "Do you really have to ask me that?"

"I am not the only one who hides from the world," he said and rolled to his side, taking her with him, so that they were still joined. "You aren't what you seem, either."

She frowned, though to her delight and amazement she could feel him growing hard within her again. Extraordinary, that she, plain, Rebecca Talbot, had this effect on him. It gave her a feeling of power such as she had never known. "What do you mean?"

"I believe I'm seeing the real Rebecca right now."

"Oh, no!" she exclaimed, shocked. "This—I've never acted like this with anyone!"

His eyes twinkled. "Glad I am of that, lass." He propped himself on his elbow, tracing lazy circles around her nipple. "But still, *leannan,* I think ye really aren't what ye seem. Mayhap ye don't realize it yourself."

She opened her mouth to answer and then hesitated. It was true that she'd often felt there were two of her, the Rebecca she showed to the world, and the woman she hid inside. But how did he know that? "I don't know who I am anymore. If someone had told me a month ago I'd be like this!"

He grinned. "You wouldn't have believed it."

"Mercy, no! It's not real."

"But that's where you're wrong, *leannan.*" His face sobered. "I think this is the real woman I'm seeing. Now, lass," he went on as she opened her mouth to protest, "think of how we met. Ye didn't plan to interfere, on St. Thomas."

"No," she said slowly. "If I'd had time to think, I surely wouldn't have."

"Ye acted on something inside ye. And when you came to my bed, Rebecca"—his voice was husky—"that wasn't because of a bargain. And ye know it. Ah, now, don't look at me like that, lass. It isn't so bad."

"But it is!" she burst out. "A proper lady would never behave like this."

To her consternation, he let out a laugh. "Is that what ye think ye are? A proper lady?"

"Yes! And I am one!"

"Nay, lass." Laughter shone in his eyes, and something else, something she thought might be affection. "You're a woman, and that is much better."

"As you're a pirate, I'd expect you to think so."

Again he laughed. "Rebecca, Rebecca. Do ye not know how beautiful ye are like this? Any man would want ye. Even a proper gentleman."

Her face burned. That was exactly the problem, though she didn't expect him to understand that. "It's—difficult for women," she began, her voice halting. "If we behave like this we're called terrible names."

"Who called ye names, Rebecca?"

She shook her head. "We must always be on guard and behave a certain way. Like ladies. There's no in-between. Even you"—she raised her eyes to his accusingly—"had second thoughts when you learned I'd had a child."

"Aye, lass, I did," he admitted. "But only because I didn't expect it. I like ye like this." He brushed a strand of hair away from her face. "I like the woman you really are."

Her breath caught. "Do—do you?"

"Aye," he said and flexed his hips, making her gasp again. "You like that, eh?"

"Brendan—"

"Ah, yes, and ye like this, too." He lowered his mouth to her breast, and the feelings spiraled within her again, blotting out everything. That he and she both wore disguises of a sort no longer mattered. He was right. *This* was right, she thought, rolling with him onto her back and moving in time to the thrust of his hips, loving him, loving him. Clutching at his shoulders, she squeezed her eyes shut and gave herself up to him.

Brendan perched on the foretopsail yard, staring out at an empty sea, the sun beating down on him. Any day now, and he'd spot the ship carrying Ezra Talbot, assuming it hadn't been delayed by bad weather or other factors. He had been told to take hostages and so he had, but he didn't like it. He liked it less now that he'd come to know Rebecca so well. When the time came for him to collect her ransom, could he do it?

He left off scanning the sea to look below, to the deck, where he saw an unusual sight. Seated daintily on upturned barrels were Amelia and Rebecca, with Tyner standing guard, and Starkey, the second mate, talking with them. The crew seemed to go about their appointed tasks, but even from up here Brendan could see the fascinated way the men glanced at the women. Letting them come on deck probably hadn't been such a good idea, and yet he couldn't stop looking at them himself. At Rebecca. And though he knew it was a terrible thing he'd done to her, taking her captive, for his own sake he couldn't regret it.

So why, he wondered, leaning back against the mast, did he feel such a hollow sensation of impending doom? Danger, it screamed at him, and in the past he'd always heeded his instincts. This time he'd ignored them, going blindly and headlong into an infatuation with a woman. Aye, infatuation, and novelty. Rebecca was unlike any woman he'd ever known. She was quick-witted and made him laugh, and her warm, lush body excited him as few things ever had. Even sitting up here he felt stirrings of warmth, and that wouldn't do. A seaman had to be alert at every moment he was aloft, or disaster would happen. If he weren't careful, Rebecca could be the death of him.

It couldn't work, of course. He was who he was, and she was a lady. He'd no doubt of that, for all her misgivings. She would go back to her safe, comfortable home, while his future was uncertain at best. He'd taken chances with Rebecca, aye, too many, revealing too much of himself to her. No one knew him as she did; no one held such power over him. For a man who had been alone for so many years, it was a little frightening.

Something fluttered on the horizon, far to the west. Brendan's gaze sharpened, but it was gone—no, there it was. Raising his spyglass, he peered in the distance, and his lips tightened. A sail. Might be nothing, just a trader, or maybe a British warship, but he didn't think so. He had a sinking suspicion that Talbot was on his way to collect his daughters.

On the deck below, Rebecca turned her face to the sun, enjoying the unaccustomed warmth and light. Heaven, after weeks of being locked in a small cabin. Beside her Amelia was smiling up at Mr. Starkey and chattering away; he, poor man, looked dazed, as most men did when they came within Amelia's orbit. She didn't mind. There was no harm in it, not with Tyner and Sam and even Brendan standing guard. Amelia deserved a bit of fun after what she'd been through. For herself, Rebecca didn't want a group of admiring men about her. Her gaze went up to the mast where Brendan perched, though the height made her shudder. She was interested in just one man.

Amelia's gaze followed hers. "Heavens, he's up so high!" she said. "Isn't that dangerous?"

"Not for the cap'n, no," Starkey said promptly. "Knows what he's doin' up there. Never seen a finer seaman, and I've served with plenty in my time." He hawked, as if about to spit, and then appeared to think better of it. "Whenever I hear he's mustering a crew, I sign on with him."

"Doesn't he keep the same men from voyage to voyage?" Rebecca asked, her attention caught. Like Sam and Tyner, Starkey seemed a pleasant man. What had induced him to turn pirate?

"No, not him." He hawked again, and this time took out a crumpled, stained kerchief. "Excuse me," he said, blowing his nose lustily. "Cap'n don't go out that often. Don't need to, with the prizes he takes. And when the voyage is over he flies away, just like the raven they call him."

Rebecca shivered again, in spite of the heat of the day. In the past few weeks she thought she'd come to know Brendan well, yet much of his life was still a mystery to her. "You're English, Mr. Starkey, aren't you? Did you serve in the navy?"

His face darkened. "Aye, that I did, and a worse time of it I never had. Hard work on low rations, manning a gun on a second-rater, and they let me go without so much as a farthing when this happened." He held up his left arm, and for the first time Rebecca realized that most of his hand was missing. "If not for the cap'n, I wouldn't have work."

Amelia's eyes brimmed with sympathy. "That must have been terrible, Mr. Starkey," she said with such warmth that he turned red. "But surely you didn't have to become a pirate."

"Well, miss, it's like this. I like bein' at sea, and the cap'n gave me a chance. He gave a lot of men here a chance. Look at Sam, there. Won't tell you what happened to him, too awful for ladies to hear, but who would have taken him on, I ask you that? Or Ramshead, there, with his peg leg? And he's got deserters from His Majesty's bloody—sorry, ladies—Navy, them who'd be hung if they were caught. Good men, all, but only the cap'n would take 'em on."

"So that is why everyone is so loyal to him," Rebecca murmured.

"Aye, miss. He treats us well, keeps us fed, and gives us work. What more could a body ask?"

"Starkey," a voice drawled, and Rebecca looked up to see Brendan. She hadn't seen him descend the mast. "Ye talk too much, did ye know that?"

"Aw, there's no harm in it, Cap'n," Starkey said, not a whit abashed by the reprimand. "Just talkin' to the ladies."

"Mm-hm." Brendan looked unconvinced. "Time for change of watch," he added as the ship's bell struck eight times, and Starkey, muttering something, hurried away.

"He's very nice," Amelia said tentatively, for she had yet to overcome her wariness of Brendan.

"Nice?" Brendan's eye crinkled, though he didn't smile. "I'm not sure as I'd say that, but, aye, he's a hard worker. Are ye ladies comfortable?"

"Oh, yes, 'tis ever so nice to be outside again, I'd quite forgotten what it was like." Brendan smiled as Amelia chattered on, and then glanced over at Rebecca. She returned his look.

"Sail ho!" the lookout cried high above.

"I know," Brendan called back. "Saw him ten minutes ago."

"Another ship?" Amelia's eyes were wide. "Oh, not another battle!"

"I don't know. Ladies, if you'll excuse me, I have to take the noon sights." Executing a neat bow, he turned and headed toward the stern of the ship.

"The sights?" Amelia's brow was wrinkled. "What does that mean?"

"Navigation," Rebecca said absently, watching him walk away. "He is a fraud."

"Becky!" Amelia stared at her. "Whatever do you mean?"

"Hm? Oh, nothing." Rebecca busied herself with arranging her skirts in precise pleats, only now realizing she'd spoken her thoughts aloud. Who was Brendan Fitzpatrick? She'd puzzled over that many a time, but she was no closer to an answer. A pirate who didn't act like it. An Irishman who sometimes sounded English. A hard man who yet crewed his ship with men others rejected. And something more, something she sensed, from his occasional silences, from a certain look in his eye. Something he took pains to keep hidden. She needed to solve the puzzle he posed. If she could, perhaps there would be a way for them to be together, after all.

The ship heeled, making both girls grab on to the edge of the hatch cover where they sat to keep from falling, as the long main boom swung over. "We're changing course," Rebecca said. "I wonder why."

"Becky." Amelia's voice was hesitant. "Forgive me if I'm prying, but—is he nice to you?"

Into Rebecca's mind flashed, unbidden, an image of Brendan looming over her, his face serious and tender as he made love to her. She flushed. "He treats me well enough," she answered vaguely. "Don't worry about me, Amelia."

"But I do! I don't like it, Becky." She pouted, her chin outthrust. "How do you think it makes me feel that you're doing—that—for me?"

"For both of us, Amelia." She spoke sharply, wishing Amelia had never had to know anything about the bargain. Thank heavens she had no idea how matters really stood. "This is really none of your concern."

"But you're my sister!"

"And I'll do what I think is best for both of us."

"Cap'n," the lookout called from above, and Brendan, who had just put away his sextant in its mahogany case, walked amidships and looked up, hands on hips. "She's in sight now."

"Can you make her out?" he asked.

"Aye, but not well. Full-rigged, Cap'n, might be R.N."

"R.N.?" Amelia whispered.

"Royal Navy," Rebecca said and felt again that same chill of foreboding that had shivered through her when they'd last encountered a ship.

"What flag is she flying?" Brendan called.

"Can't see that, Cap'n—hey, wait." The lookout leaned forward. "There's a pennant, looks like it's from the mainmast. House flag, mebbe. Must be big, to see it so clear."

"What is it?"

"White ground, Cap'n, with a black circle and something red inside the circle. Can't tell what."

White with a black circle, and a red shape inside the circle. Rebecca's head jerked up. Mercy, it sounded like— "Captain?" she said, and Brendan turned to her. There were lines on his face she'd never noticed before. "Is it—"

"Aye," he said, and his voice was heavy. "Looks like one of your father's ships."

Rebecca and Amelia were below, locked into quarters on Brendan's orders. Alone, he paced the deck near the helm, quietly issuing occasional orders to the helmsman. Already his crew was preparing for battle, dragging out the heavy guns and standing near, ready to fire on his order. And, all the time, the other ship approached.

Night was nearing, and Brendan judged that the other ship wouldn't be close enough for the exchange to be made until the morrow. If it was the ship he awaited. Though he could now clearly see the house flag flying from its mainmast, identifying it as a ship owned by Ezra Talbot, still he felt uneasy. From the little he knew of Talbot, the man wasn't one to part with his money easily, no matter how much his daughters meant to him. It could be a ruse: lure in the *Raven* with false promises of paying the ransom, and then blast them out of the water. Brendan doubted, however, that that would happen with the two girls on board. They were, he thought heavily, his main protection from imminent destruction.

"Steady on," he murmured to the helmsman, gaze fixed on the approaching ship. Not so distant now, and his crew was quiet, tense. "Sam." He looked up as the big man neared him, face watchful. "Signal her."

Sam nodded and turned away, clapping his hands sharply twice. At once a gunnery crew on the port side went into action, loading shot into the gun and touching fire to the fuse. The gun boomed, and the shot fell harmlessly into the ocean. A few moments more, and then the house flag on the other ship was suddenly lowered. Brendan's lips thinned. It was the signal he had specified in his ransom letter.

"Five degrees nor'nor'east," he muttered to the helmsman. "Sam. Ready the signal flags. When she's closer, find out who she is."

Sam nodded and clambered down a hatch, emerging several moments later with tightly furled flags under his arms. Each one bore a different symbol and had its own meaning, making up a code understood by mariners everywhere. Brendan had no intention of allowing the other ship close enough for verbal exchange, not without some assurance of his safety. "Now, Sam."

Sam nodded and began hoisting the flags on a halyard from the mainmast. It was a long process, but finally the question was asked: the identity of the other ship, and her business. Standing by the railing, tight-lipped, Brendan peered through his spyglass, straining to see the answering message. At last it came. The *Commonweal,* owner Talbot, out of Georgetown, to rescue the Talbot sisters.

Brendan nodded once, sharply. "Acknowledge, Sam, and tell them to keep their distance."

Acknowledged, came the reply.

"If they do not follow instructions completely, the sisters will suffer. Do it," he said as Sam looked at him, and then raised his spyglass again. This time the answer was a bit slower in coming, and when it did it was terse. *Acknowledged.*

Brendan grunted, and then proceeded to set the terms of the exchange. The two ships to stand off through the night. Ezra Talbot to come alone, and with the ransom. Then, and only then, would the sisters be released into his keeping.

Acknowledged.

He grunted again. "Eight bells tomorrow morning, Sam," he said, and turned from the railing, having no stomach for this, though his face remained impassive. Aye, it was what he'd set out to do; what he must, for his sake and the sake of his mission, see through to the end, but he didn't like it. He was bartering with Rebecca's life, and the thought made him feel low, small. If he was successful, tomorrow she would be gone.

"Maintain course," he said to the helmsman. "Keep the distance between her and us."

"Aye, Cap'n."

"Carry on, Sam," he said and trudged down the companionway leading below.

At his door he paused a moment, and then, squaring his shoulders, unlocked it. "Rebecca."

She looked up from her seat on the bench beneath the stern window, her face drawn. "It's my father, isn't it?"

He stopped by the door, the keys jingling in his pocket, unsure how to react. He'd expected jubilation or anger, not this calm quiet. "Yes."

"So we're to be ransomed?"

"Aye. Tomorrow morning."

"Just like that?" She whirled off the bench, and he realized that his first impression had been wrong. She was angrier than he ever would have expected. "You'll barter me—us—just like that?"

"Rebecca." He made his voice patient, gentle. "Ye knew this was going to happen."

"It didn't mean anything to you, did it?" Her voice was high and tight. "These past weeks, they meant nothing—"

"*Leannan,* ye know that's not so."

"Don't you call me that! I'm not your *leannan,* not if you can treat me so."

"Do you think I have a choice?"

"Don't you?" she retorted.

He did. By God, he did. He stood very still as the idea burst into his mind, so audacious and yet so right that he knew he'd been considering it for a very long time. Before he quite knew what he was doing, he strode across the room to her, gripping her shoulders. "Yes. There's a choice, but it's not mine." He gazed at her intently. "Stay with me, Rebecca."

Chapter 14

❧

Rebecca's breath drew in sharply. "Wh-what?"

"Stay with me." His voice was urgent, his grip hard. "Don't go tomorrow."

"But, the ransom—"

"The devil take the ransom! I'll forfeit it."

"Oh, no." She twisted away "I'll not let you do that to my sister."

"It's not your sister I want to keep, *leannan*."

She spun back toward him. "You mean—"

"I mean I'll let her go. But you, lass." He closed the distance between them with one quick stride, hauling her into his arms. "Don't leave me. Stay with me. It's not such a bad life I'm offering you," he went on before she could speak. "I've a home, you'll lack for nothing, I promise you. Only stay with me, lass."

It was tempting. Oh, it was tempting. She felt the rough weave of his shirt under her fingertips and squeezed her eyes shut. To stay with him forever. Would it be forever? He'd said nothing of marriage, and without that he would be free to sail away and leave her. And then where would she be? But, oh, while it lasted it would be bliss. No one had ever made her feel as he did; no one ever would again, so alive, so vital and necessary and needed. Wasn't she? "Brendan." Her voice was quiet. "Will you take off the eyepatch?"

He hesitated, and then looked away. "I'm sorry, lass. I can't."

"I see." She pulled back, drifting over to the tiny-paned window. "You really don't trust me."

"Ah, *leannan,* it's not that—"

"Then what is it?" She whirled to face him. "What life do you offer me, if you hide from me?"

His face was inscrutable. "Not just from you, lass."

"But, don't you see, I should be the one who does know! Oh, it's hopeless." She turned, hugging herself, blinking hard against tears. "You'll never understand."

"I do understand." His voice was gravelly as he stood beside her, his hand on her shoulder. "Rebecca, lass, I've reasons, but I can't tell you. No," he said as she looked up at him. "I can't say more than that."

"Would you, if you could?"

"Yes," he said simply.

Rebecca lowered her eyes, gnawing at her lips, and at that moment the other ship came into view, far astern. Her breath caught in her throat. "Is that—my father?"

"Yes."

"If I go with you, where will I live? In the Caribbean?" He didn't answer, and she took that as assent. Oh, this was unfair! She wanted to be with him, but just as strong was the pull she felt toward her father, her sister. All her life she'd taken care of Amelia. She couldn't leave her to face alone the scandal that would erupt at home. And Father . . . She bit her lips again. If she went with Brendan, she would never see her father again. "No," she said, twisting away from him. "I can't."

"Lass." He held out his arms. "Don't. Don't do this. What can I say to change your mind?"

You could say you love me, she thought, though even that wouldn't be enough. He didn't need her, not in the way Amelia did, or her father. Not in the same way she needed him. "No," she said, and the finality of it brought tears to her eyes. "I can't."

"Leannan—"

"I can't!" she cried and threw herself into his arms. "I want to, but I can't, oh, God, Brendan—"

His hands were on her, frantic, roaming over her back, her breasts, her hips. "You've been hurt once, lass, I know that, but I wouldn't leave you—"

"I know." She tangled his hair in her fingers and reached up to kiss him, desperate, knowing only that she needed him, now. Instantly his mouth slammed down on hers, hard, his tongue probing, taking her mouth with quick, possessive strokes, as he would take her body. She strained against him, pulling at his shirt, pressing her hips closer to his, feeling the bulge of his desire, hot and hard and surging against her. His hands were at the buttons of her gown, pulling, tearing, and she didn't care. Nothing mattered, but him.

With a wordless growl, he picked her up in his arms and strode across the room, dropping her onto the bed, so that her legs dangled over the side. She began to scramble backward, but he was there, standing between her legs, bracing himself over her with one hand, while his other reached for the buttons on his breeches. "No, let me," she said, reaching out her hand and brushing it against the taut bulge.

"Rebecca—"

"I want to." Her fingers were steady as she undid the buttons, though her heart pounded and need pooled low in her stomach. His eyes were squeezed shut, the muscles in his neck standing out, corded, and when she reached in to cradle him in her hand, hot iron sheathed in velvet, he let out that wordless growl again. Before she could react he had pushed her skirts roughly up to her waist and was positioning himself between her legs, the tip of his shaft just touching her. Exquisite agony, but she wasn't ready. Not quite yet.

She drew back. "Take it off," she ordered.

He looked down at her. "What?"

"That damned eyepatch. I'd like to do this for once knowing you're not hiding from me."

"Ah, lass." He dropped his head, bending to nuzzle her throat. "Don't do this."

"Brendan—"

"We only have now, lass. Don't ruin it."

Ruin it! she thought. But before she could say anything he had grasped her hips in his hands, pulling her to him, and she, helpless against the need he awoke in her, raised herself, waiting, until at last he thrust into her.

Fast and furious, and she met him stroke for stroke, her hips churning against him, harder, faster. Her gaze never left his, until at last the need within her became too urgent, too overwhelming. She closed her eyes and arched her head back, crying out as the climax swept over her. She was his. Oh, God help her, she was his. And that thought was all it took for her tears to start flowing.

"Rebecca." His voice was rough, urgent. "Lass, I'm sorry, I know I was too quick. Did I hurt you? If I did I—"

"N-no," she choked out, her eyes misted with tears. He was still above her, within her, and oh, dear God, she wanted him there forever. "I—don't want to leave you." The sobs came faster, harder. "Oh, Brendan, I don't want to go!"

"Oh, lass." The bed shifted as he came onto it with her, withdrawing from her body, leaving her empty, drained. But then he was gathering her into his arms, his hands awkwardly patting her back. "You were right. The life I have to offer you—it's not for you."

"Yes, it is," she sobbed, perversely certain now that nothing would suit her more than a precarious existence as the Raven's woman.

"No," he rumbled. "I can't do that to you, lass. Take you away from everything you've ever known, from your family." He rocked her back and forth. "It's no kind of life for you."

"I'd manage."

"I know you would." He planted a quick kiss on her forehead. "But you shouldn't have to. You deserve the best. If I was free, Rebecca—"

She reared back from him. "Dear God, you're not married!"

"No." The horror in her voice made him want to smile, but the devil take it, this was no laughing matter. "No, lass, there's no one else. Only you."

"Then what holds you back?"

He frowned. It was tempting. To tell her the truth, to see her face when she realized he wasn't quite what he seemed—but tomorrow she would leave him. It would be safer for her if she knew nothing. "Never mind, *leannan*," he said brushing a finger across her lips. "Never mind."

Her eyes pooled with tears again. "It's going to happen tomorrow, isn't it?"

His heart thudded heavily in his chest. "Yes."

"Then love me, Brendan." She curled her hand around his neck, bringing his head down to her. "Love me."

And, God help him, he did.

The morning sun rose on a peaceful scene: a square-rigged ship, yards backed to keep her in place; and a black, sleek brigantine, sails loosely furled, dancing about at the mercy of the waves, as if in impatience. From one ship to another a boat was being rowed, a solitary passenger within. Ezra Talbot was coming to collect his daughters.

Brendan stood impassively by the helm, watching the boat approach. His crew was in readiness, training the long guns on the other ship; in the rigging and on the yardarms, pistols, and knives at the ready, should there be trickery. And, in the midst of this, guarded and apparently held captive by Sam, were the Talbot sisters.

Brendan spared only a glance for the young women. More than that, and he might just change his mind, might just give the order that would keep Rebecca with him forever. For he didn't want to let her go. He wanted to grab her and hold her and be with her for the rest of his life, and that was stunning. Never in his life had he felt this way about any woman. Why now, with this plain, prim girl, his captive?

The longboat bumped into the ship's hull, and a rope ladder was tossed overboard. Beside Rebecca, Amelia let out a cry, grasping Rebecca's arm tighter. "He's really here!"

"Yes," Rebecca said, looking at the other ship, at the rail where her father would appear in a moment, even at Sam. Anywhere, but at Brendan. He appeared a most thorough-going rogue this morning, clad in black breeches and white shirt, and not by so much as a glance or a gesture had he acknowledged her presence. It was just as well. If he did, likely she'd run screaming to him, begging him to let her stay. And that, she knew, was not possible.

A hand appeared on the railing, square, work-roughened, and a moment later Ezra Talbot drew himself up. "You, there!" he barked at a seaman. "Give me a hand."

The seaman looked uncertainly from him to Brendan, who nodded, and then held out his hand warily, expecting a trap. Instead, Ezra clambered onto the deck over the rail, hampered by the large black valise he carried. He jerked back as the seaman reached for it. "Touch this and you'll regret it," he growled. "It belongs to me."

"No, sir." Brendan's voice was at its silkiest, and its most dangerous. "I believe it's mine. Starkey." He gestured toward the second mate. "Check him for weapons."

Ezra glared at Brendan as Starkey patted him down. "You! I have some words for you, sir."

Unbelievably, Brendan's lips tucked back in what might have been a smile. "Undoubtedly. The money, sir."

"Not until I am assured my daughters are safe."

"Your daughters are there." Brendan waved a hand negligently in the girls' direction. "They've been well treated."

"Huh. Am I supposed to believe that?"

"Believe what you wish." Brendan held out his hand. "The money, sir. When I have made certain it is all there your daughters will be returned to you."

Ezra's glare grew fierce, and with a mutter he handed over the valise. "Tyner," Brendan said, holding out the valise, "check this."

"Aye, Cap'n." Tyner scuttled over and crouched over the valise, pursing his mouth in a silent whistle as he opened it. "Let me take it down to the cabin, Cap'n, and count it. But it looks good, that it does." He cackled gleefully. "Gold coins, and plenty o' them."

The crew muttered in reaction, and Brendan's gaze swept over them sharply. His eye met Rebecca's. For a moment only they stared at each other; for just that moment all else on the ship was forgotten, unimportant. Then he looked away. "We'll wait for Tyner," Brendan said. "Offer ye a drink?"

"No," Ezra growled. "Give me my daughters and let us get off this God-cursed ship."

"In a moment." Brendan lounged back, hands in pockets. "When I am assured the money is all there."

"You'll hang for this." Ezra's hands were balled into fists, and though he was shorter than Brendan, he seemed not in the least intimidated. "I'll see to it."

"Ye may try. Yes, Tyner?" This as Tyner stuck his head through the hatch leading below.

"Did a quick count, Cap'n," Tyner called. "Looks like it's all there."

"Of course it's there," Ezra snapped. "I am a man of my word, sir."

"And I of mine."

"Huh."

"Sam, bring our guests here," he commanded. "Your daughters, sir."

"Oh, Papa!" Amelia ran across the deck, launching herself into Ezra's arms. "Oh, Papa, I missed you so!"

"And I, you." He held her a little away from him, scanning her face, and Brendan's feelings toward the man softened just a bit. Whatever else he was, he did care for his daughters. "Are you hurt? Did this barbarian touch you—"

"No, Papa! Becky took care of me." Amelia turned, her smile radiant. "Aren't you going to hug her, too?"

"Took care of you, did she?" Ezra roared, startling everyone aboard and causing Rebecca to jump back, just as she was about to kiss his cheek. "If she took such care of you, why are you here?"

Rebecca hunched her shoulders. "That's not fair. I couldn't help what happened."

"I told you to watch out for your sister, girl, not let her get in such a mess as this."

"But that isn't fair, Papa!" Amelia exclaimed, clutching at his arm. "You don't know the sacrifices she made for me! If not for me, she wouldn't have had to stay with the Raven in his cabin—"

"Amelia!" Rebecca said sharply, too late. "We'll discuss that later."

"She did what?" Ezra's voice was a growl as he advanced toward Rebecca. "Is it true, girl? Did you disgrace yourself with him? Answer me!"

Rebecca was pale. "I did what I had to, to protect Amelia."

"You little slut!" he roared and raised his hand.

Rebecca saw the blow coming and flinched, raising her arms to protect herself, a reflex action from long experience. When nothing happened, she at last glanced up, to see a strong, brown hand gripping Ezra's upraised arm.

"Careful there, boyo." Brendan's voice was deceptively soft, his hold on Ezra's forearm deceptively easy.

Ezra jerked back, his glare murderous, but Brendan's grip held. Only the whitening of Brendan's knuckles showed any strain, as the two men battled in silence, Ezra pulling back, Brendan holding on. Then, with a sudden movement, Ezra twisted away—or had Brendan released him? Rebecca never knew for certain. "I'll have none of that on my ship."

"Damn you!" Ezra hissed, a sure sign of his anger, for he rarely swore. "I'll punish my daughters as I wish."

"Not on my ship, you won't." Brendan's voice was clipped. "And if you expect to live to tell about this day, 'tis best ye go now, boyo. Before I lose my temper."

"You'll pay for this, pirate." Ezra's hands were balled into ineffectual fists at his side. "If I do nothing else, I'll make sure you pay."

"Ye scare me, boyo." Brendan's gaze flicked toward Rebecca, and then away. "Go now, before I lose my patience."

"Gladly." Ezra gave him one more long look, and then turned. "Amelia. Rebecca. Let us leave this cursed ship."

"Yes, Papa." Amelia took his arm and crossed with him to the railing, though not before turning and giving Brendan a parting glance. Not so Rebecca. Head down, she followed, awaiting her turn as Ezra helped Amelia climb onto the rope ladder. There was utter silence, and utter tension. None of the chaos she had half expected, and certainly no joy. She'd been reunited with her father and soon would be safe home. And never had she felt so wretched.

"Rebecca." Brendan's voice, stopping her as she was about to clamber over the railing onto the rope ladder. She looked up and met his gaze, cool, inscrutable. "You don't have to go."

For a long, long moment she looked back at him, committing every detail to memory: his wind-ruffled hair, strong features, bright blue eye, stormy now with emotion. She remembered again the feeling of his arms around her, the strength of his body as he made her his. Oh, she remembered! And she must remember this, too, this last glimpse of him, so roguish, so handsome, and so lost to her. Memory was all she would have, for the rest of her life.

"Go, girl," Ezra growled, and it broke the spell. Averting her head, Rebecca stepped out, and began the long, precarious climb down the rope ladder to the waiting boat, below. Her time on the *Raven* was done.

Brendan stood unmoving, fists on hips, and only someone who knew him well would have guessed at the emotions within him, the aching, spreading emptiness. Aye, and why should she stay? He'd nothing to offer her, nothing but disgrace and scandal. No wonder if she chose safety and familiarity. But to choose that vicious bastard over him—his fists tightened. Talbot would hurt her. Devil take it, why had she gone with him?

Bring her back. Aye, he could, he had the men and the weapons. Bring the boat back and keep her with him. But it would do him no good. She'd made her choice, and it wasn't him. "Let go sails," he called to Sam, and the men who stood at the ready began to pull on the lines. Sail blossomed from the yardarms, from the mainmast, and the *Raven*, feeling the wind, danced upon the water. Brendan watched it as if from a distance. His ship's beauty no longer had the power to move him.

"Boat's away, Cap'n," a seaman called from the rail.

"Aye, and so are we. Starb'd tack," he said, and the yards of the foremast were braced, the fore and main booms swung over. The ship heeled as the sails caught the wind and the rigging sang in harmony with the water rushing past their bows. And, before the longboat carrying the Talbots had covered even half the distance to the *Commonweal*, the *Raven* was speeding away. Rebecca was gone.

Chapter 15

~

Brendan stepped off the schooner's gangplank onto the wharf at Georgetown and stood for a moment, getting his bearings. Stretching before him was Water Street, with wharves on the Potomac side, where vessels of every kind were docked. To his left were warehouses and shops and an occasional dwelling, though this had long since ceased to be a fashionable neighborhood. This was the working part of town, the part where tobacco and grain and other goods were loaded and valued and sold. Government officials, and those who could afford it, lived on the bluffs overlooking the river. It was there that Brendan's attention focused. Up there was the man he had come to see. Up there, also, was Rebecca.

Brendan's lips thinned. Just over a month had passed since she'd left the *Raven*, and it seemed like all eternity. Just over a month since he had been quite himself. To see him one would never associate him with the notorious pirate known as the Raven, whose latest exploits were the talk of Washington City. His expression was mild; his hair was cropped; and his coat of blue superfine was well cut and practical. His boots had been polished to a high gleam, and as he strode along he swung his rosewood walking stick, with only a slight trace of the seaman's rolling gait. No one gave him a second look as he passed by, and that was how he wanted it. His business was important, and secret.

Using his walking stick for leverage, Brendan climbed the hill leading from the waterfront, until at last he stood on a street of pleasant brick houses and overarching elms. Across Rock Creek the capital city was struggling to be born.

Someday, perhaps, Washington City would fulfill the dreams of its founders, but just now it was a vista of muddy swamps and rutted roads. The few buildings, the admittedly splendid Capitol building and the president's house, looked as if they had been dropped from above by a careless giant child. Beyond those, there were a few homes, numerous boarding-houses, and some shops. It was no wonder that so many government officials chose to live in Georgetown, including the man he had come to see.

His house was pleasant, unassuming, of the same salmon-colored brick as the sidewalk, with white trim and green shutters. As Brendan started up the stone steps, his hand on the wrought-iron railing, the door opened, making all his defenses go up. His approach had been watched.

"Come in, my boy, come in," George Abbott said, smiling. Brendan didn't have to look closely to know that the smile didn't reach the man's eyes. It rarely did. "Did you have a good trip?"

"Tolerable." Brendan removed his curly-brimmed beaver hat, looking around for a place to put it, since none of his host's servants were visible.

"I'll take that." Abbott held out his hand for the hat. "I gave my butler the day off," he said over his shoulder as he led Brendan into a cluttered, book-lined room off the hall, and Brendan understood instantly. Abbott wanted there to be no chance of their discussion being overheard. For though he held no title in the government, he was nonetheless crucial to it. With the tension building between the United States and Europe, his task was delicate: gathering intelligence. His duty was to find people willing to act as spies. Brendan, as the Raven, had worked under him for several years.

"Thank you." Brendan moved a stack of books from a burgundy leather wing chair and sat down, surveying the room, which he'd seen only once before. Like its owner, it was untidy, with papers everywhere, strewn on the dusty surface of the mahogany library table, on chairs, even on the floor, evidence of a manuscript in progress. Where there were no papers there were books, except for a table holding a chess set of black-and-white marble. Rebecca would love this room, he thought, and forced his thoughts on to another subject. Rebecca was in the past.

"So." Abbott sat facing him, a deceptively genial soul in

a crumpled dressing gown worn over a wrinkled shirt, and with his hair in a fringe on his balding head. Only his eyes belied the facade of placid amiability; they were dark, sharp, and somehow cold. They were, Brendan thought, the eyes of a shark. "It's a month since the Raven disappeared." He loaded his pipe with tobacco, appearing not to notice the flakes sifting down onto his sleeve. "You caused quite a commotion, my boy."

Brendan leaned back. "So I understand."

"Never thought Talbot would cause such a fuss. Did you know he's circulated posters offering a reward for your capture?"

"The devil he has!" Brendan said, startled. "Where?"

"With any ship that leaves port, and all around town. I have one here." Brendan took the paper Abbott handed him in silence, and frowned at it. In large type, the poster proclaimed that a reward of one thousand dollars was offered for the capture of the Raven, dead or alive. Above that was a crudely drawn picture of a vicious-looking rogue. Brendan relaxed. The only resemblance to himself he could see was the eyepatch. "The devil take it."

"Exactly. Hand me the tinder, will you, my boy? Thank you." He struck a flint and set it to the tobacco. "Pity you had to take his daughters."

"As you told me to take hostages, I did so," Brendan said through gritted teeth. "To cover our real purpose. The Talbot sisters were the only hostages available."

Abbott drew on the pipe and exhaled a long stream of smoke. "I may have said something like that, yes. It was important no one knew it was Neville we really wanted. Important to you, too, my boy, and don't forget that. But, 'pon my soul!" He lowered the pipe. "Two young ladies! Not done, my boy, not done at all."

Brendan regarded him coolly. No, not done, but that hadn't stopped him from taking them, had it? Nor had it kept him from making Rebecca his. *Ah, Rebecca.* "Were Neville's papers worth it, sir?"

Abbott looked up from relighting his pipe, his eyes sharp. "You didn't read them?"

"No, sir."

"Good. Neville's been deported, by the way. Almost as soon as he returned." He glared at the pipe. "Damn thing never would draw right. Yes, valuable papers," he went on.

Though I must own I was surprised when you sent them by courier, rather than deliver them yourself."

"I thought to avoid Washington City for a time." Brendan studied his fingernails. "Didn't want to chance running into Talbot."

"Ah, yes. Him." He drew on the pipe again, and this time made a satisfied sound. "You may be interested to know that Neville's papers contained a list of people sympathetic to the British side. Handy to have, should there be war. We'll know the traitors to look out for." He puffed in contented silence. "Talbot was on the list."

"The devil he was!" Brendan exclaimed.

"Oh, yes. We've known about him for years. One of the reasons there's so much fuss just now is that he applied to the British legation for help when his daughters were taken. Of course, they came to us." He blew out smoke. "Very sticky situation."

"I can imagine."

"Both sides calling for the Raven's head. It might be best if you disappear for a while, my boy."

Brendan sat hunched over, his hands loosely clasped between his knees. "And do what?"

"What you've always done when the Raven isn't about. Now. Tell me all that happened, exactly."

What he'd always done? Abbott was damned cavalier about his safety. There was a price on his head, and his services to his government were now a liability. None of that seemed to bother Abbott, however. But then, Brendan had known exactly what he was getting into when he'd offered himself for this work. "The first I realized the Talbot sisters would be aboard the *Curlew* was in St. Thomas," he began, and went on to relate all that had happened over the next month. He left out nothing, even admitting that he'd kept Rebecca in the cabin with him, to keep her and her sister safe. But he did not say a word of what had happened between him and her. He did not tell of how she had so unexpectedly enchanted him, of how in her arms he'd found a paradise he'd never known existed. Nor did he say that his life since she'd left had been bleak and gray, that he no longer took pleasure in steering his ship, or in the mission he'd successfully completed. He most especially said nothing about his strong, nearly overpowering need to see Rebecca.

Abbott's lips were pursed when Brendan finished talking, and his pipe had gone cold. "Not good," he said, the genial note gone from his voice. "Do you know what the talk is of the Talbot sisters?"

"No, sir."

"That they were both ravaged repeatedly while aboard your ship."

Brendan sat bolt upright. "They weren't!"

"I know that." Abbott held up his hand in a conciliatory gesture as Brendan rose and paced to the window. "To be fair, most don't believe it. The younger sister has received naught but sympathy."

Brendan spun around. "And Rebecca?" he demanded.

Abbott concentrated on relighting his pipe. "Said to be confined to her room." He puffed on the pipe. "Talbot is a vindictive man."

Brendan swore, making Abbott look at him in surprise. "Damn him. If he's hurt her—"

"I hope you're not thinking of doing something foolish." Abbott's drawl stopped Brendan at the door. "Such as going to see her."

"That is what I was thinking, yes."

"Very foolish, my boy. You'd be recognized in an instant, and what then?" Abbott looked up at him, his eyes shrewd. "We couldn't do anything to rescue you. Not without acknowledging that the government has actually authorized the use of pirates against a country that technically isn't our enemy." He set the pipe down. "And what would that do to our other agents?"

Brendan walked slowly back into the room. Like it or not, Abbott was right. There was a larger issue at stake than his feelings for Rebecca. If his part in gathering intelligence became known, that of the other agents Abbott controlled might soon be compromised, as well. And there would go an important weapon against England. "Devil take it," he said, throwing himself into the chair. "I can't just do nothing."

"You have to." Abbott's voice was almost gentle. "Things will have to sort themselves out."

"But, dammit—"

"In the meantime, we'll have to think about what to do with you." He leaned back, puffing on the pipe. "I think, my boy, that the Raven has outlived his usefulness."

* * *

Rebecca sat in a straight chair by the window in her room, looking longingly out at the activity on Prospect Street, and down the hill to the broad Potomac beyond. Three weeks she had been locked in this hot, airless room, while the world outside her burst with life. In some ways, it was a relief. She could imagine the gossip and innuendo being spread about her, especially after her previous suspected fall from grace. Not that anyone knew what had really happened, but that, she had learned to her pain, didn't stop the gossips.

In quite another way, however, it was sheer torture. It wasn't just being locked up, far more a captive here than ever she had been on the *Raven*; it wasn't just being cut off from Amelia, nor was it her meager diet. It wasn't even the estrangement between her and her father, who had yet to forgive her for her actions aboard the *Raven*. It was the enforced inactivity, with nothing to do save a little reading, and that only in the Bible. For, without something to keep her mind occupied, Rebecca was slowly, and quite definitely, going mad.

She did not think about Brendan. That was a conscious decision she had made when she'd stepped into the *Commonweal*'s boat and realized that she had made a terrible mistake. She did not think about her weeks on the *Raven*. She simply did not, by the expedient of reciting every prayer she had ever heard, singing every hymn she'd ever sung, whenever thoughts of Brendan threatened. Such piety pleased her father, who saw it as a sign of repentance, but she knew better. It was the only way she could keep from dwelling on a time, a place, a person, now lost to her.

The nights, however, were different. At night, in her dreams, she saw again the cozy cabin aboard the *Raven*; heard seabirds overhead and felt the ship rock her to sleep. In her dreams she saw a bright blue eye, hair as dark as a raven's wing, a merry smile. She felt strong arms about her and a muscular body pressed close to hers; she smelled the salt of the sea and the essence that was Brendan's alone. And she heard a voice calling her sweet names: lass, *leannan*. In her dreams she remembered everything, and when she awoke, it was to grief so vast and so deep she feared she would drown in it.

She didn't. Instead, she submerged it again, deep inside, only to be swamped anew whenever it resurfaced. If Father would only let her out, things would be better. She could keep busy with running the house and chaperoning Amelia. Father, however, wanted to be certain she wasn't increasing before he allowed that. She had told him aboard the *Commonweal* that she wasn't, and again here at home, but he seemed not to believe her. Nor did he listen when she told him she was glad of it, perhaps because he knew it was a lie. That she wasn't carrying Brendan's child was one of her greatest griefs. Being unmarried and pregnant would have been difficult, and yet still she yearned for it. She yearned to have a child created by the love she and Brendan had shared. Now she never would.

A key clicked in the lock, and she turned her head, welcoming any distraction from the tedium of her captivity. It would be Martha, their maid, bringing her her dinner of weak tea and gruel. Rebecca detested the stuff, but she had to eat. Father apparently hoped hunger would make her submissive. To her surprise, however, it was Ezra who stepped into the room, locking the door behind him.

"Father." She rose, her legs trembling from inactivity and hunger and a little bit of fear. "Is something wrong?"

"No." He gestured her away from the chair and sat there himself, leaving her to stand; one was not allowed to sit on the beds in the Talbot house. "Have you repented, girl?"

Rebecca's lips thinned. So that was what he wanted. She should have guessed. It was the same question he'd asked her every day since the rescue. Usually, though, he visited her in the evening. "There's nothing to repent, Father," she said as she always did. "I did what I had to do."

"What you wanted to do," he sneered. "Little slut, just like your mother."

"My mother has nothing to do with this."

Ezra surged to his feet. "You dare to speak to me in such a way?"

"Yes." Rebecca stood her ground; giving in would not make matters any better. "You know why I did what I did."

"Huh. Because you'll chase after any man," he grunted, but he sat again, mopping at his forehead with a handkerchief. "Continue to defy me in such a way, Rebecca, and I'll see to it you stay in this room."

"You can't keep me locked up forever!" she burst out. "Who will take care of Amelia?"

"As for that, I'm not certain I care for your influence on her. Lord Blaine will not marry her now, you know."

"You can hardly blame me for that."

"Can I not?" He studied her. "It would have been best if I had made you stay in the country after your bastard died, instead of letting you return—but I did not come up here to discuss that." He leaned back, hands laced over his belly, eyes glittering oddly. "I have decided that you may leave your room."

"Father! Oh, thank you."

"Do not thank me. I have not forgiven you, girl."

Her eyes were downcast. "No, Father."

"What you did was unforgivable. However, since there seems to be no consequences, there is no longer any need to keep you hidden. You are lucky no one knows you consorted with the Raven."

"Yes, Father."

"They only suspect it. I would like to make you deal with the scandal yourself."

Rebecca's hands curled into fists. "Yes, Father."

"But that would only hurt Amelia's reputation, so I will not. But you will behave yourself in future, girl, or you'll find yourself out on the streets. Do you understand?"

"Yes, Father."

"Good." He rose. "I'll expect you belowstairs to see to the ordering of the house."

"Yes, Father."

"And there is something else." He stopped by the door, his eyes glittering again. "Some news."

"Yes?"

"About the Raven."

Rebecca looked up. "What about him?"

"The navy caught up with him two weeks ago. United States, not British." He made a face. "Regardless, they did their duty."

Rebecca's grip tightened. "What—what happened?"

"There was a battle. The *Raven* sank—"

"No!"

"—with all hands," he went on inexorably. "Everyone."

"Papa." Rebecca forced the words out through dry lips. "Are you telling me—"

"Yes." For the first time, he smiled, and it was a chilling sight. "The Raven is dead."

Part II

Chapter 16

~

Washington City, May, 1812

The day so many had awaited had come: the day of the annual horse race. At the National Race Course, some miles north of the Capitol, were gathered nearly every resident of Washington City. Mrs. Madison, along with her coterie of friends, Mrs. Smith and Mrs. Thornton, sat in their carriages, while Mrs. Law, proud of her riding, was on horseback. President Madison, not known for his love of sport, was here also, seated upon a fine gelding. On the other side of the track were the ordinary people, the tradesmen and merchants and the like, while farther down slaves and freedmen alike gathered together, all betting boisterously on the outcome of today's events. Within the enclosure were booths selling refreshments, and on their wide plank roofs people stood to gain a better view of the track. Even the members of the British legation were present, Sir Augustus Foster, the British minister, with his staff, in spite of the tension between the United States and England that seemed to be leading inexorably to war. For this one day enmity had been put aside. Washington City had gone to the races.

Amelia alighted from the Talbots' traveling coach and grasped Rebecca's hand. "Oh, just look at this!" she exclaimed. "I vow I haven't been this excited since we stopped attending Mrs. Madison's levees."

"And well that we did," Ezra said, taking Amelia's arm and leaving Rebecca to trail behind. "Never did trust the

Democrats. Jemmy Madison will have us in a war before we can blink, see if he doesn't."

"Oh, Papa," Amelia said, but indulgently. For once Ezra sounded genial, his complaints more automatic than heartfelt. "I vow, to hear you speak, the world will come to an end! Rebecca?" She twisted to look over her shoulder. "There you are, I feared we'd quite lost you."

"Not a prayer of that," Rebecca muttered, raising the skirts of her gray silk sarcenet dress as she stepped around some horse droppings. Oh, to be anywhere else but here. Unlike Amelia, she had been relieved when Father, a staunch Federalist, had decreed that they would no longer attend the levees Mrs. Madison held every Wednesday evening at the President's House. If it had been up to her, they wouldn't be here today, either. Not that she begrudged Amelia, sparkling and pretty in her new high-waisted walking dress of sky blue mull, her pleasure, but social life was a trial for Rebecca. No one quite knew what had happened aboard the *Raven*, but that hadn't stopped anyone from speculating. Added to that were the unconfirmed rumors of Rebecca's earlier fall from grace. Though she was not ostracized by society, most people were wary of her. Trailing behind Amelia and her father, Rebecca made her way through the crowd, past vendors hawking lemonade and beer, much in demand on this warm day, and greeting acquaintances, a smile fixed on her face. No one actually snubbed her; some even returned the smile. Still, she could feel the coolness, as palpable as a blanket of snow. Her transgressions had been neither forgiven nor forgotten. It was not going to be a pleasant afternoon.

Amelia was craning her head to see past a tall man standing ahead of her as they neared the track. "I wonder which one is Mr. Brand? Papa? Do you see him?"

"No, and you will act with decorum, miss," Ezra growled, glaring at Rebecca. "See to it that your sister behaves."

"Of course I'll behave, I'm not a child. But, Papa, you've made me so curious." She twined her arm through his and smiled up at him. "Proclaiming that you've found an eligible gentleman for me."

"I said no such thing," Ezra huffed, but his face had softened. "He seems suitable, and at least he lives fairly close, in Baltimore."

"Unlike the viscount," Amelia murmured, with just a

trace of sadness. Rebecca frowned. The Viscount Blaine, to whom Amelia had been betrothed last year, had, as she'd feared, wanted a bride of spotless reputation, not someone who had spent time on a pirate ship. Rebecca wouldn't forgive him that, even if she never met him.

"I'll not have you go so far away again. Not when—"

"Not even to England, Father?" Rebecca said softly.

Ezra glared at her. "Mind your tongue, miss," he snapped. "I'll not countenance any impertinence from you."

Rebecca's eyes dropped. "No, Father."

"If I thought Amelia would be safe traveling to England I'd allow it, but you, of all people, know the danger."

"Yes, Father."

"Mind your manners today. I'll not have people whispering about us because you do not know how to behave. You are lucky to be allowed in polite society at all, girl."

Rebecca's eyes flashed, but she kept her voice demure. "Yes, Father."

"Oh, look!" Amelia's voice broke in. "There is Mr. Collins. Papa, let us go say hello to him."

Ezra glared across the crowd. "So it is," he said shortly. "Very well. But only for a minute."

Amelia threw Rebecca a speaking look over her shoulder as Ezra escorted her through the crowd, and Rebecca bit back a smile. Amelia, recovering quickly from the viscount's defection, had found solace in the admiration of other young men and had set her sights on James Collins, who worked under Mr. Monroe, the Secretary of State, and so far had found it heavy going. He was older than her usual beaux, for one thing, and for another treated her as he might a sister, with amused tolerance. As a result, Amelia was determined to bring him to heel, not quite aware that he didn't look at her as a man did his sister. It wouldn't be a bad match, Rebecca mused. Collins came from a good Maryland family, and his chances of advancement in the government were said to be excellent. Just now he was standing with a group of people, Mr. Monroe and Mr. Abbott, a noted scholar, among them. Not her father's favorite people, and that was another reason Amelia gravitated to Collins. For things had changed in the past year. Among other things, Amelia had grown up.

Inching her way behind Amelia and her father, occasionally clasping her fingers together to adjust the fit of her gloves, Rebecca let her mind wander. Not too far away; that was dangerous and must never be allowed. No, she kept her mind on things that were close at hand, mundane. Just now she wondered about this Mr. Brand Father wished Amelia to meet. He was a shipowner from Baltimore, a widower, come to Washington City to try to procure a license from the British to trade with the French. The odd thing was, he was English himself. Oh, he had become an American citizen, but Father brushed that off. Once an Englishman, always an Englishman, he said, and Rebecca suspected that that alone made Mr. Brand a suitable marital prospect. Never mind that he might be old for Amelia, as Rebecca suspected he was; quite likely portly, and possibly balding. He was English-born, and that was enough for Ezra.

The crowd parted slightly, and Rebecca, who had been gazing ahead without really seeing anything, suddenly focused. Near the railing, his back to her, stood a man, broad-shouldered in a burgundy coat, a tall beaver hat upon his head. The shape of those shoulders and the way he stood were so achingly familiar that Rebecca's breath caught painfully in her chest. Brendan. It wasn't him, of course. Brendan was dead, and a year later, that still hurt. A year later, it still seemed unreal. For sometimes, as now, she saw someone who walked as he had, or who appeared to have the same color hair, the same shape. The same wide shoulders, that had loomed over her as he made her his own—

No. Rebecca turned her head sharply away. Rarely did she allow herself to think about Brendan. Not when it hurt so much.

Ezra managed at last to pull Amelia away from Mr. Collins, and to guide her over to where the members of the British legation stood. Sir Augustus and the others greeted them cordially enough, but in spite of Ezra's friendliness, kept a distance. Rebecca had noticed it before; that in spite of Father's well-known regard for England and all things English, the British were disinclined to accept him as one of their own. "Father"—she leaned forward to speak in his ear— "should we be here?"

"Of course we should, girl." Ezra glared at her. "Everyone is here."

"Yes, but, Father, with the situation as it is—don't you think we're rather among the enemy here?"

"Nonsense, girl. I have always been a friend to England

and always will be. Now. You watch over your sister, and I will bring Mr. Brand to you."

Amelia took Rebecca's arm, as they stood a little apart from the British. "That wasn't very wise, Becky. You know how Father feels about England."

Rebecca sighed. "Yes, I know. But look around us, Melia!" She gestured toward the British. "No one else is as friendly to them as Father. No American, that is. And with things as they are, with members of Congress yelling for war and all the trouble at sea, we can't be too welcome here, either. I feel almost like a traitor."

"Oh, pooh!" Amelia flicked invisible lint off the fingers of her glove. "I refuse to talk of such things today. All I see"—a smile twinkled in her eyes—"are some uncommonly attractive men."

"Amelia," Rebecca chided.

"Really. Oh, I do wish you had a better gown, Becky. Something colorful and pretty."

"Nonsense. I am only here as your companion."

"Well, you should be looking for a husband yourself. Or are you going to spend the rest of your life catering to Papa's every whim? He won't thank you for it, you know."

"Amelia! Father is grateful for all I've done."

"If you keep wasting time looking after him, you'll never find someone for yourself. He doesn't give a fig for you, Rebecca, and you know it."

"Amelia!" Rebecca gasped, and at that moment Amelia clutched her arm.

"Shh. Papa is coming back, I can just see him—that must be Mr. Brand behind him." She stood on tiptoe. "You're taller than me, Becky, can you see?"

"No." Rebecca scowled. "I am appalled at what you just said. Father loves me."

"Hush, Becky, this isn't the place to discuss it," Amelia said. "Why, he's younger than I expected, and I think possibly handsome, too."

Rebecca glanced away, and her heart lurched. With her father leading the way through the crowd, her view of Mr. Brand was blocked, but what she saw of him was sickeningly familiar. Dark hair, burgundy coat. The man who had reminded her of Brendan. "I feel distinctly unwell," she said, and at that moment her father reached them.

"Mr. Marcus Brand," he said, his voice jovial. "May I present to you my daughters. Rebecca, Amelia."

Amelia had already dropped into a curtsy, and belatedly remembering her manners, Rebecca joined her. Foolish to be in such a tizzy over a man who likely bore no real resemblance to Brendan; besides, he'd probably not take a second look at her, not with Amelia looking so charming. Strengthened by the thought, Rebecca rose from her curtsy—and looked directly into the bright blue eye of Brendan Fitzpatrick.

Chapter 17

〜

Amelia recovered first. "Why, you look like someone we once knew!" she exclaimed. "Doesn't he, Becky?"

Marcus's eyebrow lifted. "Indeed?" he said, and his cool drawl, so unlike Brendan's musical lilt, brought Rebecca to earth with a thud. Of course he wasn't Brendan. This man had two good eyes, and besides, Bendan was dead, she reminded herself for the second time that day. That had never hurt so much as it did now.

"Yes, but ..." Faced with Marcus's coolness, Amelia glanced beseechingly at Rebecca. "Don't you see it, Becky?"

"I'm not certain Mr. Brand would appreciate the comparison, Amelia," she said, giving her sister a warning look. The resemblance was strong, in his features and his build, and yet, now that she was close to this man, she could see differences. His hair was cropped, unlike Brendan's, and though it was black it was liberally sprinkled with gray, especially at the temples. His eyes, neither one covered by an eyepatch, were blue, as well, but cold. He held himself differently, rather stiffly, arms close to his side, and his voice was clipped, almost brusque. Not at all like Brendan's. "Perhaps you've been told, sir, that you resemble Brendan Fitzpatrick. He was known as the Raven."

Marcus's lips pursed in distaste, in a way Brendan's never would have. "Nasty fellow. The world is well rid of him."

"Exactly what I say," Ezra put in, his voice booming, and clapped Marcus on the shoulder. Marcus winced, and with exquisite delicacy edged away from Ezra's hand. "A thorough villain if ever I met one. I apologize if my daughters have offended you. It will not happen again."

"I trust not. How did two such refined ladies come to make the acquaintance of such a villain?"

Amelia smiled up at him. "My sister and I were guests of his for a time."

Marcus glanced briefly toward Rebecca, and in his eyes she could read nothing. "Indeed? How unfortunate for you. I trust he didn't harm you."

"Oh, no, in fact he treated us rather well. Though it was, of course, unpleasant being captive."

His face softened at last. "I would imagine so. It is very warm. Shall we see if we can procure something to drink, Miss Talbot?"

Amelia smiled up at him through her lashes and placed her hand on his arm. "I would enjoy that, sir. You are from Baltimore?" she asked as they moved away.

"Strange." Ezra stared at them with narrowed eyes. "I never noticed the resemblance before, but now you mention it, there's something. Shape of the face, perhaps."

"He doesn't walk like the Raven," Rebecca blurted.

Ezra shot her a look. "We will not talk of him, girl."

"I wasn't. Believe me, Father, I'm as surprised as you are." She watched as Marcus procured a cup of lemonade from a vendor for Amelia and stood talking with her, his lips tucked back in what might be a smile. Nothing at all like Brendan, who had been open and honest in his expressions and movements. Funny, for a moment she'd thought he'd been asking her to walk with him, rather than Amelia. "I wonder if he's related in some way."

Ezra snorted. "If he is, I shall discover it. I don't want Amelia allied with such a family."

"Who is he, Father?"

"I know only what I told you. He's from Baltimore, owns ships, same as me. Born in England, but came here some years back. His wife died a few years ago, yellow fever, I believe. He's said to be prosperous." His eyes narrowed. "He looks it."

"He does," Rebecca agreed, taking in at last the cut and quality of his clothing, from the coat of burgundy superfine, to the intricately tied cravat, to the pristine buff pantaloons. His legs in the tight trousers were finely shaped, well-muscled, she thought, and then quickly dragged her mind to more suitable subjects. "Baltimore isn't so very far."

"No. Though even that is a distance to send Amelia."

"If she's happy, Father."

"True. If she's happy. And you'll not do anything to ruin that."

"I?" She looked up in surprise. "What would I do?"

"I know you, girl, and your ways. I only hope he doesn't take a disgust of us when he hears of your reputation."

That hurt. Rebecca bit her lip and looked away from him, regretting the rare moments of companionship, now lost, and her gaze encountered Marcus's. His was still unreadable, and yet for a moment she thought something flickered there. Then, inclining his head to her, he returned his attention to Amelia.

"Who is that fellow with Miss Amelia?" a voice said behind her, and she turned to see a man in the scarlet uniform of a British soldier.

"Lieutenant Dee," she said, trying to force some warmth into her voice. "What a surprise to see you. Shouldn't you be on duty at the legation?"

"Not today. Servant, Talbot." Dee bowed to each in turn. He was in charge of a contingent of soldiers protecting the British legation, where the Talbots had met him. "He looks familiar."

"A Mr. Marcus Brand from Baltimore. We were just introduced."

"Marcus Brand. I will be da—excuse me, Miss Talbot." A frown appeared between Dee's brows. "What is he doing here?"

"Rebecca's looking particularly fine today, isn't she?" Ezra's voice boomed, and she winced, both at her father's crudity and at the look Dee bent upon her. Though her gown was cut full, with long sleeves and high neck, she felt as if it were transparent, so closely did he look at her. It was not a pleasant feeling.

"Miss Talbot could never be anything but lovely," he said.

Rebecca put up her chin. "Thank you, sir. You are too kind."

"My Rebecca is a fine woman," Ezra said, making Rebecca look at him in surprise. "She'll make some lucky man a fine wife, sir."

"I don't doubt it, sir. A man would count himself lucky to have her."

Rebecca opened her mouth to protest, stunned by her father's sudden praise, appalled by Dee's interest, but the return of her sister with Marcus saved her. "Have you met Mr. Brand, sir?" she asked, her voice just a bit shaky.

"As it happens." Dee bowed punctiliously. "Well met, cousin."

"Indeed. I did not know you were here." Marcus, sounding bored, raised a quizzing glass and stared at the other man through it. The action drew Rebecca's attention to his hands. Square, brown, work-hardened hands that didn't belong to a man as indolent as Mr. Brand appeared to be. Hands that were so familiar that the sight made her dizzy.

"You are cousins?" Amelia put in brightly.

"Distant," Lieutenant Dee said. "We haven't seen each other in years. Although . . ."

"Indeed," Marcus drawled. "Not since I left England. Are you feeling unwell, Miss Talbot?"

Pulling herself out of her reverie, Rebecca looked up into his eyes, seeing there an expression she didn't understand, but which held her. So like Brendan . . . "Miss Talbot?"

"I—I'm sorry. 'Tis a trifle warm. That is all."

"Becky, you do look pale," Amelia put in, her face creased with concern. "Are you sure you're all right?"

"Perhaps a cold drink would restore you, Miss Talbot," Dee put in. "I will get you some lemonade."

"No, don't," Rebecca protested, but in vain, as Dee set off. "I'm fine, really."

"Well, you don't look it," Amelia said in the suddenly mature tones she'd adopted more and more this past year. "Papa, I think we should go home."

"Oh, no—"

"Go home? When the races haven't even begun?" Ezra said. "When I haven't spoken to Sir Augustus about my license?"

"Trust me, sir, he'll not have much to say to you on that," Marcus said. "I've spoken with him myself."

Ezra turned his attention to Marcus, to Rebecca's relief. "Have you, sir?"

"Indeed. There is not a chance the British will grant us licenses to trade freely, or lift the orders-in-council. The Royal Navy will continue to harass neutral shipping."

Ezra's eyes narrowed. "But you're British, sir."

"No, sir. American." He flicked a piece of lint from his sleeve. "If I may say so, Miss Talbot does look pale. I wouldn't keep her standing, sir."

Ezra opened his mouth, and then nodded. "Perhaps you're right. Rebecca, there are trees over there. Best you go sit in the shade."

"I'll escort you," Marcus said as Rebecca turned.

"Oh, no, you needn't do that," she protested. If she had to spend another moment in his company she thought she might scream.

"It will be my pleasure. Madam?"

He held his arm out to her. There was nothing she could do but place her fingers on it and let him lead her through the crowd. She kept her touch as light as possible, but she was aware of the hard-muscled strength of his arm, unexpected in a man so stylishly dressed, and who held himself so rigidly. Uncomfortably aware, and uncomfortably warm. She was greatly relieved when they cleared the crowd and reached the shade of a beech tree on a slight rise overlooking the racetrack.

"Thank you, sir." She turned to him, wanting him only to go. Wanting him to be another man. "I appreciate your courtesy. I will be fine."

"I wouldn't think of leaving you alone." Grimacing at the dirt beneath the tree, he took out a spotless handkerchief and spread it on the ground. "Here, sit down, Miss Talbot."

"But—"

"It will make you feel better," he said with such a note of command in his voice that, much to her surprise, she did so. A moment later he joined her, grimacing again and sitting stiffly. So unlike Brendan, who would have simply sprawled.

For a moment there was silence, while Rebecca cast around for something to say. This man was daunting in more ways than one. "So you are in Washington City for business, sir?" she said finally.

"I came because I couldn't stay away."

Rebecca blinked, staring at him. "I beg your pardon?"

"Like your father, I need a license from the British to trade where I will," he said, his voice clipped again. She had imagined it, then, the intensity in his tone, the lilt. "Though I doubt they'll grant it."

"Oh, of course. You did say that," she babbled. "And how do you find the city, sir?"

"The city of magnificent morasses?" he said, and she looked up to see a twinkle in his eyes. Slight, but a twinkle, nonetheless, and the corner of his mouth was tucked back. "Is that not what L'Enfant called it when he planned it?"

"I believe he said 'magnificent vistas,' sir."

"Ah." Marcus nodded. "But he didn't anticipate a five-mile journey between buildings."

Rebecca's lips twitched. The distances one had to travel in Washington City were among the residents' most prominent complaints. "It isn't quite that bad, sir."

"Perhaps." He paused. "Three miles?"

She laughed, startling herself. When was the last time she had laughed? "Do you dare to speak so slightingly of my city, sir?" she said, trying to sound repressive, and failing.

"Yes, I dare," he said, and this time his smile was broad. "Hot, swampy, pestilential—altogether a most charming place."

Rebecca couldn't help it; she returned the smile. "Oh, infinitely charming. Particularly when the canal near Pennsylvania Avenue floods."

The twinkle in his eye deepened. "I fear I missed that. I've frequented only the British legation and the President's House."

"Paltry," Rebecca proclaimed, realizing with surprise that she was enjoying herself.

"I hope to remedy the situation soon," he said, and at that moment a roar went up from the crowd. From their vantage point, Rebecca and Marcus could see the first race beginning, the horses galloping along the turf.

"I'm keeping you from the races. I am sorry." She turned back to see him regarding her intently. Her hand went to her hat. "What?"

"You have unusual hair, Miss Talbot. If I may make a personal comment."

"I wish you wouldn't." She picked at the fingers of her gray kid gloves. She wished he didn't have a sense of humor, that he wasn't so handsome or, when he made up his mind to it, so charming. Because she was starting to feel again, and it hurt.

"It needed saying." He paused. "You are uncomfortable with me. Why?"

Startled, Rebecca looked up. "I'm not."

"If you keep on as you are, your gloves will be in shreds," he said gently. "Is it because I resemble that scoundrel?"

Lips tightening, she looked down at her hands. "Yes." Partly.

"He must have hurt you."

"No. To the contrary. He was very kind."

"Kind?" His voice rose with scorn. "A pirate?"

"Yes. Kind." She could endure this no longer. "I am feeling better, sir. If you would see me back to my father?"

He seemed about to say something, and then nodded. "Of course." Rising, he held his hand out to her to help her up, and she took it. Like his arm, it was unexpectedly warm and strong; the hand of a man who worked hard, in contrast with his dandified appearance. Even through her glove his touch burned, and, startled, she looked up at him to see him regarding her with that intent blue gaze. For a moment she couldn't look away, and then another roar went up from the crowd, distracting him, giving her the chance to study him. So like Brendan, and yet unlike, too.

Carefully, she pulled her hand free. "Thank you, sir."

He nodded, bent to collect his handkerchief, and then grasped her elbow, escorting her down the slope to the milling crowd. Oh, she wished he wouldn't! And, oh, she wished his touch didn't affect her so, with warmth that spread through her body, thawing feelings and emotions that had been encased in ice for too long. Of all men, why this one?

They reached the crowd just as the second race began. Much to Rebecca's relief, Marcus left her with her father, and then, with a bow, turned away to talk with Mr. St. John, a member of the British legation. She was glad of the noise, of people shouting as the horses thundered past, glad of the chaos that masked and matched her feelings. Marcus had reawakened feelings best left alone, and it hurt. Oh, it hurt. It wouldn't be quite so bad if she knew she wouldn't see him again, but she would. Father had chosen him as a suitor for Amelia, and that only intensified the pain. Never before had she been jealous of Amelia; never had she begrudged her anything. Now, though, she did. Marcus Brand would be courting her sister, and how would she deal with that?

Some distance away, Marcus glanced back at the Talbot sisters. There was, as he'd noticed earlier, something about the older girl. Not a girl. A woman, who had been through a trial by fire. And yet still she could laugh, though he knew his appearance had been a shock to her. Admirable. She had courage, and somewhere within her there was fire.

"Excuse me, Mr. St. John. Sir," a voice spoke behind him, and he turned, along with St. John, to see Dee. "Sir Augustus would like a word with you, Mr. St. John."

"Thank you, Lieutenant. I'll go to him directly. My apologies, sir." Hillary St. John turned to Marcus. "Even on race day, it seems there's business to be done."

Marcus nodded. "I shall watch the races. That is what we're here for, isn't it?"

"Among other things." St. John made his way through the crowd, and Marcus turned his attention back to the racecourse, where the horses were gathered for another heat.

"Trust a bad penny to turn up," Dee said.

Marcus's gaze flicked over him, bored. "We never had much to say to each other, Jeremiah. Shall we keep it that way?"

"You'd like that, wouldn't you? Wouldn't want all your fine new friends"—he encompassed the crowd with a sweep of his hand—"to know what a scoundrel you are."

Marcus swung his quizzing glass back and forth. "I don't believe I like the tone of your voice," he said mildly. "As I recall, I bloodied your nose more than once when we were growing up."

Dee's face darkened. "For which our uncle never seemed to punish you, though he was quick enough to do so with me."

"Perhaps you deserved it."

"Damn you!" Dee hissed, stepping forward. "I should—"

"It matters not." Marcus brushed a piece of lint off his arm. "Neither of us were heirs to his earldom."

"Maybe not, but you were his favorite. Don't deny it. You were the one he educated, the one he wished could be his heir. But he changed his opinion of you." Dee's face grew smug. "When you deserted your mother."

"I did not desert her," Marcus snapped. "I was impressed into the navy. And I've always wondered"—his gaze, steely now, bored into Dee—"how the press gang knew where I'd be."

Dee shrugged. "A puzzle, isn't it."

"Indeed." Marcus's voice was silky. "But I've not forgotten it, Jeremiah, or that she died alone."

"You've done well for yourself." Dee's gaze moved contemptuously over Marcus's fine clothes, and he frowned. "In Baltimore?"

"Mostly."

Dee's frown deepened. "If I didn't know better, I'd think I'd seen you since—"

"Have you known the Talbots long?" Marcus said abruptly.

Dee nodded. "The older girl is mine."

"I beg your pardon?"

"Talbot'll see to it the younger one's properly married. But Rebecca"—his face twisted into a leer—"now she's a different kettle of fish altogether."

Marcus toyed with his quizzing glass, swinging it idly on its chain. "Indeed?"

"Oh, yes. She's ripe for the plucking. Actually, she's been plucked once or twice already, it is believed."

"You are insulting a lady, sir."

"Lady? Ha. Not her. Everyone knows what she is, it's only because she comes from a good family that she's not totally ostracized. But that doesn't matter to me." The leer faded, to be replaced by the intent look of a hunter after prey. "I intend to have her."

Marcus raised his quizzing glass and stared at Dee through it, knowing that his eye would appear grossly magnified. "Indeed?" he said frostily.

"Indeed. And when I'm done with her, maybe I'll let you have a try."

"My apologies for leaving, sir," St. John said as he rejoined them, saving Dee from receiving yet another bloody nose at Marcus's hands. "There should be no more interruptions. Ah! The horses are off."

Marcus let the quizzing glass drop and very deliberately turned his back on Dee. "Which are you backing?" he asked as if nothing untoward had occurred.

"The bay. He's from Tayloe's stables, said to be fast."

"We have met since," Dee said abruptly.

Marcus did not turn around. "We have not."

"We have." Dee's face was dark at Marcus's intentional snubbing. "And I'll remember. I never forget things like that."

"Isn't there someplace you should be, Lieutenant?" St. John put in.

"Yes, sir." Dee saluted. "But if I were you, sir, I'd be careful of the company I keep," he said and stalked away.

"My word!" St. John stared after him. "Of all the insults—"

"Pay him no mind." Marcus pretended to concentrate on the race, now under way. "I will, I assure you."

"I apologize for him, sir." St. John turned back to him. "The lieutenant can be rather strange."

"Think nothing of it. Although I do imagine you have abler men than that in your army. And your navy, as well."

"Of course, sir!" St. John's chest puffed up. "Our navy is the finest in the world."

"So it is. Can't imagine how the American Navy expects to beat it, even with the new ships," he said absently.

St. John stiffened. "Excuse me?"

Marcus glanced at him. "Don't you know? It's no secret."

"No, sir. I'd not heard of any new ships being built for your navy."

Marcus shrugged. "Perhaps I didn't hear aright, then. There's a ship being built in a yard near Baltimore. Someone told me it's to be a ninety-gun, and there are more being built in other yards."

"The same as our second-rater," St. John muttered. "Bigger than anything the Americans have now."

"It is just a rumor," Marcus said quickly, looking alarmed. "Do not take it seriously, sir. I'd not like to add to the tension."

"No, no, you haven't." St. John turned. "Excuse me, I see Sir Augustus signaling to me. I must see what he wants."

"Of course." Marcus watched as St. John crossed to the group of British diplomats, his lips tucked back in what might have been a smile. That was a day's work well done.

Satisfied with himself, Marcus returned his attention to the racetrack, and his gaze encountered Rebecca. She was staring at him, lips caught between her teeth, a little frown puckering her brow, though when she saw him watching she quickly turned away. Marcus's ebullient mood faded. For there lay a greater danger than even that posed by Dee. And just how was he going to handle it?

The clock in the circulating library chimed, making Rebecca start. Later than she'd realized, and if she wasn't home to see to dinner, Father would be displeased. Still, she was loath to return home. It was a warm day, and Bridge Street was a-bustle, with people visiting the shops, and carriages and drays trundling along the cobblestones. Outside Suter's Tavern a man idled on a bench, while underneath the shade of a dogwood tree in full bloom a dog lolled, panting. There was so much life and energy that Rebecca longed to go out in it, be a part of it, even though she knew she never could be. Her past misdeeds and her father's obduracy kept her confined to the house she now regarded as a prison.

Sighing, she paid for her books and hurried out the door. She was brought up short when a man suddenly loomed up before her. "Oh!" she exclaimed, her parcels tumbling to the ground. "Excuse me—"

"The fault was mine." Marcus Brand bent and began gathering everything up with an elegance of motion that was graceful, but quite unlike the way Brendan would have crouched in the same situation. But she must stop comparing him to Brendan, even if the resemblance was startling. "My apologies. I did not mean to bowl you over." He rose, and she thought she saw that twinkle in his eyes again. "Excuse me, is something wrong?" he added.

"Wrong? Oh, no." She stepped back, flushing, realizing she'd been staring. "I'm sorry, you startled me. If you'll just give me my purchases, I won't keep you."

"Nonsense." The word was clipped. "I'll see you home."

"Oh, no, that won't be necessary—"

"It will be my pleasure." He grasped her arm firmly. Uncomfortably aware of the warmth of his touch, Rebecca had no choice but to walk along with him. Why in heaven's name did he wish to stay with her? "I've a carriage here."

Rebecca stopped, her eyes widening just a bit at the sight of the carriage to which he led her. It was a gig, perched high above the street on two wheels, their spokes picked out in yellow. Altogether a dashing and stylish vehicle, exactly what she should have expected from him. What startled her was how much she suddenly wished to drive in it. "Yours, sir?"

"I find it convenient, with the distances between here and the Capitol." With a hand on her elbow he helped her into the carriage and then climbed in beside her, taking up the reins with quick, competent motions. Once again she focused on his hands and had to look away, suddenly dizzy.

Trying to block out her awareness of the man beside her, Rebecca concentrated on the passing scene and the novelty of traveling in such a way. Marcus drove expertly, threading the gig past heavy carts stopped before Georgetown Market, and picking up pace when the street ahead was clear. To either side of her, shops and homes and trees fairly flew by, and the wind in her face carried with it a hint of coolness from the river below. For the first time in nearly a year she felt alive, exhilarated, and it was all because of the man beside her. Pulling at the fingers of her gloves, Rebecca dared to glance at him from under the brim of her bonnet. If he didn't plan to speak with her, why had he taken her up?

"Do you have business in Georgetown, sir?" she asked.

"No. I lodge here, with a Mrs. Sally, near Holy Hill," he said, naming the area of Georgetown where the college was located. "Did you not know?" he went on, at what must have been her evident surprise.

"No. Why should I? I thought perhaps you were staying near the British legation."

"Ah. Is that disapproval I hear?"

"Far be it from me to disapprove of anything you do, sir."

"But you do. I am sorry, madam."

Something in his voice made her look up to see that his eyes were twinkling. It was the outside of enough. "Pray don't mock me, Mr. Brand," she said, shifting away from him on the dark blue leather seat.

"Ah. I was right."

She shouldn't ask, she knew she shouldn't, but she couldn't help it. "About what?"

"About your hair. You've a temper."

Her lips firmed. In her mind she heard another voice, saying much the same thing. "You hardly know me well enough to make such a personal comment, sir."

"Does no one ever tease you, Miss Talbot?"

"No." Her voice was flat. "No one."

"Then your life must be dull."

"I enjoy my life," she said, but even to her own ears she sounded unconvincing. "You've no right to imply otherwise."

"No, I suppose I don't," he said with absolutely no hint of apology. "Do you enjoy reading?"

"Yes." She turned to him. She didn't know this man. She didn't know if she could trust him. "Please, when you next see my father, don't tell him we met at the circulating library."

He frowned. "Why not?"

"He doesn't approve of novel reading. Or poetry. Or anything that is not serious or religious."

"But you read them anyway."

"Just in this past year. Do you read poetry, sir?" she asked before he could question that statement.

"Some, though I prefer history."

A little imp inside her pushed her on. "Do you know John Donne?"

"A bit. 'Death be not proud, though some have called thee—' "

"Yes, I know that one," she said, deeply, irrationally disappointed. In her mind she again heard another voice, similar in timbre but not in cadence, reciting quite different lines. If she had needed another reminder that he was not Brendan, she had it. "I turn here, sir."

He nodded, turning the gig with ease onto the hilly street, climbing away from the waterfront and the bustling business district. The homes here were larger, with more space between them. "Have I offended you in some way?"

She didn't look at him. "No."

"I have, haven't I." He stopped the gig, laying his hand on her arm. "Your eyes give you away. No, don't look away." His own eyes were soft. "Whatever I did, I'm sorry, lass."

Her head jerked up. "*What* did you call me?"

" 'Lass.' " He frowned, and then his face cleared. "Too informal, I know, for our acquaintance. My apologies. It is what I call my sister."

"Oh." She looked away, unreasonably disappointed. She did not wish him to regard her as a sister, and that was a shock. "We are nearly to my house. You may let me down here."

"Very well. I shall come with you."

"You needn't," she protested.

"I would like to," he said. He tied the reins to a hitching post and helped her down, not releasing her arm, even when she again stood on solid ground. It was too much. The feelings his touch evoked in her were too much. She pulled away. "What do you want of me, Mr. Brand?"

He looked surprised. "The pleasure of your company,

madam, nothing more. I enjoyed meeting you and your sister the other day."

"Oh," she said flatly. "I see."

"Do you? And what, precisely, do you see?"

"I am not stupid, Mr. Brand—"

"No, you've reminded me of that."

"—and I've spoken with my father about this. Do you intend to court my sister?"

"What? No." He shook his head. "No, Miss Talbot, I can assure you that I definitely do not intend to do so."

She pulled at her gloves again, confused at the emotions within her. "Then I suggest you not toy with her affections."

"I won't. The truth is, she's not the one I'm interested in." He paused, but she didn't respond, staring straight ahead. "Do you not care who has taken my fancy?"

"No."

"Pity, but I'll tell you, anyway. You, Rebecca." He paused. "I want you."

Chapter 18

~

Rebecca stood still on the brick sidewalk, so stunned that for a moment she couldn't breathe, and then she began pulling her parcels from Marcus's arms. "Ooh! You—you men!"

"What did I say, lass?" he asked, sounding bewildered.

"Don't you dare call me that." She glared at him with hands on hips, not caring that her parcels had tumbled to the ground again. "You've heard stories about me, haven't you? You've heard what people say about my past and you think that means—that means—well, I'm not!" She crouched to pick up her parcels, her vision blurred with tears. "I am not available."

"I didn't think you were, lass," he said very gently, crouching across from her, and her hands stilled on the parcels. "Look at me. Look at me, Rebecca."

She kept her head bent. "I did not give you leave to use my name."

"No, you did not. Come, let me help you with those." Gathering her parcels, he rose easily, and she had no choice but to follow suit. "It seems I must beg your apologies yet again, Miss Talbot. I feel as if I've known you forever."

She looked sharply up at him; looming against the sky, he looked so like Brendan she could almost believe he stood there. "You're very like him," she said in a low voice.

"Who?"

"Bren—the Raven."

"Is that a compliment?"

"And yet, you're not." Her brow wrinkled in a frown, as she catalogued yet again the differences in speech, manner, and dress. She couldn't imagine a gentleman such as Marcus Brand captaining a pirate ship. Or, could she? Perhaps she could. For, as Brendan had, he held himself with authority and confidence. It only added to her confusion. "It's very strange," she murmured.

"Not really. No, I'll hold onto these. You really must learn to hold onto your parcels, Miss Talbot."

"I must—!"

"There's a legend in my family, whether 'tis true or not, I don't know, that we are descended from pirates. Perhaps your Raven—Fitzpatrick, did you say?"

"Yes. Brendan Fitzpatrick. And he's not my Raven."

"Perhaps he's a distant relation. Brendan? Hm."

"What?" she asked when he didn't go on.

"Mm? Nothing." His lips tucked back in what she was beginning to recognize was a smile. "Just that it's curious. 'Brendan' is a form of 'Brand,' and they both mean the same thing."

"Which is?"

"I doubt you'll like this." He paused. "The raven."

"You're jesting!"

"No." His face was serious. "You are right, Miss Talbot. I have heard about you."

Rebecca flinched and turned away. "I see."

"No, you do not." He caught her arm, and she stilled, not wanting to look at him for fear of what she would see in his face. "It must have been hard for you."

Absurdly she felt tears prickling at her eyes. "It was."

"I'm sorry for it."

"Why?" She looked up at last, puzzled at the sympathy she heard in his voice. "It wasn't your fault, what happened, or that everyone's believed the worst of me since."

"No. But, still, I'm sorry you had to go through such an ordeal."

"Thank you," she said after a moment, glad her voice didn't shake and betray how close to tears she was. In the past year, against the censure and ostracism she had faced, she had never once let herself give in. She had not given anyone the satisfaction of breaking down. One kind comment from this man, though, and her emotions became unbalanced. She didn't think it was because he resembled Brendan, or, at least, not for that reason alone. For she could not deny the truth, not even to herself. She was attracted to Marcus Brand, for all the good it would do her.

Rebecca stopped before her house, debating on inviting him in. Father would likely be pleased to see him, and Amelia, and that was part of the problem. She didn't think she could bear watching Amelia flirt with him. "Thank you for escorting me—"

"Don't thank me," he interrupted, his voice so rough that she stared at him. His eyes were intent, his face almost stern, a sharp contrast to the urbanity of his earlier pose. Pose? she thought sharply, but had no time to ponder the thought. "I wanted to do it. Rebecca"—he caught her hand in a tight grip—I haven't been honest with you. There's something I must tell you—"

"Ah, there you are," a voice said behind them, and they turned, startled, to see Ezra on the doorstep. "Good morning. A pleasure to see you again, sir. We never did finish our discussion on the embargo."

"No, sir." Marcus released Rebecca's hand, she thought with reluctance. What had he been about to say? "We never did."

"Well, come in. Rebecca! What are you thinking of, girl, keeping our guest standing outside? Come in and get him something cool to drink."

Rebecca jumped at the rebuke. "Yes, Father," she said, hurrying up the curved stairs. Marcus followed her more slowly.

"And see to Martha. She'll need your help with dinner, girl."

"Yes, Father."

"Where do you want these, Miss Talbot?" Marcus asked.

"Rebecca can take them," Ezra interrupted. "She does little enough around here as it is."

"Yes, of course." Rebecca's cheeks burned as she reached for the parcels, and her eyes wouldn't meet Marcus's.

"I don't mind, sir." Marcus kept his voice affable, though inside he burned with anger. She was a different person around her father, and he didn't like it. 'It will be easier if I just put them where they're needed."

"Oh, very well." Ezra sounded disgruntled. "Rebecca will show you."

Marcus nodded. "Miss Talbot?"

"This way." Rebecca led him under an arched entranceway and down some stairs; as with most other houses in Georgetown, the kitchen was in the cellar. An enormous fireplace took up most of one wall, making the room stifling hot, in spite of the door opened to the outside. "Martha is our maid. Father doesn't hold with keeping slaves, and I must say I agree with him. This is most kind of you sir, I would imagine you're not made to go into too many kitchens!" she chattered. "There, on the table will be fine. Thank you, Mr. Brand."

Marcus set the parcels on the trestle table, frowning. "Does he talk like that to you all the time?"

"Like what?" she asked.

"There you are, miss," a cheerful voice said, and a thin black woman came in from the door leading outside. "Got some fine peas in the garden, miss. Did you get the leg of lamb?"

"Yes, Martha." Rebecca brushed impatiently at a strand of hair, her eyes so haunted that Marcus felt a ridiculous urge to smooth it back himself. But her father awaited him. Staying here would only complicate matters for her. "Thank you again, sir."

He bowed. "My pleasure, madam," he said and went back up to the first floor.

Ezra was waiting for him in the hall, at the door to a well-appointed study, looking out on to the side garden. A luxurious oriental carpet was on the floor, and on the heavy mahogany desk were a silver inkstand and a leather letter box. Rebecca had to make do with only one servant, but Talbot apparently saw to his own comfort. "There you are," Ezra's voice boomed out. "I was about to go looking for you. She wasn't flirting with you, was she?"

Marcus looked up sharply as he settled into a comfortable leather wing chair. "Who?" he asked, crossing his legs and affecting a pose of cool indifference.

"My daughter." Ezra made a face. "Daughter of Satan, I sometimes think she is."

"Sir!" Marcus was genuinely shocked. "Miss Talbot strikes me as a fine young lady."

"Yes, that she does, doesn't she." Ezra leaned back in a chair next to Marcus, folding his hands on his ample stomach. "Deceptive, ain't she? If you didn't know—" He looked up, eyes keen under his brows. "You've heard the stories?"

"About the pirate? Yes. Hardly her fault, sir. Everyone knows what a danger the Raven was."

Ezra snorted. "Her behavior was disgraceful. If it had been just that one time I could forgive her, considering the circumstances, but . . ." He shook his head. "There's no help for it. The girl is wanton."

"Are you saying this has happened before?" Marcus asked.

"No, no, I'm not saying that," Ezra said, his face suddenly wary. "Rebecca spent some time with her mother's family a few years back, and people have put the worst construction on it. It was, unfortunately, after her romance had broken up. If I didn't need her to look after Amelia, I'd have cast her off then."

Slowly, smoothly, Marcus raised his quizzing glass and studied Ezra through it. "A remarkable thing to say."

"Mayhap. You condemn me for it? But you weren't here, sir, when she made me a laughingstock. I told her he'd never marry her."

"Who?"

"Lord Everett. Here on a visit, some years back. He was a baronet, heir to an earldom. Stands to reason a man like that wouldn't tie himself to an American. But, would she listen to me? No. I tell you, sir, she deserved what happened to her."

As carefully as he had taken it out, Marcus put the quizzing glass away. "Losing her reputation seems like punishment enough."

"No, sir." Ezra's voice was grim. " 'Else she wouldn't have fallen again. She's flighty, like her mother."

"How is that, sir?"

Ezra's eyes went blank. "Past history. I doubt Rebecca will change. I thought she'd learned her lesson when Everett returned to England—"

"He isn't dead?"

"Yes." Ezra frowned at him. "Why do you ask?"

"I wondered why you didn't see that he married her."

Ezra stiffened. "I tried, sir, but he would not. He was already betrothed. His death came later." He shrugged. "It matters not. She has shown she cannot be trusted, and that is why I must be stern with her."

"She has shown she trusts too easily," Marcus said, his voice tight.

Ezra frowned at him again. "I hope, sir, that this hasn't given you a disgust of my family. Amelia is entirely different, I assure you. Her mother was not like Rebecca's, and she has been raised carefully."

"I would never hold what you have said against Miss Amelia." Marcus rose, disgusted with the conversation. "I must be leaving."

"Now? But you just got here."

"I'm sorry. I've business to attend to." He strode out into the hall just as Rebecca entered, carrying a tray.

"But surely you can stay for a cool drink," Ezra expostulated, following him.

"I haven't time. Miss Talbot"—Marcus stopped, nodding at her—"a pleasure to see you again."

"And you, sir," Rebecca said, her heart sinking. His face was tight, his eyes cold. Oh, what had Father told him to make him look at her in such a way? "You are leaving already?"

"Yes," he said curtly, and then, as if aware of the effect of his tone, smiled. "I hope to see you again soon."

Rebecca set the tray down on the hall table and dropped a curtsy. "And I you, sir."

"Good day." He bowed to them both and walked out the door, closing it very carefully behind him.

"Well"—Rebecca turned away, dismayed by the look on Marcus's face—"I'll just return this to the kitchen, then."

"Look at me, girl."

Rebecca turned, startled. "Yes, Father?"

"What did you say to him?" he roared, and his hand clouted her across the face.

Marcus strode toward the river and his lodgings, having returned the gig to the livery stable, his face smooth, only the quick, agitated swing of his walking stick betraying his anger. Ezra Talbot was a dolt, and Marcus would take great pleasure in throttling him. Rebecca was a sweet, gentle woman, and yet her father talked of her as if she were a whore. Treated her that way, too. What did her past matter? His own past was checkered, and yet no one held that against him. It all made him wish he'd returned to Washington City sooner.

The door to the tall brick house near the river opened as he reached it, and Mrs. Sally, his landlady, stood there, her apple cheeks puckered. "Oh, Mr. Brand. You are home at last."

"As you see, madam." In spite of his anger, Marcus bit back a smile. Mrs. Sally was an elderly widow who had been forced by finances to let out rooms in her house. She had a penchant for the dramatic, and immense curiosity, which he suspected he would soon find a liability. Yet he couldn't bring himself to snub her. "Is something wrong?" he asked as he entered the house, doffing his hat.

"A message came for you, sir, not ten minutes past," she whispered conspiratorially, handing him a note. "A most arrogant man delivered it. I do dislike the English, don't you?"

"Did he say aught to insult you?" Marcus's voice was absent as he glanced down at the note, recognizing the handwriting. At least the wax seal wasn't broken. To his knowledge Mrs. Sally couldn't read, which was one reason he lodged here, but in his work he knew too well that no one could be trusted completely.

"He didn't have to say anything. The very way he looked at me was an insult." Mrs. Sally's chins quivered in outrage. "I hope, sir, that you will not be inviting him to this house."

Marcus had broken the seal and was scanning the note. "I will endeavor not to. I must go out again, ma'am."

"Again?" Her face puckered in dismay. "But I made some lemonade, 'tis nice and cool—"

"I am sorry," he said gently. It seemed he was not fated to receive any cool drinks today, he thought with a flash of amusement. "I promise I will sit with you when I return, and we will have a long chat."

"Oh, very well. But please do walk slowly, sir. Mr. Sally was taken from me on a day like today. His heart, you know."

"Yes, ma'am." He opened the door and then turned. "Ma'am, you are acquainted with Rebecca Talbot?"

Mrs. Sally's face screwed up in a frown, and he braced himself. "Oh, that poor girl."

"Ma'am?"

"Wickedly deceived she was by that Englishman, and him calling himself a lord! And, of course, there's what happened with the pirate."

"Not her fault."

"No, it wasn't, but the way her father carried on . . ." Her lips compressed. "I do not care to speak ill of anyone, sir, but I must tell you that my dear Joshua never liked Mr. Talbot."

"An indictment, indeed." Marcus's voice was grave, though he wanted to kiss her for coming to Rebecca's defense.

"Oh, yes. Mr. Sally did always say there was something strange about the manner of Mrs. Talbot's death. The first Mrs. Talbot, that is."

Marcus was very still. "In what way, ma'am?"

"Well—far be it from me to gossip, sir, but 'twas a terrible scandal at the time. She ran off with an actor, can you fancy that? Oh, it was quite a shock, and Rebecca just a babe at the time. Though, there, mayhap the poor woman meant to come back. We'd word, later, that they both died."

Marcus stirred uneasily. "How?"

Mrs. Sally's face puckered in a frown. "Now that is what always bothered Mr. Sally, since Mr. Talbot was gone from home at the time."

"Are you saying he killed them?" Marcus said sharply.

"Oh, gracious, no! At least, there is no indication he did. No, no, that would be a terrible thing to accuse anyone of." She stepped back. "I mustn't keep you, you've something you must do."

"I fear so." His voice was grim. "Don't wait dinner for me, ma'am. I don't know how long I'll be," he said and went out, his thoughts churning. Talbot was a menace. He didn't need Mrs. Sally to tell him that, and it meant he had to do something. Damn the danger to his mission. He had to do something about Rebecca.

"Becky?" Amelia said outside Rebecca's bedroom door that afternoon. "Lieutenant Dee is below to see you."

"Tell him I'm indisposed," Rebecca answered, her voice muffled.

"I'll do no such thing." Amelia walked in, hands on hips. "I agree that what Papa did to you is horrid, but I think you should stop feeling sorry for yourself."

Rebecca lowered the damp cloth she held to her cheek in the hope of lessening the throbbing and bruising. "I don't feel that way at all, Amelia. But can you blame me for not wanting to be seen like this?"

Amelia held her ground. "Other people should see how Papa treats you."

"They'll only wonder what I did to deserve it," she said gently. "I'm afraid my reputation's past mending."

"Well, it isn't fair! I think you should come down and see Lieutenant Dee."

"Amelia—"

"It's high time you had someone show an interest in you, Becky. Heaven knows I have enough suitors. And if Papa has his way," she wrinkled her nose, "I'll marry that Mr. Brand."

"Don't you like him?"

"He's well enough, I suppose." She shrugged. "But not for me. He's far too old. Oh, Becky, do come down! You know I can't entertain a man alone."

Rebecca eyed her with alarm. "Amelia, you haven't a *tendre* for Lieutenant Dee, have you?"

"No, silly, he's your beau! Do come down. Please?"

"Oh, very well," Rebecca said, unreasonably cheered. It shouldn't matter that her sister had no interest in Mr. Brand, and yet it did. Rising, she followed Amelia downstairs and into the parlor.

"Lieutenant Dee," she said, smiling, and he bowed in return. He was a well-enough-looking man, she thought, sitting, as they exchanged pleasantries. Not very tall, but solidly built, with even, regular features. There was the scar, and his light brown hair, which he kept pushing back with quick, impatient gestures, was thinning, but, really, those were minor defects. She wondered why she couldn't like him.

"What happened to your face, Miss Talbot?" he asked as she poured him a cup of tea.

"I walked into a door. Terribly clumsy of me." Her fingers brushed against his as she handed him the cup, and she pulled back, restraining herself from shuddering.

"You should be careful." His eyes, dark and penetrating, seemed to bore through her, and she busied herself with tidying the tea tray. Mercy, why did he have to look at her in such a way? "An attractive woman like you. I am surprised that I am the only gentleman here today."

"Oh, but we've had callers already," Amelia chattered. "Mrs. Harrison was by this morning, and Mr. Collins said he might call this afternoon." Her cheeks dimpled. "And Mr. Brand has already been here, though that was to see Papa."

"Brand?" Dee looked sharply up from his cup. "What did he want?"

"Why, I don't know." She frowned. "Does it matter?"

"It might." He set the cup down on the pie crust table. "I must tell you, I don't like the man."

"But he is your cousin, sir."

"And that means I know him. I don't like the way he looks at you, Miss Talbot."

"Me?" Rebecca said in surprise, feeling her cheeks color. For she knew quite well how Mr. Brand looked at her, and even now the memory made her feel warm.

"Yes. I do not trust him, and not just because I know him. There is something else." He leaned forward. "What do you know of him?"

"Just what you do, sir, that he is a shipowner from Baltimore. More tea?"

"No. No." He rose and stalked about the room, snapping his fingers. "He reminds me of someone, but I cannot think quite who—good God." He stopped still. "The Raven."

Rebecca nearly choked on her tea. "Yes, of course," she managed to get out. "Did you not realize that?"

"No, how could I?"

"But I understand you encountered him in the past."

Dee's fingers went to his scar and then dropped. "It was dark, and events happened fast," he said stiffly.

Rebecca picked up her embroidery. "Oh."

"I made it my mission, then, to catch him." His fists clenched and unclenched, and his eyes were distant. "And I nearly succeeded. But he blasted the hell—excuse me, ladies—out of the warship I was on. You must remember that. It was when the dastard held you captive."

She looked up in surprise, remembering the *Raven*'s encounter with a British man-of-war. Remembering, too, her foreboding, and glad that Brendan hadn't fallen to this man. "You were on that ship, sir?"

"Yes. And if I could have rescued you, I would have." His eyes still held that burning, distant look. "He should pay for what he did."

"He's dead, sir," she said softly and felt again the pain of that knowledge, fresh and newly sharp.

"Is he?"

"What do you mean?" Amelia asked.

"There can be no doubt," Rebecca put in. "We had the news of the battle not long after we returned home."

"But no one saw him. His body was never found, did you know that?"

Rebecca bent her head, concentrating fiercely on her stitching. Oh, yes, she knew that, and it had given her many a nightmare. Brendan was presumed drowned, lost in a watery grave. There had been no one to bless his departure, no one to say prayers over him. Except her. "I don't know why you're so concerned, sir."

"Are you saying he's the Raven?" Amelia said at the same time.

"He isn't!" Rebecca exclaimed.

"He could be. And you'd know, wouldn't you?" He spun to face her. "You could identify him."

"Funny, I don't even think he looks much like the Raven anymore," Amelia said into the stillness that followed. "I did at first, but the more I see him the more I can see 'tis a superficial resemblance."

"He's really not like the Raven at all," Rebecca said calmly, securing her needle in her fabric and rising. "I do hope you will excuse us, sir, but I need to see to supper."

"What? Oh, of course." Dee reached for his hat. "But, never fear, dear ladies. If he is the Raven, I shall protect you," he said, and executing a short bow, he went out.

"Oh, Becky." Amelia's voice was glum. "I'm sorry I made you come down. But I do wish you could find someone suitable."

"I'm quite content," Rebecca said, smiling in spite of the fear fluttering inside her. Mr. Brand wasn't the Raven. Of course he wasn't. Resemblance aside, there were too many things against it. But . . . She shivered. But Lieutenant Dee was a strange man, and by what he had just said, vindictive. No matter if Mr. Brand was the Raven or not. He was in danger, and she, Rebecca, was the only one who could do anything about it.

Marcus pulled off the cravat he had tied so carefully hours before, and tossed it onto a chair. Hell of a day, he thought, idly scratching his chest as he stood by the window. Below him on the street, the lamplighter made his rounds, the glow of the lamps soft in the deepening twilight. A woman huddled in a hooded cloak, strange in this warmth, hurried by, briefly catching his eye. Strange. It almost looked like Rebecca.

Grimacing, he turned away from the window, this time shedding the finely tailored coat. He was in a bad case if every woman he saw reminded him of Rebecca. True it was that he'd lain in wait for her this morning; true that his rage at her father still burned. As he had been reminded quite forcefully this afternoon, however, he had other things to think about, and no business jeopardizing his goals. Except that to Marcus, Rebecca was one of his goals.

There was a knock on his door. "Yes?"

Mrs. Sally stepped into the room, frowning in disapproval. "There's a young person here to see you, Mr. Brand."

"A young person?"

"She is wearing a cloak that covers her face, and she will not give her name." Mrs. Sally's pale blue eyes were clouded with distress. "Really, Mr. Brand, I know that you are a charming man, but I cannot countenance such goings-on in my house. If Mr. Sally were alive—"

"Easy, ma'am." He rested his hand on her shoulder. "Be assured that I would never do anything Mr. Sally would disapprove." Poor Mr. Sally must have led a dreadfully dull life.

Mrs. Sally's face eased. "Of course. You are a gentleman, sir. But I do not like young women coming to the house like this. So forward."

"I'll see her and send her on her way," he said, patting her shoulder reassuringly. "Where is she?"

"In the parlor. You won't let her come here again?"

"No, Mrs. Sally, I won't." Because he had enough complications in his life without some unknown woman adding more. He reached for his coat, started to shrug into it, and then laid it down again. Whoever the woman was, she'd come here uninvited. He was not going to go to any trouble for her.

Mrs. Sally's parlor was illuminated by a single candle in a brass holder shielded by a glass globe when Marcus quietly opened the door. The dim light threw shadows over the wainscoted walls and the rosewood settee and chairs, and only faintly touched on a woman standing near the fireplace. The woman he had seen outside, he realized, his unease deepening. Danger. "You wish to see me?" he said, his voice cool.

The woman swung around from the plain paneled fireplace. "Oh! I didn't hear you come in—"

"Rebecca?" In two swift strides he crossed the room to her. "Good God, what are you doing here?"

"I had to come. Please don't be angry."

"I'm not, but if you were seen—"

" 'Tis why I wore the cloak." She laughed, a little sound of self-deprecation. "I probably attracted more attention with it, but I didn't want anyone to know who I was."

"What do you here?" he asked. In the last few moments he had somehow possessed himself of her hands, and he didn't wish to let them go.

"I had to see you. To warn you."

"Of what?"

"You may be in danger. Lieutenant Dee—you remember him?"

"Unfortunately, yes. What of him?"

"He thinks you're the Raven."

Marcus laughed. "Me? Whatever gave him that idea?"

"It's not funny!" She pulled her hands free and stepped back, the hood slipping a little from her head. "He has a reason to want revenge, 'twas the Raven who scarred his face. And, last year, he nearly caught the Raven when my sister and I were captives."

"He did?"

"Yes, he was on a British man-of-war. Don't you see?" She pushed at the hood, revealing her face at last. "If he thinks you're the Raven he'll stop at nothing—"

"What is that?" he interrupted.

"What?"

"That." His fingers reached out to touch a dark spot on her face, and she flinched. "My God."

" 'Tis nothing—"

"Who did this to you?" His voice was quiet, but with an edge that made her tense with wariness. Just so had she heard Brendan speak, at his most dangerous.

"It doesn't signify—"

"Damn it, it does signify." In the dim light, his eyes were a fiery blue. "Did Dee do this?"

"Mercy, no!" She stared at him. "Why would he?"

"Because he—never mind. Who did it?"

"No one. I walked into a door."

"You did not." He grasped her shoulders. "Tell me the truth, Rebecca, so that I may go after the bastard—"

"Would you?"

"Devil take it, of course I would!" he roared. "Whoever did this to you should be keelhauled."

" 'Tis really nothing," she said, staring up at him, feeling the ice that had encased her heart for the past year begin to melt. When was the last time someone had come to her defense? "And it's not as if it's the first time."

"It was your father. My God. It was, wasn't it?"

"Yes." Flushing, she let her gaze drop, unable to meet his eyes for the shame flooding through her. And that, of course, made matters worse, because she encountered the open neck of his shirt, and the bronzed skin beneath. Dressed as he was, without his coat or cravat, he looked far more approachable than before, and more than ever like Brendan.

"Never mind what happened to me," she said impatiently. "What are you going to do about Lieutenant Dee?"

"Dee? Nothing."

"But he thinks—"

"Dee and I grew up together," he interrupted her. "I know how to handle him."

Her gaze was searching "If that is so, why would he think such a thing of you?"

He shrugged. "We were never fond of each other. Actually, I wouldn't be surprised if there's some relation between the Raven and us. My grandfather had holdings in Ireland."

"Oh?" Her cheeks pinkened as she took his meaning. "Oh."

"I don't care about Dee," he said, catching at her arm as she turned away. "Why did your father do this to you?"

"It matters not," she said dully.

"It does matter. Look at me, Rebecca. Look at me." He nudged her chin up with his hand. "Your father and I had a talk today."

"Oh?" Better he knew the worst about her now, before she came to care about him too much. It would hurt less that way. "I can imagine what he said."

"Aye. A lot of nonsense. The man doesn't know what a treasure he has."

She stared at him. "Me?"

"Yes, lass, you," he said and dropped a kiss on her forehead.

Startled, she pulled away. "What did you do that for?"

He was smiling, a warm, gentle smile that made her feel warm all over, and she realized for the first time that he had a dimple. "I wanted to."

"Ooh!" She spun about, her back to him. "You believed everything he said, didn't you? Everything you've heard from everyone. That I'm wanton, loose, a fallen woman—"

"No, Rebecca." He laid a hand on her shoulder. She stayed still, unresponsive. "I make up my own mind about things and people." His fingers were stroking the side of her neck now, and she bent her head in instinctive response. "I trust my own judgment. And what it's telling me about you . . ."

"Yes?" she prompted through dry lips.

"Is that you are a very warm, and very attractive woman. And what's past, is past."

"You're very generous."

"No, lass. I'm very selfish." And with that he turned her to him, the pressure on her shoulder gentle, but inexorable. His face was serious, intent, and his eyes—mercy! She knew well what that look in a man's eyes meant. For her it had meant heaven, and hell, and she wasn't sure if one was worth the other. Except that, somehow, she couldn't break free.

His head was bent, his mouth a mere whisper away from hers. "There is fire in you," he murmured.

Rebecca jerked back, memory flooding through her. Brendan's voice, saying that exact same thing. Brendan, calling her "lass," using words of the sea in ordinary conversation. Brendan was dead, she knew that, and yet . . . "Brendan?"

Chapter 19

Marcus paused. "I beg your pardon?"

"I am sorry." Rebecca turned away, her heart thudding sickly. "So sorry, but you look like him."

"Who?"

"The Raven. Sometimes you act like him, and sometimes you sound so like him—"

"You loved him."

"No! He was a pirate. But he was not as black as he's been painted, and—"

"You loved him."

Rebecca turned away. "It matters not," she said, her voice dull.

"Aye, Rebecca. It matters not."

She turned to look at him, her eyes wide and puzzled, those deep, sea green eyes in which a man could drown. "You shouldn't be here, lass. Time you were getting home."

"I—yes, you're right." Hastily she pulled her hood over her head, hiding that glorious hair from his view. "I won't come here again."

"That's just as well," he agreed gravely. "I'll see you home."

"Oh, no! If we're seen together—"

" 'Tis dark. No one will know us." He paused as she stood there, biting her lips. "What is it, lass?"

"I can't," she whispered. "You're too much like him."

"The Raven is dead, lass," he said and saw her shoulders slump. Marcus Brand, however, was very much alive, and able to pursue whomever he wished.

" 'Tis late," Rebecca said, breaking into his thought as she turned toward the door. "I'm sorry I disturbed you."

"Come, lass." He caught her arm. "Don't go like this. Let me see you home."

"Well—"

"I'll just get my coat."

At that, her eyes flicked up at him. "Very well."

"Wait right here. I'll be down in a moment." Touching her cheek with a fingertip, he went out, running up the stairs to his room to get his coat and hat. A gentleman such as Marcus Brand would never go out improperly attired. When he returned downstairs, however, it was to see the parlor door standing open, and Mrs. Sally locking the front door with a massive key.

"Why, there you are, Mr. Brand. I thought you'd gone out with the young woman," she said.

He stopped on the bottom stair, unreasonably disappointed. "She's gone?"

"Why, yes. When I heard the front door close, I came out to see what had happened. I hope you don't think I was prying."

"No, of course not, ma'am."

"Is something wrong?" Her face was creased with concern. "Are you in trouble, Mr. Brand?"

"No, ma'am."

"Notes from people, unsuitable visitors at all hours—" Her hands fluttered in the air. "I really don't know what Mr. Sally would do."

Marcus bit back a smile. "Be at ease, ma'am. I am not in any kind of trouble." At least, not the kind she thought. "I'll bid you good night," he said and bent over her hand. It had the desired result; her face cleared and she dimpled up at him, as flirtatious as a young girl. It made him smile, and that, lately, was rare enough.

Later, however, alone in his room, he stood again at his window, and his face was grim. He was, indeed, in trouble. Just what was he going to do about it? Nothing, for now. He turned away from the window with a shrug. Things would happen as they would.

And, across the street from the small, neat brick house, a man stepped out of the shadows, and stared up at Marcus's window for a long, long time.

* * *

The city was abuzz. The ship *Hornet* had returned from England, bearing with it dispatches for Sir Augustus Foster. Outside the President's House, and across President's Square, where the British legation was located, men gathered together, talking and speculating. Everyone knew the importance of the messages. If the British government had decided to ease its stand on neutral trade, allowing United States ships to go where they would, all would be well. If not, it could mean war.

Marcus strode along the stone sidewalk to the legation, walking stick swinging in his hand, cursing to himself as he stepped to avoid a cow that refused to budge from his path, for farm animals were allowed to roam freely in the capital. He, as much as anyone, needed to know what the dispatches contained. Nothing less than his future was at stake. He turned in at the gate, only to find his way suddenly blocked by a red-coated soldier holding a musket across his chest. "You!" the soldier spat.

"Jeremiah." Marcus stepped back, leaning on the gold head of his walking stick and regarding the other man coolly. "Finally performing your duty, I see."

Dee's face grew dark. "I always do my duty, sir. And if that duty is to deal with you—"

"Indeed?" Marcus had taken out his quizzing glass and was studying Dee through it. "Is it your duty to accost peaceful gentlemen? Our countries are not at war yet."

"It matters not. My duty is to protect the legation. And we, sir, have always been enemies."

"Indeed." Marcus's voice was frosty, though he knew he'd best be careful. With the dark light of zeal in his eyes, Dee could be dangerous. "I have business here."

"Indeed?" Dee said. "With whom?"

"With Mr. St. John. If you send to him, you will see I'm right."

Dee glared at him and then wheeled, speaking harshly to another soldier. The soldier nodded, saluted, and went into the mission. All the time Marcus stood, apparently at ease, watching everything about him coolly. And all the time, his instincts screamed at him. Danger. Dee was a threat. It exhilarated him, made him feel alive, as he hadn't in many a long day. Here was a challenge to be met, and be damned if he didn't do it.

The soldier came back and muttered something to Dee.

Still glaring at Marcus, Dee slowly lowered his musket and stepped aside. "Mr. St. John has said you may go in," he said grudgingly.

"Thank you." Marcus tipped the brim of his hat with his walking stick and saw the other man's face darken. His shoulder blades tightened, crawled, as he passed Dee on the walkway and went up the stairs, as if an attack would come at any moment. Only when he was inside did he relax, though not completely. He hadn't come here to bait Dee, enjoyable though that might be. He had more important tasks.

Once the building housing the British legation had been two houses, until the wall between had been knocked down. Now, though it was sizable, it seemed small, cramped, with a crowd of people milling about the hallway and in the reception rooms. Over the heads of the crowd he saw St. John, talking to a group of men and looking harassed. He raised his walking stick, signaling to him. St. John detached himself from the men and with some difficulty pushed his way through the crowd into the hall. "Mr. Brand," he said. "My apologies. I forgot you were to come here today. Everything is at sixes and sevens, as you can see."

"Indeed." Marcus nodded. "The news?"

St. John shook his head. "Not good, I fear. The government is holding firm. The orders-in-council will stay in force."

"Indeed." The two men stood in silence for a moment. So. The laws so hated by Americans, the ones that interfered with their trade and which encouraged British naval captains to abduct American seamen from their own ships, were not to be repealed, after years of delicate diplomacy and maneuvering. It could mean only one thing. "Then it's war."

"I fear so." St. John pinched tiredly at the bridge of his nose. "If they only knew at home what you Americans feel—but come, we can't talk here." Tilting his head, he indicated the corridor leading to the back of the house, relatively empty. "As to your request, Mr. Brand, I fear we can't honor it now."

"That is of no moment." Marcus leaned on his walking stick, watching the other man, gauging him. "I find it extremely irresponsible of my country to go to war with yours, when you have all you can do fighting Napoleon."

"Yes, that's true," St. John burst out. "He is evil, sir, I do not hesitate to say so. We are fighting for the very liberty of the world, and to have the Americans pestering us at this time is hard—but I am sorry, sir. I forgot myself."

"I may be an American citizen, sir, but I was born in England. Damned if I want to see her lose to Bonaparte." Which was quite true. "I came here to help."

St. John frowned as he leaned forward. "In what way, sir?"

Marcus's voice lowered, and he leaned forward as well. "I would like to offer my services to your country."

St. John glanced quickly around, and then let out his breath. No one was nearby to overhear. "A startling proposition. Come, let us go into this butler's pantry." He gestured to a long, narrow room opening off the hall. "We can discuss this in privacy."

In an alcove under the stairs, away from the bustle and chaos, Rebecca, her eyes wide at what she had just heard, sat frozen. No one had noticed her sitting there, and that was how she wanted it. It hadn't been her idea to come to the legation today, but her father's. Since he was afflicted with the gout, he needed her along. She had expected to be bored, even with the novel she had slipped into her reticule, and quite possibly angered by what she heard, but never, never had she expected this. Marcus Brand was a spy.

Closing her eyes, she rested her head on her hands, not knowing whether to laugh or to cry. Oh, her choice of men was abysmal. First Robbie's father, and then Brendan, and now this. Not that there was anything between her and Mr. Brand. He had indicated an interest in her, however, and there was no doubt she was attracted to him. And not just because of his resemblance to Brendan. He had an appeal of his own, in his wit and his honor and his courage. There was much she didn't know about him, much that was a mystery. But, this. This was something she could never have anticipated.

Brendan would never have done such a thing, she thought with a rush of the sweet pain that accompanied her memories of him. Not he, who had hated the British. Though he'd been a pirate, he'd been open about it. A spy was something else altogether. Not just a spy, either, but a traitor. Marcus might be English by birth, but he was a citizen of the country he was now betraying. It could not be tolerated. Something would have to be done about it.

Oh, but not by her! She shrank back in the chair, her

whole being revolting against the thought of betraying
Marcus. For such it would be. And yet how could she protect a traitor when her country stood poised on the edge of
a war it seemed unlikely to win? If only it had been someone else besides Marcus. If only he didn't remind her so of
Brendan.

"Rebecca!" Ezra's voice roared through the commotion in
the hall, making her head jerk up. The novel fell to the floor,
and she hastily retrieved it, shoving it into her reticule.
"Damme, where is the girl?"

"Here, Father." Rebecca emerged from under the stairs,
smoothing her skirts. "Do you wish to leave?"

"Damme, of course I wish to." He leaned heavily on the
arm she held out to him, and began to hobble on his band-
aged foot. "The fools won't listen to reason."

"Which is?"

"Never you mind that. But I'm working on it, girl, you
may be certain of that." He paused at the top of the stairs.
"Damme, where is our carriage? I can't walk far with my
foot like this."

"I'll see it's called for." Rebecca spoke to the soldier on
guard. Below her, near the gate, stood Lieutenant Dee,
watching her in a peculiarly intent way that made her shudder. She had hoped she wouldn't encounter him today. She
couldn't deal with him just now.

"There'll be guests for supper this evening, girl," Ezra
growled when she turned back to him. "Just you make certain the food is edible."

"It will be, Father."

"Ha! I don't know what's got into you lately, girl." He
peered at her from under bushy eyebrows. "You're getting
flighty. Like your mother."

Once that would have been the worst insult he could have
paid her. Now it was almost a compliment. At times like this
she could well understand why her mother had left. "There's
the carriage, Father," she said and set about the difficult, delicate task of easing him down the stairs. Dealing with her father was one thing; easy, almost, if done right. If she didn't
mind suppressing all her own desires and thoughts and im-
pulses. She just wished he would show her some affection or
appreciation from time to time. Dealing with the problem
that had been foisted on her was, however, quite another
matter. What she was to do about Marcus, she didn't know,

she thought, as she and Jacob, their manservant, helped Ezra into the carriage. She had learned a bitter lesson today, one she should have learned a long time ago. Where men were concerned, her judgment was poor. It would be best if she trusted none of them. Not Lieutenant Dee, and not, she thought with a little pang, Marcus. She was destined to live her life alone.

Marcus climbed the curving stairs of the Talbot house on Prospect Street and rapped on the door with the head of his walking stick. Truth to tell, he wasn't looking forward to this meeting with Talbot and his cohorts, but it had been suggested to him that it might be useful to know what went on here. Talbot's sympathies toward the British were well known, and his influence in the shipping community, wide. Knowing what he planned might come in very useful, indeed.

The door opened. "Oh!" Rebecca exclaimed, her hand flying to her lips. Her cheeks were flushed and her hair was tucked up under a cap, with a few tendrils escaping. She looked altogether entrancing. "Mr. Brand. I didn't expect to see you." She stepped aside to let him enter. "Are you here to meet with Father and the others?"

"I've been invited, yes," he said noncommittally, handing his hat and walking stick to the maid who had glided silently into the hall. "You look charming this evening, Rebecca."

Rebecca's flush deepened. "I—thank you. Come. They're in the parlor." Abruptly she turned and led him down the hall, her skirts twitching. He watched the sway of her hips with growing enjoyment. Perhaps being here wouldn't be so difficult, after all.

"Wait." He put his hand on her arm as she reached for the handle of the door opening off the hall. "Are you joining us?"

"Oh, no. This is for Father's acquaintances, only. They will be discussing politics, and—"

"And you, as a proper lady, do not understand politics."

"Of course I do!" she flared, looking up at him at last, her eyes flashing green fire.

He couldn't help it; he grinned. "You are very easy to tease, Rebecca."

"And you, sir, are no gentleman." She opened the door. "Do please go in."

"And leave you in peace?" he muttered, passing by her. She flushed again, but this time he forced himself not to look at her.

Talbot, leaning heavily on a cane, was crossing the room to him. "Come in, come in," he boomed. "Good to have you join us. Rebecca!"

She turned in the doorway. "Yes, Father?"

"Where is the wine, girl, and the cheese?"

"I'll get them, Father."

"Good Gad, I should hope so. You try my patience, girl."

"I'm sorry, Father," she murmured and swept out of the room, closing the door behind her.

Marcus's lips tightened. The room was filled with other men, and no one seemed the least surprised by Ezra's behavior. That meant it wasn't unusual. Devil take it, why did the man treat her so? Even more perplexing, why did Rebecca allow it?

He was given no time to ponder this, however, for Ezra was bringing him around the room, introducing him to the other men. Marcus recognized the names; Robert Swift owned a fortune in shipping, while Bryan Powell was a plantation owner who had seen his exports of tobacco reduced in the past years of agricultural depression. In addition, there were other merchants and farmers, and even a clergyman. None of them surprised him, Marcus reflected, sitting in a wing chair and listening to the conversation that rolled about the room. He'd expected to see them all.

"Mr. Brand owns ships in Baltimore," Ezra explained to the room at large. "I asked him here tonight because he has as much stake as anyone in what we plan."

"Did you manage to get your ships away before the embargo was enforced?" Swift asked, leaning forward.

"No, I had not that fortune," Marcus answered with studied coolness, wondering what, precisely, the group's plans were.

"Pity." Swift sat back. "Here everyone knew about it before Jemmy Madison did. Got my ships away, and off to England."

"You trade with England, sir?"

"Certainly. What, do you think I'm going to aid those damned Frenchies?" He snorted. "I like a profit as much as the next man, but damned if I'll help them fight England."

"You ask me, it's France we should be fighting," another

man said, and voices rose in a babble of argument and agreement. In all the commotion, Marcus was the only one who noticed Rebecca slip into the room, carrying a silver tray with a crystal decanter of wine, and a fine cheddar. "I'll just have Martha light the candles," she murmured, and fled the room.

Marcus began to rise, and then stopped. He wasn't here to see her, much as he wanted to. "It seems to me, gentlemen, that today's news makes the issue of who we fight obvious," he said, quietly, but with an edge that cut through the hubbub.

Immediately the voices rose again, and Marcus sat back to listen. These men were known British sympathizers, and no admirers of James Madison, and yet even they seemed disgusted by the British government's recalcitrance.

"Why won't they listen to us?" one man said, his voice rising above the others. "God knows we've all protested the policies, and so has the government. But they keep on their merry way."

"They are fighting a war, sir," Ezra said, his usually round face looking pinched.

"True, but the Royal Navy's stopped my ships more than once and taken off men."

"If they are deserters, then they deserve to be taken off," Marcus said, and appalled silence fell over the room.

"Obviously you haven't had your trade interfered with," Swift said, his voice perceptibly cooler.

Marcus studied his fingernails. "Are you for England, sir?"

"Of course I am, or I wouldn't be here. But facts are facts, man, and the truth is they've taken off as many Americans as English. And meddled with our trade in the process."

"Our own nation's done much of that." Marcus looked up. "But then, you seem not to care if trade with Britain is allowed or not."

"Demmed embargo is foolish," Powell said, his face growing red. "Everyone knows Madison will agree to war to be reelected. We have fools governing us."

"Which is why I've called you all together here today," Ezra said, more smoothly than Marcus had ever heard him. "To discuss today's news and decide what to do about it."

"What can we do?" one of the farmers said sourly. "Britain won't repeal the orders-in-council."

"Demme, you'd think they'd know better. It's like the stamp act, forty years ago," Powell put in, referring to the taxation law that had been one of the causes of the revolution. "They wouldn't listen to us then, and look where that led."

"A good point," Ezra said. "As good now as then."

Marcus stared at him, not sure he'd understood aright. "What do you mean, sir?"

"I mean"—Ezra leaned forward, hands fisted on knees—"that what worked then might very well work now. I mean, gentlemen, that we shouldn't tolerate the government's stupidity any longer. It is time for us to stage another revolution."

Swift stared at him. "Are you saying—"

"What I am saying, gentlemen, is that our government has proven to be ineffective." His gaze swept around the room, and the light in his eyes blazed brighter. The light of fanaticism, Marcus realized. Of madness. "In short, it is high time we overthrew the government."

In the hall outside the parlor, Rebecca sagged against the wall, hand to her mouth to keep from crying out in protest. If Father knew she was here there'd be the devil to pay, but she had to know what he was up to. Never had she expected this. It was treason, and Marcus was in there with him. Oh, dear God, there were two men in her life, and both were traitors.

Marcus wasn't in her life, she reminded herself, and wasn't that a good thing? Now he couldn't hurt her. Someone should know about him—but if she said anything, her father's freedom would be jeopardized. What was she to do?

Martha walked into the dim hall, bearing flint and tinder. "Miss?" she said when she saw Rebecca leaning against the wall. "You gave me a turn. You all right?"

"Yes." Rebecca hurriedly straightened and stepped away from the door. "Yes, I'm—knock before you go in, Martha."

"But, miss, no one'll pay me any mind—"

"Tonight they will. Knock first." She didn't want Martha to be involved in whatever was being plotted inside the parlor. "I'll be in the garden," she said and fled.

Marcus found her there a long time later. She was sitting beneath the grape arbor, gazing through the deepening dusk at nothing. "Rebecca?" he said, and she jumped. "My apologies. I didn't mean to startle you."

"I didn't expect to see you." Hand on heart, she stared up at him, a dark shape silhouetted against the lighter sky. If she didn't know better she would almost think it was Brendan, so similar was Marcus's build to his. "Surely the meeting isn't over already?"

"Some minutes ago." He sounded grim. "May I join you?"

"Of course," she said with little enthusiasm, shifting on the bench to make room for him. He was dangerous, this man, to her heart, to the very foundation of her life. "I heard what my father suggested."

"Did you? Listening at the keyhole, were you?"

She flushed, but kept her gaze steady. "No. I had the door open a crack."

"Even better."

"Pray do not mock me. What he suggested was appalling."

"I agree," he said quietly.

"I beg your pardon?"

"I agree with you, Rebecca."

"Oh?" She leaned back, regarding him. "Why? Isn't the plan extreme enough for you? Or do you believe we should never have separated from England to begin with?"

"Rebecca." He laid his hand on hers. "I'm not your enemy."

She gave a harsh laugh. "Oh, no, sir, on that you are wrong."

"I don't agree with your father," he said with forced patience. "Revolution isn't the answer. But neither is war."

"What other course is there, sir?"

"God knows." He stared off across the garden, perfumed with the lemony scent of magnolias. "I don't deny that I agree with the British on many things, but their stubbornness is causing serious trouble."

She studied his profile. His disagreement with her father was a point in his favor. And yet, what had he been doing at the British legation this afternoon? "Do the other gentlemen agree with Father?"

"No. They were as stunned as I. No one seemed to know quite what to say, and then your sister came into the room."

Rebecca sat up straighter. "She did?"

"Yes. It gave everyone the excuse to leave. Except"—he turned to look at her—"that I wanted to see you."

"What did Amelia want?" she asked, refusing to be diverted.

"Something about permission for an excursion to Mount Vernon."

"Oh. That. Yes, her friends plan that for several days hence."

"Will you be going?"

"Yes, I plan to."

"Good." He grinned, his teeth showing white in the darkness. "Then you might be interested in knowing I've been invited along. By your father." He paused. "I accepted."

"Oh."

"Fair warning, Rebecca." His grin widened, deepening his dimple. "You've the chance to cry off. But"—he reached out to toy with a tendril of her hair—"I hope you don't."

Rebecca jerked away. "You presume a good deal, sir."

"Do I? You are a beautiful woman, Rebecca."

"Oh, nonsense," she said, edging away from him. True, she no longer considered herself unattractive; that was Brendan's gift to her. She did not trust this man, however. "I don't know why you say such things, sir, but I wish you would stop."

"Why?" He moved closer to her. "I find you attractive, Rebecca, and I think you feel the same about me."

"No."

"But I think you do, you know." His voice turned coaxing as he continued to play with her hair, tugging at it and then releasing it, so that it bounced back into a curl. "And I think we would be very good together."

She sat very stiff. "I have already told you, sir. In spite of what you may have heard about me, I am no man's for the taking."

"I don't think that, Rebecca," he said, exasperated. "That's not what I want from you."

That made her look at him. "No?"

"No." His gaze bore into hers. "Oh, hell, I don't know what I want," he muttered, and with that swooped down and captured her lips.

Chapter 20

~

Rebecca was instantly lost, engulfed in a rising tide of feelings such as she hadn't felt in so long, so long. Marcus's lips moved over hers, caressing, nibbling, and when his tongue flicked out, tracing the seam of her closed lips, she gave herself up to him utterly, opening her mouth and clutching at his shoulders. Oh, she'd missed that, being held, being loved, and it was so sweet that the pain of the year past was nearly forgotten. "Brendan," she murmured between kisses. "Oh, Brendan."

Marcus jerked back. "What did you say?" he demanded.

She looked up at him with dazed eyes, wondering why he'd stopped, wishing he'd kiss her again. "Marcus."

His hand moved up, pulling off her cap, settling on her hair. "You are a beautiful and desirable woman, Rebecca. Never forget that for a moment." He bent his head again, but this time he'd given her a chance. This time some sanity had crept into the madness.

"No," she said and pushed him away. She was a little surprised when he released her, and not a little disappointed. "This can't happen."

"It has happened," he pointed out.

She hugged herself. "Once. That's all."

"You're attracted to me, Rebecca. You can't deny it."

"No, I can't," she said. It was the simple truth. She was attracted to him. It wasn't wantonness; if that were so, she'd have thrown herself at any man. Instead, she had withstood temptation, until now. And if he didn't look so much like

Brendan, would the attraction still be there? "I am attracted to you, but that's as far as it can go."

"For God's sake, Rebecca." He took a quick turn about the garden, hand thrust into his hair. "Why not? There's nothing wrong in this."

Oh, but there was. He was a traitor. She would not make another unfortunate choice. "Nevertheless, it will go no further. I am pledged to stay with my father."

He stared at her. "I beg your pardon?"

"I said—"

"I heard what you said. For God's sake, Rebecca!" He reached her in one quick stride, grasping her by her arms and pulling her against him. "Why do you want to stay with that old man?"

"He loves me."

Marcus swore, making her blink. "The way he treats you? My God, Rebecca, are you blind?"

"He loves me," she repeated, pulling away. "He needs me. I can't leave him."

"Rebecca—"

"I know he seems hard at times, but I've tried him much. 'Tis why he doesn't show his real feelings for me."

Marcus stared at her. "Let me understand this. He has yet to forgive you for the past, and yet you claim he loves you."

"Yes."

"No. That's not love, Rebecca. God knows what it is, but it's not love."

"But you don't love me either, do you, Mr. Brand?"

"A moment ago you were calling me Marcus."

"You didn't answer my question." She paused, waiting, but he remained silent. "I am very flattered by your attentions, sir, but—"

He caught her to him again and planted a quick, hard kiss on her mouth. "This isn't the end of it, Rebecca," he said, and releasing her, turned on his heel and walked away.

Her knees too weak to support her, Rebecca sank onto the bench, pressing her fingers to her lips. They tingled still from his kiss; her body still felt the imprint of his against her, his broad chest, his muscled thighs, and—her cheeks grew pink—his evident desire for her. The thought of it made her giggle. She'd never thought herself a woman to inspire strong passions, but mercy! Tonight she'd certainly inflamed Mr. Brand. And he, a traitor.

Rebecca returned to earth with a thud. He might not fall in with her father's treasonous scheme, but he was, nevertheless, a traitor. She must never forget that, even as something within her ached for him, yearned for him. He was betraying his country, and that meant that; no matter what she felt, what she wanted, she could never give into him. But, oh mercy, what did she do now?

Marcus strode along in the soft spring darkness, his emotions in turmoil. Anger, frustration, exhilaration all mingled in a combination that could not be soothed. He wanted her. God help him, he wanted Rebecca, and if she hadn't stopped him tonight, there was no saying what would have happened. Just as well she had; he was going to do this right. The last thing she needed was to have another man seeming to want her for one thing only. She deserved better than that.

But, the devil take it, what was this idea she had about her father? The man mistreated her, and still she clung to him. Marcus had never seen the like. If circumstances were normal he could take things more slowly, ease her away from Ezra. Not with matters as they were, though, and with Ezra's behavior being so irrational. And that was something he'd have to deal with.

A footstep crunched in the shadows behind him, and he whirled. A click, and the sword that was concealed in his walking stick, held at the ready, flicked out. "Who is it?" he called sharply, for footpads were a problem in Washington City and were not unknown in Georgetown. "Show yourself."

"Marcus." A man stepped forward, his bearing military, precise. "Good evening."

"Jeremiah." Marcus lowered the walking stick, though he didn't retract the sword. "What do you here?"

"The same as you. Enjoying a fine evening."

Marcus remained still, weighing the possibilities of a fight and gauging the other man's strengths and weaknesses. "Far from the legation, aren't you?"

"That's my business."

"Come to the point," Marcus said, suddenly impatient. "We dislike each other. I find your following me damned suspicious."

"You wish me to come to the point? Very well." Dee leaned forward on the balls of his feet, and Marcus tightened his grip on the walking stick. "It is this. Stay away from Rebecca Talbot. She is mine."

"No, sir, she is not," Marcus answered crisply. "Not while I have anything to say in the matter."

"But you don't." Dee's voice was soft, putting Marcus's guard up higher. Danger. "I saw her first, and I'll not let you take her away from me."

Marcus crossed his arms, dangling the walking stick. "Then you have a fight on your hands."

"One I will win. Just as England will, if there is a war."

"I doubt it."

"Oh, we shall. Even if you do build new ships."

Marcus glanced sharply at him. "You may be surprised, sir, at our navy."

"So you say." Dee's brows lowered. "I do not know what game you play, sir, but I am not fooled by you. If you continue to come to the legation, you'll suffer for it."

"Indeed?"

"Indeed. I shall see to it. We do not take kindly to American spies."

Marcus laughed, a genuine sound of delight. "Do make up your mind. First you think me a man long dead, and now a spy."

"You may be both."

"Your imagination is boundless," Marcus said, amused no longer. "I have no wish to prolong this conversation. Good night, sir." He began to turn, and then stopped. "And be warned. If you continue to follow me, I know how to use this." He raised the walking stick and the sword clicked out again. "I will not hesitate." He waited and then turned again, walking away with feigned nonchalance, though the skin between his shoulder blades crawled. Dee would have no scruples about attacking him from behind. Only when he had gone some distance, with no footsteps following, did he relax.

Dee was a threat, he thought, swinging onto the stairs at his lodgings and opening the door. A threat to him and what he needed to accomplish; more importantly, a threat to Rebecca. As he returned Mrs. Sally's greeting and listened patiently to her prattle on about her activities, he pondered the matter. Somehow, Dee would have to be dealt with.

* * *

"Oh, Mr. Collins, don't we have just the perfect day for this?" Amelia said, smiling up at Gilbert Collins as they stood together on the wharf, awaiting the boat to take them downriver to Mount Vernon. "It will be ever so nice to be out of the city for a time."

"Indeed," Marcus said, very low, in Rebecca's ear.

She started, looking at him with wide eyes. "Oh, Mr. Brand. I didn't hear you."

"My apologies. I didn't mean to startle you." He made her a correct bow, but the look in his eyes as he straightened, intent and warm, flustered her.

She looked away, feeling more than a trifle warm herself. "I am sorry my father talked you into this."

It was his turn to look surprised. "Why? Do you not want me here, Rebecca?"

"I never said—it has naught to do with me. I mean—you must find this dreadfully boring. All these young people." She gestured toward the group of people gathered together, chatting. They were a mixed lot, ranging from a very young lady new to society, to her parents, Mr. and Mrs. Bayard, along to act as chaperons. Everyone was well known to Rebecca; some she even considered friends. And yet she felt as if there were a wall between her and them. Only with the man beside her was that sense of distance lessened. "It is good of you to come."

"I wanted to. I never have seen Mount Vernon, you know, except from the river." Something glimmered in his eyes; a smile, perhaps. "And I am not ancient yet."

"I didn't mean—"

"In fact, I am acquainted with some of the gentlemen. Mr. Collins, for one."

"Oh." Rebecca averted her head. Three days had passed, and still she hadn't decided what to do about Marcus. If he was a spy, he should be stopped. A quiet word from her to Mr. Collins, who worked under the Secretary of State, would likely take care of that. If only she weren't so drawn to Marcus.

"Is he your sister's beau?" Marcus went on, apparently unaware of Rebecca's discomfort.

"Mr. Collins? Mercy, no. Papa has decided—"

He looked at her, brows raised inquiringly. "What? That I would be a perfect match for her? Yes, I know about that. Your father is not a subtle man, Rebecca."

"I am mortified." Rebecca put her hands to her flushed cheeks. "I shall die of it."

Much to her surprise, he chuckled. "Your father has the right idea, Rebecca. But the wrong daughter."

"Mr. Brand—"

"Marcus." His hand shot out and gripped her arm, gentle in spite of its firmness. "My name is Marcus. Say it."

My name is Brendan. The memory drifted back to her, sweet and painful. "I cannot." With great dignity, she withdrew her arm. "It wouldn't be polite."

"Hang being polite," he said in a low growl. "Rebecca—"

"Becky?" Amelia's voice, high and questioning. "Time for us to go aboard."

"Yes, Amelia." Rebecca stepped away from Marcus, both glad and sorry for the reprieve. "I shall be there directly. Let me see to the food. Please leave me alone." This in a hiss to Marcus, who followed her across the wharf.

"Why do you end up doing the work?" he asked, not a whit abashed.

"Someone has to."

"Yes, but why you? Aren't you to have a life, too, Rebecca?"

"Martha, is all ready?" she said briskly.

"Yes, miss." Martha dropped a quick curtsy to Marcus. "Me and Jacob, we'll get everything on the boat."

"Thank you."

"Ship," Marcus muttered, taking her arm as she turned away. "This is a ship."

She glanced at him, trying again to free her arm, but without success. "What is the difference?"

"A ship is large enough to carry boats. Careful, there."

He helped her step onto the gangplank with such care that she felt almost delicate, a novel sensation for one as tall as she. "Rather a circular definition, sir."

"Indeed," he said, but his eyes glimmered again. His gaze swept over the river schooner, taking in the raked masts, the jutting bowsprit, the neatly curled lines and clean decks. "She's trim."

His hand on her elbow, she walked across the deck to a hatch cover and sat, his care still making her feel dainty, cared-for, protected. Cherished. "You like ships, sir?"

"Always." He braced his hand on the mast as the lines holding the schooner to the wharf were let go and she moved with the current. "I grew up near Bristol, used to see the ships coming up the Avon when I was young. I would climb the highest tree, and pretend I was in the crow's nest."

She followed his gaze to the top of the mast and shuddered, remembering Brendan's habit of perching so high, and her fear for him. In the end, though, it wasn't a fall that had claimed him. "Have you a family still in England, sir?"

"No." His eyes darkened. "There was only my mother, and she's gone."

"And your sister."

"Who? Oh, yes, her, too. Haven't seen her in so long I'd forgotten."

Rebecca frowned. His life sounded lonely, much like Brendan's. She really didn't want to hear any more. Dangerous, to be close to a man again. Especially this man. "I am curious, sir, why you continue to live here when you still love England."

Something in her tone must have caught him, for the look he gave her was decidedly wary. "I left England long ago. This is my home now."

"And yet you speak fondly of it, sir."

"Perhaps. But it's past." He held his hand out to her and waited. After a moment, she placed her hand in his, as if without her conscious volition. As if he had somehow drawn her to him. "The past is past, Rebecca."

She looked up at him, helpless, her gaze caught by the same force that had drawn at her hand, and felt something inside her give way. Some hard little knot of pain eased, dissolved, leaving her feeling lighter, younger. Hopeful, for the first time in years. She could have let it go long ago, but she hadn't wanted to, she realized dimly. Until this man came along. "Yes," she said, her fingers curling ever so slightly on his. "The past is past."

The fifteen-mile journey downriver passed quickly, the ship moving well with the steady breeze and the brisk current. They passed Washington City and saw the President's House on the banks of the river. Past Alexandria, like Georgetown a thriving port, the views grew rural, of stretches of forest and open, rolling land on either side. Occasionally there was a glimpse of some great plantation house, high on a hill, and of workers toiling in the fields. Rebecca had not been this way since her return home in disgrace nearly a year ago, and now she saw it through new eyes. She had not expected to enjoy this excursion but, unexpectedly, she was.

In late morning they docked at last at Mount Vernon's wharf, and tumbled out onto the property, Amelia surrounded by her friends. "She's well liked," Marcus commented as he and Rebecca followed behind the others, climbing the hilly path between high, wooded banks. "Especially by the young men."

Rebecca smiled. Among the group of young people indulgently watched over by Mrs. Bayard, Amelia stood out, a bright spring jonquil in her yellow frock and matching bonnet. The young men were clustered about her, but in a testimonial to Amelia's character, so were the young ladies. "She is a sweet girl," she agreed. "I feel very proud of her."

"An odd thing to say."

"Why?"

"You talk as if you're her mother, rather than her sister."

"Her care has been my responsibility for many years, sir."

"And always will be," he muttered.

Rebecca stared at him. "I beg your pardon?"

"When is it your turn to live, Rebecca? When will you have a life?"

She averted her head; she'd had a life already, and look to what it had led. "I'm quite happy."

"Are you?" He stopped, and as he was holding onto her elbow, she had no choice but to stop as well. Farther ahead on the path, the others moved on, out of sight beyond a curve. "Look at me."

"Mercy, Mr. Brand—"

"Look at me." He swung her around to face him. "You deserve more, Rebecca. You deserve to have your own life, not to live in someone else's shadow."

"I'm not—"

"When will you stop punishing yourself for the past?"

"What in the world do you mean?"

He gestured with his hand, so like Brendan that for a moment she was assailed by déjà vu. But Brendan's hair had been coal black, not streaked with gray; he had spoken with an Irish lilt. So different, they were, and their similarities only heightened the differences. "The past, Rebecca. We both know what I'm talking about. You're punishing yourself for it, aren't you?"

"No."

"Hiding away, doing your father's bidding, acting old before your time, never letting yourself have a normal life. For God's sake, Rebecca. It's all past."

Had she ever thought this man lacking in emotion? He wasn't, today. His eyes shone with the fervor of his beliefs; his hands gripped her arms. Curiously, it calmed her. "You know nothing of me, sir."

"I know what I've seen."

"I do what I do because I wish it. You see," she went on before he could interrupt, "someone once told me to forgive myself." She paused. "I have."

"Have you?" His gaze was unreadable. "You have no regrets?"

"There are some things I wish I could change. I would have my son back, if I could." She raised her chin, wondering what his reaction was to that; seeing only the same impenetrable gaze. So he knew she had a child. "I regret none of it."

"Then why do you live as you do? You must have other choices—"

"Choices? What choice does a woman alone have, sir? I would have no home. No, sir. I have no choices."

"You do." His grip tightened. "I've offered you one."

Her heart contracted. Tempting, so tempting. She didn't love him; love had died with Brendan. But, oh, she was attracted to him, and he was right. She did want her own home, her own family. If only she hadn't seen him at the British legation. "So we're back to that."

"Yes." His hands gentled, slid down to grasp hers. "I meant what I said, Rebecca. I'm attracted to you."

"Why?" she asked bluntly.

"Because you're strong and brave and beautiful."

"And what do you offer me, sir? Certainly nothing to make me change my mind."

"No?" His gaze was piercing. "I want you, Rebecca, and I suspect that you want me."

She bit her lips. Want. Not need, and certainly not love. She accepted that men found her attractive, but, oh, why couldn't they wish for more of her? "My answer remains no, Mr. Brand," she said, pulling her hands away.

"I won't stop trying," he said behind her.

"My answer will remain the same," she called over her shoulder, and hurried on, along the sun-dappled path, seeing neither the trees arching overhead, nor the wood violets and day lilies in the undergrowth. At last she reached the top of the hill, and the group of people who waited there.

Amelia eyed Rebecca curiously as she joined them. "Is something wrong?" she asked.

"Nothing." Rebecca strove to keep her voice normal, in spite of the past emotional moments and the exertion of climbing the hill. "Mr. Brand and I were remarking on the view."

Amelia's gaze flicked past her to Marcus, just coming into view and looking remarkably unruffled, the wretch. "Do you mean"—Amelia's voice lowered—"he didn't try to kiss you?"

"Amelia!" Rebecca exclaimed, and several of the others turned to look, smiling a little.

"Well, he should. He's being remarkably behind-hand."

"Amelia, we hardly know each other," she hissed.

"And he's been pursuing you since we met." Her eyes crinkled. "What would Papa think, do you imagine, if you made a match of it with Mr. Brand, and I with Mr. Collins?"

"Mercy! He'd have an apoplexy." Rebecca frowned, alerted by something in Amelia's voice. Mr. Collins would be a good match for Amelia; he was ambitious and of good family, and in his presence Amelia seemed steadier. But then, she had changed from the girl who had once wanted to marry an English lord she didn't know. "Amelia, are you and Mr. Collins—"

"Papa said an odd thing today," Amelia interrupted, the mischief gone from her eyes. "He asked me if I would like to live in the President's House."

"He was jesting, Amelia."

"No. He was serious. And his eyes looked strange, Becky. I cannot describe it, but—they scared me."

A chill ran down Rebecca's spine, in spite of the warmth of the day. She had no chance to say anything, however, for Marcus joined them at that moment. "Ladies? I believe they're organizing the tour."

"Oh. Yes." Rebecca looked once more at Amelia and then turned away, a determined smile on her face. She would endure this, but after today she would have little to do with Marcus Brand. For the sake of her heart, she had to.

Mount Vernon was no shrine to the late General Washington, but a working farm; the current owner, Judge Bushrod Washington, a justice on the Supreme Court, lived in Washington City. Behind the great house there were an icehouse, a spinning house, stables, and paddocks; a flower garden and a kitchen garden, and even a bowling green, making the plantation a town within itself. Because the Bayards were acquainted with Judge Washington, the group toured the house itself, though little remained of the general's possessions. His globe of the world was still there, and the key to the Bastille, given him by Lafayette. The furnishings, however, were a hodgepodge mixture chosen for function and comfort, and in the general's study were empty shelves, his carefully chosen library having been bought by, of all places, the Boston Atheneum. Finally the party left the house and came to the family tomb overlooking the Potomac. They stood in respectful silence for a moment and then turned away, their chatter all the more hectic because of the silence.

Martha and the other servants had set out the food under a grove of trees, and here they settled for their picnic. Below them opened a sweeping vista of the hill down to the river, sparkling in the sun, and the rolling countryside beyond. Rebecca deliberately chose to sit with Mrs. Bayard; she was nonetheless surprised when Marcus joined the younger people, sitting next to Miss Fairfax, after Amelia the loveliest girl there. As she ate the repast of cold ham and chicken, followed by fresh fruit and a trifle and washed down with lemonade (discreetly strengthened for the men), Rebecca watched him, though she hadn't meant to. She watched as Miss Fairfax, wary at first, soon began to smile and then to flirt. Her lips tightened as Marcus showed every sign of flirting back, and her heart contracted when he leaned over to say something to Miss Fairfax that had her simpering and smiling. Determinedly she looked away and started a conversation with Mrs. Bayard. Marcus was not important to her. She would not let his behavior bother her.

Luncheon was over, and the party was sitting, somnolent, under the trees. Gilbert Collins had taken out a knife and was carving away at a chip of wood. "That's a fine-looking blade," Marcus said, and the sound of his voice made Rebecca look up.

Gilbert looked pleased at the compliment, but didn't relinquish the knife for inspection. "It was my father's. He gave it to me sometime back."

"Tell him why," Mr. Parke suggested, and there were some sniggers. "Remember? You took it to play mumbledypeg when he said you couldn't," he said, referring to the game of knife throwing.

"So did you. How old were we? Ten? Twelve?

"Yes, but I didn't catch my aunt in the—in a delicate portion of her anatomy."

"She shouldn't have been in the garden!" Gilbert said hotly, while the men hooted with laughter and the ladies, pretending embarrassment, looked down and bit back smiles.

"Wasn't she hurt?" Marcus asked.

"With all the petticoats she wore? No. But I was," Gilbert said ruefully, his hand going to his backside before he remembered himself. "After my father learned about it I couldn't sit down for a week."

"I like your Aunt Lucy," Mr. Parke said. "But sometimes she does need taking down a peg or two."

Everyone groaned at the pun, and clicking his knife closed, Gilbert tossed it in the air. "How long has it been since you played?" he asked, looking at Parke.

"Are you challenging me?" Parke answered.

"Yes."

"I'm said to be rather good with a knife myself," Marcus said, rising to his feet. "Shall we make it a competition?"

"Oh, dear, here they go," Mrs. Bayard groaned as her husband joined the group. "Sometimes men are such little boys. Which one has the longer knife. Or sword."

Startled, Rebecca looked at her, and then decided that she'd imagined the double meaning. How well did Marcus use his blade—*stop it,* she commanded herself, feeling the color rise in her cheeks.

The men gathered in an informal group, coats off, cravats loosened. Rebecca looked up to see muscles rippling across Marcus's taut shoulders, and warmth started low in her belly. Always he was dressed so proper, and now she had seen him in only his shirt twice: here, and when she had gone to Mrs. Sally's to warn him. Just the thought of how he had looked then, with his shirt open at the throat, was enough to make the heat within her intensify. But then, she thought, trying desperately to regain some control of herself, she had never denied that he was a fine-looking man.

The rules had quickly been decided. Each man would throw his knife, with those throwing the longest going on to compete against each other. "Best two out of three, gentlemen?" Marcus said, and took out his knife, flicking out the blade. Rebecca gazed at it absently, and then suddenly straightened, Mother of pearl handle; distinctive silver scrollwork on the hilt and along the tip of the handle. She had seen the very same knife flash in a sunny Caribbean lane; seen it clamped between the teeth of a ruthless pirate come to take captives. *Brendan's knife.* It couldn't be, but it was.

"Dear? Are you all right?" Mrs. Bayard asked.

"What? Oh, yes, fine."

"You look a trifle pale."

"It is probably the heat. Pray don't worry. I am fine." Brendan's knife. How could it be, unless his personal effects had been sold—but the *Raven* had gone down with all hands. Her heart thudded sickly. Brendan's knife, in the hands of a man who looked so like him it made her heart ache. Dear heavens. No one had ever found Brendan's body. Common enough at sea, but what if—no, it was impossible. But . . .

Her thoughts were jumbled as she watched the competition, sharpening only when it was Marcus's turn. He threw it with the cool competence she'd expected of him, and yet also with controlled savagery, joy in the game, and determination to win. And win he did, his knife going the farthest in the preliminary round, and in the following games. It flew cleanly, gracefully through the air, falling precisely, tip into the soft grass, each and every time. At competition's end he was proclaimed the winner, with promises of future matches to come.

The men returned to the ladies, perspiring, grumbling as they struggled into their coats, but looking far more relaxed and cheerful. The ladies clustered about them, talking, with most of the attention reserved for Marcus. Rebecca stood aside, watching as he shrugged into his coat, straightened his cravat, smoothed down his hair. He was the picture of cool, controlled elegance again, and if she hadn't seen it she would never have guessed at the keenly honed danger within him.

His gaze caught hers. "Well, Rebecca?" he said, walking over to her. "Don't you have something to say? Some comment or criticism?"

"No."

"No?" He grinned. "Dare I hope you actually approve of something I did?"

"Yes." She paused, watching him. "You throw very well, Brendan."

"Thank you," he said absently, and then his head snapped up. His gaze caught hers, and in his eyes she saw a terrible knowledge. Dear heaven. She was right. Why she hadn't seen it before she didn't know, but Marcus Brand was, indeed, Brendan Fitzpatrick, the Raven.

Chapter 21

~

"Excuse me," Marcus said politely. "What did you call me?"

"You heard me." This couldn't be happening. It couldn't be, not when she had just decided to face her future at last. Yet here was her past, undeniably real and solid.

"Yes." His voice was clipped. "You made a mistake, Rebecca. No man likes being called by another's name."

" 'Twas no mistake." She faced him squarely in spite of the feeling that this was a bizarre dream. "Brendan." She hadn't really believed it, she thought, heart pounding, hadn't really expected he'd answer to the name. But he had. He was—"Brendan."

"Ah, lass," he said, dropping the clipped accent along with his studied pose of coolness. "I can explain—"

It was too much. She turned and ran, blindly, not caring where she was going. She knew only that she had to escape, from the pain, from the knowledge that it had all been a lie.

"The devil take it," Marcus swore.

"Rebecca?" Amelia called at the same time, staring after her sister, blundering down the hill. "Where is she going?"

"She must be unwell." Marcus's mouth was a thin, grim slash. "I'll go to her."

"I'll come—"

"No." His voice cut across hers. "I'll go alone."

"Well, if you think that's best," she said, puzzled. "But please do bring her back."

Marcus nodded and set off at an easy lope. Keep it slow, careful; show none of his panic. Devil take it, he'd known he would someday have to tell her the truth, but not like this. Not when she was unprepared and vulnerable. She'd been hurt badly in her life, and most of it had been by him.

He caught up with her at the river's edge, her shoulders heaving. "Rebecca," he said, reaching out a hand to place it on her shoulder, and she spun away from him.

"Don't you touch me!" she hissed, and in her eyes he saw pure agony. "Don't you come near me, you, you—liar!"

"Rebecca, if you'll let me explain—"

"It was all lies, wasn't it?" Her voice was high and tight. "That eyepatch you wore and wouldn't let me see under—all lies, all of it, on the *Raven,* and here—"

"No, *leannan,* it wasn't—"

"Don't call me that! Don't ever call me that again. God." She turned her back to him, arms wrapped about herself, head back, as if searching the sky for answers. "God."

"I'm sorry," he said helplessly. He had an explanation composed for such a contingency, but the words would be flat, stale. For the truth was, he had lied to her. He still was. "If I could undo it, Rebecca, I would, but—"

"All of it?" she demanded, looking at him.

"No. Not all of it." He paused. "I asked you to stay with me, Rebecca."

"Yes. As a pirate's woman. Or so I believed," she said bitterly. "What is your name? I don't even know that."

"It is Marcus Brand."

"Then Brendan Fitzpatrick never really existed."

"Oh, he was real enough. I—"

"I mourned you!" She spun around again, hands on hips, and he caught the glitter of unshed tears in her eyes. "When everyone else rejoiced that the Raven was dead, when everyone told me I must be relieved—relieved!—I mourned you. This past year has been hell."

"I'm sorry," he said again. "Sorry for the scandal you had to face."

"I don't give that for scandal." She snapped her fingers. "But you—knowing you—Brendan wasn't in the world anymore—I loved you!" she cried, and now the tears streamed down her cheeks. "And all the time, I loved someone who never existed."

"I'm real, Rebecca," he said urgently. "I'm right here."

"But who are you? Marcus, or Brendan?"

"Both," he said after a moment. He'd never thought about it before. "Rebecca, you must believe me. I never meant to hurt you."

"Where have you been this year past?"

That was a hard one. "In Baltimore."

"Baltimore." She stared at him. "You were safe in Baltimore, when all the time I imagined you in a watery grave, with the fish all around, and—"

"Ah, lass, don't—"

"Baltimore!" She spat it out. "Couldn't you even let me know you were all right?"

"I wanted to. I came to Georgetown again and again, just to catch a glimpse of you, to make sure you were all right—"

"Why?" she demanded. "Just tell me why you did it."

"I can't."

"Can't, or won't?"

"Can't." He stared at her. "It's not my secret to tell."

"Oh, yes." She gave a bitter laugh. "Oh, yes, I understand. 'Tis because you're a spy. Oh, don't worry," she went on as his head jerked up. "I haven't told anyone. Yet."

"Who told you that?" he said, his voice dangerously quiet.

"No one. I saw it for myself. At the British legation. Offering your services to Mr. St. John."

"Oh. That." Relief made him light-headed. "I can explain that."

"The way you can explain everything else? I don't think so."

"Rebecca." His voice was low and urgent. "This isn't the place, but I can explain it all to you, if you'll give me a chance—"

"Here you are," a voice called behind them. Startled, they turned to see Mr. Bayard approaching, puffing with exertion. "Mrs. Bayard sent me to find you. Are you all right, Rebecca?"

"Miss Talbot is feeling unwell," Marcus said before Rebecca could answer.

" 'Twas the knives," she said flatly. "They reminded me of the Raven."

"Ah. No wonder you were upset." Mr. Bayard patted her shoulders in an avuncular manner. "You've had a hard time of it, no mistaking that, but it's over. The scoundrel's dead."

Rebecca stared at Marcus. "Yes."

"Come. It's getting late. Mrs. Bayard thinks we should head home."

"Of course." Rebecca turned, ignoring Marcus. "Shall we return to the others?"

Mr. Bayard grimaced. " 'Tis a long walk up that hill. No, better if we go directly to the wharf. Come, my dear, lean on me. We'll see you safely home. Are you coming, sir?" he called over his shoulder.

Marcus started. "Yes, in a moment."

"Well, don't take too long. It takes a while to get back up-river, with the current against us."

"I'll be along directly." Marcus watched helplessly as Rebecca walked away, wanting to run after her; knowing it would do no good. She wanted nothing to do with him, and he couldn't blame her. Her accusations were true. He had lied. But the devil take it! He stared at the broad reach of the river, hands balled into fists. He'd never meant her to be hurt. If things had gone right—but they hadn't, and there was naught he could do about it now. The damage was done. He doubted it would ever be repaired.

Marcus slammed the door of George Abbott's study behind him, cutting off Abbott's butler and glaring at the old man. "I have to tell Rebecca the truth."

"Do you, now." Abbott methodically removed his wire-rimmed spectacles and laid down his pen on the desk, as if such an intrusion were a usual occurrence of an evening. "It's all right, Peter." This to his butler, wearing full livery, who was looking in at the door, his dark face concerned. "I don't mind seeing Mr. Brand. Close the door. Now." He looked up at Marcus, his hands folded on the papers strewn across his desk. "What's all this?"

Marcus paced away from the desk. "She found out."

That made Abbott straighten. "How?"

Marcus grimaced. "A mistake on my part. She recognized my knife." Tersely he told Abbott what had happened, and Rebecca's reaction. "I have to tell her the truth," he said when he finished.

"Hm." Abbott leaned back in his chair, tapping his folded spectacles against his lips. "Things could be worse. She thinks you're spying for the British."

"Worse." Marcus stared at him. "I've made her life a living hell. If I'd only gone to her last year—"

"You would have been captured and hung," Abbott said succinctly. "You know that we put it about that the Raven was dead to protect you."

"Not just me."

"You also know I wanted you to stay in Baltimore."

"Devil take it, I couldn't take anymore!" Marcus burst

out. Did Abbott have a heart? Did he have blood pumping in his veins, or ice water? Only the cause mattered to him, not people. "I couldn't stay away from her any longer."

"You hardly tried," Abbott said dryly. "All those times you came to Georgetown, against my express orders—"

"The devil take your orders." Marcus's fists bunched. If the year past had been hell for Rebecca, it hadn't been easy for him, either, knowing she was so close, and wanting her, wanting her. Knowing at the same time that to go to her was to court his own death, and to put other United States agents into difficulties. He had taken up the threads of the life he led as Marcus Brand, successful shipowner and eminently respectable merchant, but it was an empty life, hollow. Nor had he been with another woman, something that startled him when he thought about it, but which seemed right, proper. There was only one woman he wanted. Rebecca.

"I'm no fool." His voice was low. "I've no desire to hang. But no one recognized me."

"Except the Talbot girl," Abbott said dryly.

"She won't say anything," Marcus said with a confidence that startled him. After her outburst today, there was no telling what she would do, and yet he couldn't believe that the woman he'd known aboard the *Raven* would betray him.

Abbott drummed his fingers on the desk. "And if she did, it will only reveal you as a British spy. Which you are not. It may be as well to remove you, now."

"No." He was through letting Abbott run his life. "Not with things as they are. Besides, the British trust me. I have them believing we're building a fleet of warships."

Abbott shook his head. "They'll find out soon enough that's a ruse. No, my boy. You've been useful, but it's time for you to go."

"No." Marcus stood his ground. "Not this time."

Abbott leaned back, sighing. "We've been over this. If it's revealed we've placed spies in the legation—"

"War is inevitable. You know that as well as I. I heard today the President is drafting his request to Congress to declare war."

Abbott sighed again and put his spectacles on, looping them over his ears. "I see I can't persuade you. Very well. But I can't protect you, either." He looked up, and his eyes behind his spectacles were sharp and shrewd and cold. "Spying is one thing. Piracy is another. If you're caught, there's nothing I can do for you."

"If I'm caught, I'll take care of myself," Marcus said grimly, reaching for his hat. "Servant, Abbott." He nodded at the other man and left the room.

He was on his own now, he thought as he strode along the street. On his own, and unprotected. He was not going to turn tail and run, however, not this time; he was not going to cower in Baltimore, despising himself for a coward. He had work yet to do, false information to feed to the British; gleaning anything he could from them in return. In addition, he wanted to keep an eye on Ezra, with his mad scheme for revolution. All those paled in importance, however, against his feelings for Rebecca. She mattered most. She was why he must stay, danger to him or not. He was not going to leave her again.

He stopped, looking from his vantage point on the hill across the Potomac, past Mason's Island and into Virginia. He had found her again, and he wasn't going to let her go. If she allowed it. Because, after today, he doubted she'd ever speak to him again.

Rebecca stood back and surveyed the dining table, making sure all was in place: her mother's china; the good silver; flowers in a crystal bowl as a centerpiece. Fresh wax candles had been placed in the many-armed brass chandelier above the table, and in the silver holders on the sideboard. There was to be a guest for supper, Father had told her, and she was to make certain everything was right. Where his own comforts were concerned, Ezra didn't stint. Thus she had planned her menu carefully, choosing a fine Virginia ham, as well as a good roast beef, oyster pie, fresh vegetables, hot Sally Lunn bread, and a pudding for the sweet. Father would select the wines, including a robust port for after dinner, when he and his guest would smoke their cigars and talk. All was ready, now, awaiting only the guest's arrival.

"Becky?" Amelia peeked into the dining room. "Oh, how pretty everything looks! But you're surely not wearing that gown, are you?"

"Yes, why not?" she asked absently, listing in her mind what remained to be done.

"Don't you want to look your best for Mr. Brand?"

"Mr. Brand!" Rebecca gripped the back of a chair so hard her knuckles were white. "He's not our guest, is he?"

"Yes, silly." Amelia looked at her curiously. "Did you not know?"

"No." Rebecca glanced wildly around, seeking escape, fighting the urge to sweep everything off the table, china and cutlery and all, and then run from the house. From him. She didn't want to see Marcus again, didn't want to be reminded that all she'd thought was real and true and good in her life had been a sham. He had indeed turned out to be the pirate she'd first thought him.

Amelia eyed her curiously. "What happened between you and him at Mount Vernon?"

"Nothing."

"Don't gammon me. I know something did, you were so pale and he was so quiet." She paused. "Did he try to make love to you?"

"Good God, no!"

"There's no need to swear."

"Amelia, there is not now, and never will be, anything between me and that—that man. And I won't let you marry him."

"Oh, I've no plans to," Amelia said cheerfully. "He's much too old for me. And, to tell you the truth, he reminds me too much of the Raven. I don't think I could live with that. Oh, Becky. Is that the problem?"

"What?"

"You loved him, didn't you?"

"Who? Marcus?"

"No, silly. The Raven."

Rebecca closed her eyes as the pain assailed her again, and turned away. "I thought I did," she said in a low voice. "Now I don't know what to believe."

Amelia frowned. "I'm not sure I understand, but it's all past, Becky. Surely it's time you stopped being so sad."

"Sad!" Rebecca whirled around. "I am not sad. I am angry, and I thank God for it." Anger was cleaner, less draining, than sadness. Being angry was, in a way, oddly healing; it had broken her out of her long mourning at last. Mourning not just for Brendan, but for what she had lost.

Amelia wrinkled her nose. "If you say so. Now, please, do at least put on your gray sarcenet. There's time—oh." From the hallway came the sound of the door knocker falling. "Do you suppose that's him?"

"Most likely." Rebecca straightened, calm now that the moment of confrontation had come. She continued calm as she heard Marcus's voice in the hall. "Come. We should greet him."

"You're very pale, Becky. You aren't sickening for something, are you?"

"No. Quite honestly, Amelia, I feel better than I have in a year." How she would face Marcus, or what the future would hold, she didn't know, but at least she knew she had the strength to deal with both.

"Ah, there you are," Ezra said, the expansive, genial host as Amelia and Rebecca walked into the parlor. "Amelia, you are in looks tonight."

"Thank you, Papa. Mr. Brand." She smiled at him, but without any of her usual dimpling.

"Miss Amelia. Miss Talbot." Marcus bowed to them, and Rebecca's feeling of unreality deepened. He was attired properly and stylishly in burgundy coat and fawn-colored trousers. Part of her wished that she had, indeed, changed her frock; the rest of her wondered at the transformation in him. Brendan would never have dressed so, or been so stiff. And when had his hair gone so gray? He acted his part well, did Marcus Brand. Or had he been acting as the Raven? It was enough to give her the headache.

"Rebecca." Ezra's voice was sharp. "Answer when you are spoken to, girl."

"I am sorry," she said, belatedly realizing that Marcus had said something. "I fear I wasn't attending. You were saying?"

"Merely inquiring as to your health, ma'am. Are you recovered from the other day?"

She looked him straight in the eye. "Not as much as I would like."

"I am sorry for it."

"What is this?" Ezra demanded. "Are you ill, girl?"

"Something Miss Talbot ate disagreed with her," Marcus put in before she could answer, and she glared at him. She was quite capable of taking care of herself.

"Ah. So that is what happened." Ezra sat back, looking satisfied. "I knew there was something."

"Papa, Mr. Brand was quite kind to Rebecca," Amelia put in. "When she took ill."

"Yes, he was quite honorable," Rebecca said and had the satisfaction of seeing Marcus flinch.

"Was he, now." Ezra's satisfied air had been replaced by a speculative look. "I believe—yes, what is it?" This as Jacob, their manservant, appeared in the doorway.

"Dinner, sir," Jacob said.

"Good." Ezra grunted as he rose to his feet. "Well, no matter, no matter. Rebecca is well now, sir."

"I am glad of it," Marcus said gravely, standing back to let Rebecca precede him from the parlor. She felt his gaze on her almost as a caress as she followed Ezra to the dining room. It made her want to squirm.

At supper she sat between Marcus and her father, with Amelia facing her. She kept her head down throughout the meal, looking at neither man, until something her father said at the end of the meal caught her attention. "You say you are returning to Baltimore, sir?"

Rebecca's head jerked up. He was leaving. She should be glad. "Are you?" she asked before she could stop herself.

"I may have to." Marcus reached for an orange from the silver bowl Jacob had placed on the table and began peeling it with his thumbnail. Without intending to, Rebecca focused on his hands. Brendan's hands, she thought, and forced her gaze away. "My chances of obtaining a license to trade are slight. I've ships I need to oversee, and crews to hire, in case—"

"In case of what, sir?" Amelia asked.

"In case of war. But we needn't talk of that."

"My girls are aware of what is happening," Ezra put in. "Been thinking about this myself. What do you plan to do, should war break out?"

"Arm them, of course, and if necessary offer their services."

"Exactly what I thought." Ezra nodded. "To the navy, though they've enough ships."

"I thought we had few ships," Rebecca said.

"Use your head, girl. Not the American Navy."

Rebecca gasped as the implications of his words struck her. "Father! You'd offer them to the British? And"—she swung to face Marcus—"you, too?"

He shrugged in reply. "Can't afford to have them standing idle. If they can bring in some profit—"

"Profit!" She lunged up from her chair, knowing she was behaving badly, and not caring. Brendan had been a man of no country, and an enemy to the British. Now, when the Americans needed every resource, he was turning traitor. "It's treason."

"Do you dare to question me, girl?" Ezra growled, standing also.

"Yes." She faced him steadily. "It's wrong, Father, you know it is."

"Wrong?" he thundered. "You dare to speak to me of what is wrong, when you chase after every man you meet?"

"Papa," Amelia gasped.

"That's a lie!" Rebecca cried, goaded beyond endurance. "I never did—"

"I am not a liar!" Ezra roared, and his hand came crashing down.

Rebecca ducked, hands flung over her head to ward off the blow. It didn't come. After a moment she looked up. Marcus's hand held Ezra's arm suspended, and the two men were glaring at each other. "Easy there, sir," Marcus said, his voice soft, yet edged with steel. "Not done, you know, in front of guests."

"Let—me—go." Ezra twisted away, his look murderous, and then abruptly dropped into his chair, his face stunned.

"Papa?" Amelia leaned over. "Are you well?"

"What? Oh, yes, yes." He straightened, and though the stunned look had left his face, there was something still in his eyes. "I apologize for my daughter, sir. Sometimes she goads me beyond endurance."

"Excuse me," Rebecca murmured, more goaded than anyone could ever know, holding back the tears that threatened. "I'll just clear the table for the sweet."

"I can't stay, I fear." Marcus, too, rose, and though she could feel his gaze on her, she didn't look up. "I've another appointment. Sir?" He looked toward Ezra. "I understand there was something you wished to discuss with me?"

"Hm? Oh." Ezra looked up and got up from the table. "It will keep. But now I have some thinking to do." He rambled out of the room. "A deal of thinking."

Rebecca stared after him worriedly. "Melia, go after him, make sure he's all right. I'll just see Mr. Brand to the door." She turned back to him. "I am sorry about this, sir."

He gazed at her intently from across the table. "It wasn't your fault. Rebecca—"

"Oh, but it was, sir." She gave a short, bitter laugh. "I seem to goad him more and more often, but this I couldn't let pass."

"This happens often?" Marcus interrupted.

"Not so very, no. It's just—" She frowned. "His temper is so unpredictable lately. I never know what will set it off."

"Rebecca." He leaned forward, hands braced on the table. "You know he's unstable, don't you?"

"No! Don't say that. He's a little upset—"

"Unstable. Perhaps even mad. That scheme he proposed the other evening, to lead a revolution, was pure madness. I am surprised he hasn't been arrested."

Rebecca felt her face pale. "Do you think—"

"No. But I worry about you, in this house with him."

"You needn't, sir." She straightened and turned, leading him into the hall. "I was doing quite well before you came along."

"I know that." He reached for his hat, on the hall table. "It seems I've done nothing but complicate your life, doesn't it?"

"I—yes."

"I am sorry for it. You may not believe it, but I am. But, Rebecca"—he turned to her—"everything's changing. If war's declared things could get bad here. I could keep you safe—"

"As a traitor with the British? No, thank you."

"I'm not," he began and then stopped. "Perhaps you are right."

"Perhaps I am." She opened the door. "All I know is that my life would be much better without you in it."

He paused in the doorway. "Easier, yes, Rebecca, that I can believe. But better? No. I doubt it."

"Better," she said firmly. "You've brought me nothing but sorrow and pain."

"Nothing?" His voice was soft. "Have you forgotten, *leannan*, those nights at sea?"

"Yes."

"I haven't." He took up his walking stick. "And I mean to make you remember them again. Good night, Rebecca," he said and went out.

"You mean to—" she exclaimed, but he was gone, striding along the sidewalk with a graceful, pantherish gait she recognized. Just so had she seen the Raven walk, and it deepened her confusion. Who was the real Marcus Brand: the pirate, or the traitor?

Sighing, she closed the door. She hadn't time for this. She had a house to see to and her father to settle. Not just yet, though. She cast a quick look at the closed door of the study. Let him cool down first. She headed for the dining room to help Martha with the cleaning up.

And, in his study, Ezra Talbot sat alone, brooding over the revelation he had tonight received.

Chapter 22

~

"Another note for you, Mr. Brand," Mrs. Sally said later that evening when Marcus had opened his door to her knock. "Brought by that rude Englishman again."

"Thank you, ma'am," he said, taking the note and closing the door all in one smooth motion. Abbott's choice of messenger was inspired: it added credibility to the story they were slowly creating about him, that he was sympathetic enough to the British cause to turn traitor. Too much so, he mused ruefully, breaking the wax seal on the note with his penknife. The last thing he had expected, he thought, setting the note down unread, was that Rebecca would believe him to be a spy.

He paced to his window and looked out into the soft spring twilight. Below him he could just see the river, with the lights of ships winking on it. It was a mess, this situation with Rebecca. Devil take it, he'd missed her. He hadn't expected to, but he had. He missed her rare, sweet smile, her tart comments, her quick intelligence. He missed the way he felt when he was with her, alive and exhilarated. Most of all, he missed her in his bed.

The thought brought a sharp pang of yearning, and, grimacing, he turned away from the window. In some ways he was no better than her past lover, or Lieutenant Dee; he wanted her as badly. But if simple desire were all he felt, he could slake it easily enough. There were always willing women available. He wanted more. He wanted to be with her, live with her, have children with her. He wanted, God help him, to marry her.

Stunned, he sank down onto the edge of his bed. Marriage? Good God. Always he had been free to do as he wished, to roam the sea when he wanted, to go where he would. Never had he seriously contemplated marriage. Now, though, he wanted Rebecca with him, beside him, forever. That meant marriage. The irony was, she wanted nothing to do with him.

His eyes lighted on the note, discarded on his bed table, and lips tightening, he reached for it. A few moments later he looked up, eyebrows raised. Then, deliberately, he thrust the note into the candle's flame. When it was well alight he dropped it into the fireplace, leaning his arm on the mantel and watching it burn. Another task for him, and an important one. Abbott had apparently decided he would be more useful here than in Baltimore, after all. Not that he would have gone. He was through taking orders from Abbott where Rebecca was concerned. She was his heart, his life, his soul. Shrugging into his coat again, preparatory for an evening visit to Abbott to garner more information, he made his decision. Somehow, some way, he would make Rebecca his.

Lights glowed from every window at the British legation on K Street. A different soldier was on sentry duty this evening, allowing Marcus in with little trouble. Inside, everything glittered. As if nothing untoward had occurred, as if events were not leading inexorably toward war, Sir Augustus, the minister, was holding a reception.

Inside the house, a fine staircase rose to his left; to this side as well were offices, Sir Augustus's at the front. Halfway down the hall was the butler's pantry where he had offered his services to St. John. To the right were the reception rooms, crowded tonight with those of Washington society who disapproved of the President and his policies; members of the Federalist party, as well as known British sympathizers. For one bad moment Marcus thought he saw Ezra Talbot, but then the man in question turned. Someone else. The Talbots, thank God, weren't here tonight.

Hillary St. John looked at Marcus in surprise as he entered the drawing room, preparatory to paying his respects to Sir Augustus. "I didn't expect to see you here tonight," St. John said, crossing the room to him.

"Indeed? But I was invited, was I not?"

"Yes. We'd word you were returning to Baltimore."

"Not quite yet." He glanced toward the British minister, talking affably with a group of men. "I thought I'd try one last time for a license to trade."

St. John pursed his lips. "Doubtful. The talk is that your president will ask for a declaration of war at any time."

"I am not political," Marcus said absently, his gaze sweeping about the drawing room and the room beyond, where refreshments awaited. Hoping for a glimpse of Rebecca; hoping she wasn't here. "What the President does doesn't concern me."

"But won't it affect your business?"

Marcus shrugged and flicked a piece of lint off the sleeve of his coat of black superfine. "I am prepared to move my shipping to Canada, if I must."

"Are you." St. John eyed him speculatively. "Well, I will speak to Sir Augustus for you once more, but don't expect much. He's other things on his mind these days."

"Thank you." He inclined his head to St. John as he turned away, well satisfied with the evening so far. He had established his ostensible reason for being here, and strengthened his credibility with the British. It was a good start.

After greeting Sir Augustus, Marcus wandered into the other room in search of refreshment, pausing here and there to speak with people he knew. Leisurely he procured a glass of punch for himself; just as leisurely he made his way back across the room, until at last he stood in the relative coolness of the hall. It was peaceful here, with few people about, and none paying any mind to him. Marcus set his cup down on a table and glanced into the butler's pantry. Empty. His muscles tensed. It was now, or never.

Quietly and quickly he slipped into the pantry and across it, to the stairs. Not as grand as the main staircase in front, but far more suited to his purpose, quiet and private. He paused for a moment at the bottom, waiting, listening, but no sound filtered down from upstairs. Taking care to stay close to the wall, lest a board creak, he began his ascent.

Once upstairs, he stopped a moment to let his eyes become accustomed to the darkness, and to get his bearings. Here were the minister's private quarters, and more offices. Fortunately no one was about. It was the perfect opportunity for him to do a little snooping.

Third door from the stairs, to the left. Marcus counted,

turned, and found the door. The door handle was stiff under his fingers, and he exerted pressure, turning it with a click that sounded like a pistol shot. He tensed, but no one appeared to have heard; no one came to investigate. Still, his shoulder muscles remained rigid as he stepped into the room and closed the door, the latch clicking loudly again. The thing needed a good oiling. There was, thank God, a key in the lock. It turned easily, giving him a sense of safety. If he should be discovered, he would have at least a chance of escape.

No telling where the papers he sought would be. Though moonlight streamed into the room, he struck flint to tinder and lit a candle. Its feeble light shone over a tidy desk, its surface bare, except for inkstand, pens, sander, and blotter. Against the wall were bookcases, and next to the desk was a green leather chair. Marcus sat in its companion behind the desk, trying the various drawers and finding them, to his relief, unlocked. Security needed to be tightened here. But then, who would expect someone to come snooping when the house was filled with people?

"You'll know what you're looking for when you see it," Abbott had told him last night, his face creased with worry. Unusual for him, bringing the gravity of this situation home to Marcus. He had never questioned how Abbott knew about such things, about important papers or, in the past, secret agents traveling to England, who needed to be stopped. As the Raven, he had done so more than once. He suspected, though, that Abbott had installed someone in the legation. Someone who had seen papers of great importance in this very room, but who had not been able to see the details. Someone so thoroughly English that no one suspected his sympathies secretly lay with the Americans. Marcus saluted his courage, whoever he was.

A quick search of the top desk drawers yielded little. In the bottom ones he found more: a proposal for a possible blockade of the American coast, should war break out; an estimation of troop strength in Canada. Important, surely, but not vital, Marcus thought, scowling with frustration as he closed the desk drawer. Much of this information was already known. No, it had to be something different. Something new.

He found it before he quite realized it, tucked in the back of the very bottom drawer, just when he was about ready to

give up. At first he saw no significance in the sheets of
foolscap, folded together, or the top page, with its crudely
drawn map of a winding river, until suddenly he recognized
it. The Potomac, as it narrowed near Washington City and
Georgetown. And those x's here and there—good God. The
President's House. The Capitol building. The Navy Yard. It
looked like—his breath sucked in as he lifted the map and
read the words on the paper beneath. "Plans for an Invasion
of Washington City, District of Columbia."

Good God. He read quickly now, relying on his well-trained
memory to absorb the details. The Royal Navy to come up the
Potomac in force. Fort Washington on the river to be sabo-
taged beforehand, by means unmentioned. Troops to be
landed, and how many. Casualties expected, should the Americans fight back, as it was expected they would. And the ob-
jectives, the places marked with x's on the map. Mr. and Mrs.
Madison to be taken prisoner, along with the Speaker of the
House Henry Clay and members of the Cabinet. The President's House to become British headquarters for the war, and
afterward. For the goal of the plan was more far-ranging than
winning a war. Whoever had authored it intended that the
Unites States would once again be Britain's colony.

Good God, he thought again, and at that moment, heard
voices. Coming from outside? No. From the corridor, faint,
but clear. He snuffed the candle and sprang up from the
desk, standing in readiness near the window. "I tell you, sir,
I saw candlelight in the window," a voice said. Dee's voice.

"Most likely Reed, doing something Sir Augustus asked
him to do." St. John, sounding irritated. "I see no light beneath the door, Lieutenant."

"It was there. Damme, it's locked."

"No, that latch always sticks. Let me—it *is* locked."

"I'll look in the keyhole—damme, the key's in the lock."
Banging on the door. "Reed? Are you in there?"

Coolly, Marcus glanced out the window. Ivy twined on the
side of the building. Good. He took off his coat, wrapping it
about his waist, and pushed at the window. And, like the
door latch, it stuck.

For the first time he felt just a bit of panic, and sweat
trickled down between his shoulder blades. No longer caring
if he made any noise, he struck at the window frame, and the
sash at last budged, opening with a squawk. The pounding

on the door increased. They were getting ready to kick it in, he thought dispassionately, climbing out onto the sill. A good thirty feet from here to the ground; nothing to one who had once perched at the top of a ship. Grasping a vine, hoping it would hold, he began to descend, using skills learned long ago at sea. Down and down, more surefooted now, the ground coming nearer, and from a distance he heard a crash as the door in the office above at last let go.

The ground at last. Marcus jumped nimbly down, landing in a crouch, and at that moment a shout came from above. "There he is!" Involuntarily he looked up, seeing a face in the window, and then, self-preservation taking over, began to run. A cracking noise, and there was a sudden, stinging sensation of heat along his arm. Damn! He'd been shot. Another crack, and he ducked, frantically pulling at his coat. His white shirt made him too clear a target. The black coat, chosen specifically in case he had to make an escape, wrapped around him just as he reached the trees, and he melted into the shadows. He was safe for the moment, but pursuit would come quickly. And here he was, trapped in the British legation grounds, high brick walls between him and freedom, and his arm injured. How the devil was he going to get out of this?

"He's out here." Dee's voice was tense as he led the contingent of soldiers into the mission's garden. "Piper, O'Neill, see if he got over the wall there, and be careful. The rest of you move out. You know what to look for—broken branches, the ground disturbed, and the like. Weapons at the ready! We don't know if he's armed." He turned, surveying the garden. In the light of the moon shadows moved, shifted, from the trees and the bushes near the walls. It was impossible to tell where a man might be hiding. But, wherever the intruder was, Dee was determined to catch him. "Hart, Taylor, come with me, and fix bayonets."

"Yes, Lieutenant," Hart said. "Where?"

"Over here." Crouching, as if expecting an ambush at any moment, Dee loped over to the garden shed. A nod to Hart, and the door was kicked in, both soldiers jumping in, weapons at the ready.

"Empty, Lieutenant," Taylor said, looking out.

Dee grunted. "Over here," he said tersely, and set off again, this time heading for the garden's other structure. Just as they reached it the door began to open. Dee gestured frantically, and all three of them sprang forward, bayonets held high—to face Marcus, coming out of the privy, just buttoning the flap of his trousers.

"What the devil?" he said in evident surprise, pulling back from the bayonets leveled at his face. "Lieutenant? What the devil is this?"

Hart had let his musket waver, and Dee barked a command at him. "Mr. Brand. Have you been in there all this time?"

"That is an unusual question, Lieutenant," Marcus said, his voice cool. "Is there trouble? I thought I heard a shot."

"We had an intruder."

"Indeed?" Marcus straightened his cuffs. "Call your men off, Lieutenant. It's obvious it wasn't me."

"Move your arms, sir."

"I beg your pardon?"

"Move your arms, I say."

"What, do you want me to spring the seams of this coat? I'll tell you, it came dear."

"Move your arms," Dee said between his teeth. He had caught the intruder in the arm, possibly the shoulder, of that he was certain. He didn't care if Brand had reason to be in the garden. He didn't trust the man. "Now."

"Devil take it," Marcus muttered, but he complied, flapping his arms up and down. "Do you expect me to fly like a bird, Lieutenant?"

Dee stepped back. "Lower your weapons." He gave the order reluctantly, glaring at Marcus as he stepped out of the privy. He did not appreciate being made to look like a fool before his men. "Mr. Brand," he began, when at that moment there was a shout from the other side of the garden.

"Lieutenant! Over here. It looks like he went over the wall."

Dee glared at Marcus a moment longer, and then wheeled around, stalking away. Marcus watched for a moment before, straightening his cuffs again, he ambled toward the house. A close thing. Thank God he'd had the foresight to lay a false trail; thank God the privy had been there. The wound in his arm, bound by his handkerchief, throbbed, and he suspected it was bleeding afresh; but the dark material of his coat would not yet show the stain. For the moment, he was safe.

He walked back inside with his usual brisk stride, his face clear, smooth. About him people gathered in groups, whispering together, looking excited. At the bottom of the main staircase stood St. John, along with Sir Augustus, the two of them talking together and looking worried. Brazen it out, he thought as St. John turned away. "What is amiss? I heard there was an intruder."

"Yes. I've things to do, Brand, so if you'll excuse me—" St. John stopped suddenly. "Where were you?"

Marcus sighed. "Your soldiers have already questioned me. I was using the necessary. Surely you don't think I had anything to do with it?"

"No, of course not. My apologies. This has caused an uproar, as you can see." He grimaced. "I have to make sure the rest of the guests are all here."

Marcus arched an eyebrow. "I wondered how an intruder could get past your sentries. Are you saying it might be one of the guests?"

"Lord knows. Excuse me, Mr. Brand. I really do have things to see to."

"Of course." Marcus toyed idly with the cord of his quizzing glass, and then turned to a nearby gentleman, engaging him in conversation. People milled about, clearly intrigued by the evening's events, but after a time he noticed that some were leaving. It was safe for him to go, then, and not before time, either. His arm ached and throbbed abominably, making him perspire enough that more than one person had given him a second look. If Dee were to ask him to lift his arms now, he doubted he could comply.

Out into the warm spring evening again; stopped briefly by a soldier, who let him go. Swinging his walking stick, he walked across President's Square with studied insouciance, until the lights of the legation had been left behind and he had turned onto the stone walkway along Pennsylvania Avenue, the leaves of the poplar trees that lined the avenue rustling above him. Only then did he quicken his pace. He had to have help. If he returned to his lodgings, Mrs. Sally would see his bloodied linen, and he couldn't have that. Once word of that got out, Dee would quickly draw the right conclusion, and that would be that. He would have to leave Washington City, and Rebecca. There was only one person he could turn to, one person he could trust. Gritting his

teeth, knowing he might be walking into greater danger, he
set off for Georgetown.

Something pattered at Rebecca's window. Startled, she
jerked her head up, reflexively shoving the book she was
reading under her pillow. Silly, she chided herself. Father
was asleep, and she'd taken care to shield her candle. He
wouldn't know she was indulging in the forbidden pleasure
of novel reading. But what in the world had that noise been?

It came again, a tap-tapping, followed by an odd sliding
sound. Rain? It had been a clear day, without any of the
heaviness that presaged a storm. Snuffing her candle, she
eased over to the window and looked down, gasping with
surprise. In the dim moonlight she could just make out the
figure of a man, the shape of his shoulders familiar. Marcus.
What on earth?

Not stopping to think, she threw a shawl around her
shoulders and padded quietly out into the hall. In the darkness she made her way down the stairs and hesitated at the
front door. Father slept just above. If she drew the bolt, he
might hear. Instead, she slipped into the parlor, easing open
a window and putting her head out. "Marcus!" she hissed
and saw him turn toward her. "What on earth do you want?"

"I need your help." His voice was low, but it held strain.
"Could you let me in?"

She hesitated. "Around the back," she said and closed the
window, scurrying quietly into the hall and down the stairs
that led to the basement kitchen. When she opened the door
under the rear gallery he was there, a dark, looming shape,
but she felt no fear. Only exasperation and anger she had
nursed for days. And, against her will, a growing excitement.

"Thank you." Marcus dropped into a chair at the broad
trestle table. "I didn't think I'd make it this far."

"Please do keep your voice down. Martha and Jacob sleep
nearby, and I don't want them telling Father you're here."
Rebecca lit a candle. "From where?"

"The British legation."

"But that's above a mile away—mercy!" She stared at
him. He had removed his coat, and in the wavering light she
could see a spreading stain on his sleeve. "Brendan!"

He grimaced. "A little mishap. I tried binding it up with
my handkerchief, but as you can see, it wasn't enough." His

eyes met hers as she bent over to see the cause of the bleeding. "If you call me by that name in front of others, my life won't be worth a farthing."

"I am sorry." Frowning, she studied the jagged tear in the sleeve. "What caused this?"

"Pistol shot."

"Pistol shot!" Her voice rose, and he quickly put a finger to her lips, hushing her. It felt too good there, too right, and so she jerked away. "However did you manage to get yourself shot?"

"Snooping at the British legation."

"Snooping—what on earth?"

"Never mind, Rebecca." His eyes were closed. "If you can just find me something to bind this with, I'll be on my way."

"You'll do no such thing. That wound will need to be cleaned, and you can't do it yourself. Take off your shirt."

"Why, Rebecca." He was grinning at her. "Dare I hope you still care?"

"Do not try any of your foolishness with me," she retorted. "If Father finds you here this wound will be nothing. Now do take off your shirt."

"You're a hard woman." He pulled his right arm from its sleeve, struggled for a moment, and gave up. "I need help, lass," he said apologetically.

"Marcus—"

"I can't manage it, Rebecca."

She took a deep breath. "Oh, very well." After all, hadn't she taken care of Father when he was ill? This should be no different.

Oh, but it was, it was. To help him slip his shirt over his head meant that she had to stand close to him, between his legs. Her breasts, loose in her nightshift, brushed against his chest as she bent to her task, and they both pulled back. His shoulders were so broad, she thought, dazed, easing the shirt down his arm. His chest so hard with muscle, and his body so very, very warm. "I'm afraid it's stuck where the blood's dried," she said, her voice unsteady.

"Pull it off if you have to." His voice was husky, and she looked down to see him watching her with an intent look that was familiar to her. For a moment, all the hurts of the past year, all the anger faded. He wanted her. Uncomfortably warm, she lowered her eyes, only to encounter more evidence of his arousal. Oh, he wanted her, and what was worse, she wanted him. She could feel it in her knees, almost too weak to support her, in her breasts and in her belly, warm and heavy. Thoroughly rattled, she pulled on the shirt harder than she had intended, and he grunted.

"I'm sorry," she murmured. "I fear I started up the bleeding again."

"Rebecca." He caught her hand as she moved away. "We need to talk."

"Not now." She freed herself and went in search of a basin and clean rags. Oh, no, not now. She would patch him up and send him on his way, and she would not—would not!— let herself think about how very much she wanted him.

"I think we do." In the dim light his eyes were dark, unreadable. She avoided his gaze as she set about pumping water into the basin. "You don't trust me."

She bustled over to the table, setting down the basin and the cloths she had found, her shawl slipping from her shoulders. "Do you blame me?"

He sighed. "Nay, lass. If anything, I understand. But I want you to know I never meant to hurt you."

She cast him a brief, cool look, and applied herself to washing the wound. "This will sting."

Marcus's lips tightened, but other than that he gave no sign of discomfort. "I hurt you. I made your life hell this past year, and you're angry. I—"

"Of course I'm angry!" She slammed the rag into the basin, spattering them both with droplets of water. "I mourned you for a year! I thought you dead, and then one day you reappeared. But not the same, oh, no, that would have been too easy." She paced back and forth, the shawl slipping off completely, and he watched, a slight smile on his face. "No, you reappeared as a different man. Different name, different voice, different mannerisms—and just when I begin to believe you are who you say you are, just when I'm beginning to be attracted to you, you turn it all upside down again! And now you sit there and laugh at me!"

"I'm not laughing, lass." He was, though, his face stretched wide in a grin. "I've missed ye, Rebecca. Missed seeing ye like this, standing up to me, no matter what I've said or done. You're like no other woman I've ever known."

She stopped to pick up her shawl, wrapping it around her and staring at him distrustfully. "You deserve a tongue-lashing for all that you've done. But perhaps . . ." She paused. "Perhaps it wouldn't matter so, if I only know why. Is it me?" To her consternation, her voice cracked. "Am I really just the type of woman men use and leave, and now you've decided 'tis time to use me again?"

"No, lass." He was across the room to her in an instant, so close that she turned, her back to him. He put his hand on her shoulder, and she shrugged it away. "You mean a great deal to me, Rebecca. You always have." He paused. "But I wasn't free to be with you as I wished." Again, a pause. "I still am not."

"Oh, God." She turned to face him. "They say you're widowed—are you married?"

"No. There's no other woman for me. And no, I've never married, lass, no matter what story was put about. I told you the truth about that."

Rebecca searched his face, seeing only sincerity there. She wanted, needed, to believe. "What is true for you, Marcus? It seems to change."

He shook his head. "Not the basics. Not what is inside me. As for the rest"—his lips tightened—"both stories held truth. Marcus Brand's more so than the Raven's."

"Tell me." She was begging, but she didn't care. "Tell me the truth, Marcus. I need to know."

"Aye, lass." He touched her cheek with a fingertip, and she moved her head sharply away. "The truth is—"

"Sit down," she commanded. "I might as well bandage your arm while I listen."

"Ah, lass, don't pass judgment on me until you've heard it all."

"I won't. Now, sit." She stood in front of him, wrapping a cloth around his arm, forcing herself to ignore its hard-muscled strength. "You aren't from Ireland."

"No. Bristol, as I've said. My mother's maiden name was Fitzpatrick, and we were poor connections of the earls of Brand. And she did die when I was impressed by the Royal Navy."

Her lips parted in surprise. "But now you work for—"

"You do not know who I work for," he said, laying his finger across her lips again. So long since he'd touched her, since he'd had her in his arms, in his bed. It might never happen again, if he didn't convince her now. Abbott be damned, he thought, watching her as she bent over his arm again. After all she'd been through, Rebecca deserved to know the truth.

"I deserted, along with Tyner," he went on. "That much was true. When I shipped out on American ships, I earned American citizenship, and I did well for myself, lass, earning a master's rating and finally buying my own ship."

She tied the ends of the bandage in a neat knot. "There, that should hold. You'll need to be careful how you use that arm."

"Thank you, lass. Do you not wish to know the ship I bought?"

She had moved away from him and was leaning against the hutch. "I expect you'll tell me, whether I do or not."

He grinned at the tartness in her voice. "Aye, that I will. It was the *Raven,* lass."

"So even then you were planning to turn pirate."

"No." He shook his head, an action he instantly regretted, as hot pain throbbed in his arm. "She was a fine ship, and the coincidence of the name pleased me. I believe I told you once that 'Brand' means 'Raven.' "

"Yes. And Brendan does, as well."

"Yes." He nodded. "My ship was stopped at sea once, by the British. I managed to convince them I was American—I was, by then—but some of my crew wasn't so lucky. The British took them off. God knows what happened to them." He paused. " 'Twas then I decided to turn spy."

Her eyes closed. "Oh, God. I knew it—"

"You know nothing about me if you think I'd spy for the British," his voice grated. "For the Americans. Yes, stare at me, Rebecca, but 'tis true. I am a spy for the Americans."

"But—" Her eyes were huge. "I heard you. I heard you telling Mr. St. John you'd spy for him."

"A ruse, Rebecca. Just as my accent has been a ruse, and the powder to make my hair gray, and the way I dress, so the British would think me a proper gentleman and trust me."

Her brow wrinkled. "Why in the world would you want that?"

"To feed them false information. And, possibly, to get information from them."

Her breath drew in. "Is that what you were doing tonight—"

"Don't ask me that. 'Tis better if you don't know. In fact"—he grimaced—"I shouldn't have told you what I have. But I had to." He held her gaze with his own, and this time thought he saw the faint, first stirrings of trust. "You know why, don't you?"

She shook her head. "I don't know anything anymore. On the *Raven*—were you spying then?"

He shifted in the chair, trying to ease his arm to a more comfortable position. "In a way. Sometimes there'd be documents or people we couldn't allow to reach England. That was when the *Raven* would come out, and only then. The rest of it—all made up, Rebecca, so I would be seen as a fierce pirate. I never went out only to plunder other ships. I regretted anyone who was hurt because of me. I still do." He watched her. "I was never as black as I was painted."

Her lips were pursed in a frown. "So that is why you wore the eyepatch."

Hope rose within him. "As a disguise. Yes. No one ever looked beyond it." He paused. "Except for you, Rebecca. You don't know how I hated wearing it around you."

"Did we have to be stopped from reaching England? Amelia and me?"

"No." He paused, wondering how much to tell her. "Someone else did, and to cover that, I was told to take hostages. You were a pawn, Rebecca," he said gently.

"Oh." She turned, her arms wrapped around herself. "And when you took me to your bed—was I a pawn then, too?"

"No!" He crossed the room quickly, and this time when he grasped her shoulders, she didn't turn away. "No, *leannan*, never that. Never that."

She gazed up at him, eyes huge, and her tongue flicked out to moisten her bottom lip. The action sent shafts of flame through him. "You never did tell me what that means."

"Sweetheart." He gazed down at her lips, full and lush, and, in his memory, so sweet. "Beloved," he said, and, unable to resist any longer, caught her up against his chest in his good arm, and brought his mouth down on hers.

Chapter 23

~

He kissed her as if he were a starving man, and she his first taste of food. He kissed as if he were dying of thirst, sucking at her lips, drawing the essence of life from her and yet sending it surging through her veins. She responded to his quick hunger, insistent, demanding, pressed against him. His arms around her were rock hard, his chest rock solid, and though she had learned the hard way he couldn't be trusted, still she leaned against him, a wall sheltering her from all the storms of the past years. She kissed him with all her pent-up emotions, the hurt and the anger, and yes, even the love that hadn't died. She kissed him and held him with all her heart and body and soul, her arms about his neck, her back bent as he pressed savage, desperate kisses along her throat, the line of her jaw, her mouth again. And she kissed him, at last, with all the passion she had once denied, and the sure knowledge that this was right. This was where she belonged, in his arms. In her pirate's arms.

"Brendan," she gasped when he at last released her lips, giving her a chance to breathe. "Oh, Brendan, I've missed you so—"

"Devil take it," he growled, and in the next moment she was held away from him, his hands gripping her upper arms.

She blinked up at him, coldness already seeping in. "What—"

"My name is Marcus," he said in that same harsh voice. "Not Brendan. Brendan Fitzpatrick never existed."

"But he did." The coldness was gone, replaced by liquid

fire. "He does. Here." She laid her hand over his heart, feeling for the first time in so long the heat of his skin, the crisp curls of hair. "He is part of you—Marcus," she said and was rewarded by being hauled into his arms again. Marcus. The name sang through her. Not Brendan Fitzpatrick, the Raven, a pirate, but Marcus Brand, respectable shipowner and spy.

Laughter shook her, and once again he held her at arm's length, wincing at the motion. "What?" he demanded.

"I—I thought I was in love with a pirate," she gasped between bursts of giggles, "and now I find out he's only a—a spy!"

"It's not funny," he said, but she saw the corner of his lips twitch.

"Proper, respectable Rebecca Talbot," she went on, still helplessly caught in the grip of mirth. "The men she chooses—"

"The man." He caught her up against him, holding her in a fierce, tight grip. She would have bruises on her arms come morning, but she didn't care. "One man. Say it."

"One man," she agreed happily. "Only you. Oh, Marcus!" She threw her arms around his neck, and he grunted, making her pull back. "Oh, heavens, I forgot. Your arm—am I hurting you?"

His eye twinkled. "If you'd kiss me again, I'd forget it, too."

"Enough of that," she said severely, though she smiled as she peered at the bandage. To her relief, it remained pristine. "I don't want anything to happen to you. To have found you again—it's a miracle."

"No, it's not, lass." The seriousness in his eyes dampened her mirth. "I should have come to you sooner."

"Why didn't you?"

"Abb—my superior was afraid I'd be recognized. He wasn't afraid for me, mind," he said, his lips twisted, "but for his other spies. But, devil take it, Rebecca!" He glared at her as if she were the cause of his anger. "I should have come to you sooner. I should have known I could trust you."

"Yes. You can." Her smile was serene. Her last question had been answered. "But what of Amelia, or my father? He didn't recognize you, but he'd see you dead if he knew. And there's Lieutenant Dee, too."

"I know." Running a hand through his hair, he glanced

distractedly about the kitchen. "I shouldn't stay any longer.
I might have been followed here."

"By whom?"

He shook his head. "Where is my shirt?"

"You can't put that back on. Go out with that all bloody,
and you'll be announcing to the world that it was you at the
British legation. No. I'll get you one of my father's shirts."

"Rebecca." There was a slight smile on his face. "Are you
collaborating with me?"

"Yes. Pray don't mock me, Mr. Brand. At the moment I'm
not sure whether to kiss you or hit you! Putting yourself in
such danger."

" 'Tis glad I am to know ye care, lass," he said, the lilt of
the old brogue in his voice.

"You'll not get around me, Marcus," she said, her severity
belied by the softness in her eyes. "Sit. I'll find a shirt for
you," she said, and whisked out of the kitchen into an ad-
joining room. "There's one here fresh-laundered, and I'll see
what I can do about yours." She held the shirt out to him as
she returned to the room. It was coarse homespun, far different from the fine linen he usually wore, but adequate for the
purpose. "You'll need a sling, too."

"No." With Rebecca's help, he struggled into the shirt. "If
Dee sees that, he'll know for certain he hit me."

Her hands stilled on his sleeves. "He knows?"

"Not for certain." He laid his hand over hers reassuringly.
"I laid a false trail. But you were right, lass. He does suspect
me."

"He won't learn of you from me." Her gaze was clear and
steady. "That I promise."

"I know, lass." He dropped a quick, hard kiss on her lips.
"Help me with my coat, and I'll be gone."

"And about time, too. Disturbing my night as you have."

He grinned. "I'll disturb all your nights if you like, lass,"
he whispered, his mouth deliberately grazing her ear.

"Ooh." She pushed at his chest, but she was smiling.
"You are an arrogant, annoying man, and you should
leave—"

"I will." He caught her around the waist with his good
arm. "But not for long, *leannan*," he said, bending his head
to hers again. A long, slow kiss, with lips moving against
lips, tongue lazily caressing tongue; a kiss of passion, and
promise for the future. "I'll not leave you this time."

"I know." Shakily she clutched at his shirtfront, his sleeves, his hands, as he pulled back, not wanting to let him go; knowing she must. "You'll be careful?"

"Always." He kissed her once more and then stepped back. Rebecca almost cried out in protest. If he didn't leave now, she would never let him go. "Good night, lass."

"Good night, *leannan*," she whispered, and the door closed at last behind him.

The candle flame flickered, and then burned steadily. He was gone, and the kitchen suddenly seemed large, echoing. Empty. Quickly she bent to snuff the flame and made her way through the darkened house to her room. He was gone, but he would be back. She knew that now, and if she still didn't quite believe his story, still didn't quite trust him, her heart felt otherwise. Her heart knew only that she felt alive again, as she hadn't in nearly a year, and it didn't count the cost. But she would have to.

Wondering yet again at her judgment in men, Rebecca slipped into her room, padding across to the window and searching the street in vain for a sign of him. First a pirate, and now a spy. Her pirate. She wouldn't, she realized as she climbed at last into bed, have him any other way.

The British legation was in an uproar. How the devil, Sir Augustus wanted to know, had an intruder gained access to the building, let alone that particular office? And did they have any idea yet what he'd sought, or who, for that matter, it had been? The questions were asked and repeated, through that night and the day that followed, and the person who should have known the answers didn't. Lieutenant Dee, in charge of security for the legation, had no more knowledge than anyone else. Only suspicions.

"I tell you, I know who it is, sir," he said, standing stiff at attention in Sir Augustus's office. "Marcus Brand."

"And have you proof to back that up?" Sir Augustus snapped. The effects of a night with very little sleep showed in his weary face and the slump of his shoulders, but his eyes were keen and sharp as he sat at his desk, glaring up at Dee. "Mr. Brand has proven to be a good friend to us."

"And a good source of information," St. John said quietly from his chair across the room. "We've need of men like him."

"With all due respect, sirs, he's not what he appears," Dee

said, hiding his scorn. Diplomats were duplicitous, so steeped in evasions and half-truths that they could no longer spot reality.

Sir Augustus sighed and leaned back in his chair. "If that is so, who is he, then?"

"The Raven."

"Excuse me?"

"So you've said before," St. John put in. "Besides the fact that the Raven is dead, you've no proof of that, either."

"I have indications." Dee stared straight ahead. "I've looked into his background—"

"By whose leave?" Sir Augustus said sharply.

"By yours, sir." Dee's voice held mild surprise. "As I do with every stranger who enters the legation. It is my duty." Sir Augustus grunted, and so Dee went on. "There have been times when he's been missing from Baltimore for months at a stretch, and no one knows where he goes."

"Hardly criminal."

"He is the exact image of the Raven," Dee plowed on and fingered the scar on his cheek, until he remembered his duty and snapped to attention. "Remember, I had an encounter with him."

"It is not enough." Sir Augustus rose, slapping his hands down on his desk. "Not to accuse someone who has caused us no harm, and who, God help us, is a connection of an earl. And I do not understand why you are accusing your own cousin of such a thing. No," he went on, holding up his hand as Dee began to protest. "Find proof the Americans lied about the Raven's death, find someone who can verify his identity—do any of those, and then we'll see. Until you do, you will not harass Mr. Brand." He looked at Dee from under lowered brows. "I trust I make myself clear?"

"Yes, sir."

"Good. You are dismissed."

"Sir." Dee saluted smartly and left the room, his face impassive. Only his eyes, gleaming with anticipation, gave him away. Find someone who knew the Raven's identity? He could do that, and more. He could find someone to lead him directly to the Raven. Rebecca Talbot.

Word of the incident at the British legation spread quickly through the city, and speculation as to the identity of the intruder was widespread. Just as widespread were the opinions, with the Americans being gleeful at England's embarrassment, while those who favored England thundered that such acts of espionage between two countries ostensibly at peace were unconscionable. Sir Augustus had protested the incident to James Monroe, the Secretary of State, to no avail. Barring the capture of the intruder, the incident was being explained as a simple burglary, though nothing had been taken.

Two days after the incident, two days after Marcus had come to her, Rebecca set out alone to do the day's marketing, since Martha had taken an ague and was bedridden. Summer was upon them, and in her long-sleeved gown of tan broadcloth she was already uncomfortably warm. If she could she would discard the hated bonnet and gloves, but always she was conscious of a need to be on her best behavior. Except that, lately, the rewards for that no longer mattered so much. There was no joy in it, not when compared to the thrill of Marcus's illicit and exciting kisses.

A noise behind her, as of a footfall, made her look back as she turned from High Street onto Bridge Street, where the shops were located, but she saw no one. Frowning, she continued on. Odd, but she'd had the strange feeling the last few days of being observed, an almost palpable sensation of eyes watching her every move. Once or twice she had even caught a glimpse of someone from her bedroom window, but always, he melted into the shadows beneath the trees opposite before she could identify him. It made her uneasy. Who could be following her, and why?

She forgot her concerns for a while in the butcher shop, where she spent some time selecting a choice bit of beef for dinner. Likely it would aggravate Father's gout, but he was in such a testy mood lately that she was doing all she could to appease him. Not that she expected gratitude from him anymore, but having him calm made her life easier. Like every other British sympathizer in the city, he was in arms about the intrusion at the mission. On a more personal level, he no longer received visits from friends and associates as he had. Not since he'd made his outlandish proposal for revolution.

There was something else, though, something she couldn't quite put her finger on. Sometimes she would look up to see him watching her, a speculative gleam in his eyes. It was all very odd, the unseen follower, her father's behavior. At the center of it, she was certain, was Marcus. No wonder if she felt so uneasy.

The cut of beef at last selected, she instructed the butcher to deliver it to her home. That errand done, she stepped out into the street in time to see a man wearing a familiar red uniform turn quickly away from the tiny-paned shop window. Incredulity rose within her, and with it, dread, forming a thick lump in her throat. Was Dee following her? "Lieutenant Dee?" she said, gathering her courage. "Is that you?"

He turned. "Miss Talbot," he said, bowing correctly, but his gaze, as always, traveled over her in a way that made her skin crawl. "How do you today?"

It was too much: the scene with Marcus and her own uncertainties; the unseen watcher; her father's behavior. Now this, and her feeling that he had been watching her through the shop window. "Have you been following me?" she demanded.

"I?" He seemed surprised, but his eyes were sharp and knowing. "Why would I do such a thing? Though I must admit"—his smile twisted into a leer—"that if I did I would have a most enjoyable view."

Rebecca drew herself up to her full height. "You are insulting, sir."

"My apologies." He bowed again. "I did not mean to be."

Rebecca compressed her lips. She had never liked the lieutenant, with his fanatic's eyes and his knowing leer; nor did she trust him. "If you are doing so, please cease at once. I do not like it."

"Rebecca, Rebecca." He shook his head, smiling. "You should be complimented. You are a most attractive woman."

"Nevertheless, sir, I would appreciate it if you would leave me alone."

"So that you can go to the Raven?"

She stopped, the lump in her throat increasing. He couldn't know anything. "The Raven is dead," she said, her voice muffled in what she hoped he would take as grief.

"All the more reason, my dear, for you to welcome my attentions."

She sensed, rather than heard, him come up behind her, felt it in the way her skin tightened and crawled. "Thank you, sir, but I think not."

"He won't marry you, you know," he said abruptly.

"I beg your pardon."

"The Raven. Marcus Brand, or whatever he calls himself these days."

It was exactly her fear, but she had more pride than to show it. "I do not know why you continue to insist that Mr. Brand is the Raven, since everyone knows the Raven is dead. And his interest in me is hardly any of your concern."

"Oh, but it is, Rebecca." He was close behind her again, and she glanced wildly around, hoping someone would come to her aid. "Because you are mine—"

"I am not."

"—and because he is a spy."

She spun around, and her shock was not feigned. "A spy!"

"Yes. A spy. He thinks he's clever, but I know." He grinned, and not for the first time she noted how crooked and yellowed his teeth were. "He'll be arrested very soon, Rebecca, and then where will you be? Much better if you choose me."

Arrested. Her stomach churned. Marcus, arrested. If his identity were discovered, he would be hanged. Dear God, she couldn't allow it. No matter what else lay between them she suddenly had no doubts that he had told the truth the other evening. He was who he said, and he had behaved as he had for the sake of his country. And he had come to her, trusting her with his life. Pride swelled through her, for the work he did, for his trust in her. "I find this a distasteful conversation, sir. You will excuse me—what on earth?"

The stage from Washington City, driven at breakneck pace, careened over the bridge spanning Rock Creek, swaying as it turned onto Bridge Street, and stopped before Suter's Tavern. The driver jumped down, shouting and waving his arms wildly. "A madman," Dee said.

"Can you hear what he's saying?" Rebecca asked, the tension between them forgotten for the moment.

"No, he's—listen!" He went very still, and now Rebecca could hear the words, too. The words all of Washington City had been awaiting, but which still came as a surprise.

"It's happened," she said, stepping away from Dee, her enemy now in more ways than one. "The President has asked Congress to declare war on England."

Rebecca hurried through the darkened streets, cloak pulled closely about her in spite of the warm evening. It wasn't safe to be out after sunset, and if she were noticed and recognized, her already damaged reputation would take a fatal blow. None of that stopped her. She had to get to Marcus, to warn him, before it was too late.

It had been a difficult day. The news that the President had addressed Congress had stunned the city, though everyone had expected it. Nearly everyone. Ezra had gone into a rage when he'd heard the news, ranting about the stupidity of such an act and what it would do to his business. In his anger he'd struck out at the closest target. Rebecca considered herself lucky to have escaped with just a glancing blow to the side of her head. Only liberal helpings of wine had calmed him, sending him at last into a stupor from which she hoped he wouldn't emerge until the morning.

Ahead the street ended at the bluff above the river. Scattered lights glimmered on the Virginia shore, while even at this distance the toneless, musical clink of boats moving at anchor reached her. Otherwise, it was quiet, since term had ended at the nearby college, and no one else was about. Rebecca stopped a moment, glancing back, but she saw no one, heard no footsteps. By slipping out the back gate she had, she thought, managed to elude any pursuer. She was now nearly to her destination.

The realization brought her up short, her stomach quivering with nerves and fear and anticipation. The Sally house, where Marcus lodged. She stood on the brick sidewalk beneath the elm trees, gazing up at the house, tall, of brick, with a dormered third story. Now that she was here, what would she do? Panic had sent her here, the terror that he would be arrested for his activities intensified by the day's events. She had to warn him. Staring at the darkened house, though, she hadn't a clue how.

Footsteps rang out on the pavement. In the still night air they resounded like pistol shots, seeming to come from nowhere, and everywhere. She shrank back against a tree, panic bubbling within her again, and it was only by an act of will that she stayed quiet, hidden. There! A man striding along, across the street, there—and in an instant, Rebecca was out of her hiding place and scurrying across the cobbled street. She knew that walk, knew the shape of that body as intimately as she did her own. "Marcus," she gasped.

He whirled to face her, dropping into a crouch, and the walking stick he usually held so negligently was suddenly thrust outward. From its base protruded a wicked-looking blade, gleaming even in the dim light. Rebecca stopped dead. This was not Marcus Brand, gentleman merchant, she confronted. This was the Raven.

Marcus recovered first, springing the last few steps to where she stood, swaying, in the street. "Rebecca." His voice was low, harsh, as he caught her about the waist. "What the devil are you doing here?"

Relief made her giddy. "I had to see you," she gasped, her voice high and uneven. "I had to tell you—"

"Hush." He glanced quickly around, alert, wary, and abruptly she remembered the danger he stood in. The danger they both were in. "Not here."

She leaned her head against him. "Where, then?"

"Devil take it." He frowned up at the Sally house. "My room. But you'll have to be very quiet. If Mrs. Sally knew—"

"She'll be awake." Rebecca straightened, faced with a new problem. "She'll be there to see you when you go in."

"Devil take it, she will. But I don't want to leave you out here." His face thunderous, he gave her a little shake. "What are you doing here? Don't you know 'tis dangerous?"

"There's more danger to you, Marcus. I saw Lieutenant Dee today, and—"

"He won't have you." Marcus caught her up against him, making her gasp in surprise. "You're mine."

"Well, of course I am." She stared at him, wide-eyed. "Why in the world would you think otherwise?"

"Then, what—"

"He knows who you are. Oh, Marcus, I've been so frightened for you."

"There's no need to be, lass. I can handle myself. But, come, we can't stay here." He pulled away and caught her hand. "We'll go into the garden. Quietly, now." He cast a glance up at the house as he led her past it, into the back. "That woman has the ears of a cat."

"Then I shouldn't stay, if it'll be a danger to you."

"To me!" Hands on her shoulders, he pushed her down onto a bench beneath a latticed trellis, heavy with the scents of roses and honeysuckle. "You're the one who shouldn't be abroad—but never mind that. I'll go in, and then come back for you. Will you be all right here?"

Rebecca's pride had returned, along with her composure. "Of course."

"Good girl."

"I am not a girl, sir. I am a woman."

His teeth gleamed in the darkness. "That I know. Now stay here and be quiet. I'll be back quick as I can." Bending to drop a brief, possessive kiss on her lips, he turned and strode away, leaving her alone, but not lonely. She had found him again. Brendan, Marcus, the Raven—it mattered not what he called himself. She was his, and, please God, he was hers.

It seemed an eternity, waiting there in that flower-perfumed arbor, but at last she heard the click of a door latch and the sound of feet walking softly along the brick path toward her. "It's best we stay here," Marcus whispered. "Mrs. Sally is abed, but I doubt she's asleep yet."

"It doesn't matter," Rebecca said. "I thought I'd never see you in time. Marcus, there's—mpf!" This as he caught her up in his arms and slammed his mouth down on hers. In spite of her fears, in spite of the urgency that had driven her on, she responded, threading her fingers into his hair, moving against him, wanting to be closer, and closer still. When at last he raised his head her lips tingled, her gown was in disarray, and the most intimate parts of her body throbbed from his rough, urgent caresses. She wanted to sing out in gladness, exultation. It had been so long, so long! "Marcus," she gasped, offering up her lips again. "Oh, Marcus."

"You're mine," he muttered before ravaging her mouth with his again, before sending his hands on a mission to rove and explore and fondle. "You were made for this."

She jerked back. "I was made for more than this, Marcus Brand."

"Aye." His eyes twinkled. "I know that, lass. But you were made for this"—his hands traced a slow path over her breasts—"with me."

She was. Oh, she was. Her eyes fluttered shut, her head arched back, and the feelings spiraled within her, the need, the desire, urging her to give in to him, now. Only a small voice in her mind remained to remind her of all this had led to in the past. "Maybe I am." She pushed at his chest, and, startled, he let her go. "Maybe that is all I'm good for."

"Rebecca, I didn't mean that—"

"But it's not what I came for." She stared at him measuringly. "And the truth is, Marcus, Brendan, whoever you are—the truth is, I don't trust you."

Chapter 24

~

For a moment silence rang between them, and then Marcus turned away. "I suppose I don't blame you for that," he said, running a hand through his hair. "It's little I've done to earn your trust. Come, sit down." He gestured toward the bench. "I know you didn't come here to be ravished."

"No, I did not." She settled herself primly on the bench, arranging the folds of her skirt about her. "I came because I am concerned about your safety."

He leaned against the arbor, and though his eyes glittered she could read nothing in them. "I can handle myself, Rebecca."

"I know you can. But I don't trust Lieutenant Dee." She leaned forward. "He's wanted revenge against you for a long time, and he'll take it any way he can. I tell you, Marcus, he told me today you'd be arrested for spying."

"He has no proof."

"It won't stop him. Oh, why won't you listen to me?"

"I am listening, and believe me, I don't underestimate him. But he is a risk I have to take."

"As I was?"

"Yes," he said after a moment.

She looked down at her skirt, pleating it between her fingers. "Did—did what we have ever mean anything to you?"

"The devil take it, Rebecca, you know it did!"

"Pray do not swear."

"And pray do not act prim and prissy with me," he shot back. "I like you better when you're honest."

"Honest! You're a fine one to talk."

"Yes. Honest. When you're yourself, not acting like a cold, frigid spinster."

"Frigid—!" She stared at him. "Of all the nerve—"

"Ha." He was grinning. "Didn't like that, did you?"

She closed her mouth with a snap. "Listen to you talk about honesty, with all the lies you've lived."

A curious silence fell between them. "You've not forgiven me, have you, lass."

Rebecca bit her lips. "No," she said, slowly. "I suppose I haven't." She lowered her face, wondering why she felt so wretched, so guilty. Why should she forgive him, after all she'd been through? The past year, thinking he was dead— that was the worst, of course. Knowing she'd never see him again; dragging through her days with no reason to live, except that she didn't like the alternative. Enduring her father's scorn, and never, ever, being allowed to cry. No hope, no light, no color in her life; only the memory of those weeks aboard a pirate ship, when she had come so briefly, unexpectedly, alive. And then to learn it was all a lie. "I can't seem to put it behind me."

Marcus muttered something she didn't catch. "I beg your pardon?" she said.

He swung to face her. "I said you're just like your father."

"What? How?"

"Cold and unforgiving."

"I am not!" She jumped to her feet, hands clenched. "I am not like him."

"You are. You'll nurse your grievances to the grave."

"I have cause."

"So does he," he retorted. "Or he thinks he does."

"I—" Rebecca began, and fell silent. "Am I really like him?"

"No." His face softened, and yet his stance remained rigid, implacable. "But you will be if you go on like this. Think on that, Rebecca. Think of your life, lonely, alone, afraid to love. And then think about forgiveness."

She swallowed hard and extended her hands to him beseechingly. "Marcus, I don't want to be this way—"

"But you are," he said flatly. "You shouldn't be here. I'll see you home."

"I'd rather stay," she murmured, greatly daring, wanting only to feel his arms about her again.

Something flickered in his eyes, but he shook his head.

"When you can come to me with nothing between us, Rebecca, then you can stay."

"But you're the one who lied!"

"Aye. And I've suffered for it, too." He stalked to her. "Do you think this year past was easy for me? Wanting you, knowing you were near, but not being able even to see you? And then when I did, it was as a man you didn't know. Devil take it, Rebecca, it was hard for me aboard the *Raven*! I knew what I was doing to you. But I couldn't help myself. Neither could you." He stared down at her. "At least be honest with yourself about that."

She gazed down at his hands, seeing them through a blur of tears. "I have been. But—"

"No more 'buts.' " He sounded weary as he took her arm. " 'Tis late. I'll see you home."

Rebecca glanced up at his set face and discarded any idea of attempting to win him over again. He'd made up his mind, and nothing would sway him. "I knew as soon as I left the *Raven* I'd made a mistake," she said in a small voice. "I knew I should have stayed with you."

"But you didn't," he said and reached for her arm. "And it's past."

Rebecca pressed her lips together to hold back tears. It was past. If only she could put it behind her, as he seemed to have done. But she couldn't. Not without some indication that it wouldn't happen again, that she could trust him. She loved him with all her being, all her soul, but she couldn't trust him, and that hurt.

Marcus was watching her, one eyebrow raised quizzically. "Ready?" he whispered.

Nodding, Rebecca put her hand on his arm and let him lead her out of the garden.

With the President having addressed Congress, what happened next was inevitable. In mid-June, the United States declared war on England. The British legation staff increased their guard and began packing, against the day when they would be ordered to leave. In high spirits, the Americans made plans to invade and annex Canada. And with the navy so pitifully small, anyone who owned any sort of vessel applied immediately for a letter-of-marque to become a privateer.

"Hell and damnation!" Ezra roared when the news

reached him. He stomped through the house into the kitchen, where Rebecca, face flushed with heat, calmly continued peeling potatoes for dinner. She had heard the news earlier when doing the marketing. "We've an idiot for president. I swear if I didn't have this foot"—he pointed down at his gouty foot, swollen and sore again—"I would do something about him."

"Father." Rebecca frowned. "You knew this was coming."

"Do not talk back to me. This is a disaster, girl." He glared at her. "How am I supposed to get my ships to sea?"

Rebecca concentrated on the potato in her hand. "Turn then into privateers."

"Have you run mad? I'll not fight against England, no while there's breath in my body. They need my help, not my opposition."

Rebecca set the paring knife down. "That's treason."

"Do not speak to me of treason." He leaned over, his face close to her, the smells of sour wine and perspiration making her nauseous. "You are the traitor."

Rebecca drew back. "I? What did I do?"

"Consorting with the enemy. Don't think I haven't seen you. That Brand fellow. I was deceived in him, and you hang all over him like a bitch in heat."

"I do not!"

"Aye, I thought I could trust him, and now I hear he's gone and turned privateer with all the rest."

Rebecca shot to her feet, her chair falling back. "He hasn't!"

"He has." There was an odd look on his face, almost of satisfaction. "And what is a privateer, but a legal pirate?"

Marcus had turned privateer. He would be leaving her, and he hadn't said a word to her. "You'll never forgive me for that, will you?"

"What you did was unforgivable."

"I did it because," she began and stopped. She had explained her actions aboard the *Raven* again and again, and always to the same effect. Father neither listened to her, nor believed her. He hadn't forgiven her.

Just as she hadn't forgiven Marcus his transgressions. Moving automatically, she righted the chair and sank into it. She hadn't forgiven him, and now he was leaving. Fool! She'd been foolish to let the past come between them. Lies? Yes, but necessary ones, and not uttered to hurt her. Since then he had been nothing but honest, except about leaving. In the face of that, how could she continue to hold a grudge?

"Are you listening to me, girl?" Ezra's demand penetrated into her consciousness. "I am talking to you. And what are you smiling about?"

Rebecca rose. She *was* smiling, she realized, and she couldn't seem to stop. She didn't want to. "About forgiveness, Father." To his evident surprise, she kissed him on the cheek. "You should consider it," she said and floated out the door into the garden, feeling light, free, at peace. Feeling like herself, for the first time in ages. Why, forgiveness was easy, she thought as she drifted out onto the street, not caring that she had neither bonnet nor gloves. Easy, and right. Why had she not seen it before?

The pleasant daze continued as she ambled uphill along First Street, heading toward the river. Heading for the Sally house, and Marcus. She noticed neither people staring at her, nor greetings called to her, but continued on, confident at last of the future. The past was over, done. There was only now.

It was only when she had let the door knocker fall several times at the Sally house, with no answer, that her curious, inviolate sense of rightness began to fade. No one there. Had Marcus left already, without saying good-bye? Panicking, she grasped the knocker again, banging it down in a fusillade of short, sharp raps, and nearly fell forward when the door was abruptly opened.

"What the devil?" Marcus stood there, in shirtsleeves, hair disordered. "Rebecca?"

"Oh, Marcus!" She launched herself at him. He fell back into the hall, taking her with him. "I was so frightened."

Marcus cast a quick glance out into the street before closing the door. "About what, lass?"

"That you had gone."

He grimaced. Something else for her to hold against him. "You heard of that, did you?"

"Yes." She gazed up at him, and, unbelievably, her eyes were shining, a clear, sparkling emerald. "And I couldn't let you go without doing this." Standing on tiptoes, she reached up and pressed her lips to his, using all the persuasion that he had taught her. *Little witch,* he thought, but his arms came down around her. His Rebecca. Devil take it, but it was good to have her in his arms again, and that was dangerous.

Summoning all his strength, he pushed her away. "This changes nothing, lass," he said sternly.

"But you're wrong." Again she stretched up to kiss him. "Everything's changed."

"Devil take it, Rebecca!" He pushed her away. "Do you know what you're doing to me?"

A slow, secretive smile spread across her face. "Yes."

He couldn't help it; he grinned. "Ah, lass. For a prim spinster, you do some bold things."

"I am not a prim spinster." She moved against him, her smile widening. "At least, not prim."

"No?"

"No." Her smile faded. "You were right, Marcus. I haven't been honest with myself. And the way I felt about you . . ." She swallowed, hard. "It was myself I couldn't forgive, not you."

"Oh, lass—"

"For behaving as I did, for worrying my father, for"—she swallowed again—"for falling in love with you."

He could endure no more. Heedless of where they were, that Mrs. Sally might walk in at any moment, he pulled her to him and brought his mouth down on hers. She responded eagerly, the feel of her breasts and hips so warm, so close, inflaming him. God help him, but he wanted her. And yet, if they were dealing in truths, he had a few to confess.

He tore his mouth from hers and stood, his forehead to hers, breathing harshly. "You were right, too," he said, his voice low. "I did lie to you."

"Because you had to."

"No. Not at the end, on the *Raven*. I could have trusted you. I just thought"—his mouth twisted in frustration—"that it would be better for you if you didn't know."

"And it probably was," she said softly. "What I found hardest to forgive was that you let me believe you were dead."

Was. Past tense. At some point in the past few days, she had put the past behind her. It filled him with a tremendous lightness, making him want to laugh aloud. "I didn't want to hurt you." His voice was low. "I'm sorry that you were. But the truth is, Rebecca . . ."

"Yes?" she said when he didn't go on.

"You scared the life out of me."

"I did? Why?"

"Don't you know?"

"No."

"Because of this," he said and kissed her again. Because she made him feel things he had felt for no other woman. For a man who prized his freedom, that was frightening, indeed.

"Oh, Marcus," she began when he lowered his head to press kisses on her throat. "I think—Marcus!"

He raised his head, caught by her urgency. "What?" he asked, and then he heard the voices outside. "Devil take it, Mrs. Sally's come back." He caught her hand. "Come on."

"Where?" she gasped as he pulled her up the stairs.

"To my room. She can't see you here."

"But—"

"Hush." He placed his hand over her mouth as the front door opened. Standing in absolute silence on the second-floor landing, they listened as Mrs. Sally chattered on to her maid about the high cost of goods and the insulting attitudes of the shopkeepers, and did she think that nice Mr. Brand was home? Rebecca bit back giggles at that one; she loved Marcus, thought him a wonderful man, but nice? "Might as well call a raven a pretty bird," she whispered unsteadily.

Marcus gave her a little shake, and they waited until the voices below faded before they moved across the hall to his room. "That was close," he said, closing the door behind them and pulling her into his arms. "If she finds out you're here, your reputation would be ruined."

"Hang my reputation."

"You don't mean that."

"Marcus, my reputation was ruined long ago. Nothing I've done has fixed it." She drew back. "And as I once said to you, might as well be hanged for a sheep as a lamb."

He grinned. "Is that so?"

"Yes, it's so." She reached up to smooth back a strand of his hair, touch his cheek, the corner of his eye. "Do you know, I rather miss the eyepatch."

"I could put it back on."

"No. I like you this way." She peered up at him. "No more hiding?"

"No. No more hiding," he said and bent his head for a long, slow, thorough kiss. No hiding, no barriers. No secrets.

Just Rebecca, in his arms, in his life. He would never leave
her again. Never.

And because he had made that pledge at last, of a sudden
he couldn't have enough of her: of her breasts, heavy in his
hands; of her hands clutching at him; of the feel and the
scent and the taste of her. "Too many damned buttons on
this dress," he muttered, his fingers clumsy as they struggled
with the long line of buttons that fastened down her back.
But then they were undone, and his touch was gliding over
her skin, satin soft and warm. He tugged at the gown and
she helped, shifting in his embrace as he lowered it down
her shoulders, down her arms, his hands skimming over her
breasts. It fell to the floor, useless, discarded, and in a moment later her petticoat followed. Her breasts, full and
round, were in his hands again, and he bent to kiss each
hardened tip, feeling her hands tug at his hair, hearing her
soft exclamation of pleasure. His Rebecca. His *leannan,* his
heart.

The door handle turned suddenly, making them both
tense. "Mr. Brand? Are you there?" came a querulous voice.
"Now why did he lock his door?"

Rebecca buried her head against his shoulder, and he
could feel her shaking. Tears? Concerned, he looked down,
to see her face twisted with mirth. The little witch was
laughing. The very ridiculousness of their being caught in
such a situation struck him, and he clapped a hand to his
mouth.

Rebecca looked up, eyes sparkling, seeing the retribution
he promised in his eyes, and not caring. With great delicacy
she undid the laces of his shirt, and bent to taste his salty
sweet skin, her tongue flicking out in delicate circles. He
groaned, a muffled sound behind his hand. "Witch," he
whispered when they at last heard Mrs. Sally walking away.
He caught her face in his hands and forced her to face him.
"I could strangle you."

"You won't," she whispered back. "There are other things
you'd rather do to me."

His eyes roved over her, as warm and arousing as a touch.
"Yes," he said, and lifting her in his arms, carried her over
to the bed.

She lay back, watching as he shed his shirt and trousers,
holding her arms up to him as he settled onto the bed with
her, above her, his weight a delicious burden. Loose, wanton

behavior, and yet it felt right, inevitable, and all the more delicious for being done in utter silence. He rubbed her nipples, stroked her hips, her thighs, and her gasps of delight were muffled against his shoulder; she curled her fingers around his manhood, feeling the pulsing strength of him, feeling him tense with the effort not to groan aloud. She bit her lips to hold back her cry of pleasure as he entered her; swallowed the whimpers that rose, unbidden, as she moved with him, faster, urgently. The ache, the pleasure, grew, spiraled, lifting her higher, and then she was at the peak, crying out her joy into his mouth. She belonged to him. It was no good denying the truth. She was his.

"Lord," Marcus said in a low voice long moments later, raising his head to look at her. "What you do to me."

She shifted, feeling him still inside her, and glad of it. "What?" she asked, feathering her fingers through his hair. "What do I do to you?"

He shook his head, bent to kiss her. "If you don't know by now, I don't know how to tell you."

She knew. Oh, she knew, and the knowledge was delicious. She encircled his shoulders with her arms. Outside were the normal sounds of life going on, of people and carriages passing by, and faint, far away, came the fluting tones of Mrs. Sally's voice. None of it mattered. Only now, and this man.

He mumbled something, and she turned her head. "What?"

He lifted his head. "I said I'll have to get you out of here somehow. But don't worry, *leannan*." He placed his fingers on her lips, as if aware of the dismay his words had caused her. "I'm not leaving you."

"I know."

"I'll never leave you again."

"I know," she said again, but in truth, she didn't. The loving was over. Reality had to be faced. "Marcus? I heard something today."

His lips slid along the side of her jaw. "Yes, love?"

Love. That one word almost stopped her. "I heard you plan to become a privateer."

He went still in her arms, and then lifted his head again. "Who told you that?"

"It doesn't matter. Is it true?"

"Aye, lass," he said and rolled off her. She almost whimpered at the loss of him, even though he immediately gathered her close to his side. "I have to do what I can do to help. We're at war, Rebecca."

"I know, but"—her fingers toyed with the crisp curls on his chest—"can't you do something from your home? Can't you stay there and run your business?"

"There's no business for a man like me at times like this, Rebecca. The best thing I can do, for my country and myself, is to go out as a privateer.

"Against England."

"I have to, Rebecca."

Her heart thudded slowly, painfully. Of course he did. If he did as she asked, he wouldn't be the man she loved. But the parting was coming, no matter what he had said. "I know."

"But not alone." He shifted, and suddenly she was atop him, staring down at him in surprise. "I'll not leave you behind. You'll be with me."

"Oh, Marcus." She squeezed her eyes shut. "I can't. Don't you realize that?"

"You can." He moved his hand to her shoulder, shaking her a little. "You're a grown woman. You can do what you want."

"No. I have obligations."

"Yes. To me."

She lifted her hand, stroked it down his cheek, delighting in the feel of skin roughened by the sun. "You don't need me, Marcus," she said softly.

"The devil I don't!" he exclaimed and tumbled her over, rising from the bed, magnificently naked, magnificently male. "Do you know what my life's been like without you? It's been—"

"Empty," she finished for him. "Lower your voice, Marcus."

"I don't want to lower my voice," he grumbled, but he sat on the edge of the bed, head down. "I need you, Rebecca. I've been alone too long, lonely too long, and the only thing I've cared about is getting revenge on a country that doesn't care if I exist. But, you." He twisted and bent over her, fisting his hands in her hair. "The day I met you, everything changed. Lord, I didn't know what was happening to me, but I do now. There's more to life than I've ever known." He paused, his face working with emotion. "Show it to me, Rebecca."

She closed her eyes tightly, hearing in her mind a similar plea aboard the *Raven*. Need, and want. Not love. "I want to." Her voice was a whisper as she traced the outline of his lips with her fingertips. "But I can't. No, please, hear me out." This as he shifted away. "Times will be hard. Amelia needs me more than ever—"

"Amelia's grown up," he growled.

"Yes. But she still needs me. And my father." She frowned. "I'm worried about him. He's not himself."

He muttered something in reply. "I beg your pardon?" she said.

"I said, if he's not himself, that's a good thing." He glared at her. "Dammit, Rebecca, you're going to waste your life on that old man."

"He's my father."

"And he treats you like dirt."

"He loves me!"

"I haven't seen any signs of it."

"He does. When I was a little girl, no one could have asked for a better father. He had two daughters to care for and no wife, and he was wonderful."

"Devil take it, Rebecca, he's not wonderful now."

"Does that mean I should just abandon him? Should I walk away because things have gotten difficult?"

"Things have gotten impossible. He doesn't give a damn for you. When are you going to admit that?"

She flinched. "You're wrong—"

"I'm not." He swung around and sat up. "We had this argument before, on the *Raven*. And you've admitted that what you did then was a mistake."

She didn't answer right away. "Leaving you was a mistake. But if I hadn't done what I did—Marcus, I don't know if I could have lived with myself. I don't know if I could, now."

"I'd make you forget him."

"Maybe. For a while." She looked up at him, longing to touch his back, hunched and strained. But she didn't dare. She didn't have the courage.

"So it comes to this." His voice was flat. "You're choosing him over me."

"Marcus, you once chose your country over me."

"That's different."

"I don't think so."

"Devil take it, Rebecca," he said, turning toward her. She saw anger in his eyes, passion, fear. "I could force you to come along."

She shifted on the bed, intrigued by the idea in spite of herself. "Abduct me, you mean?"

"Yes. I've done it before."

"So you have." A smile curved her lips and then faded. "It wouldn't work. I'd only resent you."

"Devil take it." He pounded his fists on his thighs. "Don't do this, Rebecca."

"When the war is over—"

"And when will that be? And what excuse will you find then? No." He rose. "Now or never, Rebecca."

She swallowed hard. It had an awful, final ring. "I'm sorry, Marcus," she whispered.

"Sorry," he snorted and began pulling on shirt and trousers. "Get dressed."

"I could stay awhile longer—"

"No. If you won't stay with me forever, then that's not enough. Get dressed."

Rebecca closed her eyes against a sudden rush of tears, then rose. In silence she found her petticoat and gown and slipped into them, turning her back for him to fasten the buttons, a very different experience than when he had undone them. In silence she followed him out into the hall and down the stairs, and, at last, out into the street. Silently she walked along beside him, her hand on his tense arm, until they drew near her house. And it was in silence that she watched as he bowed, turned, and walked away from her, though inside she screamed. *Marcus!* She wanted to run after him. *Oh, Marcus, come back, I was wrong.*

But she didn't. Instead, she stayed still at the top of the hill, watching his figure growing ever distant. Only when he had turned a corner and gone from her sight did she turn, dry-eyed from pain too deep for tears. Marcus was gone. She was alone.

Chapter 25

~

Georgetown, July, 1814

Rebecca trudged up the hill to Prospect Street, her marketing basket light and her spirits low. Behind and below her the Potomac sparkled in the sunlight, and where it had once been filled with ships at anchor, now there were few: her father's, rotting at anchor, his plans for transferring them to Canadian ownership having fallen through. Times were hard, and the brunt of the problems had fallen on Rebecca. On her was the task of finding food, beyond the chickens they kept and what they grew in their garden.

The war was not going well for the Americans. The early naval successes over the British were now a thing of the past, with most of the American frigates being blockaded, and the invasion of Canada had failed. In Europe, Napoleon's abdication had freed Wellington's seasoned troops to fight in the Americas; rumor had it that they were already in Bermuda, preparing to invade from Canada. The blockade extended along the entire coast, and with the British marauding at will throughout Chesapeake Bay, exports from other countries had been cut off. Sugar was scarce, and so was coffee; and the tobacco that once provided livelihoods for so many went unharvested. In the spring plans had been made for the defense of Washington City, and soldiers now drilled in President's Square, bringing home to everyone just how close the war was. There was little money in the Talbot household, and less life, and as she approached the house she had once loved, Rebecca felt as if she were entering a mausoleum.

To her surprise, Amelia was standing in the front hall when she entered, fussing with her bonnet and surrounded by bandboxes and trunks. "What in the world?" Rebecca exclaimed. "Amelia, what is all this?"

"I'm leaving." Amelia put her chin up defiantly. "And nothing you can say will stop me."

"Leaving!" Rebecca dropped into the chair that stood in the hall. "Amelia, you can't."

"Oh, can't I." Amelia's voice was grim, making Rebecca look at her as she hadn't in too long. Why, Amelia had grown up. She wasn't a girl, but a woman. The two years past had brought more changes than Rebecca had realized. "I've thought this over, Becky, and I've decided I will not stay in this—this tomb!—any longer."

Rebecca closed her eyes, tired, so tired, only vaguely surprised that Amelia's thoughts echoed hers. "I know it hasn't been too lively around here, Melia, and there's been little fun, but—"

"Fun! Is that what you think I want?" Amelia crouched before her, her face incredulous. "I need more than fun. I need a life. Oh, Becky! Just look around." Her gesture encompassed more than the hall, dusty in spite of all Rebecca's best efforts, for the lack of income had forced them to let Martha and Jacob go. It took in the entire house; the closed doors, the curtains, drawn at Ezra's command, the darkness. "I can't live like this. Papa never comes out of his study anymore, and when he does he doesn't talk, and, Becky, you"— she reached out to grasp Rebecca's hands—"you're growing just like him."

Rebecca pulled her hands away. "I'm not."

"You are. You never smile anymore, and I don't know when I last heard you laugh. Not since you sent Marcus away."

Rebecca started. "You know about that?"

"I saw you." Amelia's voice softened. "The day war was declared. Oh, Becky! Why didn't you go with him?"

"He didn't love me, Amelia."

Amelia snorted. "The way he looked at you? You were blind, Rebecca, and foolish." She stood up, drawing on her gloves. "I'm not going to make the same mistake."

Rebecca blinked at her. "Where will you go? To your mother's family?"

"No." Amelia finished buttoning her gloves. "Gilbert Collins has asked me to marry him. I've finally agreed."

"Mr. Collins! Oh, Amelia. Why didn't you tell me?"

Amelia glanced at her from the mirror. "He's been asking me for a long time, but I couldn't. I thought you needed me. Now I know . . ."

"What?" Rebecca said when she didn't go on.

"You're like Papa, nursing your hurts and not letting anyone close."

"That's not fair!"

"No? Look at me, Rebecca. I'm not a timid little girl anymore. I've grown up. But you don't treat me that way."

"I'll change—"

"I wish you could. Oh, Becky! Do you think I like leaving like this? I almost asked you to stand up with me at my wedding, except . . ."

"What?"

"I didn't think you'd agree."

Rebecca swallowed around a lump in her throat. "I'm sorry, Amelia. You know I would, but . . ." Her voice trailed off as she glanced at the study door. "If he disapproves of your marriage, there'll be no living with him."

"Then come with us. Oh! I hear a carriage." Amelia flew to the door and looked out the sidelight. " 'Tis Gilbert. Oh, Becky!" She spun around, catching Rebecca's hands in hers. "Come with me. You can stay with us."

"I can't, Amelia." Rebecca rose, unsteadily. "I wish I could, but—I can't. Someone has to look after Father."

"Becky." Amelia's eyes filled with tears, and she reached up to touch Rebecca's cheek. "Why is it always you who has to carry the burdens?"

"Because someone has to. Oh, Amelia!" She caught her sister close, squeezing her eyes shut. "I'm glad for you, truly, I am. But I'll be so lonely."

"Find out where Marcus is and go to him."

The lump in her throat grew larger. "I doubt he'd have me now."

"I think you're wrong." The sound of the door knocker echoed in the hall. "That's Gilbert. I must go. Rebecca, please, please, change your mind."

"I can't. Does Father know?"

"That I'm leaving? Yes. I went into his study and told him. He just looked at me, but he knew what I was saying."

"Oh, dear. I don't know what he'll do now."

The door knocker sounded again. "I must go. Wish me happy, Becky."

"You know I do." Rebecca pulled her sister close and then, as abruptly, released her. "Be happy," she whispered and fled up the stairs to her room. She couldn't bear to watch another loved one leave her.

In the upstairs hallway she listened to the muted voices below, and then the click of the door latch as Amelia left. Alone. All gone now, her son, Amelia, and Marcus. At tear slid down her cheek, and she blinked furiously, determined not to give in to self-pity. No matter that she woke nights aching for Marcus, yearning for his touch; no matter that she went through her days aimlessly, existing only because she had to. The choice had been hers. But if she had it to do over—no. She shook her head. Even now, she didn't know if she'd do it differently. She loved Marcus, needed him; without him she was dying a slow death. She didn't know, though, if she could have lived with herself, had she abandoned her father and sister. They had needed her then. Father still needed her now.

Straightening, she brushed a hand across her face, wiping away any trace of tears, and went downstairs to make the dinner her father would probably ignore and she would only pick at. She had to make the best of things, but, oh, she was so lonely. And she doubted it would ever get any better.

The sleek black ship had docked at Alexandria, several miles below Washington City on the Potomac, and discharged its cargo: coffee, fresh oranges, sugar. She was a smuggler, bringing in the goods made scarce by the British blockade, and her captain was a respectable man. A far cry, Marcus thought, turning for one last look at his ship as he headed up King Street, from the days when he'd been a hated and feared pirate. If he could, though, he would bring those days back. They had brought him Rebecca.

"Be ye goin' to see her this time, Cap'n?" Tyner asked, scurrying to keep up with Marcus's long strides.

"I don't know," Marcus said shortly.

"About time ye did. Ye haven't been a joy to be around."

"Tyner—"

"Nay, I'll speak my mind on this, Cap'n. Lettin' her go was a mistake. Both times."

"She chose her father," Marcus said through gritted teeth. Aye, and not just once. Time after time in the last years he'd written to her, and not once had she replied.

"She had no choice." Tyner retorted. "What did ye offer her, Cap'n? Life on a pirate ship? All the time worryin' and wonderin' if ye were alive, or comin' back to her? Did ye even ask her to wed?"

"Devil take it, Tyner, 'tis none of your concern!"

"Mebbe not." Tyner nodded. "But I don't like seein' ye unhappy, Cap'n, and ye are." He paused, as if waiting for a reply. "Go to her, Cap'n. Ye know ye want to."

Marcus stood still, gazing ahead without seeing anything. Oh, yes, he wanted to. That was the problem. Twice he'd asked Rebecca to stay with him, and twice she had refused. If he went to her he'd ask her yet again. Only a fool would put himself through that. "Maybe," he said slowly.

"Boat leaves in half hour, Cap'n. Ye could be in Georgetown this afternoon."

"Damn you, Tyner," he said, but without any heat. "You won't give me any peace until I do go, will you?"

Tyner grinned up at him. "No, Cap'n, that I won't. Ye're makin' the right decision," he called as Marcus abruptly hefted his ditty bag and began heading back down the hill, toward the waterfront. "And this time, ask her to marry ye."

Passersby hearing the exchange grinned at Marcus, and he gave them a sheepish smile in return. Marry? Aye, maybe. Hard to do, though, when there was so much left for him to do, and such a need for his services. It was making him into a rich man, but that wasn't his main reason for smuggling. Privateering had been profitable, too, but not nearly as satisfying as he'd expected. Smuggling was different, a war of wits between him and the British ships roaming the coast, a battle he had so far won. It had been close this time, with that British corvette hot on his heels, but his ship was a fine one, as fast as could be. Once again, he'd escaped. Now he was walking into a different kind of trap. The strange thing was, he thought as he boarded the schooner that would take him upriver to Georgetown, he didn't mind at all.

Rebecca sat by the base of a broad oak tree, knees drawn up, watching a swan glide on the serene surface of the little lake nearby. It was peaceful here, the only sounds birdsong and the wind rustling in the leaves overhead. Cooler, as well, with the lawn a verdant green. Rebecca glanced at the wind-ruffled grass a few feet away, her heart skipping a beat. Few would realize that the slight mound was a grave, for it was unmarked, but its location was graven on her heart. Her son was buried there.

She looked at the grave for a moment, and then away. Odd, but the pain of her son's death had grown distant. It would always be with her, but she had more recent disasters to consider. Amelia was married, and happily ensconced in a snug little house on F Street, not far from the President's House. She missed her sister in the dark tomb her house had become. Papa stayed in his study all the time, coming out only to sleep. What he did in there all day she didn't know; he had a great many papers lying around, but he took pains to cover them when Rebecca brought him his meals on a tray. When he did talk it was about the war, never about Amelia. More obdurate than ever, he behaved as if she had never existed, and Rebecca, for all her pleading, could not make him change his mind. Thus her visits to her sister were clandestine and brief, and yet she continued to make them. They were the only light spots in a dark, dark life.

Branches rustled nearby, and she glanced up incuriously to see who else had come to pay his respects to the dead. A man, carelessly attired in a coat of navy blue that needed a good sponging, with longish black hair, and broad shoulders—she stiffened. It couldn't be, but it was. Marcus.

She didn't move, utterly convinced he was an apparition, though he walked toward her. "Hello, Rebecca," he said, his voice very gentle.

"Marcus." She said it without surprise. "Am I imagining you?"

"No." He dropped down onto one knee before her. "I'm here." He glanced toward the grave. "There was no answer at your house. A neighbor told me you might be here."

"We had to let Martha go." She glanced toward the headstone, too. "I spend a fair amount of time here. 'Tis peaceful."

"It's dead, Rebecca."

She shrugged. "It doesn't seem to make much difference."

"No? You've changed, lass."

"So have you." Only now did she turn to look at him, tall

and broad and strong, like the oak at her back. If only he were as dependable. "You look like the Raven again. Your hair is all dark."

He shook his head. "No. Not the Raven, and not the fop I was before. This is me, Rebecca."

"At last."

"Yes, lass."

She looked away again, and now it was his turn to study her. Thin, so thin, her face almost gaunt, and pale. Her eyes were dull; even her hair seemed to have lost its sheen. Devil take it, what had happened to his Rebecca? "You've been through a tough time, lass."

She blinked, and he realized his words had brought her nearly to tears. "There's been worse."

"Not that I've heard." Gently he laid his hand on hers, clasped around her knees, but after a few moments, she withdrew. "You don't seem surprised to see me."

"Nothing seems to surprise me anymore." Again she turned to look at him. "Why are you here?"

"I just brought a load of goods into Alexandria."

"The spoils of privateering?"

"No, lass. Legitimate goods, from the Indies. I brought them through the blockade." He smiled suddenly. "From St. Thomas. Do you remember it, Rebecca—"

"Oh, don't!" she burst out. "Please, just—don't."

"I can't help it," he said, his voice low. "I think of you all the time, Rebecca. No, don't turn from me. I hear your voice in the wind, see your eyes in the sea, wake in the night and want you there beside me. I've missed you, *leannan*." More than she knew; more than he could say. "I should never have left you."

"Don't," she said again.

He pressed on. At least she'd shown some emotion, rather than that dull hopelessness. "You're all I think about, Rebecca. What I do, I do only because I have to, but if I could, I would take you away with me, hold you, kiss you, make you my own—no, don't pull away." This as she jerked back. "I won't hurt you. If I could, I'd shelter you from anything that ever hurt you, Rebecca. I would."

"But you don't love me!" she cried, and her face twisted. "You talk of taking me away, but it's never more than talk, with no promises, no mention of the future—"

"Oh, lass—"

"—and I know why. I'm not good enough, am I? Even for a pirate and a spy, my past is too much and—"

"Devil take it, Rebecca! I don't give that for your past." He snapped his fingers. "Is that what you've been thinking?"

"'Tis the truth. Oh, God." She rested her head on her knees, the tears she'd held back coming out in great, gulping sobs. "Why couldn't you love me?"

He sat very still, and he knew at last, under the shade of the oak tree, that he did love her. That he had loved her for a very long time. Why else would he feel as he did, empty, without her beside him? Why else would he keep coming back to her? And why, he wondered, reaching out for her, hadn't he seen it before? "Ah, *leannan*," he said, gathering her into his arms. He expected her to struggle, but she lay against him limply, her only movement the convulsions of her sobs. "*Leannan, mo cridhe*," he crooned, rocking her back and forth. "Of course I love ye. Of course I do."

"No, you don't," she sobbed, her head resting against his chest. "You're saying it to make me stop crying."

"Rebecca." He pulled a little away, making his voice stern. "Did we, or did we not, agree to be honest with each other?"

She looked up at him, her breath coming in little gasps, and in her eyes he saw something new: the fragile beginnings of hope. "Y-yes."

"Then do ye really think I'd lie to ye?"

"It's funny."

"What is?" he said, startled.

"On the *Raven*, when you were emotional, you sounded English. Now the brogue is back."

"Is it? But ye bring it out in me, *leannan*. The joy and the laughter, the music." He smiled at her, taking out his handkerchief to wipe away her tears. "The love."

"I think," she said, her voice as stern as his had been, "that you have kissed the Blarney Stone."

He couldn't help it; he gave a startled bark of laughter, a sound not often heard in that hallowed place. "Rebecca, Rebecca." He rocked her in his arms again. "How have I lived without you?"

"I don't know." She reached up to touch his cheek tentatively, as if still not believing the reality of him. "I don't know how I lived without you."

He sobered. "It's been bad, Rebecca."

She sighed, looking away. "Bad enough. Amelia's married, and Father pretends she doesn't exist. Father pretends," she said, her voice low, "that very little exists."

He had a sudden thought. "Rebecca, I wrote to you. Did you ever get my letters?"

"No." She stared at him. "You wrote me?"

"Aye. Did you really think I'd leave you like that, lass?"

She glanced away. "Yes. I thought you had."

"Devil take it." His lips thinned. "Your father must have taken the letters. Has he hurt you?"

"No. Mostly he's left me alone. And that's the problem." Her eyes filled with tears again. "I've been so lonely, Marcus."

"Aye, I know it, lass." Tenderly he brushed her tears away. "But that's done. Marry me, Rebecca."

Her eyes grew wide. "I—you mean that?"

"Aye. Marry me. I'll take you to my home. It's a modest place, not like your father's, but it will be yours. You'll be my wife. And the mother of my children."

Rebecca's lashes fluttered down. So much to take in, and none of it seemed quite real. "I—oh, I want to, Marcus! But I can't."

"Rebecca—"

"It's not my father," she rushed on, the words tumbling out. "Since the war started he's hardly noticed I'm alive. All he needs is someone to see that he's fed and has clothes to wear. It's me. I don't know why, Marcus, I truly don't, but—I can't." She looked up at him, pleading for understanding. "I just can't."

"If I give ye time, lass, will that do it?" he said, his voice low.

She gripped his arm. "You promise me you'll come back?"

"Lass, I don't think I'm ever going to leave you."

"Well, that might cause problems," she said dryly. "Even Father might notice if you started living at our house."

"Don't jest," he said severely, though he was smiling. "Is it all a bit too much, lass?"

"Yes." She looked at him in wonder. "That's it. How did you know?"

"Never mind." He shook his head. "Aye, lass, I'll give ye time. But not too much, mind." The look in his eyes warm, tender, belied the menace in his voice. "Because you're mine."

"Aye, Cap'n. And you," she said, turning to him and placing her hands on his shoulders, "are mine. Now. Are you ever going to kiss me?"

"It's a kiss you want, then? I think I can oblige. Come here."

She went into his arms like coming home. They closed about her, welcoming her, sheltering her, and in his embrace the miseries of the past years began to drain away. She kissed him with all the longing, all the abandon she had denied, all the passion she now admitted lay within her, and gloried in it. This wasn't wanton. This was love, and if he didn't really mean what he had said, if he didn't really love her, what she felt was real and true. The consequences no longer mattered. She loved this man.

At length Marcus drew back, eyes glittering. "Ah, lass," he murmured, reaching out idly to cup her breast. She shivered as his thumbnail ran lazy circles about the tip, feeling as if she were going to dissolve into a pool of need and desire right there. "Do ye know what ye do to me?"

"I've an idea."

"An idea, is it?" He leaned back against the tree, legs sprawled, arms about her waist where she faced him, half kneeling, half leaning on him. In such an intimate position she couldn't help but be aware of his reactions; yet when he took her hand and led it downward, pressing it against the bulge in his trousers, she didn't protest. "That, lass. That is what you do to me."

"Good," she said, letting her fingers play as they would, and smiling as a groan came from his lips. It felt strange, smiling, it had been so long. Strange, but good.

"Little witch," he muttered and hauled her close again. His kiss burned through her, and long-dormant nerves and responses, the very fiber of her, began to stir in a rush of sensation. Painful, this coming back to life, feeling again, when she had tried so hard not to feel anything for so long. Painful, but good, and right. And as he'd said a moment earlier, too much.

Rebecca pulled away this time, averting her head when he would have kissed her again, so that his lips only grazed her cheek. "Not here, Marcus," she whispered.

She could feel him regarding her. "No, not here," he agreed finally.

"And not now."

That took him longer to answer. "It's been two years, lass."

"I know." She looked down at her hands, now resting on her lap. "But I can't."

His lips tightened, but he nodded. "Aye. If you can't, you can't. Don't look at me like that, lass."

"Like what?"

"All big-eyed and sad. I'm not angry with you."

"I didn't think you were." She toyed with the laces of his shirt. "But you'll be leaving again, won't you?"

"Soon," he admitted. "But I'm not leaving you, lass, I promise you that. I'll be back." His eyes searched her face. "I will, Rebecca."

"When?"

He shifted beneath her, and again she felt his desire, setting off sparks within her. "I don't know, and that's the truth. But soon. Soon as I can get to the Indies and back, Rebecca." He caught her chin in his hand, forcing her to face him. "My roving days are over."

"I'm sorry for it."

"Why?" he said, startled. "I thought you'd be pleased."

"Oh, I am, but ..." She lifted her eyes to study him, rakish-looking with his open shirt and long hair. "I loved the pirate, too."

"He's here." He pressed her hand to his heart. "I suspect, lass, there's a bit of the pirate in you, too."

"Mercy, no! A plain, prim spinster like me?"

"Not plain, and not prim." He punctuated each word with a kiss.

"But a spinster, nevertheless."

"Not for long," he said, rising to his knees. "We'd best go, lass. If we stay here no telling what will happen."

She felt her cheeks color. Oh, she knew quite well what would happen, and in spite of her earlier refusal, she wanted it, too. "I suppose I should be getting home to see to supper." She held her hand up to him, and he helped her up. "Though Father probably won't eat it."

He frowned. "Lass, isn't there someplace else you can go? To your sister's, perhaps?"

"No." She shook her head, bending down to retrieve her bonnet. "No, I'll see it through, Marcus."

"I never have understood why you wanted to stay with the old man," he muttered.

Truth to tell, neither did she anymore, except that he was her father. "I know. Let's not argue about it, Marcus." She placed a finger on his lips. "We've found each other. That's all that matters."

He frowned. "Aye, lass, but I worry about your safety."

"I'm all right. Where do you go now?"

"Back to Alexandria, and my ship. I'm sorry, lass, but I will come back."

"I know you will," she said, believing it at last.

"Come." He held out his arm. "I'll see you home."

"Gladly, sir," Rebecca said and placed her hand on his arm, letting him lead her out to the street. Hope, so long dead within her, was blossoming again. Hope for the future, hope for a life filled with love and laughter and babies. She cast one quick glance over her shoulder at the cemetery, saying good-bye to her son, to her past. Then, smiling up at Marcus, she tucked her arm closer to his, and they walked on, facing their future.

And because they were so involved with each other, neither noticed the man who slipped from beneath the trees behind them and ambled along, following them.

Jeremiah Dee sat up straight, hand slamming onto the table in the seedy tavern where he now made his home. "You saw him? Where?"

"With her, mate." The little man sitting at ease across from him, his hair lank and greasy and his clothes stained, grinned. "Hot night, mate. A cold beer would taste good."

"Drinking is evil," Dee said, but nevertheless he signaled to the barkeep, who came over with a pewter tankard. "Now, Simms, tell me all."

Simms took a deep draught of the beer and exhaled in satisfaction, wiping his arm across his mouth. "Ah, that was good. What'll I get for all my work?"

"We discussed payment." Dee eyed the man distastefully. A distressing business, but with his country at war someone had to keep an eye on the upstart Americans. Someone had to prove that Marcus Brand was not an upstanding citizen, but the Raven. When war had been declared and the need for espionage became apparent, Dee had jumped at the chance given to him, volunteering to serve behind enemy lines. In the last two years he had put together a network of agents and had managed to find out some valuable information. His headquarters was at this tavern deep in the Maryland countryside, a lucky find, for the barkeep had been born in England and had no use for Mr. Madison's war, as he called it. Few questioned Dee's comings and goings; fewer still even talked with him, and that was how he liked it. He had a mission to perform, a destiny to fulfill.

"Aye, we did." Simms took another deep draft, banged the tankard down, and signaled to the barkeep. "But I deserve extra for this."

"You'll get what we agreed upon, and no more," Dee said coldly.

Tension flickered between them, not broken by the barkeep coming back with the refilled tankard, until, at last, the man looked away. "Well, mate, it's like this. I've been following the Talbot wench, like you said. Not that she ever does much. Stays home, mostly. But today she went to that cemetery again." He paused to take a sip. "Not much to her, but it's been a long time since I've had a woman—"

"She's not to be touched."

"If you say so, Lieutenant." His face darkened. "But I've got something to settle with her."

Dee felt a flicker of satisfaction. God was smiling on his mission; how else to explain this stroke of luck? When he had been in need of someone to keep watch on Rebecca, lest the Raven return to her, in another tavern he had found Simms, deserter from the Royal Navy, with a grudge of his own against both Rebecca and the Raven. "Never mind that," he said and withdrew a coin from his pocket. Simms's eyes grew larger. "Tell me what happened."

"Well, mate, it was like this. I followed her to that cemetery, like you said, and I thought it was going to be a dull one. But then he showed up."

"Who?"

"Him. The one you told me about. And I'll tell you somethin'. He's the Raven, sure enough. Even without the eyepatch, I'd recognize him anywhere. Didn't I serve under him?" His face darkened. "Aye, and didn't he try to cheat me at cards on St. Thomas? Nearly had him, I did, and good riddance, except *she* came along and knocked me down. Still don't know how she did it." He glared into his tankard. "Thought he was going to cut my balls off."

Dee leaned back. "You'll get your revenge, Simms. That I promise. With your information we can bring him down."

"And you'll let me have at him, first," Simms said, banging the tankard down again.

Dee hesitated and then nodded. Why not agree with him? Simms didn't need to know that Dee had other plans for him. "Yes." He pushed the coins across the table and rose. "A good job, Simms, and there's a bit extra there for you."

Simms smiled with satisfaction. "Now that's right generous of you, mate. Appreciate it."

"You earned it. We'll get him yet." Dee inclined his head and then turned, stalking out of the smoky, beery tavern, though the heavy air outside offered little relief. Barbarous country, this, he thought, looking up at the stars. But he'd not have to endure it for long. The Raven was within his grasp. Soon he'd have his revenge.

Chapter 26

~

"Becky?" Amelia's voice rang through the house, and in the parlor Rebecca dropped her dust rag in surprise. "Where are you—oh, there!"

"Amelia." Rebecca hurried across the room to embrace her sister and then drew back. Amelia was garbed in a fashionable ensemble of pale blue trimmed with darker blue ribbon, a shawl tossed about her shoulders and a chip straw bonnet upon her head, while she—well, the less said about her frock, the better. "I'd hug you, but I'm all over dust. You look so pretty, Melia."

"I wish I could say the same for you. Whatever are you doing?"

"Oh, I thought I'd give the house a good turnout."

"In this heat? Can't you wait till the fall?"

"Yes, well, I let it go in the spring, and last fall, too."

Amelia tilted her head to the side. "You look different, Becky. I don't quite know how, but you're different."

Rebecca smiled and shrugged, imitating Marcus's mannerism. She knew what the difference was. She was happy. It had been several weeks since she had seen Marcus, but she had faith in him. She had no doubt that soon he would come sailing up the river to her again. The thought made her feel alive, vital, as she hadn't in much too long. "Nothing has changed. Oh, but do come in, Melia. I fear the only clean chair I can offer you is in the kitchen, but I know you won't stand on ceremony."

"Well"—Amelia glanced back over her shoulder, and her smile dimmed—"I cannot stay very long, Becky. Gilbert is waiting for me outside, and if I'm not out in a little while he'll come for me."

Rebecca frowned. "Why?"

"Because—" Again she looked over her shoulder. "I need to see Papa."

"Oh, Melia." Rebecca grasped her hands. "I'm not sure he'll see you."

"I need to tell him—oh, Becky, I can't keep it from you!" she exclaimed, her face glowing. "I'm increasing."

"Oh, Melia." Rebecca caught Amelia up in a hug, ignoring the pang that went through her. Her sister was going to be a mother, while her own arms were empty. "That's wonderful."

"Yes. I thought if Papa knew he's to have a grandchild, he would forgive me."

Rebecca bit her lips as that pang went through her again. He had had a grandchild once, and never had he forgiven Rebecca for it. It still hurt.

"Becky? Are you listening to me?"

"What? Oh, I'm sorry, Melia." Once her father had loved her. She continued to insist to Marcus that he did still, in the face of all the evidence to the contrary. All these years, could she have been wrong? "What did you say?"

"Will you tell him I'm here? If I go in unannounced—he's in his study, isn't he?—I fear he'll have an apoplexy."

"He may not wish to see you, Melia," Rebecca said as gently as possible. "He doesn't forgive easily."

"He'll forgive me," Amelia said with touching confidence.

Rebecca bit her lips and then nodded. "Very well. Wait here. I'll go to him."

In the hall Rebecca untied her apron and pulled the kerchief from her head, smoothing her hair with nervous hands. She saw little of her father these days, and when she did he was distant, remote. Yet sometimes there was a fire in his eyes that made her wonder uneasily what emotions burned inside him. Raising her hand, she knocked on the door and at his answering growl went into the study.

Ezra looked up from behind his desk, his eyes red-rimmed and hostile. Papers were everywhere, on the desk, on the floor, on the chairs, some in place so long that they were covered with thick layers of dust, for he would not allow her in here to clean. As Rebecca closed the door behind her, she saw out of the corner of her eye that he was slipping one paper over another, making her wonder, yet again, what he did all day. "Well? What is it?" Ezra growled. "Speak up, girl."

Rebecca lifted her chin. Like all of them, her father had changed; he was no longer stout, and what hair he had left was completely white. Yet one thing remained the same, and that was his unpredictable temper. "There's someone here to see you, Father," she said finally.

Ezra grunted and returned his attention to the paper before him. "Tell whoever it is to go away."

Her lips tightened. He had to know who it was. "Father, it's Amelia. She—"

"I will not see her!"

"But she's your daughter—"

"I have no daughter." He rose so abruptly that she took a step back. "Don't you understand, girl? I have no daughter by that name."

"You're wrong." Rebecca stood her ground, fighting for Amelia, where she had never fought for herself. "She's as much your daughter as I am, even if she married someone you don't approve of. She's come here to tell you something—"

"I tell you I won't see her!" he roared, and the silver inkstand, once prized by him because it had been a gift from Amelia's mother, whizzed through the air. It struck the paneling scant inches from where Rebecca stood, spattering her and everything else with ink. "Now get out of here, girl, before I forget myself."

Rebecca glared at him and then turned on her heel, stalking out of the room. Stupid, stubborn old man, she fumed, slamming the door behind her. And dangerous. If he were to throw something at Amelia in her condition, what would happen?

Amelia was standing in the hall, her face pale. "Oh, Becky!" she gasped. "What did he do?"

"Threw the inkstand." Rebecca grimaced down at the black stains on her dress. "I'll never get these out."

"And it's on your face. Oh, Becky." Amelia's eyes filled with tears. "I never meant for anything to happen to you."

Rebecca shook her head. "Nothing has. But I think you'd best go, and let me try to persuade him. Another day—"

"He won't change. Becky"—Amelia grasped her hands—"you can't stay here. I fear for what he'll do to you."

"He won't hurt me, Melia."

"Come home with me and Gilbert. He won't mind. We've discussed it, Becky, and he thinks you should, too."

"No." Gently, Rebecca pulled her hand free. "I can't go, Amelia. Who will take care of Father? Lord knows what he'd do if I left."

"He is a mean, selfish, stubborn old man, and I don't understand why you are sacrificing yourself in this way."

"I'm not. Believe me, I'm not." She cast a quick glance over her shoulder at the study door, and her voice lowered to a whisper. "I've plans for the future. No, I can't tell you what they are, but trust me, Amelia. I will be all right."

The front door opened. "Amelia?" a masculine voice called.

"Yes, Gilbert." Amelia crossed to her husband. "Oh, Gilbert, do please tell Becky she must come with us."

"No," Rebecca said as he opened his mouth to speak. "I've made up my mind on this, Melia, and you can't change it. But you'd best go." Again she looked back at the study door. "If Father hears you, I don't know what he'll do. And you wouldn't want anything happening to Amelia, would you?"

Gilbert started to answer and then shook his head. "No. But you know you can come to us if you have to."

"Yes, I do know that." Rebecca shepherded them toward the door, listening to their protestations and agreeing, soothingly, that yes, they were right, wanting them only to be gone. Wanting Amelia to be safe. It was a relief to close the door at last behind them, leaving her alone in this dark, miserable home. But not for long.

Not stopping to think, she crossed the hall and crashed the study door open. "You're wrong," she announced, marching across the room and planting her hands on Ezra's desk, leaning forward. "You are a stupid, stubborn, bitter old man, and you are wrong. I've stood by you all these years, but this is the outside of enough! I'll not stand for anymore, do you hear me?"

Ezra said nothing; merely sat back and studied her, an odd glitter in his eyes. "All these years," she went on, heedless, years of hurts and slights rising up to fuel her anger, "all these years, I have waited for one little sign from you that you forgave me, that you even still cared. Well, I will not wait any longer. Not after today." She straightened, suddenly tired, her energy and anger draining away. "Marcus Brand has asked me to marry him. When he returns, I intend to tell him that I will."

With that, she turned and left the room, closing the study door very quietly behind her. Ezra continued to sit still for a few moments, his face impassive, and then reached for a fresh sheet of paper. Rather than retrieve the inkstand, he had opened a new bottle of ink. He dipped into it, the tip of his quill scratching across the paper. When he was done he folded the paper and sealed it, and then sat back looking at the direction with great satisfaction. Rebecca thought she could defy him, did she? She would learn. Chuckling a bit, he tossed the letter onto the desk, and the direction was clear to see: a tavern deep in the Maryland countryside.

The night was hot, sticky. Rebecca tossed in her bed, trying to sleep, but memory of the day's events, combined with the heat, prevented her. Amelia was right, she thought, sitting up and punching her pillow. She couldn't stay here any longer. Oh, if only Marcus were here ... And, as if the thought had summoned him, she heard a pattering at her window.

Jumping up from the bed, she ran across the room, wincing as she trod on a pebble that had come in through the open window. Not caring, she hopped on her other foot, until at last she reached the window and leaned out, her heart swelling with joy. In the dim light she could just make him out, standing below her, a finger to his lips and a basket of some kind in his other hand. Eagerly she waved to him, and he gestured to her to come to him.

She needed no second invitation. Stopping only to toss a shawl about her shoulders, she ran out of her room, tripping lightly down the back stairs and out to the garden. At the sight of her he let the basket drop and opened his arms wide, and she flew into them. "Oh, Marcus!" she gasped. "I'm so glad to see you—"

"And you." He lowered his head and took her mouth in a fierce kiss of possession, of need, sending flames through her. "God, Rebecca." He crushed her to him. "I thought I'd never get back to you."

"But you're here, you're here." It was almost a song, and, indeed, she felt like singing. "Do you want to come in?"

"Better not. Unless"—he held her a bit away from him—"you wish to put some clothes on?"

She beamed up at him. "No."

"Good. I like ye like this, lass," he said, hugging her again. "All soft and warm. You've put some weight back on."

'Yes." Her fingers dug into his shoulders as reality intruded. "I knew I'd need to be strong."

"That you are, and brave. I—what's this?" This as his seeking fingers, exploring her face, found and stopped at a dark stain. "The devil take it, did he hit you again?"

"No, Marcus! It's ink," she said hastily. "He threw the inkstand, and it will not wash off. I assure you, I'm fine."

"I would like to teach him a lesson."

"Not now." She cast a glance back at the house. All remained dark, but sounds carried on the still night air. "Come. Let's go into the arbor. Come," she repeated, tugging at his arm as he continued to glare at the house. "We'll have privacy there."

"Devil take it," he said, but he turned at last. "But one day, Rebecca, I'll make him pay for what he's done to you."

"Yes, Marcus. Here, sit on the bench. What did you bring?"

"Supper."

"Supper?"

"Aye." He set the basket down in the arbor. "A good wine, and other treats. And"—his eyes gleamed, "something for us to sit on."

Rebecca eyed the blanket folded atop the basket and then glanced up again. To sit on, indeed! She suspected he had very different ideas. "A practical idea," she said, nodding, giving away none of her excitement.

"Practical." He caught her up again, whirling her around. "My beautiful, practical, proper Rebecca."

Her laugh was breathless as she supported herself above him, her hands on his shoulders. "My pirate."

"Aye. That I am." His grip loosened, tightened, allowing her to slide down against him, until her face was level with his and her toes still danced above the ground. "And don't ye forget it."

She kissed him lightly, playfully. "I'm not likely to, am I? You've already threatened to abduct me again."

Another playful kiss, this one initiated by him. "Aye. And I'll do so if I have to."

"You don't." She nibbled at his lower lip, darting away when he would have deepened the kiss.

"I'll wager you'd like me to."

"Why, Mr. Brand! I am a proper, practical lady—"

"Woman," he corrected, and this time his kiss was longer, harder. "My woman."

She tossed her head. "Sure of yourself, aren't you?"

His eyes glinted again. "When I have you in my arms like this, all warm and soft and willing—aye, I'm sure of myself." Another kiss, longer yet, and when he raised his head the playfulness was gone from his face. "I'm not letting you go again, Rebecca."

"Good," she murmured and hooked her arms around his neck, bringing his face down to hers. She, too, was done with playing and teasing. She wanted him, and if these few stolen moments were all they had, she would make the most of them.

The kisses increased in length, in number. His tongue darted in past her lips; hers tangled with his and followed, as his hands molded her to him. His caresses were quick, hard, impatient, and yet they inflamed her, making her cry out softly as he caught her nipple between thumb and forefinger; making him gasp when she moved her hips against his. And then it was all frenzy, all need. He tore at the ribbons that held her nightshift closed, pushing it off her shoulders. He warmed her with his body, his hands, his mouth. She clung to him, not letting go when he bent to shake out the blanket and lay it on the ground with quick, impatient movements, not even when he laid her atop it. Her fingers, eager, clumsy, pulled the lacings of his shirt, at the buttons of his breeches, caressed and surrounded his hardness, full and surging in her hands. He was above her, and then, with one quick, smooth thrust, within her, driving deep, driving home, and it was too much, it was enough. She shattered into a thousand tiny pieces, losing herself and not caring. She knew who she was. She was the Raven's woman, now and forever.

The stars twinkled above, distant and eternal. Rebecca lay still, combing her fingers through his thick hair, feeling his weight upon her, welcoming it. Such a fool she'd been, ever letting him go. Such a fool, desperately searching for long-lost propriety and the love her father wouldn't give her. "Welcome home, sailor," she whispered.

He raised his head to look at her, his eyes dark, unfathomable. "I'll give you a home, Rebecca," he said, his voice husky. "Not a bed in a pirate ship, or a rented room, or the hard ground. A real home."

She smoothed his hair back from his forehead. "I don't regret any of it."

"I know." He dropped a kiss on her shoulder, and she shivered in delight. "Nevertheless, you deserve more. You were made for loving." His hands swept down, bracketed her hips, though she was already as close to him as she could be. "For loving and being loved. And you'll catch cold if we stay like this."

"No," she protested as he rolled off her, but too late; he had already climbed to his feet, with the grace of a cat, and was distractedly searching the arbor for their clothes. She sighed. Her pirate could be a stubborn man. Best to humor him. She reached for his trousers, holding them up to him.

"Thank you, lass." He knelt beside her. "Sit up," he commanded, and dropped her nightshift over her head, pausing to tie the ribbons just so. How odd, that his dressing her felt as sweet and intimate as his undressing her had.

"I told Father today that I plan to marry you," she said calmly.

His fingers stilled on the ribbons, and then his hands gripped her arms. "Did you? Did you really?"

"Yes. I—"

"What did he say?"

"Nothing. He just looked at me." The crisp curls on his chest were too inviting to resist. She let her fingers drift through them, feeling him shudder in response. "I don't know what he's thinking anymore, except when he gets angry. He refused to see Amelia today."

"He is a hard, unforgiving man."

"Because he's been hurt."

"Devil take it, Rebecca, I wish you would stop making excuses for him. What did you ever do to hurt him?"

"Not me. I don't know much about his life, Marcus, but I do know it hurt him terribly when my mother left him."

"And it hurt you."

"Of course it did." She looked away. "I spent a long time wondering what I'd done to send her away."

"For God's sake, Rebecca—"

"It's only lately I realized that it wasn't me. It was him. Or maybe something in her. I don't know." She gazed up at him. "What I think now is that he doesn't want to lose me."

"For God's sake," he said again.

"I'm serious. I don't think he wanted to lose Amelia, either."

"Then why cut her out of his life? Why treat you as he does?"

"Because it hurts less."

"That's foolish—"

"Yes. But 'tis the only thing I can think of."

"People don't act that way. If they love someone they forgive them."

"Most people. Not him. And not me." She looked away. "I would have been just like him if you hadn't talked to me about forgiveness. 'Tis why I understand him." She turned back to face him. "I'm asking you for time, Marcus."

"What?"

"Time. I need more."

"I didn't intend to take you away immediately," he said, deliberately cruel, and regretted it as soon as he saw her flinch. "Ah, lass, I'm sorry for that. I want you with me. You know that. But it seems you always choose him over me."

"No." She shook her head. "Not this time. At least, not for long. Let me talk to him, Marcus. He did like you once."

Marcus frowned. "I don't like it."

"Why not?"

"I've got this feeling that if I don't take you away soon, I never will."

"Silly." She laid her finger on his lips. "You know I'm yours."

"Aye. But I worry about you here, with the British in the Chesapeake. Talk is they'll invade."

"Everyone says they'll go to Baltimore or Annapolis."

"With the capital so close? I think they'll come here, Rebecca." His gaze was somber. "Even if they don't, your father will do what he can to come between us, and what will you do then? Who will you choose?"

"You."

"Will you?"

"Yes. And if he doesn't agree—the next time you come,
I'll go with you."

"Let me talk to him, Rebecca."

"No!" She eyed him with undisguised alarm. " 'Twill do
no good. Let me do it, Marcus. I know how to manage him."

"You haven't done a good job so far," he pointed out.

"That's not fair."

"Isn't it? I'm offering you myself, a home, everything I
have, and still you choose him."

"But not for long! I told you . . ." She dropped her head
to her knees. "Must we quarrel," she said in a very small
voice, "when you'll be leaving me again?"

"It's your fault that I do."

"Don't put this on me, Marcus Brand!" she flared, his Rebecca again, glorious in her indignation as she faced him,
hands on hips. "You were a wandering man before I met
you."

"Aye. And now I've the wish to settle down. Ah, lass." He
caught her hand and brought it to his lips, his anger fading.
She'd been through a lot, his Rebecca, and he was the cause
of much of it. If she needed time, why not let her have it?
Even if the old instincts within him clamored. Danger, danger. "You're right. I don't want to quarrel with you."

Her fingers feathered through his hair. 'What do you want
to do?" she asked softly.

"Make love to you again," he said and pulled her close.
And for a little while they forgot about all else.

"Good morning," Ezra's voice boomed from the doorway
to the kitchen the following morning.

Startled, Rebecca dropped the pewter dish she was drying.
"Father," she gasped, bending to pick up the dish, still
rolling on the floor with a metallic ring. "What on earth—"

"Can't a man go where he will in his own house?" Grimacing, he sat at the table. "It is still my house."

"Of course it is." Automatically she wiped the dish,
though it was dry. "But you usually stay in your study—"

"Who are you to tell me what to do, girl?"

Rebecca lifted another dish, holding it before her like a
shield. "I'm sorry, Father."

"You should be. Blast." He lowered his head, rubbing at
his forehead with thumb and forefinger. "This isn't how I
meant to go on."

Carefully she laid the plate down so it made no noise. The situation was fragile, fraught with possibilities of disaster, and she wished to do nothing to disturb him. Not when he was at last talking to her again. "How did you mean to go on?" she asked finally.

He glanced away. "I made a mistake yesterday."

Rebecca felt her eyes widen. "With Amelia? Yes."

"Blast it." He pounded the table with his fist. "I wanted her to marry well," he said, glaring at her. "Is that a crime?"

"No, Father." She kept her voice soothing. "But she's happy, you know."

"Married to a clerk."

"Well, he does come from a good family, and there are those who say his career is on the rise." She gathered her courage. For Amelia, she could fight. "He's really a good man, Father. You'd know that if you gave him a chance."

He muttered something, very low. "Excuse me?" she said.

"I said he took my daughter away." He glared at her again. "Why should I give him a chance?"

"Oh, Father." She sat across from him, laying her hand on his. To her surprise, he didn't pull back. "You haven't lost her. She very much wants to make amends with you. If you'll let her."

Ezra looked away. "If you ask her to come, will she?"

Hope soared within Rebecca. "Yes. But I think she'd like it better if the invitation came from you. And"—greatly daring—"to her and her husband, both."

"Blast," he grumbled. "You're a hard woman, Rebecca."

"With you, someone has to be," she retorted.

"Mayhap," he said, pushing himself up with his hands braced on the table. "All right. I'll write to them."

"Oh, Father! She'll be so happy. And you won't regret it, either."

"I pray not."' He stopped in the doorway, fixing her with a look. "As for you."

She stiffened, her fingers unconsciously twisting in the cloth. "Yes, Father."

"Blast it," he muttered and turned away. "Tell your Mr. Brand I approve of your marriage."

Chapter 27

❧

"Father!" Rebecca couldn't help herself. She flew to him, though she stopped shy of touching him. "Oh, do you really mean it?"

"I rarely say things I don't mean, girl."

"But why? What changed your mind?"

"Don't vex me with questions," he grumbled. "I haven't changed my mind. Always approved of Mr. Brand."

"But not for me."

"No. But seeing as your sister is married to someone else, why not you?"

"Thank you, Father," she said, choking back a laugh at this less-than-enthusiastic response to her marital prospects. "I know I'm not his ideal match, but I will strive to do better."

"This is not a topic for levity."

"No, Father."

"There's too much of that in you, levity. Best you curb it."

"Yes, Father. Will you be wanting to see Mar—Mr. Brand?"

He turned. "Is he here?"

She thought of Marcus, in Alexandria, readying his ship for another voyage. A message would reach him that afternoon. It would mean that she and Marcus no longer would have to hide their love. She should send a note immediately—and yet, she hesitated. "Father, are you sure about this?"

"I told you, girl. I have decided, and I will not change my

mind." He, too, hesitated. "No, I do not want to see him yet. Isn't it enough I have to deal with the man-milliner Amelia's married?"

"Father! He's nothing of the sort," she said, relieved and disappointed at once. Why the relief, she didn't know, except that this entire morning had been very strange. Father wasn't the only one who would need time to adjust. "When next he's home, then."

Ezra turned in the doorway. "Is he still privateering?"

"No. Smuggling," she said with some pride.

"Smuggling. Dangerous business, that. The English would probably like to take him."

"Do you think he's in danger?"

"If the English invade and he's here, then yes, he'd be in danger."

She frowned. "Father, no one thinks there'll be an invasion."

"Open your eyes, girl! You told me yourself Wellington's troops are said to be in Bermuda. Oh, yes, I hear everything you say to me. I hear more than you think."

"Of course," she murmured, frowning. "Everyone thinks they'll head to Baltimore, but I suppose 'tis possible they'll come to Washington City." If so, Marcus would be in danger. "He said he'd let me know when he returns."

Ezra's eyes gleamed. "Did he? Good. I'll much anticipate seeing him again."

"Then you really do approve of the match?"

"Must you continue to plague me with questions?" he roared. She held her ground, expecting a blow. "If you must know, it's high time you married, and someone to steady you, too. Good gad, girl, you've always been—"

"Flighty," she said flatly.

"Yes, flighty. Like your mother. You've proven that enough in the past."

"I've stayed with you, and believe me, it's not been easy," she retorted. "That's not being flighty."

"It was your duty. Now"—he turned toward the stairs—"I've work to do. See to it I'm not disturbed."

"No, Father," she murmured. Well, what had she expected? That he would suddenly say he had misjudged her all these years, that he loved her and wished her to be happy? Foolish of her. Father hadn't changed. Yet, whatever his motives were, the results were the same. She was going to marry Marcus.

Hugging herself with happiness, she whirled around. At last it was all coming right for her. She would marry Marcus, be his wife, bear his children. And he should know. If she wrote to him right now, he would get the message before he left, she thought, running up the stairs.

And, in his study, Ezra set the seal on a letter and smiled to himself.

Rebecca turned to the mirror in the fashionable dressmaker's shop, and gasped. "Oh, Amelia! Are you sure?"

"Perfectly." Amelia beamed at her from a gilt-and-white chair. "It suits you wonderfully, Becky. I knew it would."

Rebecca spread her fingers over her exposed chest. "It doesn't look like me at all."

"Yes it does, silly. It's just that you've hidden yourself in all those drab grays and browns all these years. I knew that shade of green would be perfect. It's so rich and dark. See how it brings out your eyes? The highlights of your hair?"

Rebecca shifted her fingers and instantly put them in place again. " 'Tis not my hair I'm worried about," she muttered. "Amelia, what will people think if I appear in a gown so low?"

"Silly! Who's to see you but us and Mr. Brand? I do think it's wonderful you're marrying him. I knew you had an affection for him."

"Please do lower your voice," Rebecca murmured, casting a quick glance about the dressing room. She and Amelia were alone, but beyond the curtained doorway were the dressmaker, her assistants, and various customers, among them the most stylish ladies in the city. The shop was, in short, a hotbed of gossip. "I don't care to have my affairs discussed in public."

"Oh, but, Becky, 'tis such happy news." Amelia began to pull the pins from Rebecca's hair. "Don't struggle, you'll hurt yourself. If we dress your hair differently—yes, like that. 'Tis high time you looked pretty. When you asked me to help you with your clothes, I had such ideas! I still do."

"That is what worries me," Rebecca said tartly, pulling away. "I meant that perhaps you could help me with choosing fabrics and with the sewing! Not this. I shall look like mutton dressed as lamb."

Amelia let out a silvery peal of laughter. "Don't be silly! You look lovely."

"And the cost—"

"Gilbert and I are happy to do it for you, after what you've done for us. Now. Look in the mirror again." She turned Rebecca around. "Put your hand down and look, and tell me what you really see."

Rebecca bit her lips, but did as Amelia bade, lowering her hand and forcing herself to study her reflection. The gown of rich forest green silk was simply made, high-waisted and with short, close sleeves edged with lace. The skirt was full, as her dresses usually were, but, unlike those, this one didn't hide her shape. Instead, it dipped where her waist did, flared where her hips flared, and fell in graceful folds to the floor. And, oh, it was so low! Father would have an apoplexy when he saw it. As for Marcus—well, he'd seen her in less, hadn't he? The thought sent color surging into her face and made her study the gown more objectively. Low in the bodice, yes, but she'd seen worse than that in society, and she could always wear a shawl. And Amelia was right. The color did suit her. Altogether a most wonderful, beautiful gown, and she wanted it as she had never wanted anything in her life. "Perhaps if I tuck in a bit of lace, here," she murmured, tugging at the bodice.

"You'll do no such thing! It's perfectly fine. Doesn't Mr. Brand deserve to see you in something pretty for a change?"

Rebecca studied herself and decided. "Yes. He does. Oh, thank you, Melia." She turned to hug her sister. "He'll be so surprised."

"Good." Amelia's eyes twinkled. "That's how to go on, Becky. Keep surprising him."

"Mm." Rebecca's hand drifted down to her stomach, and then away. "I do so long to see him. It's been nearly three weeks."

"Have you heard from him?"

"No. Just that message last week that he hoped to be here soon." She viewed her reflection from the side, arching back to see the hem of the gown. "I do hope he's not in any danger. If there's an invasion—"

"Oh, pooh! There won't be."

"But if there is, the British will come up the Potomac." She shivered, in spite of the heat of the day. "I fear for what will happen to Marcus."

"There won't be an invasion," Amelia announced. "Gilbert says that Mr. Monroe doesn't think it, and he doesn't, either."

Rebecca turned from the mirror. "Wellington's troops are in Bermuda."

"What if they are? Gilbert says they won't come here. Baltimore or New York are more likely targets."

"But Washington City is the capital."

"And otherwise of little importance. What is here, Becky? A few buildings, nothing more, and everyone in Congress has gone home for the summer. You are worrying yourself needlessly," Amelia said, sounding like the elder of the two. "Nothing will happen."

Rebecca faced her reflection again, her eyes dark. But she did have to worry, with Marcus somewhere upon the high seas, and the might of the British fleet against him. He had escaped the British before, but the danger was always there. And there was one more thing to consider. Her hand slipped down to her stomach again, reassuringly, protectively. She thought she might be pregnant.

She didn't know for certain, of course; it was much too early for that. Still, the signs were there. Her monthly cycle was never late, and yet here she was, nearly a week overdue. Hope bloomed within her, fragile, almost painful. To have a child again, to hold it in her arms, suckle it, keep it safe from harm—and this time she would, she told herself, staring at her reflection and seeing, not a fashionable gown, but a determined woman. For this was Marcus's child. Nothing was going to take it away from her.

"I think," Amelia was saying to the dressmaker, who had just come in, "that it needs to be taken in a bit at the waist. And perhaps the neckline lowered just a bit—"

"No." Rebecca fixed her with a stern look. "It is fine as it is."

Amelia dimpled. "I thought I'd try."

Rebecca gave her another look and then turned to the dressmaker. "It is a lovely gown, but it won't be necessary to take it in. If it can be ready by—mercy, what is that?"

"I don't know." The dressmaker's brow wrinkled at the sound of shouting coming from the front of the shop. "But I will not have such a disturbance in my shop," she said and bustled out of the room.

Amelia's fingers worked quickly at the buttons that fastened down the back of the gown. "It is a bit loose, Becky. Why not let her adjust it?"

"I like it now." Rebecca took one last look at herself before Amelia helped her pull the gown over her head, and her heart beat a little faster. Oh, she hoped Marcus liked it. She hoped he would be as happy about her news as she was.

The shouting outside increased, accompanied by the heavy rumble of carriage wheels and the staccato rhythm of horses' hooves. "Mercy, whatever can be going on?" Rebecca said, slipping into her ordinary and very dull day dress of gray broadcloth.

"I'll just go see." Amelia went out, leaving Rebecca to contemplate her reflection again as she put her hair up into its usual tight knot. Marcus was right. There was another Rebecca inside her, the real Rebecca. She was tired of wearing prim clothing, tired of pretending to be something she wasn't. Thank God for Marcus. Because of him, the deception was nearly over.

She was just putting the last hairpin in place when the curtain opened and Amelia came back in. "Did you find out what it was—Amelia! You're so pale."

Amelia dropped onto the chair as Rebecca, concerned, hovered over her. "Oh, Becky!" she wailed. " 'Tis the most terrible thing."

"It can't be that bad," Rebecca said, speaking soothingly, out of long habit.

"Oh, but it is. The British Army has landed at Benedict."

Rebecca gasped, groping for a chair herself, her knees suddenly weak. "They can't have. It's so close."

"But that's what everyone's saying. Oh, Becky!" She raised wide, frightened eyes. "They're going to invade us."

Marcus whistled as he jumped nimbly from his ship's rail to the wharf in Alexandria. Another run made right under the noses of the British Navy. Good cargo this time, too, and it should bring him a decent profit. Tyner would supervise the unloading. For too long now he had given over his life to his country, and while it was the right thing to do, it meant he'd had to neglect other things. He'd had to neglect Rebecca. No more, though. He didn't like the looks of things, with the British Army having sailed from Bermuda, and the fleet that patrolled the Chesapeake. He had to get

Rebecca to safety. This time when he went to her he would take her with him, and there'd be no arguing about it.

Alexandria's streets seemed unusually busy. Marcus frowned as he pushed his way past a group of people, on his way to the wharf where he would get the Georgetown boat. There were a great many wagons, fully loaded with what appeared to be household goods, trundling down to the waterfront to have their contents loaded into vessels of various sizes. Even odder was that the wagons were accompanied by families, silent children and pale, frightened-looking women. In the distance a church bell pealed, and as he watched, a company of militia, ragtag in uniform but with muskets held against their shoulders, marched by. For some reason, Alexandria was in retreat.

His frown deepening, he took off his hat and wiped at the sweat that had accumulated on his brow. "What's about?" he called to a man walking alongside a wagon. "Is there an outbreak of fever?"

"Fever? No, man." The other man stared at him. "Where have you been, that you've not heard?"

"At sea. Not heard what?"

"About the British. Word came yesterday they landed in Maryland—"

"The devil they did!"

"—and it looks as if they'll march on Washington City."

"Are you certain of this?"

"No, but if you've family, get them to safety. I am," the man said and turned away, shouting at the wagon's driver.

Marcus swore again and turned, running toward the Georgetown boat. There was only one person he cared about, one precious woman. No matter the danger to himself, should the British discover who he was. He had to get to Rebecca.

Rebecca stood by her bedroom window, looking out at the activity on the street. An eerie calm had descended over Washington City, as if everyone were holding their breath. Yesterday many people, including Amelia, had been evacuated, heading for safety in the surrounding countryside, but as yet the government was standing firm. There was little to do now but wait for word. There was little she could do but to wait for Marcus.

Biting her lips, Rebecca turned from the window and left

her room. Since the news had come yesterday of the possible invasion, Father had left his study only once, and that, to her surprise, had been to go into the town. He had returned home as surly and uncommunicative as ever. Not a word to her of reassurance, of instruction, and she could bear it no longer. Hesitating just a moment, she knocked firmly on the door of his study and went in.

Ezra looked up as she came in, his eyes flat. "Well? What is it, girl?"

"What do you think we should do?" she asked. "If we're to leave I'll have to see to the packing."

"We'll not leave," he said and bent his head to his papers again.

"But if the British get past our defenses and invade—"

"They won't harm us. We've their word that no civilian will be hurt."

"This is war, Father. Who knows what will happen?"

"They won't harm me!" he roared. "Haven't I supported them all this time? They will not hurt their friends." Oddly, he smiled. "What they will do is help."

Rebecca frowned. "I'm not sure I understand."

"It matters not. Now"—he placed his hands flat on the desktop—"we will not leave, and that is all I have to say on the matter, girl. Besides, don't you want to be here when your Mr. Brand comes?"

"I rather hope he doesn't."

"Oh? Having second thoughts, are you?"

"No," she said firmly. Once having received her father's approval, she wasn't about to forfeit it. "But I fear for him if he does come here."

"If he doesn't, he is a coward."

"He's no coward," she flared.

"Then don't fret." He picked up his quill. "Go, girl, and leave me in peace. I've things to do."

She frowned, and then shrugged. He was as obstinate as ever. "One more thing. We may have to have the rat catcher in."

Ezra looked up, eyes glittering. "What is that to me?"

"I just thought you should know. I heard some scratching sounds in the storeroom this morning."

"See to it, girl, and don't bother me about it." He waved his hand in dismissal. "Now, go," he said, and she at last left the room.

In the hallway Rebecca headed for the kitchen and then turned on her heel, instead opening the front door and looking out. Prospect Street, on the hill above the merchant's district, was usually quiet, but today there were more people on the street than usual. She hailed a man passing by, her neighbor, and he stopped at the bottom of the stairs. "Any news?"

"None." He squinted up at her against the late afternoon sun. "None new, at least. If you listen to rumors the British have returned to their ships, or they're almost to Bladensburg, or they've turned for Baltimore. No one seems to know."

Rebecca hugged herself, shivering, though the day was hot and sultry. "Is there any idea when we will know?"

"Probably not until they're on our doorsteps. As for me, I'm taking Charlotte and the children to her mother's home in Rockville."

Rebecca nodded. "Father won't leave."

The man glanced toward the house, and his face hardened. "No offense meant, Rebecca, but likely he'll welcome them with open arms. You should have gone with your sister."

"I probably should have." Rebecca sighed. And she might have, except that Marcus might come here yet. "Thank you, Mr. Harris. I won't keep you."

"Good day to you. Keep safe," he said and turned away.

Safe. Rebecca bit her lips. There was still time for her to go to safety in the country with Amelia. What of her father, though? And what of Marcus, who would endanger himself should he come here? She glanced down the street to see a man just reaching the crest of the hill. He looked familiar, though he was still too distant for her to see clearly. Most likely her imagination was at work, because she so wanted to see him. Still, she went down the stairs, standing on the brick walk and shading her eyes, and then beginning to walk toward him. And then running. It *was* Marcus. She knew his walk, his build, the angle of his head. It was him. "Marcus!" she cried and threw herself into his arms.

"My *leannan*." He tightened his grip and then pushed her a little away. "You're well? Safe? All I heard in Alexandria was talk of invasion."

"Yes, 'tis all we talk of, too. Oh, Marcus!" She peered up at him. "Should you be here? Is it safe for you?"

"Yes, why wouldn't it be?" He released her and took her arm. "But I'm not letting you stay here."

"I'm quite safe. But what if they capture you, Marcus? You'll be a prize for them."

"What, for smuggling? They've no proof."

"Would they need proof in wartime?"

"And as for privateering, it's legal, lass."

"Marcus." She turned, gripping his hands. "What if they find out about the Raven?"

"They won't, lass." His hold was reassuring. "How will they? They've had years to find me out, and they haven't."

Rebecca glanced up at her house. The windows stood open, and though they had kept their voices low, Father might have heard. "We mustn't talk of this here," she said, leading him toward the front stairs. "But you must promise me, Marcus, that if they invade, you'll leave."

"I'd never be such a coward." He followed her inside to the paneled hallway. "Did your father know I was coming?"

"Yes, I told him yesterday you might be here today. Marcus, won't you reconsider—"

"No, not without you."

She hesitated, hand raised to knock on the door of her father's study. "Very well."

"Rebecca"—he gripped her shoulders—"are you saying you'll come with me at last?" he said, his voice low.

"Yes." She reached up to give him a quick kiss. "I won't let you leave me again."

"Good." There was a decided gleam in his eyes as he reached for her, but she eluded his hands, smiling.

"Not here," she whispered, pointing toward the study door. "Not now."

"Later?" he whispered back. "Mayhap out in the arbor."

Her cheeks turned pink, and her hand fluttered to her stomach. Now was not the time to tell him, though. "Let me tell Father you're here. Father?" She knocked on the door. "Mr. Brand is here."

"Well, what are you waiting for, girl?" Ezra's voice came from the room. "Bring him in."

Marcus looked at her with eyebrows raised. "You heard him," she said as she opened the door. "Go in."

"Don't fret, lass," he said, his hand on her back as she entered the room. "I'm right behind you."

What happened next occurred so fast that Rebecca would later remember it only with great difficulty. She had only a moment to note that her father was standing behind the desk, grinning triumphantly, before the study door was suddenly slammed behind her. She whirled, and a hand grasped her arm, pulling her off balance and into the room, away from Marcus. At the same moment, two men jumped upon him, and though he had already reacted, dropping into a crouch and going for his knife, they had prepared the ambush well and had already brought up their muskets, clubbing him with the butts. She cried out, and the man who held her spun her around so that she was held, hard, against his chest. Stunned, she raised dazed eyes to her captor's face. Lieutenant Dee.

His strange, dark eyes gleamed. "Welcome, Miss Talbot. We've been waiting for you."

"But—" She looked in bewilderment at Ezra. "Father? What—"

"Be still, girl, and you won't be hurt. Got him?" Ezra asked, leaning over the desk, and she saw that Marcus was down on the floor, very still. She cried out, and Dee's grip on her tightened.

"Got him," one of the men answered, reaching down to haul Marcus to his feet. Blood trickled from his temple and his lips and his face was dazed. When he saw her, though, he surged forward against his captors' grasp. "Damn! Hold still," the man said, and his partner clubbed Marcus with his musket.

Again Rebecca cried out, bucking forward, and again Dee pulled her back. "I don't think he'll be giving you any problems," he said, and at the sound of a clicking noise near her ear Rebecca looked up, to see a pistol leveled at her head. "Will you, boyo?"

Marcus looked up, and in his eyes was such rage that Dee took a step back, dragging Rebecca with him. "Damn you, Jeremiah," he growled. "You're a rotten coward, hiding behind a woman. Let her go."

"Oh, no, boyo. That's what you called me once. Do you remember?" He grinned, his breath foul on Rebecca's neck. "Give it up. You're caught."

"You did this, didn't you?" Marcus snarled, glaring at Ezra. "This is your doing."

"So it is." Ezra sat back in his chair. "I've waited a long time for this moment. Gentlemen." His smile was smug. "I present to you Brendan Fitzpatrick. The Raven."

Chapter 28

❧

Rebecca pounded once more on her bedroom door with both fists, and then, letting them drop to her side, leaned her forehead against the door. It was no good. No one would come, no one would heed her calls. It was as it had been when first she had returned from the voyage on the *Raven*. She was a prisoner in her house, and her captor was her father.

Oh, she should have expected this! Whirling around, she stalked to her window and looked down, coming again to the conclusion she had reached earlier: too far to jump, and too difficult to climb. To attempt to escape that way would only endanger her unborn child, and it wouldn't help Marcus at all. Wherever he was.

The events in Ezra's study had happened so quickly and so brutally that she was still shaking from them. It wasn't until the other two men—soldiers working as spies, Ezra had announced with pride—had taken Marcus, wrists bound, from the room, that Dee finally removed the pistol from her head and released her. Even now, though, sickeningly, she could still feel the imprint of him against her, and his unexpected arousal. She was in peril from Dee, but the greater danger was to Marcus. She wasn't even certain he was still alive.

At that thought she moaned and sank onto her knees, fist to her mouth. If he was dead, what would she do? He was her life, and she, so foolish, had sent him away, time and again. Now, when finally she was ready to commit to him, it was too late. He had been betrayed and captured, and was lost to her. And all because of her father.

The key turned in the lock. She raised her head, wary, wondering what she could use as a weapon. She did not relax even when Ezra walked in, locking the door behind him. Her father, the man she had tried so hard to love, for whom she had given up all else in hopes that someday he would return that love. Her father, her betrayer. "Go away," she said, averting her head.

"That's no way to speak to me," Ezra said, sounding more genial than he had in many a day. "Look at me, girl."

Rebecca's hands clenched into fists. "I do not want to look at you."

"You will. When you are over your sulk. Ah, but that feels good." Ezra sank into the chair. "It has been a long day, but profitable."

Rebecca knelt where she was, hands on her knees, staring stonily ahead. "You lied to me."

"Lied? When did I do that?"

"Saying you approved of my marriage. It was all a ruse, wasn't it? To get Marcus here." She looked up at him at last, searching his face in bewilderment. "Why? Why did you do it?"

Ezra leaned back, hands clasped on his stomach. "I told him he'd pay. Took three years, but he has."

"Revenge?" Her voice rose. "You've done this for revenge?"

"That, and other reasons."

"But he isn't who you think—"

"Spare me that, Rebecca," he said dryly. "I am not stupid. I admit I should have recognized him straight off, but I didn't. It was the lack of the eyepatch, I expect. Clever move on his part, that. No, he had me fooled. Until he dared to interfere with my chastising you."

"What? When was that?"

"You do not remember? I was going to punish you, as you deserved, and he dared to stop me. Just as he did on that cursed ship of his."

Rebecca gazed blankly ahead, dimly remembering a night when Marcus had protected her from Ezra's wrath by preventing him from striking her. Yes, and he'd done so aboard the *Raven*, too. But surely that wasn't enough. "But, Father, that's not proof—"

"Do you think I'm stupid, girl? Of course it isn't. I bided my time," he went on with quiet relish. "Asked questions of the right people, and found out that your Marcus Brand tended to disappear, just at the time when the Raven was roaming the sea. And I figured out from things that were said that there never was a battle at sea where the *Raven* was captured. It was all a lie, but I"—he pointed to himself, face smug—"saw through it. You figure it out, girl."

Rebecca bit her lips. It did come together, and it didn't matter that the theory was thin of proof. Marcus was the Raven, and if the British troubled themselves, they'd find men a-plenty to testify to it. "You're overlooking one thing, Father," she said at last, glaring defiantly at him. "The British have no right to take him prisoner."

"Yet. And he is not their prisoner." His mouth stretched wide in a cruel smile. "He is mine."

"Where?"

"In the strong room in the cellar, girl, where else? There he'll stay until the British take over. And what do you think those rats were you heard? The soldiers were hidden there, until Fitzpatrick returned."

"Brand," she said automatically. "Fitzpatrick isn't his real name."

"It matters not what his name is." Ezra rose. "He is the Raven, and he will hang for it."

"Damn you." Her voice was low. "I will never forgive you for this."

Surprisingly, Ezra let out a booming laugh. "As if that matters to me! Get up, girl. High time you fixed supper."

"I will not."

"Then you will starve, and so will your Mr. Brand."

Rebecca's legs were stiff as she got to her feet. "Aren't you afraid of what I'll do?"

His grin stretched broader. "Afraid? No. If you do anything to ruin this for me, Brand will suffer. You may depend upon that." He stopped, staring at her from under his brows. "You will behave, will you not?"

"Yes, Father," Rebecca said finally, lowering her head so that he wouldn't see her expression. This was not the end of it. There had to be a way to set Marcus free, a way they could both escape. She would find it, she vowed. She had to. Because if she didn't, Marcus would die.

Ezra went down the stairs with a lighter tread than he'd used in years. Entering his study, he saw Dee sitting behind his desk, booted feet propped up on the mahogany surface and a cheroot in his mouth. "Shouldn't you be guarding our guest?" he said, arms akimbo, looking pointedly at Dee's boots.

Dee blew out a stream of smoke. "He won't escape. Clever of you to have the strong room built. I trust you have just the one key?"

"You have it." But he wasn't about to hand total control of the Raven over to Dee. No, Ezra had a score to settle with that blackguard, not the least of which was the seduction of his daughter.

"I've been looking at your plan, here." Dee leaned forward to riffle some papers on the desk. Ezra tensed. When he'd left the study, his plan had been tucked away in a locked drawer. "Ambitious, wouldn't you say?"

"But not beyond reach." Ezra sank slowly into a chair, forgetting for the moment that he wasn't the guest in this room. He had yet to discuss his plan with anyone; Dee was the perfect person to hear it first. "When your country wins this war you'll need someone you can trust in place, and who better than one who knows the area?"

"Who better, indeed." Dee swung his legs off the desk and rose. "I believe you are right. I've no doubt that Swift and Kelly are guarding our guest well, but I think I shall see to his care myself." Executing a neat bow, he went out, leaving Ezra in the delusion that he was still in control of his house.

Fool, Dee thought, striding down the hall and wrenching open the cellar door. Foolish of Talbot to be so trusting, to believe that the British would allow him any sort of authority when they did, at last, conquer this wild country. Not when Talbot had already proven himself to be a traitor. No, when he wrote his report about this glorious mission, he wouldn't recommend Talbot for any commendation at all. As for Rebecca—Dee smiled secretively. He expected little opposition from Talbot, but Rebecca might cause trouble. He rather hoped she would. He would very much enjoy subduing her.

His bootheels clattered on the cellar stairs, and the two sentries snapped to attention. Good. They were good men, had to be to survive as secret agents in a hostile country, but they knew their better when they met him. From the first, Dee had been in charge of this mission, one they thought

was sanctioned by the government. It was he who had discovered the Raven's whereabouts; he who had kept in touch
with Talbot, a valuable ally; he who had made the plans and
recruited these two. It was his mission, and when the time
came, he'd not share the glory. "How is the prisoner?" he
asked curtly.

"Quiet, sir," Swift said, facing forward, posture stiff. "Not
a sound out of him."

"Good." Dee glanced in through the little barred window
in the heavy iron door. Strange thing to find in a strong
room door, almost as if Talbot had considered using the
room for a cell when he'd built it. In the shadows he could
see the Raven sprawled on the dirt floor, and the sight
aroused both satisfaction and annoyance. The dreaded Raven
wasn't so mighty, after all. "It's time I interviewed him," he
said, taking the key from his pocket. "Have you supped?"

"No, sir," Kelly replied.

"Go, do so now. He'll cause me no problem," he went on
as he saw Swift about to object. "That is an order."

"Yes, sir." Swift's voice was wooden, causing Dee's lips
to twitch in annoyance, but after a moment the two men
trudged up the stairs in search of food. Dee fitted the key in
the lock, smiling to himself. Good. This moment, long-
awaited, was for him alone.

For a moment after closing and locking the strong room
door behind him, Dee frowned down at the still figure of the
Raven, absentmindedly stroking the scar on his cheek. The
man was crafty. It would be best to be on his guard.
"Brand," he said harshly, "get up."

There was no response. Dee frowned down at him, and
then hefted the wooden bucket that stood in a corner, dump-
ing water over Marcus's head. "Do you hear me, Brand? I
said, get up."

Marcus moaned, but otherwise stayed still. Frowning, Dee
bent over him, and suddenly his collar was caught in a stran-
glehold. He clawed at it, trying to breathe, trying to dislodge
Marcus's hands, but Marcus held on, twisting the cloth, his
eyes bulging with the effort, his teeth bared. Dee tried to
yell, but the only sound he made was a kind of squawk.
Damme, he shouldn't have sent the soldiers away, he
thought frantically, and with an almost superhuman effort
bore Marcus back. Marcus grunted, his grip weakening for
just a moment, but long enough for Dee to recover. Damme,

he was not going to let his cousin get the best of him again!
Recalling all the past conflicts, all the times he had fought
Marcus in the past, he reared up, and with a mighty sweep
of his arms at last freed himself. Marcus was flung against
the wall, to lie very still.

Dee rose on unsteady legs, his breath coming in harsh
gasps, and surveyed his enemy uneasily. What new trick was
this? "Try that again," he rasped, "and you'll find me more
than ready."

There was no reply. Unsheathing his pistol, Dee aimed a
kick at Marcus's midsection. "Get up," he said coldly.

Marcus turned his head, though it seemed to take all the
strength he possessed. His gaze, fuzzy and blurred, took in
two pairs—no, one—of boots badly cracked and in need of
a polish. Devil take it, he had the monster of a headache, but
he was in command of his faculties. Jeremiah. Exactly the
sort to attack an injured man, as he had been the type to mo-
lest a helpless woman. Devil take it, was Rebecca all right?

"Jeremiah," he croaked, rising to his hands and knees,
though his head swam and his limbs trembled with the effort. He would not cower, a willing victim, before this man.
"Do you always attack helpless women?"

One booted foot swung back and then stopped, as if Dee
had thought better of it. "Ah, you think you are still in control here? Well, you are not!" His voice was harsh. "I ordered you to get up."

"Certainly, boyo," Marcus said affably. "If you'll just give
me a hand—"

"Do you take me for a fool?

"No. A cad and a coward, but not a fool."

This time when Dee's foot swung back, it didn't stop. The
toe of his boot collided solidly with Marcus's ribs, making
him collapse in a heap on the floor again, moaning in spite
of himself. "I prefer you better this way," Dee said coldly.

"Then—you really are—a coward," Marcus croaked out
and received another punishing kick for his boldness.

"Damn you. You'll pay for that, and for everything else
you've done to me."

"Don't—be too certain." The pain in Marcus's ribs was
nearly unbearable, making it difficult for him to breathe, but
he'd be damned before he let Dee see that. "My men know
where—to look for me. Told them if—I wasn't back—to

come after me. And then—we'll see—who wins this—fight."

Dee shuffled his feet and then steadied himself, laughing a little. "Then they'll be arrested, too. Haven't you heard the news? My army'll be marching into this city within a day."

"You—lie."

"And when they do, I'll gladly turn you over to them. Do you know what will happen then?" Dee's face was very close, his breath foul with tobacco smoke. "They'll hang you from the highest tree, and I'll enjoy watching. Oh, yes, that I will. Best say your prayers, Brand. You are a dead man."

"And I'll see you—in hell," Marcus grated out. His only answer was Dee's mocking laugh, as he went out and slammed the door shut. His mind, his spirit, urged him to get up, to open the door before it was too late and grab Dee, but when he tried to rise, it was only to fall back again, groaning. He was badly hurt. Devil take it, if Dee would kick an injured man, what would he do to Rebecca?

That thought did make him move. Biting his lips so hard they bled, he rolled over, slowly, slowly onto his back. There he lay for a while, dimly aware of his guards returning and looking in on him. It was a bit better this way; his breathing was easier and he could see his cell. Not good enough, though. Inch by agonizing inch, he pulled himself up, until at last he sat, panting, his back to the wall. Devil take it, he was already exhausted. What use would he be to Rebecca in this shape? But he couldn't give in. Using the wall for support, he twisted until he was on his knees, rested for he didn't know how long, and managed, at last, to bring one foot up to rest on the floor. The rough wall provided handholds; clinging to them, ignoring the screaming pain in his ribs, the swamping dizziness in his head, he pulled himself up slowly. He was standing at last, and though he had to close his eyes to shut out a whirling, spinning world, still he was on his feet. Damnably weak, but standing, and determined. The pain didn't matter, nor did the locked iron door. He knew only one thing. Somehow he was going to have to escape and rescue Rebecca from Dee.

Rebecca slept little that hot, sultry night and rose early, her spirits depressed. The day promised to be uncomfortably warm, and already she could feel her clothes sticking to her as she went downstairs, a little fearful of what she would face. To her relief, only her father was in the kitchen.

"There you are," he grunted. "I will not tolerate lying abed in my house. Now see to breakfast, girl. And prepare a chicken for dinner. We have guests."

Rebecca nodded, not wanting to acknowledge him by so much as a word or a look. He was a stranger to her, this man she had showered with love her entire life, a cold, hard stranger who cared naught for her happiness, or even her safety. And what would happen to Marcus, should she not find a way to free him? "Is Marcus well?" she asked, breaking her silence as she poured out coffee for Ezra.

He grunted, concentrating his attention on the copy of the *Times and Potowmack Packet* in his hand. "Do not concern yourself with him."

"May I see him?"

Ezra looked up. "Are you daft, girl? Of course not. You'd do well to start being nice to Lieutenant Dee instead."

"No," she said, but the protest was automatic. Foolish of her to hope that Father might relent this once. With even that slight hope dashed, depression settled upon her again in a smothering blanket. She went through her work automatically, stopping every now and then in surprise as awareness struck her. She didn't remember washing the dishes, but she must have; didn't remember gathering greens from the kitchen garden or potatoes from the root cellar; didn't even remember butchering and plucking the chicken that she held in her hand, just outside the kitchen door. Merciful, that muffling, enshrouding blanket of hopelessness, sheltering her for a time from her painful emotions, and the terror of what would happen to Marcus if she didn't do anything. Merciful, and dangerous. She was his only hope.

Head held high, thoughts clear for the first time that morning, she walked into the kitchen and stopped dead. Dee was sitting at the table, the same issue of the *Times and Potowmack Packet* in his hand. "Well, come in," he said, looking up as she stood in the doorway. "I won't bite." He smiled, displaying crooked, yellow teeth, and she barely repressed a shudder. "I'd almost think you were avoiding me."

Rebecca laid the chicken on the table and took a cleaver down from its hook in the pantry. "Whyever would you think that?" she asked, and in one quick, chopping movement brought the cleaver down. Thwack! The chicken's head was neatly severed from the rest of the body, and blood streamed across the table, toward Dee.

"Hey!" He jumped up in surprise. "Careful, there."

"My apologies, sir. Butchering a chicken is messy work. I shall try not to spatter you."

"See that you don't." He sat down again, his gaze going uneasily from the cleaver to his musket, propped against the wall. Good, Rebecca thought with grim satisfaction. Let him see she was not some weak, timid miss to be bullied into submission.

Thwack! The cleaver came down again, severing one of the chicken's legs. Thwack! The other leg. Thwack! And she wished it was Lieutenant Dee's head. He continued to watch her with wary fascination. "Have you never seen a chicken cut up before?"

He seemed to collect himself, drawing himself up straighter. "Of course I have. I never realized you were quite so—masterful, Rebecca."

"There's much you don't know about me." Thwack! The wings came off easily; no need for her to use so much force, but she wanted to.

"I would like to learn."

"Huh."

"Have I hurt you, Rebecca?" She merely stared at him at that, and so after a moment he went on. "I heard you talking to your father earlier."

"Yes, and so?"

"You wish to visit our prisoner?"

Hope flared in Rebecca's heart, fragile and painful, but she knew better than to let it show on her face. "If I say yes, you'll refuse."

"Why, Rebecca. Do I appear so cruel?"

"Yes." The cleaver came down again, slicing neatly through the chicken's breastbone. "You strike me as cruel, hard, and quite possibly deranged."

Much to her surprise, Dee let out a laugh. "A compliment, indeed! I do like the deranged. A novel touch."

"You would," she muttered.

"Do you know, Rebecca, I might just let you see him," he said, and in spite of herself she looked up. "If you're nice to me."

There was so much to answer to that that she found herself speechless, staring at him with cleaver upraised. Under her gaze Dee shifted, his eyes upon the bloody cleaver. Why, she could attack him right now, she thought, and she would happily do so, except that Marcus would suffer for it. "No," she said, finally, lowering the cleaver.

"Think before you answer. You don't wish to do something you'll regret."

"No," she said again and turned away, to the pantry, to put the chicken pieces on a plate. Thus she didn't see Dee jump up from his chair and rush across the room to her; she only heard him, and that when it was too late.

"Understand this," he hissed, grabbing her arm and turning her to him, his face very close to hers. "I've waited a long time for this, and I will not wait much longer. You will be mine, Rebecca."

"Well, well." Ezra's hearty voice came from behind Dee, preventing Rebecca from retaliating, with the cleaver so close to hand. There was a well of violence in her she had never before suspected. "Getting acquainted already?"

Dee turned, though he didn't loosen his grip on Rebecca's arm. "Your daughter is an attractive woman."

Ezra chuckled, a rusty sound. "I quite understand, sir. But mind you, I will not stand for anything before marriage. Not"—he looked sternly at Rebecca—"this time."

She returned his gaze, stony-faced. "I would as soon kiss a toad," she said clearly.

Dee's face darkened, and his grip on her arm tightened punishingly, but his voice when he spoke was almost cheerful. "Of course not before marriage, sir." He released her at last, going back into the kitchen. "By the by," he tossed back over his shoulder, "I have decided to let her visit the prisoner this afternoon."

Involuntarily Rebecca stepped forward, but Ezra spoke first. "Are you sure that's wise, sir?" he said, frowning.

"Why not?" Dee sat down, carelessly crossing his leg and swinging one booted foot to and fro. "She'll be guarded. What can she, a mere woman, do?"

"True." Ezra continued to frown. "Still, I disapprove, sir."

"This is my mission, sir." Dee's voice was silky-soft and menacing. "I shall do as I see fit."

"It's my house," Ezra blustered, but he took a step back at the look in Dee's eyes.

"So it is. But for now it is a prison, and I am the jailer.

If I say she may visit, she may visit. After all, she'll never see him again."

"True."

"And I intend to keep her very busy afterwards," he said, tossing Rebecca a twisted smile.

Rebecca's fingers curled convulsively on the doorjamb. She hated him. Oh, she hated him, and she wished she had used the cleaver when she had the chance. Alone, though, a woman among men, what would that have availed her? If Dee hadn't gotten it away from her, one of the others would have, and then where would she be? Where would Marcus be? She would have to think of another weapon.

And suddenly, looking at Dee, she knew what she had to do.

Dinner had been consumed and the dishes tidied away. Rebecca had eaten very little, though the fried chicken had turned out just right, crispy and golden brown; she hadn't the spirit for it. Yet she would have to keep up her energy for what she planned. Marcus's life depended upon it. If only it weren't so hot.

She brushed beads of sweat away from her forehead as she walked through the hall, heading for the stairs and her room. If she were to see Marcus, she wanted to look her best. As she started to ascend the stairs, however, the study door opened. "Rebecca. Come in here," Ezra said and turned away, apparently never doubting that she'd obey.

Annoyed, Rebecca went into the room. "Yes? What is it?"

"I don't like your taking that tone of voice with me, girl." Ezra sat down behind his desk, frowning at her. "But I'll forgive you this time."

"And yet you betrayed the man I wish to marry," she retorted.

Ezra waved his hand in dismissal. "Forget about him. I've better plans for you, girl."

"What? Dee?"

"Close the door," he commanded, and she obeyed, puzzled by his expression, smug and apprehensive at once. "That's better. I'd not care to have him overhear this."

"Overhear what? Father, do get to the point. I've things to do—"

"Your visit to the Raven? Dee is mad to allow that. But,

there, I suppose it will do little enough harm. After all, the man will be gone soon—"

"When?" Rebecca sat forward, hands clenched on her knees.

"When the British take the city. And when they do, my girl"—he leaned back—"I've plans for you."

"I warn you, Father, that I'll not marry Dee."

"I don't expect you to."

She gaped at him. "You don't?"

"No." From his desk drawer he took out a cheroot and lit it, the odor of fine tobacco fuming the room. "Dee is a tool. A means to an end. And that means you will be nice to him."

"Only if it means Marcus will be treated well."

"Your Marcus is a dead man. Yes, Dee has been useful." He took a long draw on the cheroot. "He'll be useful yet, in telling what I've done."

"What you've done?" she asked cautiously, for there was an odd light in his eyes.

"Yes. What do you think I've been doing here all these months?" He flourished a sheaf of papers in her face. "I've been making plans, girl, for all of us. For the government."

Rebecca frowned. "I don't understand."

"Don't you? It has become clear to me that our present form of government is ineffective." He rose and began to pace the room. "Look who we have for president. Little Jemmy Madison, who's led us into war with the one country we need as an ally. I intend to change that."

"How?" she asked through dry lips.

"How? By forming a new government, of course. You look surprised, and well you might. But this has been on my mind for a very long time."

"'Tis treason, Father," she whispered.

"No. Common sense, girl. When the British take over, they'll need someone to be in charge, someone who knows the country, the people. I intend"—he turned, bracing his hands on the back of a chair—"that person to be me."

Rebecca stared at him, knowing at last what the light in his eyes was. Insanity. "You're mad."

"Some may call me that," he agreed. "It ever has been thus with visionaries. I intend to dispense with this ridiculous system of government we've been laboring under. Imagine, the people making the rules! Nothing will ever get done that way." He paced back and forth again. "I've been thinking of this plan for a very long time, and now is my chance to implement it. The British think they'll subdue us, eh? Well, they'll soon be proven wrong. The countryside will rise up in revolt, and who will they turn to to lead them? Me." He pointed at his chest. "I will already be their leader, 'twill be natural for them to look to me. And when we've ousted the British"—his chest swelled—"who will be in place to lead our new country? Me. You've nothing to say to this?" he asked as Rebecca stared at him. "Well, no matter. You will be happy enough when it happens. King Ezra the First. Yes." He stood by the window. "It has a certain ring to it."

"Father, you can't be serious," Rebecca said, finding her voice at last.

"I am. And I will not have you disrupting my plans." He sat back, his eyes cold, yet burning. "I must think of what to do with you."

"Father—"

"I will send you away," he went on as if she hadn't spoken. "Yes. That way you will not disgrace me. And I believe I shall marry again. As king, I will need an heir."

"You have gone mad!" she exclaimed, and at that moment faint in the distance came a dull, booming sound. "What is that?"

"Ah." Ezra turned to the window. "Cannon fire, Rebecca," he said with great satisfaction. "The battle has begun."

Chapter 29

~

The battle had indeed begun. As the afternoon progressed, the sound of guns continued almost without stopping. From her window Rebecca looked out, straining to see any other signs of battle and seeing only the peaceful, if busy, streets, and the broad river beyond. Below her people congregated, and once she caught the name Bladensburg. Was that where the battle was? If so, it was very near, not five miles away. She longed to call down to the people for information, for help, but she didn't dare. A different kind of battle was being waged within this house.

She turned at a knock on her open door to see one of the soldiers. "Lieutenant Dee said as how I'm to escort you to visit the prisoner," he said.

Rebecca nodded. Even though the man was only doing what he considered to be his duty, she was not about to speak to him. Head held high, she accompanied him to the cellar. Her silence must have been daunting, for he said little on the way. "May I see him alone?" she asked as they approached the room.

"Afraid not, miss." The soldier sounded genuinely apologetic. "We can't leave the prisoner unguarded."

"Oh, for mercy's sake! What can I possibly do? I haven't a key to get him out."

"Sorry, miss." He shrugged, stopping in front of the door.

"Will you at least move away so we can have some privacy?"

The two men looked at each other, and then Swift nodded. "We'll be over there," he said, indicating the other side of the cellar with a jerk of his shoulder. "But mind you don't pass anything to him, or we'll be over like a shot. Hey, Raven! You've got a visitor." He turned. "All yours, miss."

"Thank you." Forcing herself to patience, she waited until he had moved away before turning to the door. "Marcus?" she called softly, peering through the bars.

"Rebecca?" He sounded incredulous. "What in the world—oof."

"What is it?" She could just see him, leaning against the wall. "Are you all right?"

He pushed himself away from the wall. "Aye, lass."

But he wasn't, she could see that as he hobbled toward her. "Marcus, you're hurt!"

"Nothing to signify, *leannan*." He grinned at her, puffy lip and all, as he at last reached the door. "Ah, lass, but you're a sight for sore eyes. Come to get me out, have you?"

"Oh, how can you be so cheerful?" She searched his face, seeing the swollen eye, the bruises. "When you are in such a fix?"

"I've been in worse, lass."

"Marcus. We promised to be honest with each other."

"Aye. And I tell you, I'm not done yet." His smile faded. "I'll get you out of this, Rebecca, I promise," he said, his voice low.

"You'll get me—! Marcus, how in the world can you? When you're—"

"I said I'd protect you, and I will."

Rebecca's lips tightened. "My life has been nothing but upheaval since I met you."

Surprisingly, he laughed, his hand going to his ribs. "Oof. I shouldn't have done that. But that's the Rebecca I love."

"You'll laugh yourself to the grave."

"Aye, perhaps I shall. Tell me what is going on." His face sobered. "The guns?"

"A battle. Near Bladensburg, I think."

"Any news?"

"No."

"Devil take it," he swore, catching hold of the bars. "I came here to get you out of danger and instead I've landed you in it."

"Marcus, it wasn't your fault—"

"Wasn't it? I should have known better than to trust your father."

"How could you have known he knew—"

"I should have realized something was wrong when he agreed to our marriage. He'll never let you go."

She raised her chin. "He has no say in the matter."

"I've put us in the devil of a fix. Devil take it, all the years of being careful, of watching my back, and I walk into a trap like a green lad."

"You couldn't have known—"

"And if anything happens to you because of it I won't forgive myself. Devil take it, Rebecca." He shook the bars. "If I could just get out of here—"

"Marcus"—she leaned forward, her voice a whisper—"do you trust me?"

"Aye." He frowned. "With my life, lass, but—"

"Then listen. I've a plan to get you out of here—"

'How touching," a voice came from behind them, and she whirled to see Dee. "Swift, Kelly, I thought I told you not to leave them alone."

"We are hardly alone, sir," Rebecca said icily as the two soldiers jumped forward, stammering excuses. "What do you expect me to do? After all"—her eyes lowered—"I am only a woman."

Marcus snorted. Fortunately Dee didn't appear to hear. "That is true. But I do not trust your lover. Well, cousin?" He stalked toward the cell. "Does it please you to know that Miss Talbot will soon be mine?"

"Over my dead body," Marcus said pleasantly.

"It will be, cousin. It will be."

Marcus gazed meditatively at the scar on Dee's cheek. "Do you know, I should have marked the other one while I was at it."

Dee's face darkened. "You'll regret that, Raven. I'll—"

"See you hanged. I know." Marcus yawned, and only Rebecca, watching anxiously, saw his eyelids twitch, as if in pain. " 'Tis getting a bit monotonous, boyo."

"But true, boyo," Dee said, laying ironic stress on the last word. "You forget who holds the upper hand here."

"Do you?" Marcus's face was calm. "I wouldn't be so certain."

"Sir," Swift gasped from the stairs. "I just went out to take a—to use the necessary, and I heard talking."

"Yes, so?"

"They're saying the Americans are in retreat." Dee and

Rebecca both swung to stare at him. "They fought at Bladensburg and our army scattered them, sir! They'll be in the city this night."

Dee turned back to Marcus. "Hear that, Raven? The British are coming." He laughed. "Isn't that what one of your famous patriots said? Only this time, the warning is too late. Tonight, Raven, tomorrow at the latest, I shall turn you over to them."

Marcus's gaze was steady. "We shall see."

"Indeed, we shall. Swift! Take Miss Talbot from here."

"But," Rebecca protested as Swift took her arm and pulled her away.

"Say your good-byes, Rebecca. You'll not see him again."

Rebecca bit her lips against sudden tears. "I love you, Marcus," she called, though from her position near the stairs she could see only his strong, brown hands on the iron bars.

"And I you, lass, always. And remember what I told you."

"What?"

"Watch out for pirates."

Dee swung around. "What is that supposed to mean?"

Marcus shrugged. "Whatever you think it means."

Dee stared at him for a long moment. "You'll not escape me, Raven. One way or another, I shall have my revenge."

"Mayhap."

"Lieutenant," Kelly said, standing to attention, "permission to rejoin our regiment."

Dee looked up at him, startled. "Excuse me?"

"The battle's not over, sir, not if the Americans rally. Our side needs every man."

Dee hesitated. "So it does. Very well, go on. Talbot and I can guard the prisoner."

"Thank you, sir," Kelly said and ran up the stairs.

"Letting them go? Brave of you," Marcus said, and Dee swung back toward him. "What will you do without them? You let them do the dirty work of capturing me, didn't come near me yourself until you were certain I couldn't strike back—"

"I hold the upper hand now!" Dee hissed, grabbing the iron bars and glaring at Marcus. "And don't you forget it."

Marcus stared at him a moment, and then, quite deliberately, yawned. "Mayhap," he said, turning away.

"We'll see," Dee said very quietly after a moment. "We'll see."

Marcus stood still as Dee walked away. Only when he
was certain that Dee was no longer watching him did he allow his shoulders to sag, his head to droop. It had cost him
all the strength he had to present a cheerful front to Rebecca;
a defiant one to Dee. And though he thought he had put
some heart into Rebecca, what, when it came to it, could he
actually do to help her? He kicked at the straw that made his
bed, scowling. What he had said to her, and to Dee—
bravado, all of it. That was all it could be. Because, the truth
was, he hadn't the strength to overpower Dee. Devil take it,
how was he going to get out of this fix?

Washington City was in chaos. Even in Georgetown, some
miles from the government buildings, the panic was felt as
soldiers streamed in on the Bladensburg road. They told of
a determined British assault and disorganized American
troops, of the Congreve rockets the British fired, and the effects they had on the weary, demoralized Americans. It
wasn't a defeat, it was a rout; and the retreat continued
throughout the afternoon. With it came wild rumors, that
President Madison, who had been on the field of battle, had
been captured; that Mrs. Madison had given orders to blow
up the President's House; that the British intended to im-
prison any and every government official they could find.
People evacuated the city to the relative safety of the heights
above Georgetown, or beyond, to the countryside. The British Army was on the move, and there were few not frightened by the prospect.

From his study window, Ezra looked past his garden, a
little smile on his face. He could see the river from here,
and, beyond, the capital. His, all his. The British would
soon arrive, and when they did, they would quickly recognize that in Ezra they had an able leader. Who knew what
that might lead to?

The study door opened, and he turned to see Dee walking
in without knocking. Ezra frowned, but forbore to say anything. They were, after all, partners in this splendid exercise.
"Are Swift and Kelly away?" he asked.

"Yes, sometime ago." Dee stood stiffly, militarily, and
Ezra's frown faded. "Your daughter is out of the way?"

"Locked in her room." Ezra went to stand behind his
desk, reasserting his authority. This was his house, and he

was the leader in this venture. "When do you anticipate turning the prisoner over?"

"Tomorrow at the earliest. They'll need to subdue any revolt." From his pocket he took a folded piece of paper. "As will I."

"Pardon?"

Dee unfolded the paper and held it up. "In the name of His Majesty, King George the Third," he read in a sonorous voice, "I requisition these premises for use by His Majesty's Army."

Ezra leaned forward, bracing himself on his hands. "What the devil does that mean?"

"It means, dear sir"—Dee folded the paper with exquisite care—"that I have taken over this house and all within for the use of our army."

"You can't do that!" Ezra roared.

"I can, and I have."

"If you think I'll let you get away with this—"

"You've no choice. Swift carries a message to General Ross, offering the house to them. It's no good fighting it, Talbot," Dee said, calmly and competently raising his pistol as Ezra charged around the desk. "The deed is done. This house is now British property."

Ezra stopped at the sight of the pistol. Enraged though he was, he knew he stood no chance against Dee at the moment. In a contest of strength he would win every time, of that he was confident. The pistol, however, changed the odds. "A good move," he said mildly, and had the satisfaction of seeing Dee blink with surprise. "I should have thought of it myself. It accords well with my plan."

"Your plan." Dee snorted. "Do you think anyone will take your plan seriously? Even if we wanted to take over your country again—and God knows why we would—no one would make you provisional leader. They'll pick someone younger, someone from their own ranks. Someone they can trust."

Ezra held on to his temper with a great effort. "You are wrong, sir. They will need someone who knows the country."

"Then who better than someone who has spent most of his career here? Who better than"—his chest puffed out—"me?"

"You!"

"Yes, why not me?" Dee gestured broadly with the pistol,

and Ezra shied back. "Do I not know this country? Have I not lived here in hiding for two years, listening to the people and their concerns? And have I not proven the value of my services, time and again? Oh, yes, when I bring the Raven to General Ross tomorrow, my value will be recognized. I must thank you for giving me the idea. I myself would not have thought of so daring a plot. But now that I have, who knows where it might lead? Governor Jeremiah Dee. Perhaps"—he smirked—"President Dee."

"You go too far," Ezra said, his voice gravelly.

"Do I? Do you really intend to tell me that you haven't entertained similar ideas? King Ezra. Oh, yes, I read that," he mocked as Ezra started. "A most ridiculous idea."

"Damn you," Ezra said, advancing upon him.

"Watch it." Dee raised the pistol, his eyes wild. "I'll use this if I have to."

Ezra stopped, hatred and rage boiling impotently within him. With a weapon held on him there was little he could do. But if Dee thought he could get away with this, then, by Gad, he had better think again! "I'll not stop fighting you."

Dee laughed. "You'll lose, old man. Now. Get your daughter down here. I'm hungry." He gestured with the pistol toward the door. "Go, go on."

Ezra crossed the room, glaring at Dee. "This isn't over."

Dee merely laughed. "Oh, yes, it is, old man. Now." He sobered, eyes cold and yet still wild. "Do as I say, or it will go ill with you."

Ezra glared at him one last time, and then went out to the hall. Dee thought he had won? No, he hadn't, not while Ezra Talbot drew breath. Old man, was he? Ha. With that derogatory phrase, Dee had made his final mistake. They'd see, he thought, trudging up the stairs. Oh, yes. Lieutenant Dee would see.

Night again, and Rebecca paced her room, wishing for surcease from the heat, the tension, the terror. Wishing desperately that she could turn back the clock two days and run out to warn Marcus away from this house; that she would awaken to find this had all been a dream. She knew, though, that the real horror lay ahead. Lieutenant Dee intended to turn Marcus over to the conquering army tomorrow, and there was not a thing she could do about it. After she had cooked supper, Father had returned her to her room, again locking her in. Her plan to free Marcus was useless now.

Something nudged at her memory. Father had locked her in, hadn't he? She didn't remember hearing the lock click, but at the time she'd been too distraught to notice. Of course he'd locked the door, she chided herself even as she sprinted across the room to try the handle. He wouldn't want her roaming free, and—mercy! The handle turned under her fingers, and the door opened. She was not, after all, a prisoner.

The lassitude of despair fell from her, and she was suddenly imbued with new energy. She could do it. She could put her plan into effect. Flying about the room, making her preparations, she knew she had no choice. The plan was risky, dangerous, but if it worked, Marcus would be free. She had to take the chance.

A short while later, Rebecca trod elegantly down the cellar stairs, an upraised candle in one hand and the skirts of her forest green silk gown in the other. She had purchased the gown for Marcus, and now she would use it for him, though in a far different way than she had planned. In her own way, she was going to battle.

Dee was sitting on a straight chair outside the strongroom, a lamp on the floor beside him, but he rose slowly when he saw her. "Well," he said, eyes gleaming as they raked over her, "I thought you were abed. Come to see the prisoner, have you?"

"No." Rebecca blew out the candle and bent to place it on the floor, deliberately allowing Dee a long look at her breasts before she rose. "I came to see you."

"An honor, ma'am." His voice was ironic, but already she could see the effect of her appearance on him. Inwardly she quailed, though she knew she had no choice. She had to go through with this. "May I say you look fetching in that gown."

"Rebecca?" Marcus's voice came from the strong room, sounding incredulous. "What the devil are you doing here?"

Rebecca ignored him, keeping her gaze trained on Dee. "Thank you, sir." She swayed toward him, her hips sinuous, the silk whispering as she called up all the arts of seduction she had learned from Marcus. "Is there a place, sir, where we can be private?"

"Rebecca, for God's sake—"

"Be quiet!" Dee snapped, never taking his eyes off Rebecca. "Why do you wish to be private with me, ma'am?"

"I wish"—her tongue came out and moistened her lips—"to talk with you, sir."

"We can talk here."

Rebecca cast a glance at the strong room and then turned back. "No, sir." She leaned forward to whisper in his ear. "What I must say to you is private."

"Say it." His hands gripped her suddenly, hard, cruel. "Say it here, and now."

Her eyebrows rose in imitation of Marcus's gesture. "Oh, I do like a masterful man!" she exclaimed. "Very well, sir, if you must know. Father has said that you wish to wed me."

"Rebecca," Marcus growled, and for a moment her nerve failed her.

"Yes, so?" Dee said.

"So"—she moistened her lips again—"I have been thinking. And what I have decided, sir, is that I agree. In fact, I have come here to become your wife."

Dee looked down at her, his gaze unreadable, and then, unexpectedly, put his head back and laughed. "Did you hear that, Raven? She wishes to be my wife."

"Damn you, Jeremiah, let go of her!" Marcus shouted.

"My wife. No," Dee said and bore Rebecca back. "You little fool. Did you really think I'd wed you, when I am destined for better things? When you have lain with any man available? Oh, no." He pushed her hard against the wall, his body pressing against her. "I'll not marry you."

"Then let go of me!" she cried, frightened now. This was not how she had planned this moment. "Please—"

"Oh, I'll please you," he growled, hauling her up against him with a hand on her hips, forcing her against his arousal. "And I'll take what's offered. Right here, right now."

"No."

"And your lover can watch."

"No," Rebecca protested again, fighting, struggling, but to no avail. His mouth came down on hers hard, grinding, cutting off her breath and making her want to gag. Oh, it wasn't supposed to be like this! she thought despairingly, twisting against arms that felt like the iron bars of Marcus's cell. She had planned it so carefully—but it wasn't supposed to be like this. It wasn't—

With one quick motion he bent, caught her behind the

knees with his arm, and pulled her feet out from under her, depositing her on the floor. Rebecca tried to scuttle away, but Dee was atop her, his mouth pressing on hers again, his thighs forcing her legs open, his hands everywhere, squeezing her breasts, pinching her bottom. His hips ground against her as his hand swept down her thigh, and then he suddenly went very still.

"Well, what's this?" he said conversationally.

"No." She struggled as his fingers fumbled with the garter that fastened her stocking.

"A knife." He pulled it from her garter and held it up, the blade glittering in the lamplight. "And just what were you planning to do with this?"

"To stick it in your back!" If he had cooperated. If he had agreed to do this in a more civilized manner, so that she could get him off his guard.

"You were planning to kill me? How resourceful, my dear. I suppose then you would have freed your lover."

"I should have used the cleaver this morning," she spat, and he let out a laugh.

"Bloodthirsty wench, aren't you? Well, this will be of no use to you." He raised his arm, and the knife flew, useless, across the room. "And now you will pay."

"No!" Marcus roared, shaking the bars of his cell so hard that the door rattled. "It's not her you want to pay, Jeremiah, it's me. Prove you're a man. Come after me."

Dee twisted his head, his weight still holding her prisoner, though she struggled. "You'll have your chance," he said and abruptly grabbed Rebecca's arms, holding them above her head with one hand. "Later."

"No," Rebecca moaned, whether for herself or for Marcus, she didn't know. She was going to be raped by this monster, and there wasn't a thing she could do to stop it.

"Yes." His eyes glittered, gleamed, and at that moment a shadow loomed up behind him. A long, thin object hurtled down, crashing onto Dee's head. Rebecca cried out as he went rigid, his eyes wide and startled, and then collapsed upon her, a dead weight.

"Get up, girl," a voice growled, and she looked in dazed surprise from Dee's face, next to hers, up to the man standing above her. "Get up," Ezra said again, and in his upraised hand was a poker.

Chapter 30

~

"Father!" Rebecca gasped, stunned. "What—"

"I told you to get up," he said harshly. "Good gad, must you continue to lie there like a wanton?"

"Help me get him off me—oof." She grunted as she pushed at Dee's inert body. He rolled off her to land with a satisfying thud on his back, eyes closed, arms outflung, as she scrambled to her feet. "Father, why on earth—"

"He requisitioned our house."

"So?"

"He betrayed me. He laughed at my plans."

Rebecca stared at him in astonishment as he took a ring of keys from his pocket. "And for that you did—this?"

He grunted. "Of course," he said, frowning as he sorted through the keys.

Marcus thrust his hand through the bars, and Rebecca clutched at it. "Because he laughed at your plans, and not because your daughter was in danger."

Ezra grunted, and Rebecca gave Marcus a warning look. As unpredictable as Ezra was, there was no telling what he would do. "Is he dead?" she asked.

"I doubt it," Ezra said. "If you're concerned, check for yourself."

Rebecca shuddered as she glanced back at Dee, though it was with relief that she saw his chest rise and fall. "No, he's alive."

"Good," Marcus said with quiet relish. "I don't want him to die before I make him pay."

"That, sir, will be my privilege," Ezra said. "Move away from the door, girl."

"But, Father—"

"Stand away, I say." He stepped forward as Rebecca reluctantly released Marcus's hand, fitting a key into the strongroom lock. "What?" he said as Rebecca stared at him. "You thought Dee had the only key?"

"Yes."

"I'm not that foolish, girl. And I will not be mocked." He turned the key in the lock. "Dee will pay for that."

The strongroom door swung open. Instantly Marcus jumped out, eyes wary, fists upraised. With a glad cry Rebecca ran to him, only to be stopped by the quick gesture of his hand. "Marcus—"

"Keep away," he said, his eyes on Ezra, who had gone to stand over Dee's body.

"But—"

"This isn't over." He advanced a pace toward her. "What the devil did you think you were doing?"

"I was trying to free you. Don't you see—"

"Devil take it, Rebecca, you should have realized you were no match for him."

"I didn't expect him to behave as he did," she retorted, stung. Did he think she had put herself in harm's way for her own sake? "If I could have gotten to the knife—"

"With me there to hear and see everything," he went on as if she hadn't spoken. "How do you think I felt when—"

"Quiet!" Ezra roared, and both stopped, staring at him. "I did not go through all this to listen to you squabble."

Marcus jerked his head back, reaching out for Rebecca and thrusting her behind him. "Then why did you do it? I tell you now, if you think to turn me over to the British yourself—"

"You're a pair of fools. Do you think I did this for you? How do you think Dee's superiors will react when they learn he let the Raven fly away? You"—he looked sternly at Marcus—"were the main reason he took up spying. Oh, yes, he was a spy," Ezra went on as Rebecca gasped. "But instead of doing what he was told, he decided to try to capture you." He nodded at Marcus. "Bringing you in was meant to be his triumph. Now"—he nudged Dee's leg with the toe of his boot—"it will be his downfall."

"I warn you, sir, I won't go so easily."

Ezra's gaze flicked over him, almost bored. "I care not what you do. Leave my house, and take my worthless daughter with you."

"Father!" Rebecca cried. After all that had happened that shouldn't hurt, but it did.

" 'Tis what you want, isn't it? You told me so yourself."

"Yes, but—"

"Why, lass," Marcus said, turning to her. He was smiling, the wretch. "Have ye not the courage for it?"

"It's not that," she said flatly, "and you know it."

"Aye, I do, *leannan.*" His voice had gentled. "But you know you'll never get what you've been seeking all these years."

Rebecca bit her lips. Her father's love. Marcus was right. It was lost to her now. "Father?"

"Go with him," Ezra grunted, not looking at her. " 'Tis the best thing for you."

"Are you sure?"

"I don't want you here, girl." He looked up at last, and in his eyes she saw something she hadn't seen in years, something she had never really expected to see again. At least, not for her. "He'll give you a better life than I can."

"Father?" She took a tentative step toward him, though he drew himself up. "I love you, you know."

"Go on with you." He stepped back, face stern and forbidding, making her wonder if she had imagined the look in his eyes. "You're becoming a nuisance. Best plan would be to cross the Potomac to the Virginia side," Ezra said, addressing Marcus. "You'll avoid the troops that way."

"Yes, sir, I'd thought of that." Marcus's face was inscrutable as he held out his hand. "Rebecca—"

Rebecca hesitated. This was it, then, the final choice, between the man who had given her life, and the man who had helped her to be reborn. It may have been love she'd seen in her father's eyes; it may not have been. In either case, it was the most she was ever going to get from him. "Yes," she said softly and placed her hand in Marcus's. His fingers closed over hers, and she felt more truly his, their love more truly sealed, than ever she had before.

"Go, now," Ezra said gruffly, "before the British come. You don't want to be involved in this."

"No, sir." Marcus glanced down at Rebecca, and his eyes softened. "Come, *leannan,*" he said and led her out of the cellar. The last glimpse she had of her father was of him standing over Dee, as if he had already forgotten her.

It was the work of a few moments to toss some of her belongings into a valise. Then they were out on the street, Marcus fidgeting beside her. "Come, lass, we must be away."

"I know." Rebecca looked up at her home one last time. There was nothing here for her, nothing she was leaving behind. Only her old life. "Marcus. That can't be the dawn, can it?" she asked, glancing toward the east and seeing a red glow.

"Not yet time for it—good God."

"What is it? Oh, mercy, it's—"

"Fire."

"Oh, mercy!" She stood beside him, staring, both stunned. "They've set fire to the city!"

"The bastards." From their vantage point high on the hill, they could see across to Washington City. From river's edge to Capitol Hill were fires, and as they watched yet another flame leaped into the sky. "The Navy Yard, there, on the river," Marcus said grimly. "But the others?"

"Oh, Marcus," Rebecca said, appalled. "All of Capitol Hill is in flames. And"—she turned to him, tears in her eyes—"they just fired the President's House."

"Damn them." In the reflected glow Marcus's jaw was set, but his eyes when he looked down at her were soft. "Time for us to go, lass."

She stood, stunned by the night's events, and yet knowing that there was little she could do. She had made the right choice. "Yes," she said and placed her hand in his, giving into his keeping her life, her heart, her trust. They walked away, and not once did she look back.

Epilogue

~

"Red sky at morning, sailors take warning," a voice rumbled in Rebecca's ear, and she stirred, rubbing at her eyes. Mercy, she'd fallen asleep, though she didn't know how, perched as she was upon a horse in front of Marcus. But then, the last few days had been trying, and she was worn out. "Good morning, lass."

"Morning." She yawned and then stiffened. They were at the top of a hill leading down onto cobbled city streets, with neat brick and stone dwellings on either side, their doors painted bright colors. "Oh, Marcus! Not another fire."

"Nay, lass." Marcus handled the reins with the same assurance as he handled a ship, expertly guiding the horse down the hill. " 'Tis the dawn. But with the looks of that sky, likely we'll get a storm soon."

"Another one?" she said, dismayed, for their flight from Washington City last evening had been anything but comfortable. With the Long Bridge across the Potomac burned by the British, and the ferries long since stopped, the only way for them to cross had been for Marcus to commandeer someone's boat. "Once a pirate, always a pirate," he'd said cheerfully. He hadn't been quite so cheerful, however, when the storm, presaged by the day's sultriness, broke while they were still in the middle of the river. Wet and bedraggled, they had taken shelter in a crowded inn on the Virginia shore and spent a miserable night sitting on the floor, backs propped against the wall, because there wasn't a room to be had. Finally, Marcus had made a bargain for the swaybacked horse they now rode, and they'd set off by land for

Alexandria. It was a relief to have Marcus away from the city, and danger, but she would not completely relax until they were far distant from the British forces.

"Probably," Marcus said, and she realized he was answering her question about the storm. "Best we're away before it breaks. We'll handle it better at sea."

She looked up at him questioningly. "At sea? I thought we were making for Baltimore."

"Aye, lass, and how do you think we'll get there?" They were at the bottom of the hill now, the waterfront stretching before them, the Potomac glassy in the early morning calm.

"I don't know. I didn't think—oh!" She turned to him, eyes startled as they neared a ship. "Marcus! Is it—but it can't be—"

"Aye, lass." He grinned down at her. " 'Tis the *Raven*."

"But I thought she'd been sunk."

"Now, lass, did you really think I'd let go of such a beauty?" he said, swinging down from the horse. It wasn't at the ship he looked, however, but at her. "I had to rename her, of course, but she's the *Raven*." His face softened. "Do you know what her name is?"

"No."

"Leannan."

"Oh." A lump rose in Rebecca's throat as she stared up at the ship's tall masts. The sails were tightly furled, and taut lines bound her to the dock, and yet still she seemed to fly, to soar. "Oh, she's beautiful."

"Aye, lass." Marcus gazed down at her, his eyes soft. "Welcome home," he said and caught her up in his arms, bringing his lips down onto hers. In spite of their surroundings and the people who, even so early in the morning, were about their business, Rebecca threw her arms about his neck and gave herself up to his kiss. Home for the three of them, she thought and smiled inwardly. And wouldn't he be surprised when she told him that?

"You offer me only a ship for a home?" she said with mock indignation, and his eyes flared with alarm before he saw her suppressed smile.

"Witch," he said and kissed her again, hard, stealing the breath from her. "Ye know who I am."

"Yes. A pirate. And if you don't abduct me this minute, I am going to be very annoyed."

His eyes gleamed. "Is that so?" he said and without warning swept her up into his arms and carried her across the wharf, to the narrow board that served as a gangplank.

"I object to being handled this way, sir," she said, relaxing against him after the momentary shock of finding herself airborne.

He stopped on the swaying plank. "Oh, ye do, do ye?"

"Yes."

"And how do ye wish to be treated?"

"Like this," she said, and reached up to kiss him. It was all behind her now, the pain of the past, the loss of her father's love, the prim, timid spinster she had once been. This was where she belonged, and she knew at last who she was. She was the Raven's woman, now and forever.

Author's Note

~

In writing Rebecca and Marcus's story, I took some liberties with history, and made some reasonable assumptions. While St. Thomas has traditionally been a free port, at the time of this story it was patrolled by the British and so it is unlikely that a pirate such as the Raven would have been allowed to roam free. For purposes of this story, I have changed that. Also, the annual horse race, though described much as it occurred, usually took place in autumn, not in the spring. Other liberties I took with history include the plan to invade Washington, as well as any groups that plotted against the government. Though I do not know if such things actually existed, it seemed reasonable to assume they did, and to include them in this story.

I have also included a few historical characters: President and Mrs. Madison, obviously, along with their acquaintances, and Sir Augustus Foster, British minister. All other characters are fictional.

My thanks to Meredith Bernstein, for encouraging me to chase my dream; to Jeanmarie LeMense, for taking a chance on me; and to Constance Martin, who has been a constant source of support and help. A special thanks to Bob Goldrick, who taught me chess and told me about the Fool's Game. Thanks is also due to the Silver City writers, who were the first to hear of the Raven's saga and the first to tell me to go for it. They have helped me more than they know.

I love hearing from my readers and will gladly answer all letters. My address is:

Mary Kingsley
RWA/New England Chapter
P.O. Box 1667
Framingham, MA 01701-9998

WE NEED YOUR HELP

To continue to bring you quality romance
that meets your personal expectations,
we at TOPAZ books want to hear from you.
Help us by filling out this questionnaire, and in exchange
we will give you a **free gift** as a token of our gratitude.

- Is this the first TOPAZ book you've purchased? (circle one)

    YES   NO

    The title and author of this book is: _____

- If this was not the first TOPAZ book you've purchased, how many have you bought in the past year?

    a: 0 - 5   b 6 - 10   c: more than 10   d: more than 20

- How many romances in total did you buy in the past year?

    a: 0 - 5   b: 6 - 10   c: more than 10   d: more than 20 ____

- How would you rate your overall satisfaction with this book?

    a: Excellent   b: Good   c: Fair   d: Poor

- What was the main reason you bought this book?

    a: It is a TOPAZ novel, and I know that TOPAZ stands
        for quality romance fiction
    b: I liked the cover
    c: The story-line intrigued me
    d: I love this author
    e: I really liked the setting
    f: I love the cover models
    g: Other: _____

- Where did you buy this TOPAZ novel?

    a: Bookstore   b: Airport   c: Warehouse Club
    d: Department Store   e: Supermarket   f: Drugstore
    g: Other: _____

- Did you pay the full cover price for this TOPAZ novel? (circle one)

    YES   NO

    If you did not, what price did you pay? _____

- Who are your favorite TOPAZ authors? (Please list)

- How did you first hear about TOPAZ books?

    a: I saw the books in a bookstore
    b: I saw the TOPAZ Man on TV or at a signing
    c: A friend told me about TOPAZ
    d: I saw an advertisement in_____magazine
    e: Other: _____

- What type of romance do you generally prefer?

    a: Historical   b: Contemporary
    c: Romantic Suspense   d: Paranormal (time travel,
        futuristic, vampires, ghosts, warlocks, etc.)
    d: Regency   e: Other: _____

- What historical settings do you prefer?

    a: England   b: Regency England   c: Scotland
    e: Ireland   f: America   g: Western Americana
    h: American Indian   i: Other: _____

- What type of story do you prefer?

  a: Very sexy
  c: Light and humorous
  e: Dealing with darker issues

  b: Sweet, less explicit
  d: More emotionally intense
  f: Other

- What kind of covers do you prefer?

  a: Illustrating both hero and heroine
  c: No people (art only)

  b: Hero alone
  d: Other_____

- What other genres do you like to read (circle all that apply)

  Mystery   Medical Thrillers   Science Fiction
  Suspense   Fantasy   Self-help
  Classics   General Fiction   Legal Thrillers
  Historical Fiction

- Who is your favorite author, and why?_____

  _____

- What magazines do you like to read? (circle all that apply)

  a: *People*
  c: *Entertainment Weekly*
  e: *Star*
  g: *Cosmopolitan*
  i: *Ladies' Home Journal*
  k: Other:_____

  b: *Time/Newsweek*
  d: *Romantic Times*
  f: *National Enquirer*
  h: *Woman's Day*
  j: *Redbook*

- In which region of the United States do you reside?

  a: Northeast   b: Midatlantic   c: South
  d: Midwest   e: Mountain   f: Southwest
  g: Pacific Coast

- What is your age group/sex?   a: Female   b: Male

  a: under 18   b: 19-25   c: 26-30   d: 31-35   e: 56-60
  f: 41-45   g: 46-50   h: 51-55   i: 56-60   j: Over 60

- What is your marital status?

  a: Married   b: Single   c: No longer married

- What is your current level of education?

  a: High school   b: College Degree
  c: Graduate Degree   d: Other: _____

- Do you receive the TOPAZ *Romantic Liaisons* newsletter, a quarterly newsletter with the latest information on Topaz books and authors?

  YES   NO

  If not, would you like to?   YES   NO

  Fill in the address where you would like your free gift to be sent:

  Name: _____

  Address: _____

  City:_____   Zip Code: _____

  You should receive your free gift in 6 to 8 weeks.
  Please send the completed survey to:

  Penguin USA•Mass Market
  Dept. TS
  375 Hudson St.
  New York, NY 10014